THE CHAPLAIN'S WAR

THE CHAPLAIN'S WAR

BRAD R. TORGERSEN

THE CHAPLAIN'S WAR

This is a work of fiction. All the characters and events portrayed in this book are fictional, and any resemblance to real people or incidents is purely coincidental.

Portions of this text appeared previously in slightly different form in *Analog Science Fiction and Fact* magazine as "The Chaplain's Assistant" and "The Chaplain's Legacy."

A Baen Books Original

Baen Publishing Enterprises
P.O. Box 1403
Riverdale, NY 10471
www.baen.com

ISBN: 978-1-4767-3685-3

Cover art by David Seeley

First printing, October 2014

Distributed by Simon & Schuster
1230 Avenue of the Americas
New York, NY 10020

Library of Congress Cataloging-in-Publication Data

Torgersen, Brad R.
The chaplain's war / Brad R. Torgersen.
pages cm
ISBN 978-1-4767-3685-3 (paperback)
1. Science fiction. I. Title.
PS3620.O587485C48 2014
813'.6—dc23

2014020256

10 9 8 7 6 5 4 3 2 1

Pages by Joy Freeman (www.pagesbyjoy.com)
Printed in the United States of America

To the Chaplains Corps of the United States Armed Forces, all branches; brave men and women tasked with preserving both God and hope in some of the world's most godless, hopeless places.

To my friends Larry Correia, Chuck Gannon, Mike Resnick, and Kevin J. Anderson; without whom this book would not have become a Baen book.

To editors Stanley Schmidt and Trevor Quachri; who first brought these stories to life in the pages of *Analog* magazine.

To mentor Allan Cole and also to (the late) Chris Bunch; because I was there when, "Death came quietly to The Row."

ACKNOWLEDGMENTS

A fix-up novel is a long series of stumbling steps aimed (more or less) towards an ever-shifting set of goal posts. When I wrote "The Chaplain's Assistant" in 2010 I did not plan to make a book out of it, nor had I yet conceived of the sequel novella, "The Chaplain's Legacy." Harrison Barlow (at that time) did not even have a name. He was just a guy. Someone who'd have fit right in on an episode of Mike Rowe's *Dirty Jobs*.

Ideas for expanding the story came later, in fits and starts. Largely because I liked Barlow, and I liked the central conceit of the human vs. mantis conflict. I thought it somewhat original, given the vast number of man-against-alien war stories which have been written over the years.

Eventually I had a large project on my hands, which even in its finished form needed some expert eyes to make it better. I want to thank Toni Weisskopf for providing those eyes. Toni saw what I was trying to do with this book even better than I did, and challenged me to make explicit that which I'd only previously dared to point at with a lot of prosaic road signage. I was never really sure how traditional SF audiences would react to a "church story" like this. But the fact that "The Chaplain's Assistant" scored well on the *Analog* magazine readers' choice ballot—the Analytical Laboratory, or AnLab award—and that "The Chaplain's Legacy" got me a lot of kind reader mail, told me I was on the right track. Toni simply demanded I take Harrison's journey to its logical (and inevitable) conclusion.

Better yet: since turning in the final revision for this book, "The Chaplain's Legacy" has gone on to win the AnLab award for best novella, and was also nominated for the genre's best-known award: the Hugo.

Apparently my initial misgivings about delving explicitly into the purpose and value of religion—in an ostensibly secular, post-religious, high-tech society—weren't necessary. People have told me that this is some of my best work. I hope that readers (who've read the short story and the novella both) found this expansion to their liking. I risked trying to have too much of a good thing, by enlarging 30,000 words of short fiction into almost 120,000 words of book. Along the way I not only gave Harrison Barlow a history, I also gave him a love interest. Things which were suggested by the original *Analog* magazine stories, but which never saw print until this novel came into being.

Thanks to everyone at Baen for helping me to make this book what it is. And thanks to Dave Seeley for a truly eye-popping cover!

Also, thanks to the men who worked on my behalf to not only introduce me to Toni Weisskopf, but impress upon her my bona fides as a writer worthy of investment: Larry Correia, Stan Schmidt, Mike Resnick, Kevin J. Anderson, and Chuck Gannon. Accomplished authors, all. It's been a privilege having the advice and assistance of such wonderful people.

PART ONE

The Chaplain's Assistant

CHAPTER 1

I WAS PUTTING FRESH OIL INTO CLAY LAMPS AT THE ALTAR WHEN the mantis glided into my foyer. The creature stopped for a moment, his antennae dancing in the air, sensing the few parishioners who sat on my roughly-hewn stone pews. I hadn't seen a mantis in a long time—the aliens didn't bother with humans much, now that we were shut safely behind their Wall. Like all the rest of his kind, this mantis's lower thorax was submerged into the biomechanical "saddle" of his floating mobility disc. Only this one's disc didn't appear to have any apertures for weapons—a true rarity on Purgatory.

Every human head in the building turned towards the visitor, each set of human eyes smoldering with a familiar, tired hate.

"I would speak to the Holy Man," said the mantis through the speaker box on its disc. Its fearsome, segmented beak had not moved. The disc and all the machines within it were controlled directly by the alien's brain.

When nobody got up to leave, the mantis began floating up my chapel's central aisle, the mantis's disc making a gentle humming sound.

"Alone," said the visitor, his vocoded voice approximating a commanding human tone.

Heads and eyes turned to me. I looked at the mantis, considered my options, then bowed to my flock, who reluctantly began to leave—each worshipper collecting handfuls of beads, crosses, stars, serviceman's Bibles, and various other religious items. They exited without saying a word. What else could they do? The mantes ruled Purgatory as surely as Lucifer ruled Hell.

I waited at the altar.

"You are the religious officer?" said the mantis.

"The chaplain is dead. I am—was—his assistant."

"We must speak, you and I."

Again, I noted the mantis's lack of armament.

"What can I do for you?" I said.

"I wish to understand this entity you call God."

I stared at the alien, not quite sure if I should take him seriously.

"To understand God," I said slowly, "is a skill that requires ongoing mastery."

"Which is why the other humans come here, to this structure? To learn from you."

I blushed slightly. In the two years since I'd completed the chapel—some five years after our failed invasion and subsequent capture—I'd not given so much as a single sermon. Preaching wasn't my thing. I built the chapel because the chaplain told me to before he died, and because it seemed obvious that many humans on Purgatory—men and women who had landed here, fought, been stranded and eventually imprisoned—*needed* it. With the fleets from Sol departed, and our homes many thousands of light-years away, there wasn't much left for some of us to turn to—except *Him*.

"I don't teach," I said, measuring my words against the quiet fear in my heart, "but I do provide a space for those who come to listen."

"You are being deliberately cryptic," the mantis accused.

"I mean no offense," I continued, hating the servile tone in my own voice as I spoke to the beast, "it's just that I was never trained as an instructor of worship. Like I said when you asked, I am only the assistant."

"Then what do the humans here listen to, precisely?"

"The spirit," I said.

The mantis's beak yawned wide, its serrated tractor teeth vibrating with visible annoyance. I stared into that mouth of death—remembering how many troops had been slaughtered in jaws like those—and felt myself go cold. The chaplain had often called the mantes *soulless*. At the time—before the landing—I'd thought he was speaking metaphorically. But looking at the monster in front of me I remembered the chaplain's declaration, and found it apt.

"Spirit," said the mantis. "Twice before has my kind encountered this perplexing concept."

"Oh?" I said.

"Two other sapients, one of them avian and the other amphibian."

Other aliens... *besides* the mantes? This was news.

"And what could they tell you about God?" I asked.

"Gods," my visitor corrected me. "We destroyed both species before we could collect much data on their beliefs."

"Destroyed," I said, hoping the alien's ears couldn't detect the shaking dread in my voice.

"Yes. Hundreds of your years ago, during what we call our Third Expansion into the galaxy. We thought ourselves alone, then. We had no experience with alternative intelligence. The homeworld of the avians and the homeworld of the amphibians were pleasing to the Quorum of the Select, so those worlds were annexed, cleansed of competitive life forms, and have since become major population centers for my people."

I took in this information as best I could, unsure if any human ears had ever heard anything like it. I thought of the Military Intelligence guys—all dead—who would have given their years' pay to gain the kind of information I had just gained, standing here in the drafty, ramshackle confines of my makeshift church.

I experienced a sudden leap of intuition.

"You're not a soldier," I said.

The mantis's beak snapped shut.

"Certainly not."

"What are you then, a scientist?"

The mantis seemed to contemplate this word—however it had translated for the alien's mind—and he waved a spiked forelimb in my direction.

"The best human term is *professor.* I research *and* I teach."

"I see," I said, suddenly fascinated to be meeting the first mantis I'd ever seen who was not, explicitly, trained to kill. "So you're here to research human religion?"

"Not just human religion," said the mantis, hovering closer. "I want to know about this... this *spirit* that you speak of. Is it God?"

"I guess so, but also kind of not. The spirit is... what you feel inside you when you know God is paying attention."

It was a clumsy explanation, one the Chaplain would have—no doubt—chastised me for. I'd never been much good at putting these kinds of concepts into words that helped me understand, much less helped other people understand too. And trying to explain God and the spirit to this *insect* felt a lot like explaining the beauty of orchestral music to a lawnmower.

The Professor's two serrated forelimbs thoughtfully stroked the front of his disc.

"What do the mantes believe?" I asked.

The Professor's forelimbs froze. "Nothing," he said.

"Nothing?"

"We detect neither a spirit nor a God," said the Professor, who made a second jaw-gaped show of annoyance. "The avians and the amphibians, they each built *palaces* to their gods. Whole continents and oceans mobilized in *warfare*, to determine which god was superior. Before we came and wiped them all out, down to the last chick and tadpole. Now, their flying gods and their swimming gods are recorded in the Quorum Archive, and I am left to wander here—to this desert of a planet—to quiz you, who are not even trained to give me the answers I seek."

The Professor's body language showed that his annoyance verged on anger, and I felt myself pressing my calves and the backs of my thighs into the altar, ready for the lightning blow that would sever a carotid or split my stomach open. I'd seen so many die that way, their attackers reveling in the carnage. However technologically advanced the mantes were, they still retained a degree of predatory-hindbrain joy while engaged in combat.

Noticing my alarm, the Professor floated backwards half a meter.

"Forgive me," said the alien. "I came here today seeking answers from what I had hoped would be a somewhat reliable source. It is not your fault that the eldest of the Quorum destroy things before they can learn from them. My time with you is finite, and I am impatient to learn as much as possible before the end."

"You have to leave . . . ?" I said, half-questioning.

The Professor didn't say anything for several seconds, letting the silence speak for him. My shoulders and back caved, if only a little.

"How many of the rest of us will die?" I asked, swallowing hard.

"All," said the Professor.

"All?" I said, at once sure of the answer, but still needing to ask again anyway.

"Yes, all," said the Professor. "When I got word that the Quorum had ordered this colony cleansed of competitive life forms—prior to the dispatching of the Fourth Expansion towards your other worlds—I knew that I had a very narrow window. I must study this *faith* that inhabits you humans. Before it is too late."

"We're no threat to you now," I heard myself say with hollow shock, "all of us on Purgatory, we've all been disarmed and you've made it plain that we can't hurt you. The Wall sees to that."

"I will return tomorrow, to study your other visitors in their worship," said the alien as his disc spun on its vertical axis, and he began to hover towards the exit.

"We're not a threat—!"

But my shouting was for naught. The Professor was gone.

CHAPTER 2

I DIDN'T SLEEP AT ALL THAT NIGHT. I KEPT THINKING ABOUT WHAT would happen. There were approximately six thousand of us left from the invasion, mostly men, but some women too—and now, here and there, children. All of us confined to a single semi-arid mountain valley by what we'd come to think of as The Wall—a slightly opaque curtain of energy that ringed us on all sides, with an indefinite height that faded into the sky. Rain, wind, snow, and air fell into and through The Wall, but every man or woman who had approached and touched it had been reduced to ashes.

"Selective nuclear suppression field," I'd heard one of the parishioners tell me one day—a man who'd been a pilot. "It's the same thing they mask their ships in orbit with. Our missiles couldn't ever get through. Nor the shells from the chainguns. We were smoked before we knew it."

Now, it seemed, the mantes were going to finish the job.

When morning came, there was a stiff wind coming down off the peaks from the north, and the irregularly-shaped shutters of the chapel stuttered and flapped. Such was common. Purgatory had small oceans and large deserts, with most of the livable country up in alpine territory. Why the mantes had seen it as worth defending—or why we'd seen it as worth invading—was a question I often asked myself.

Only a few people wandered in after breakfast. I had the oil lamps going to light the altar, and tried to offer my flock a smile, though I am afraid I must have looked a wreck.

The Professor showed up before lunch, getting the same kind of stabbing glares he'd gotten the day before. He hovered right up to the altar, turned, and looked at the parishioners as they looked at him, some of them glancing at me, as if to silently say, *what kind of goddamned sacrilege is this?*

Those in prayer ceased. One or two got up immediately and left.

"What is wrong?" the Professor asked me as I nibbled at some root bread and a small bowl of stew, made from native Purgatory vegetables and varmint meat—both of which we'd learned to farm. Purgatory's native fauna was on the diminutive side, and unfortunately for us, did *not* taste like chicken. You got used to it, after hunger for protein drove you to desperation. Thank heaven Purgatory wasn't short on salt.

I looked at the mantis, and pointed to the door that led to my room where I slept. He followed me back, and I closed the door behind us, light leaking around the corners of the room's shuttered, rattling window. His disc buzzed softly.

"You really don't understand religion, do you?"

"You state the obvious," he said.

"When people come here, they want to get *away* from you mantes. They want to get away from the anger and the rage and the despair."

The Professor just stared at me.

I sighed and rubbed my hands over my eyes, trying to figure out a way to penetrate his cold sensibilities.

"God is about warmth, and hope, and being able to see the future free of pain. Your coming here today is reminding everyone in the chapel of their pain, and they hate you for it. This is the one place where they think they can have a moment—just a moment, in the whole miserable world—of true peace. You're denying them that."

"I have not interfered with their activities at all," said the Professor.

"Worship is not something you do so much as it's something you feel. Your being here... It's driving out the feeling. The *spirit* is gone."

Gaping maw, vibrating saw-toothed horror.

"It doesn't help," I said, "that you told me yesterday we were going to die. I haven't said anything about it to anyone else—it would just upset them, and we clearly can't do anything about it even if we wanted to—but the people who have been here today, they know I'm bothered. Makes me wonder why you mantes let any of us live at all."

"Some of us were curious," the Professor said. "Humans are only the third sapient species we have found, after searching and colonizing thousands of star systems. Like I told you before, we annihilated the first two species without thinking more deeply about it. This time, we were determined to not make that same mistake."

"So we're good to you alive," I said, "only as long as we're of research interest."

"Do not forget, human, that it was *you* who initiated hostilities."

"Bullshit," I said. "The planets Marvelous and New America were uninhabited when our colonists got there. They didn't know about the mantes until your people showed up and blew the colonial fleets out of orbit. Sol would have been totally in the dark, except for the two picket ships that got away. Bad mistake, that. We came back hard. Showed you what we were made of."

The vestigial wings on the Professor's back opened and fluttered—a sign of extreme amusement.

"What's so funny?" I said.

"Do you know what happened to the six colonies—*mantis* colonies—that your Sol fleets attacked, in so-called reprisal?"

"We kicked your butts," I said, my voice rising.

"No, assistant-to-the-chaplain. *We wiped you out.* Those worlds remain in *our* hands, as do many others you once thought of as yours."

"Liar," I said, feeling hot in the face.

"If you've been told that your attacks against us on other worlds have been successful, then it is not I who has been lying to you. Think of your own fate, here on this planet. How successful was your fleet this time? Why would it have been any different anywhere else?"

I longed for a weapon. Any weapon.

"Our science is far advanced beyond your own. Discovery of the jump system is an easy, first step towards becoming truly technological. It in no way prepared you to deal with us at our level, and fortunately we have been able to deflect your violence and will now extinguish it from the universe."

The Professor stopped, as if noticing my posture for the first time.

"You hate me," he said.

"Yes," I told him.

"I can smell it on you. You would kill me, if you could."

"Yes," I said. Why lie now?

The Professor and his disc hovered lower, his disturbingly alien eyes looking directly into my own.

"Listen to me, assistant-to-the-chaplain. It is not I and my colleagues who orchestrate your species' destruction. The Quorum of the Select see you as animals. A pestilence. Having become aware of you, they consider you only inasmuch as they wish to eradicate your existence. But a few of us—in the schools—think differently. We suspect there is more to you than the Select believe. We suspect you have... perceptions, beyond our own."

"I don't understand," I said, still wishing for a weapon.

"This place"—the mantis spread both forelimbs and wings wide—"is an utterly absurd concept to us. A house for your God. Where you come to hear Him speak to you without words. It is madness. Yet, we remember the avians and the amphibians. We remember their cultures. It is a profound scientific deficit, that we destroyed them as quickly as we did, without first penetrating their *otherness,* such that we understood their passions."

"Our belief frightens you," I said, feeling a small surge of pride.

"Yes," said the Professor.

"Good."

"You would antagonize me?"

"What have I got to lose?" I said.

The Professor was silent for well over a minute, then rotated his disc and opened the door with a forelimb, before gliding out of my room, and back out of the chapel, which at that point was completely empty.

CHAPTER 3

THREE DAYS PASSED, AND THE PROFESSOR DID NOT RETURN. I kept his news of our impending doom to myself, still believing that if word of it leaked out, there would be more harm done than good. We still couldn't penetrate The Wall. We had no machines anymore with which to fly over it. Better, I thought, if the human population of Purgatory went on about its business, so that when the end did come, it came swiftly.

It was tough. As people came and went, I longed to share the burden of what I knew, for it crushed me inside. But I also couldn't bear to see it crush anyone else. There was nothing to be done. No defense could be raised. That part of my conscience which told me I had no right to keep the others in ignorance was in constant struggle with the other part of my conscience which couldn't bear to see what my news would surely do to the valley—assuming anyone even believed me. It was entirely possible I'd be declared mentally ill, and ignored. Hell, lots of people had already done so anyway. Not everyone in the valley thought religion was a good thing. I'd heard through the grapevine—more than once—that there were prisoners who regarded the chapel and my service as a stupid waste of time.

So I focused on my work as best I could.

Sweeping through the pews one day I knocked over a little clay figurine that one of the parishioners had left behind. I picked it up to discover that it was a crude, but recognizable, rendition of a mantis—including the requisite disc.

I stared at the figurine for a long time—the straw-and-twigs broom in my other hand momentarily forgotten. There had been occasional rumors in the valley. About a small cult of people whose beliefs centered around the idea that the mantes themselves were God's true children. Humans were merely a lower form of spiritual life whom the mantes had been sent to punish. For our weakness, decadence, and apostasy.

I'd always doubted the existence of such a group, if only because subscribing to such a belief—and speaking it openly to anyone—would have invited violence.

Still, what to make of the figurine?

I tucked it into a shirt pocket and kept sweeping. When I'd finished my job, and brushed all the sand and dirt out the back door, I went to the altar and considered. Bringing out the figurine, I compared it in my line of sight to the other objects on the altar. My hand began to tremble as I felt a hot rush of anger sweep through me. I could have crushed the little clay symbol in my fist.

But then the anger drained away as quickly as it had come. Whoever had brought the figurine had obviously not intended to leave it. In their carelessness, they'd exposed themselves to more potential harm than they knew. Besides, maybe the cult was right? All evidence since the failed invasion said the mantes really *were* superior. And now they intended to prove it once and for all.

I sighed and went back to the exact spot where the figurine had been abandoned, and put it back on the floor. In the shadow of the pew. Where nobody not deliberately looking for it would find it.

Within a day, it quietly disappeared again.

A week after the Professor's last visit, a trio of former officers appeared at my chapel door.

"Barlow," the leader said to me. He still wore his duty jacket with the name tape over the breast pocket, and the clusters of a major on his collar.

"What can I do for you?" I said, standing up from the small stool to the left of the altar where I ordinarily sat and observed the comings and goings of the parishioners.

"Sir," he said firmly.

"Beg pardon?" I said, not quite getting him.

"What can I do for you, *sir.*"

Ah. I resisted the urge to tell him to go fuck himself. While most of us had gradually relaxed out of our former rank and position, there were still a handful of stalwarts who kept their bearing. In another time and place, the major's approach might have worked. But not now. Not here. So far as we knew, we were cut off. Permanent residents. And almost nobody wanted to be under martial authority for life. Least of all me.

I waited silently. Just looking at him.

He looked back, his face getting pink.

"Is there a problem?" I finally asked, keeping my tone deliberate and even.

"Maybe," one of the other men said.

"People tell us there's been a mantis coming in here," the major said.

I walked towards him a few steps so that I could get a better look. The tape on his breast read HOFF and he looked to be in his forties. Balding. Sharp eyes. The posture of someone used to giving orders and having them obeyed. I immediately wanted him off the premises, but decided I could at least entertain a few questions. If I kept my answers circumspect enough, hopefully the trio would get bored and leave.

"It's true," I said. "There has been a mantis coming to the chapel."

"What does he want?" Hoff asked.

"He's just curious," I said.

"About what?"

"About the chapel. About churches in general. About what I do here."

"Why?"

"Couldn't begin to tell you. He's an alien, how am I supposed to know?"

"So what have you told him?"

"Nothing much. I make sure the chapel stays clean, that the lamps are lit, and that people can always come and worship whenever they want during the day."

"Anything else?"

"That's the long and the short of it."

Hoff stared at me, while his compatriots looked around the chapel's interior.

"He comes in here and asks any more questions, you notify one of us immediately."

"What for?" I asked.

"We're still at war, you know. The fact that we're long-term prisoners doesn't change anything. Though I think a whole lot of people forget this. No matter. When the Fleet returns, there'll be a reckoning. Right now I'm mostly concerned with information. You were the chaplain's assistant so I respect the fact that you've carried out the chaplain's wishes for the construction and care of this place. Hell, I admire it. At least you've done something useful. Which is more than I can say for a lot of others."

"It seemed like a good idea," I said.

"Right. So keep your ears open. A mantis comes sniffing around here, it may mean something important."

"Like what?" I asked.

"Who knows?" Hoff replied. "You just said it yourself: they're aliens. But that's not your concern. I'm giving you an order to report back on whatever you learn from the mantis. Is that understood?"

"Clearly," I said.

Hoff and his pals waited.

I think maybe they were expecting a salute?

I didn't offer one.

Eventually he muttered something about insubordination and wandered out the way he'd come in, his cronies giving me sidelong glances.

I breathed a sigh of relief and went back to my stool. I had no intention of reporting anything to those fools. Chain of command only works when everyone in it agrees to cooperate, and ours had disintegrated shortly after being captured and cordoned off behind The Wall. Since we couldn't talk to Fleet Command, and Fleet Command had probably written us all off as casualties, what more did we owe to the service?

Still, the major had made one good point.

So long as I—or any of us—possessed information of interest to the mantes on any level, there was potential bargaining power.

I dwelt on this for the rest of the day, remembering the Professor's awful promise that the Fourth Expansion would finish humanity forever.

CHAPTER 4

THAT NIGHT I WAS AWAKENED BY THE SOUND OF VOICES—TWO human, and one familiarly mechanical. I slowly got up out of my cot and stepped quietly to the doorway, where I peered out. The Professor was there, and seemed to be conversing by lamplight with a man and a woman, neither of whom I recognized.

"And what does immersion accomplish?" said the mantis.

"It takes away the sin," said the woman.

"And what is *sin?*"

"Bad choices," said the man. "When you screw up."

"Mistakes?" said the Professor.

"Yes," said the woman. "All of us make mistakes. All of God's children. Which is why we all need His forgiveness."

"And that's what the immersion in the water accomplishes?" said the Professor.

"Yes," said the man. "It's a clean start. Once a person becomes a member."

The mantis rotated his disc suddenly. He looked at the doorway.

"Assistant-to-the-chaplain, do come out and join us."

I stepped into the light, feeling stiff and frigid and wondering what time it was.

The man and woman smiled at me, then returned to talking to the mantis.

"So you see," she said, "nobody is cut off from His love. Not even you."

The Professor's antennae made an ironic display.

"Your human God claims to love me?"

"He's not just the *human* God," said the man. "He's the God of all things. Ours, yours, everyone's."

"I'm sorry, but the chapel is closed at night," I said gently.

"We know," said the woman. "We'd have kept the Professor over at our branch house, except he practically dragged us here to talk to you."

"Why did you not tell me, assistant-to-the-chaplain, that your human God comes in different flavors?"

"Flavors?" I said, yawning.

"Yes. And shapes. One deity, many forms. These two humans, their God is made of gold and holds a trumpet to his lips."

"That's not Heavenly Father," the woman reminded the alien. "That's the Angel Moroni."

Ah. I understood now. The Professor had ferreted out the Latter-Day Saints.

"Is that where you've been all week," I asked him, "over with the Mormons?"

"I have visited every religious structure in the valley," said the Professor. "Each one seems to serve a different flavor of spirit. Tonight I visited the Mormons. You do not like the Mormons?"

"I don't *not* like the Mormons, let's put it that way," I said. The chaplain himself had been a fierce Baptist. Didn't think much of the whole Joseph Smith thing, or so he'd told me a few times in confidence. Loved the people, near as I could tell, but the so-called Prophet... hogwash.

My dealings with the Mormons were few. They had their church, I had mine, and we operated at opposite ends of the valley. Seemed like a good fit. So what was the Professor doing bringing Mormons here?

"We'd better go," said the man, sensing my vibe.

I showed them out, and returned to the lamp-lit altar.

"I have learned much," said the Professor. He pointed at the altar. "Here I see multiple symbols for your flavors. The star is for Jews. The cross is used by many different subdivisions of Christianity. The smaller star with the eclipsed disc is for Muslims. The fat human who laughs is the god of the Buddhists."

"Buddhists don't really have a god like Christians or Muslims or Jews."

"But in the confines of this structure, you act as official for all of these, yes?"

"The chaplain did," I said. "I just keep the building clean and make sure everyone knows that they can come in here during daylight. It's what's called multidenominational."

"The Mormons do not come here?"

"Not usually."

"Do you compete with them? For followers?"

"What?"

"The avians and amphibians, it was a major part of their societies, to compete for and hold adherents to a particular flavor of belief."

I thought of the internecine religious struggles which plagued Earth, right up to the present. I wondered if the mantes hadn't already *cleansed* humanity's homeworld in the same manner as had been done to other species previously.

"Some places that happens," I said. "But not here. There aren't enough of us that it's worth fighting each other."

"The Muslims, at their mosque, they told me I was the devil."

I smiled a little bit. "Some Muslims are like that. They think everyone who isn't Muslim is evil. Even, sometimes, other Muslims."

"Then why do you have their symbol on your religious furniture?"

"Not all Muslims go to the mosque. Some of them—the open ones—they come here sometimes."

"But never Mormons."

"Look, I don't really know what the beliefs are of the people who come to the chapel. I don't put a sign out advertising for specific faiths. Once someone keeps coming for a while I usually talk to them and figure out what they believe, but sometimes people don't say anything at all. They come in, they sit, and whatever else they do inside their hearts and heads, well, it's not my business."

"Then how does one join your church?"

"I don't have a church to join. The building... it's separate from their belief. The word 'church' therefore has double meanings. My *chapel* just happens to service multiple religions. The others—the mosque, the synagogue—are each for one 'flavor' only."

"Fascinating," said the Professor.

"What's so urgent," I said, "that you needed to drag a couple of Mormons across the valley to talk to me in the middle of the night?"

"Tomorrow I am bringing my students. I already have permission from the Mormons for my students to attend their church. The Buddhists as well. Since the mosque is closed to us, I ask that my students be allowed to come to you to learn Islam. And Judaism. And any other flavor you can show to them."

"What about Hinduism?" I said.

"There was no building for this Hinduism."

"Hindus. They're around, though not many."

"Then yes, that too."

Dammit, where was the chaplain when I needed him? He'd have *loved* an opportunity like this. A chance to illuminate the enemy—to preach the gospel among the alien heathen. But the chaplain was dead, and I was stuck in his place. I knew just enough about the major Earth religions to get by, but that was all. I felt it was a serious mistake to attempt to teach any of the mantes about religions that I myself didn't understand beyond their basic precepts.

But first, I needed an answer of my own.

"Why should I do this for you, when your people plan to destroy my people?"

The Professor considered.

"That is a fair question, assistant-to-the-chaplain."

"Well?"

"The logical answer is, you should not."

"What if I tell you that I won't cooperate at all? Unless you promise me that you're going to go to the mantes—to this Quorum you talked about—and convince them to spare the valley. In fact, convince them to hold off on the Fourth Expansion, period."

The Professor's forelimbs made an expression of being taken aback.

"I am a scholar, not a politician," he said. "You ask me for things which I cannot promise, and may not even be able to attempt."

"You told me that enough mantes wanted to avoid the 'mistake' of killing humans before you understood us. What if you talked to and convinced *them?* How much influence does *that* body have?"

"Again, you ask for that which I cannot deliver."

"But you and your 'school' mates obviously have enough leverage to at least get your Quorum to think twice?"

The Professor's forelimbs rattled on his dish—agitation.

"No, assistant-to-the-chaplain, I cannot do it."

"Then I won't help you. In fact, I will go to the other religious leaders and I will tell all of them what I know—about the genocide that is to come—and we will all promise together to not reveal even a single additional piece of information."

"This is the second time you have pretended to antagonize me," he said.

"And this is the second time I have had to remind you that I've got nothing to lose. Can you say the same?"

The mantis stared at me, his beak opening ever so slightly. A flush of blue along the semi-soft portions of his carapace told me that I'd flustered him badly. He'd not expected me to bargain, only to obey.

"It will take time," he said.

"Take all the time you want. Just stop your people from killing us."

The Professor stared at me, then turned his head and looked long and hard at the altar: the cross and crescent and the six-pointed star gleaming slightly in the wane light from the dimming oil lamps.

"The difficulty is great," he said hesitantly. "If I return with my students, you will know your answer."

"And if you don't return at all?" I said.

"Then that too will be an answer."

He left as the last lamp flickered out, leaving me in cold darkness.

CHAPTER 5

ANOTHER WEEK PASSED. THEN TWO WEEKS. TEMPERATURES IN the valley began to drop. Purgatory's axial tilt wasn't as pronounced as Earth's, so the seasons weren't so well defined. There was no spring, summer, winter, or fall, just a warmer season and a colder season, with reflective growth and decay of alpine vegetation.

My little garden needed work as a result. I spent time carefully picking through the rows, saving every little root, bulb, and leaf that could be dried or stored for the cool months. Then I razed the rest of the plants to the ground, tilled them under, and set about sowing seeds for the stuff which would be able to survive and grow with the lower temperatures. A trick I'd learned from one of the parishioners who'd grown up on a farm on one of Earth's interstellar colonies.

A winter crop, he'd called it. Something I'd not even thought possible, having grown up on Earth, where almost everything anybody ate merely came from the store, three hundred sixty-five days a year.

One afternoon, when I'd just come inside from working in the soil, Hoff and his boys reappeared in my doorway.

"You didn't follow orders," he said to me as I wiped my hands on my overalls—the pair I saved for outside chores.

The sharpness in Hoff's tone caused the four worshippers sitting in my pews to become uncomfortable. They quickly got up and left, brushing past the indignant officer while avoiding his gaze. Which was directly upon me as I stood up from my stool and began to walk up the central aisle.

"Sir," I said, feeling a bit more conciliatory since the last time he'd visited, "you asked me to bring you any relevant information. If I had something remarkable to report, I'd have done it already."

"You're a bad liar," Hoff said. "We've been from one end of the valley to the other. We've talked to the other religious folk. We know the mantis is some kind of researcher, asking lots of questions about church stuff. Supposedly he's bringing more mantes—to study us. I'd call that pretty important information. Or are you just a dumbass who doesn't realize what he's stumbled into?"

A hot flush flowed up my neck and into my face.

"It just didn't seem relevant," I said, opening my arms wide and throwing out my hands. "How is this one mantis bringing more mantes to talk to us about our religion going to solve our mutual problem of captivity? Is it going to get us off this planet? Take us back home?"

Hoff didn't appear to have a good answer to these questions. I suspected that if he knew the full truth, it might make him more annoying than he already was. Perhaps even dangerous. I was glad I hadn't revealed a thing to any of the other congregational leaders—though I knew most of them by name. If Hoff had been curious enough to go cross-examine them, he'd have ferreted out the fact of our impending demise one way or another.

"It doesn't matter what *you* think," Hoff spat. "That's what officers are for. We do the thinking around here. You just do as you're told."

"Sir," I said, working hard to remain calm in the face of Hoff's belligerence, "since you clearly found out as much as I know from talking to the other denominations, what point would there have been in me confirming redundant information? Yes, the mantis says he's bringing more of his kind to study us. But have you seen hide or hair of that mantis since he made that promise? Neither have I. I suspect maybe we've been dealing with an eccentric. He's the first civilian mantis any of us have ever seen. Maybe he's serious, and maybe he's just a quack. I don't see how it makes a difference since he clearly can't get us off this world any more quickly than we ourselves can. Frankly, I'm glad he's gone."

Hoff walked up the aisle and met me halfway. I had him by a couple of centimeters, so he actually had to look up into my face. His jaw was clenched and I sensed from him the urge for violence. Much as the Professor had once sensed it from me. With the odds being three to one, I figured I'd get my ass handed to me if the major really wanted to pick a fight. I felt sweat springing out across my skin as we stood there in the middle of the chapel glaring at each other.

"You've been warned," he finally said. "Screw with me again, and I will make you sorry for it. Understood?"

"Yes," I said.

"Yes, *sir*?"

"Yessir."

Hoff pivoted quickly on a heel and stalked out, his henchmen following.

I braced myself on the backs of two pews, breathing deeply and heavily while the adrenaline of the moment slowly wore off.

God, I hated pricks like that.

Not all Fleet officers were as bad as Hoff. But enough of them had rubbed me wrong to make me understand that I had not been, nor would I ever be, a great soldier. Taking orders from people I judged to be idiots just wasn't my thing.

With no one in the chapel, I began to wander up and down the rows of stone benches, collecting bits of detritus that had been swept in on the feet of visitors. When noon arrived and I still had no one, I made myself a modest meal and propped a stick-built chair at the front door so that I could get a little fresh air while afternoon wore on into evening.

Purgatory's sky was dappled with clouds.

I suspected there might be rain in our future.

Heaven knew we needed it. The sparse cold-season snows on the peaks didn't last long into the warm season. The handful of valley lakes usually began to run dry just a little after the midpoint of the warm months. Thus drought was almost a perpetual state for us, making the rare thunderstorm a welcome thing.

The chapel had a catchment system which I'd engineered into the roof.

It would be nice to have fresh, relatively clean water instead of the silty stuff I was always pulling out of the distant creek.

A figure wearing a poncho and a wide grass hat walked up. The brim of the hat was pulled low so that I couldn't see the person's face.

"Did that major come to bother you?" said a woman's voice.

"Hoff?" I asked, recognizing Deacon Fulbright.

"Yeah, that's the cocksucker."

I chuckled. The Deacon had been a noncommissioned officer—and a gunner—before turning her attention to Christ. She still had her salty mouth. Whether or not she had any actual pastoral bona fides from her previous civilian life was a mystery to me. Not that anyone gave a damn here.

So much of the valley's religious fabric was like that. Once the mantes had us beaten and it was obvious we weren't going anywhere, dozens of would-be congregational leaders sprang up from the ranks.

Deacon Fulbright and I had been on good terms since the beginning.

"Come take a load off," I said to her, going inside and bringing out another stick-built chair.

She sat, and together we leaned against the wall of the chapel while the sun set.

"Hoff's trying to rally as much of the former officer corps as he can," she said.

"Is he having much success?"

"Yes and no," she said. "There are some colonels who aren't taking kindly to Hoff's attitude. I think if he keeps this up there's liable to be an ass-whippin' at his expense."

"Couldn't happen to a more deserving man," I said.

The Deacon snickered at my sarcastic comment.

I stared at the sky as the clouds continued to thicken.

A low rumble, almost so far off we couldn't hear it, told me my earlier suspicion of rain would turn out to be correct.

"Harry," she said—we only used first names when things got candid.

"Yeah?"

"Are you sure you don't know anything more than I know?"

"What *do* you know?"

"What Hoff *said* I know."

"And that's all *I* know too," I replied flatly.

She stared at me.

"You're a bad liar."

"And you're not the first one to tell me that today."

"Look, fuck the major, this is between you and me. What's really going on with this mantis and the 'students' he says he's bringing back? I talked to the Mormon Bishop two days ago and he's all excited about it. Though he said he'd expected the mantes to be here by now. That they're not here yet has him a little worried."

"You seem to think this mantis scholar tells me more than he tells you, or anyone else around here. Why?"

"Because he came to you first," she answered.

"Diane," I said, "believe me when I tell you that if I had any knowledge I thought would be good for you to know, then you'd be the first to know it. Okay? There's nothing for me to say. We're friends. I respect you."

"And I respect you," she said.

"Then let me be," I replied gently.

After a long silence, she whooshed out a frustrated breath.

"Suit yourself, Harry. I can't make you say what you don't want to say. But I trust you. Just please promise me that if you change your mind, my door will be the first one you knock on."

"I promise," I said.

"Good. Now I'd better get back before the storm hits."

"I think it's just minutes away," I said.

The Deacon stood and we exchanged farewells, before she walked away.

More rumbling in the sky, and a smattering of tiny drops on the parched soil, told me it was time to go in and close all the shutters.

CHAPTER 6

THE STORM HIT, AND HIT BIG.

Flash flooding kept us all busy for a few days while we cleaned up the mess. Thankfully my chapel didn't get damaged. *This* time. I'd not always been so lucky.

During one particularly violent downpour, a runnel was cut under the northeast corner of the building, causing the wall to crumble. I wound up having to rebuild and repair not only that corner, but the roof above it as well. It took me the better part of two weeks, during which the interior of the chapel was both drafty, and prone to gathering more than its usual layer of noxious dust.

But now, with our water supply somewhat renewed, the mood in the valley grew optimistic. Funny how our time in this place had simplified our expectations. Even something as mundane as an unusual abundance of water could be a cause for rejoicing.

Me? I remained quietly anxious.

Over the next ten days I had half a dozen repeats of the conversation I'd had with the Deacon, only with different people from different congregations around the valley. I told them all what I could—omitting the one big piece of information I dared not reveal—and life went on its merry way.

The wait become a month.

Then two months. Then three.

No sign of the Professor.

My dread of the inevitable began to deepen. The Professor had never specified when the end might come, so I had no way of knowing if this was a delay in the course of events as he'd described, or merely the running out of the proverbial sand into the bottom of the proverbial hourglass. Since he'd not come back I suspected that any hope I might kindle—and this happened more than once—was a false hope. So I stuffed it down inside and tried to be resigned to whatever fate awaited us.

If nothing else, the Professor's visits all over the valley sparked interest among the general population. My chapel's average attendance grew substantially. I wasn't sure what to think about that, other than being grateful for the increased donations of goods and food at my drop box by the front door.

I still didn't preach—would not have had the foggiest idea what to say to any of them—but I kept the chapel clean, I made sure the altar and all the objects on it were tidy and arranged according to pattern, and I welcomed in everyone who felt the need to come.

When an entire Purgatorial year passed—perhaps one and a half Earth standard—I began to wonder if the Professor really *had* been an eccentric. A nutball. Such people existed among humans, why not the mantes? He had been chasing religion, after all, and I had nothing to corroborate what he'd said. Perhaps he'd been the mantis version of a millennial—someone attracted to and fascinated by "end times" myth. Enough to spin me a story?

The first sign of the inevitable came when the hill farmers reported that The Wall was beginning to close in.

Deacon Fulbright and I rushed out to the valley rim, hiking for hours up to the peaks so that we could take a look for ourselves.

Seeing was believing.

"Christ in Heaven," she said under her breath. We were less than a meter away from The Wall—silent, shimmering, and deadly. I kicked a couple of stones up to it, one in front of the other. Perhaps three centimeters apart. As we watched, The Wall gradually and inexorably drifted over the top of the first stone, then over the top of the second. Not terribly fast. Maybe a millimeter per minute. But given the fact there was nowhere for anyone to go, it didn't matter.

The Deacon stared at me.

"You knew," she said. "You knew this would happen."

"No," I said. Which was the technical truth. The Professor had never told me the precise nature of our doom, should it come.

"You knew!"

This time she'd yelled it at me.

My cheeks reddened with shame.

"Well, okay, dammit, so maybe I did. What was I supposed to do? Go blabbing to every man, woman, and child in the valley? Who would that have helped? Would it have solved anything? It would have caused panic, that's what it would have caused. And half of them would not have wanted to believe me in any case. I'd have been cast out as a crazy and the chapel would have been shut down."

Tears stained the Deacon's face.

"I'm sorry, Diane," I said. "I really am. But I didn't *dare* tell anyone. Not even you. How could I?"

She spun away from me and began marching back down the mountainside.

"Wait!" I called after her, practically running to catch up.

When I grabbed her shoulders she threw off my hands with a violent twist of her body.

"Don't touch me," she snarled.

"I said I was sorry."

"Like it matters?"

"To me it does. Diane, think about it. We've all been trapped here for how many years now? With no sign that there will ever be any escape? People have begun families. It's not much of a life, but it's *something.* People have found ways to get by. And you and I and the rest of the religious leadership, we've been part of that. You *know* we have. Prematurely telling people what I knew about the mantes' plans would have been a gross betrayal of our service. My job—your job too—is to give everyone a mode for hope. Not all of them use it, but enough of them do that I couldn't in good conscience let them down by becoming a prophet of death."

She'd stopped in her tracks. From the side I could tell that fresh tears continued to leak from her eyes. The shuddering of her back told me all I needed to know about the anguish she must be feeling. I myself merely felt a hollowness in my chest where emotion should have been. If the news had just hit Diane like a baseball bat between the eyes, I'd had to live with it on my heart like a slow corrosive. Insidious and malignant.

"Well you can't hide the truth now," she finally said, her voice cracking. "Word's already getting around. Even the hardcore doubters will eventually come up here and confirm things for themselves. Just like we did. What's going to happen, Harry? Are we going to keep blowing sunshine up their asses, or are we going to be straight with them?"

"Didn't you once tell me you thought our incarceration was God's way of testing us?" I asked.

"Yeah," she said, snuffling. "It was easy to talk, then. The war was more or less over. The mantes seemed to have left us alone. Now? I guess this means God's passed judgment."

"Maybe," I said. "Is that what you're going to say on Sunday?"

"I don't know yet. All I know is I want to get the hell off this mountain."

She began walking again, which left me no choice but to follow her.

CHAPTER 7

FOR SEVERAL DAYS, HUNDREDS OF FEARFUL AND CURIOUS PEOPLE went up to the valley rim. When enough of them had returned with confirmation of the dreadful reality, the mood in the valley promptly shifted to alarm.

But for me? It was almost a relief. No more carrying around a silent burden.

I still didn't let on that I'd had advanced warning. And the Deacon didn't tell anyone either. Suffice to say that what others didn't know wouldn't hurt me or them.

Whether the Professor had been legit or not, he'd been unable to change the minds on his Quorum. Humanity's stay on Purgatory was coming to an end.

In the weeks that followed, attendance in the chapel went through the roof. I was forced to allow people to begin spending the night. Who was I to keep banker's hours, at a time like this? As long as people didn't leave a mess—excremental or otherwise—I let them stay as long as they wanted. It's what the chaplain would have preferred were he still alive and able to give direction. I could think of no better use for the place.

Occasional scout trips to the hills told us that the contraction of The Wall was accelerating.

By the time The Wall was in the valley floor, and closing at well over a meter per day, I had more people in the chapel than could possibly fit. I began to wonder if the combination of fear and crowding might cause a riot. But my flock was like me for the most part—calm and resigned. Maybe attempting to make some sort of final peace with the universe? Perhaps, also, we were each of us eager for the ultimate escape. It had been years since we'd walked freely on a human world, masters of our own universe. Life in the valley, controlled utterly by the mantes, had been like a living coffin.

Now it would end.

CHAPTER 8

CARRYING ON WITH BUSINESS AS USUAL WAS A STRANGE EXPERIENCE. Knowing what was to come left an aftertaste of dread in my mouth each morning. But there was always the same routine maintenance work on the chapel to be done. Rather than neglect my chores, I hurled myself into them with as much energy as I could muster. Keeping busy on productive tasks was just about the only sober way to take my mind off The Wall.

I suddenly found myself welcoming every little crack in the mortar, hole in the roof, or rotted slat of wood in the doors and shutters. Fixes that might have taken me only minutes before, now took hours. Not because I half-assed them. Far from it. I gave them the attention of a craftsman. Carefully patching and replacing as I went, so that for much of the day my mind was directly occupied.

A few of the regulars began helping me, and then, more people too. Before long everybody was in on the action. And quite quickly the chapel looked sharper than it ever had before. The place almost hummed with energy—everyone displacing his or her fear into the work itself. Including the grounds surrounding the chapel, as well as my garden.

We didn't talk about it, of course. I don't think we needed to. We could each see it in each other's eyes. To speak our thoughts would have burst the fragile, necessary bubble of suspended disbelief that seemed to be keeping our manners and our sanity intact. So we discussed our work, and patted each other encouragingly on the back when it seemed a job had been well-done, and at night I huddled on my cot and tried to console myself with the idea that even though the end was near, at least I could say I was approaching the end with dignity.

Which was more than could be said for others.

One night I saw a bearded figure shuffle through the chapel entrance. He'd not shaved in weeks and had grain alcohol on his breath.

That was one rule I chose *not* to break: no drunks in my building. People who wanted to drown their sorrows in a mug or bottle were welcome to do it somewhere else. I politely approached the man and began encouraging him to go, when I stopped cold.

"Major Hoff," I said quietly, recognizing him.

"How do you do it?" he slurred at me.

"Do what, sir?"

"How do you believe?"

"Sir?"

"God, damn you! How do you believe in God?"

I thought back to the first time the Professor had entered the chapel. I'd not had a very good answer for him then, and I didn't have a very good answer for Hoff now. The major's eyes squinted angrily up at me as I fumbled my way through an explanation, then he waved me off.

"Crap," he said. "It's all a lot of crap. Always has been."

I looked behind me to see that a small crowd of the chapel's inhabitants had gathered to see what all the fuss was about. Recognizing that he had an audience, Hoff drew himself up to as dignified a stance as he could muster and began holding forth.

"The damned bugs always did have us by the balls," he said in the too-loud volume of the generally intoxicated. "If there really was a God up there, He'd have made it so that the game was *fair*. No advantage for the mantes. Instead, they were so far ahead of us when the war started, we never really got our shot. Humanity, a day late and a dollar short. Or maybe a few hundred or a few thousand years late. Well, put your heads between your legs and kiss your butts goodbye. It's been nice knowing you assholes."

With that, Hoff turned and stepped out of the chapel.

Someone who came in later told me that the major kept walking well into the night, right up until he hit the wall.

Then, *crackle-poof*. He was gone.

By the time The Wall was clearly visible from the doorway of the chapel, people were giving themselves up to it on a regular basis. My parishioners, others from around the valley, anybody who'd just gotten tired of the waiting and decided to end it. I began to be able to tell who those people were. The pews would be packed, and someone would just stand up and slowly walk out, a look of remarkable calm on his or her face. Like Hoff, they'd keep going like that—calm, quiet, no running, right up and into The Wall. Flash. One moment, a human being. The next, a cloud of carbon molecules, decaying to submolecular nothingness.

I heard that the other church leaders began railing against this practice. Deacon Fulbright especially. Suicide was sin, and for those who walked into The Wall, it was said, there would be damnation.

"You know the rules as well as I do," she told me one night as we stood outside the packed confines of the chapel. The Wall was ghostly bright in the distance—a reminder of our coming mortality.

"I serve other people besides Christians," I reminded her. "The chaplain was very specific about his chapel being a place where everybody could come to seek spiritual solace."

"You don't have to be a Christian to see that throwing away what He gave you—a life—is a slap to His face."

"I'm not so sure about that," I told her. "I can't believe in any God that would curse a soul who picks freedom from this place, especially since we're going to die regardless. I've even considered it a few times myself: just getting up, walking out, and ending it."

"So why don't you?" she said, her voice hard and bitter.

"The only thing that stops me is my flock," I replied. "They need the chapel, and the chapel needs me, so I stay where I am."

The Deacon didn't have a response to that.

She just stared at the Wall as it rippled like a curtain.

Within a few days, she'd joined the teeming congregation already at the chapel, bringing everyone in her attenuated religious circle with her.

Every night she and I made a point of meeting outside to consider our fate—watching The Wall creep toward us.

When I could sleep I dreamt odd dreams of flying away from Purgatory on a gust of warm ether, floating to another world far, far away from anywhere I'd ever been before.

CHAPTER 9

ONE MORNING I FOUND MYSELF OUT OF BED EARLY, GETTING ready to light the altar lamps in the pre-dawn darkness, when I heard Diane shriek from the foyer.

Jumping over a few people who had curled up asleep in the central aisle, I found the Deacon leaning against the doorway and pointing into the distance. I peered out and saw nothing. Just the black shapes of the mountains, and the almost imperceptible lightening of the sky in the east.

"What?" I said, tired and puzzled.

"Look," was all she could say, her eyes bugging out at me as if I'd gone mad or blind.

Then, like a physical thunderclap, it hit me.

I was seeing nothing but mountains!

Other shouts from inside the chapel had roused my flock to their feet.

Diane and I stumbled out onto the packed earth in front of the chapel and looked to the scattering of other nearby buildings where others had also come out to see.

The Wall. It was . . . gone.

CHAPTER 10

THE PROFESSOR AND HIS STUDENTS SHOWED UP LATER THAT day. Eighty young mantes, each riding an unarmored and unarmed disc, their carapaces green whereas the Professor's was a dingier brown. Each of them very young—and eager. They congregated at the chapel, observing the mass of hundreds of humans who had come to crowd the inside and the outside of my little church, each of them giving thanks to various versions of the Lord for their salvation.

Diane was leading a particularly raucous bunch of gospel singers who were harmonizing at the top of their lungs. I'd literally never seen her so happy before.

I squeezed my way out of the building and went out to greet the Professor, waving my arms and smiling genuinely for probably the first time in almost two years.

"You were successful," I said matter-of-factly.

"For the moment," said the Professor, wings fluttering slightly. "It took a great deal of argument and debate through the university system, but together we pressed the Quorum of the Select, and they agreed to stay your communal execution."

"What of the Fourth Expansion?"

"That too has been stayed, until my students and I can complete our research here. We are to observe and learn all we can about humans: religion, culture, all of it in as natural an environment as possible."

"Is that why The Wall is gone?" I asked.

"Yes. I had to fight hardest to get that done, but my colleagues and I believe it is impossible to conduct accurate research so long as humans are trapped in a test tube. You're free to travel as far as you wish, though I would warn you that not all the mantes in this hemisphere will take kindly to seeing humans roaming freely. I would advise caution."

"And when your research is complete?"

"That will be several of your years from now, assistant-to-the-chaplain. Many things can happen in that time. Many minds can be changed."

"Mantis minds?" I said.

"Perhaps human too," said the Professor.

His wings fluttered again. And that's when I felt it start to bubble out of me. Laughter. Clean, pealing, exuberant laughter. So much that I had to bend over and drop to all fours, gasping. I finally recovered and, wiping my eyes, got back to my feet.

"Come on," I told him. "You kept your part of the bargain. I have to keep mine. You should come watch this."

PART TWO

The Chaplain's Legacy

CHAPTER 11

"CHIEF BARLOW," SAID THE FEMALE VOICE THROUGH THE WOODEN door.

Lost in thought, I didn't answer right away.

She cleared her throat, and tried again. "Warrant Officer Harrison Barlow?"

I sighed, and slowly got up from my seat at my desk in the tiny pastor's quarters of my chapel.

She'd called me chief. I wasn't used to the new rank. There had been a time when I'd happily watched my military days fade into memory. But the recent return of Earth ships to Purgatory orbit meant that many of us former prisoners of war had again been pressed into service—whether we wanted our old jobs back, or not.

I was a prior enlisted man. They could have just slapped my stripes back on me. But my apparently pivotal role—as interlocutor between humanity, and our former enemies, the mantis aliens—had necessitated something a bit more lofty.

Not like I needed the shiny silver bar on my collar. I commanded no one. The chapel, built with my own hands in the early days of my former captivity, had never needed any hierarchy. I'd constructed the place in the spirit intended by its original designer, Chaplain Thomas: *all are equal in God's sight.*

I'd have refused promotion if I'd thought Fleet Command was giving me a choice.

I opened the door.

She was young, with a startlingly beautiful face. I guessed Nile Egyptian heritage, but with something else mixed in. Not European. Southeast Asian, perhaps? Her fluent use of commercial English—that hoary old offshoot of British and American English which had dominated international human affairs for hundreds of years—gave me no hint of her nation of origin.

I looked at the captain's clusters on her collar, and tipped my head.

"Ma'am, what may I do for you at this early hour?"

"General Sakumora sent me," she said, her wide eyes staring up at me.

"And of what use may I be to the general?"

"You're the one who brokered the original cease-fire," she said. "The general is hoping you can do so again."

An instant prickling of alarm went up my spine.

"Have the mantes attacked?" I asked, not blinking.

"No," she said. "Not yet."

"What does that mean?"

"Nobody told you what's happening?"

"Ma'am, in spite of my appointment and what this starchy new uniform might indicate, I'm just a chaplain's assistant. Nobody tells me much of anything. Certainly I don't pretend to understand what Fleet Command worries about when it goes to bed at night. All I care about are the people still here, on this planet."

"And the mantis converts who come to you for religious indoctrination," she said.

"Instruction," I corrected her. "And it's not even anything so formal as that. You ought to know as well as anyone, if you've earned your commission recently, that the mantes are an utterly atheistic people. They cannot even conceive of a God, nor a soul, nor do they understand anything about Earth's varied and flavorful religious history."

Flavorful. A deliberate euphemism on my part. The mantis university Professor who'd first approached me ten Purgatorial years earlier, to study Earth's major systems of belief, had often used that word to describe our faiths. He'd considered them fascinating—a key to the utterly alien mentality of the human being.

But that had been a long time ago. The Professor, and most of his students, had gone. As had many of my parishioners, once the ships from Earth returned and it became possible for humans to go home again.

I'd chosen to remain. Despite Purgatory's hard, arid climate and the chapel's crude rock-and-mud-walled simplicity. A part of me had become invested in this place. I looked over the lovely young officer's shoulder to the chapel's lone altar, where various human religious symbols and objects were carefully placed for all to see. This early in the morning I had no flock to attend to. But soon they'd begin to trickle in, a few here and a few there. Most of them human. But not all.

"It's the mantes' difficulty with religion that brings me here now," she said. "It's been almost ten Earth years since the armistice. Fleet stealth missions indicate that the mantes are moving some of their own ships. Renewed battle exercises. The truce you won may not last much longer. Not unless someone can help the mantes get what they came here for. From you specifically."

I laughed coldly.

"I labored with the Professor," I said. "For years. He read every last line of holy text I could put in front of him. The Bible, the Torah, the Koran, the Bhagavad Gita, you name it. He soaked it up like a sponge. We engaged in various rituals, both for demonstration and also to see if he'd take to any of them. But he was as deaf to the spirit as the next mantis. They're all like that—biologically incapable of feeling what you and I might call 'faith.' The Professor eventually withdrew in confused futility."

"What about the ones who still attend?"

"They are young," I said. "Grad students. They come to the chapel for objective study, no more. Working on their equivalent of thesis papers, probably."

"General Sakumora was adamant. You must help."

I wanted to keep protesting, but the earnestness in her expression told me that there wouldn't be any point. I reached a hand up and felt the non-regulation stubble on my face. I hated shaving every day. But it looked like I was going to have to start again.

"Orders are orders, ma'am?" I said, straightening my duty topcoat.

"That's right, Chief," she said.

"Yes, ma'am. And if it's all the same to you, nobody around here calls me that."

"Then what do they call you?"

"Padre. One of my former parishioners hung that on me shortly after the cease-fire."

"Father Barlow," she said, testing it out.

"No," I said sheepishly, "just padre."

"Well, *Padre,* I'm putting us on the next flight into orbit. The General is getting ready for a summit with his counterparts in the mantes' chain of command. You and I have both been instructed to cooperate in every way—to ensure that the summit is productive."

"Are you part of the Chaplains Corps?" I asked.

"No," she said. "Fleet Intelligence."

I repressed the urge to scoff. If the military's blind hurling of the original human flotillas against Purgatory's impervious mantis defenders had been any indication, intelligence was the one thing we'd been sorely lacking.

"I don't think it will do any good," I admitted. "I tried to tell the Professor, when he started to give up hope. If mantis curiosity about human faith is the only thing holding back their war machine, then our fates truly do rest in God's hands."

She stared at me.

"But," I said, "I'll do my best."

"That's all anyone can ask," she replied.

I spent a few minutes getting word out that I would be leaving. Fleet business. The flock would have to take care of the chapel for a change. Which was fine. Some of the regulars were people I trusted implicitly. But as I walked outside to join the captain, there was a sinking feeling in my stomach. I turned my head to look at the building which had been my home for so many years, and I wondered if I'd ever see it again.

The sensation was unpleasantly familiar.

One old memory swam up from the depths of my life as I trailed the captain to the four-by-four truck that would take us to the only place on Purgatory where human spacecraft were allowed to land and take off from.

"Here we go again," I said under my breath.

CHAPTER 12

Earth, 2153 A.D.

THE WOMAN SAT AT A SINGLE TABLE IN THE HIGH SCHOOL CAFeteria. There was a wide, tall thinscreen behind her, and on the thinscreen there was a slowly revolving interstellar map. A bright blue point glowed cheerfully at the center, signifying Earth and Sol System. Smaller, green points were Earth's growing number of successful colonies around other stars. One of those colonies had a harsh red halo that throbbed ominously. A computer graphic of an extremely large starship soared slowly through the scene, towing a stylized banner that said, THE FLEET WANTS YOU!

Myself and my friends Kaffy, Ben, David, and Tia stopped short, our small trays of food momentarily forgotten. The woman in front of the star map was talking animatedly with several other students who'd come to chat her up. She wore a uniform unlike any I'd seen before. From the sound of her accent, she was from the Southeast—a bit of a drawl, worn flat by years spent living outside her home state.

Up until very recently, she'd probably been Army or Air Force. Maybe Marine Corps? I'd been barely fourteen years old when the president went on the air to tell the whole country that by joint Senatorial and Congressional order, the whole of the armed forces of the United States were being used to form the backbone of a new multinational force that would be explicitly created for fighting in outer space.

Small wonder. News of the aliens had been both exciting and disquieting. We'd always suspected they might be out there. With the new colonies putting down fresh roots since the invention of the interstellar jump system some twenty years prior, many of my middle school teachers had speculated that we'd run across non-human intelligence eventually. Probably in the form of primitives living a stone-age existence. As homo sapiens, and its cousins on the primate family tree, had done for millions of years.

But the planet Marvelous had been explicitly attacked. A planet which had shown no hint of harboring intelligent life. A threat from the stars had savaged her, leaving Earth and the other colonies scrambling to put together some kind of effective defense.

War news was something that came only in irregular bits and pieces. Since Earth itself had not been hit, what went on out in the colonies, many, many light-years from home, wasn't exactly front-page news. Once the initial furor over the alien threat had died down, most American families had gone back to business as usual. What else could be done? We watched our thinscreens and we checked the Internet and we speculated about what might happen next. But for most of us, the war was a thing happening far away, out of the realm of ordinary experience.

Tia leaned close, speaking in a whisper only the four of us could hear.

"They want troops for the colonial counteroffensive," she said.

"Who told you that?" I asked, also in a whisper.

"Nobody," she said. "But what else could it be?"

I wondered. The Fleet recruiters had been getting more numerous as our senior year at school drew to a close. One of my cousins who lived in Rhode Island and who occasionally gamed with me online said that she'd noticed the same thing at her school. Was it true that the Fleet was going to strike back? What did that mean for those of us who'd never even seen the alien threat up close?

We'd all been shown pictures, of course. The aliens individually looked for all the world like a grotesque, outsized mutation of an ordinary praying mantis. Only each one rode a man-sized flying saucer not terribly different from the kind I'd seen in some of the very archaic two-dee movies of the previous century. The images which had been brought back from Marvelous were pretty horrible. So much so that even the scientists and politicians who'd been loudly advocating for peace talks gradually piped down.

The threat was real, it was ugly, and the only question that remained was: what were humans going to do about it?

The Fleet recruiter noticed us, and beckoned us over.

We hesitantly complied.

"How are y'all doin' today?" she said, smiling. Her hair was red, and she had freckles across her cheeks.

"Okay, I guess," Ben said.

"Y'all seniors?" the recruiter asked; her name tape on her uniform read O'DONNELL.

"Yeah," Tia said.

"Got plans for after school? You know the Fleet's got countless opportunities for healthy, able-bodied young men and women like yourselves. The president's authorized nice bonuses for anyone willing to sign up with me today. You'd ship out when you graduate."

Money. That was a definite enticement. Prior to the mantis aliens making their existence known, the American economy had been locked in a rather pernicious stagflationary cycle. The advent of the interstellar jump system, and the establishment of the colonies, had destabilized most of the international stock markets. Earth's economic ship-in-a-bottle approach to commerce was being disrupted now that thousands of people were disembarking on colony boats every day, while freighters returning from the colonies were bringing goods and materials back. The United Nations had been trying to slap together an interstellar monetary committee when ships fleeing Marvelous brought word of the alien attack.

Now, things were worse. The dollar was really struggling. And jobs—any kind—were not that easy to find. Not when computers and machinery did so much of the manual labor all over the country. Many people were either technicians servicing those computers and machines, or developers, engineers, and programmers who worked on improving and refining the technology that kept much of the human race fed, housed, and clothed.

"What do you do in the Fleet?" I asked O'Donnell.

"Well, before I was Fleet, I was Navy, and when I was Navy, I was a maintenance expert out on one of the submarines. Submarine life is a lot like life on the starships, you know. They snatched up as many of us submariners as they could get their hands on, when the Fleet was initially launched. I did some time converting my skills over to spacecraft, and then I got put into recruiting."

"Sounds like you don't stay in one spot too long," Kaffy said.

"Not so far," O'Donnell said. "So, can I show you a few videos? Interest you in what the Fleet has to offer?"

"Maybe later," I said. "We're going to be late for class if we don't get something to eat, and soon."

"Well, that's fine, but here, let me give you these," O'Donnell said, handing us all thin little pieces of plastic about the size of a standard credit or debit card. The card was silver, with a holographic logo on it that moved when you faced the card in different directions. The logo appeared to be a hawk or eagle, stylized of course, with its eyes and beak looking fierce. Under the bird was a small globe of Earth, shielded from above by the bird's protectively-arched wings. The bird's talons held what appeared to be a sword on the left, and a cluster of rockets on the right.

We mumbled our thanks, and went to sit at a table.

"No way," Ben said as he slipped bites of school lunch spaghetti into his mouth.

"You're not interested in going to space?" David asked.

"Not like that," Ben said, shaking his head.

"I've got an older cousin who signed up," Kaffy said. "He left home three weeks ago. My aunt and uncle don't hear from him much, though they say he says the training is tough."

"Military training is always tough," I said, chewing on a piece of cold garlic bread.

"How would you know?" Tia teased. "Playing war hero in VR isn't like the real thing, you know."

I scowled at Tia, and flipped her my middle finger.

She laughed, and up-ended her bottle of fruit juice with her right hand, flipping me back with her left.

"Too bad the mantis aliens aren't just VR," David said, his face growing sober. "I mean, really, what do any of us know about the aliens anyway? One colony has been attacked, so far. How many of the others will be attacked? Maybe they're under attack right now?"

"If it were that bad," Kaffy said, "Don't you think they'd be here already? Invading Earth?"

"Maybe," I said. "Or maybe we just happened to settle some planets that the aliens thought were theirs to begin with."

"Doesn't matter now," Ben said. "War is war. We fight, or we lose."

"Spoken like a man who just said he'd never go to space as a soldier," Tia said, turning her sarcasm on our mutual friend.

"Hey, if the battle comes to Earth, I'll do what I have to, just like everyone else," Ben said defensively. "I'm just not in a hurry to go up and be roach food, you know what I mean?"

We all nodded our heads.

It was easy to talk options, with the mantis threat almost entirely removed from our daily lives.

Still, I kept looking over my shoulder at the Fleet recruiter.

When I went home that night, I sat on the family living room couch and flipped the recruiter's card over and over and over in my fingers. Mom and Dad were still at work, and wouldn't be home until later. I noticed that the card had a chip in it.

I eyed the Total Entertainment System in the corner of the living room.

Like most virtual reality units on the market, the TES looked a lot like a huge egg, with two steps leading up to the hatch in the side. I got up and slowly went over to the unit, eyeing the small slot on the TES's control panel—a slot just big enough to accept the card the recruiter had given me.

I looked up through the numerous clear windows that made up the arched ceiling above my head, and noticed the moon was just starting to come out. The Fleet often did training exercises there now. Spacesuited infantry and armor units, practicing for the day when they might be hurled into battle against the mantis hordes.

I slipped the recruiter's card into the slot on the TES, climbed in, sat down, and shut the hatch.

It was a little unnerving, being in the TES unsupervised. Mom and Dad had very strict rules about that. I'd been punished more than once. It was easy to get lost in the virtual environment. For hours, or even days. VR had become so realistic that habitual users risked drifting over into disconnect: a clinically diagnosed condition, which left the user believing that not only was the VR experience more real than real, it was also preferable to real.

I inhaled once, then used my fingers in the air to swipe and drag the VR digital menus until the TES booted up whatever program was on the card in the exterior slot.

Almost instantly, I was plunged into a total surround starscape, with impressive full orchestra music that piped through the stereo speakers on either side of my head rest.

"A challenge awaits," said a deep baritone voice. "The galaxy needs men and women who can meet that challenge."

A planet appeared, then grew larger. It was Earth, if I had the shapes of the continents right. Then the view zoomed down into Earth orbit, where several asteroids from the asteroid belt had been artificially inserted. The view zoomed in again, and showed the shipyards on the surfaces of the asteroids. The spines and ribs of numerous large vessels were being busily constructed, while other ships—further along in the construction process—were being detached and floated into formation for their final fittings.

"The Fleet is humanity's sword and shield against all dangerous life before us," the voice boomed. "Millions of men and women from across the solar system, and also the colonies, are doing their part to ensure that humanity is protected. Our lives kept safe and secure."

Suddenly the view rapidly dropped past the asteroid shipyards, down a dizzying number of kilometers, through the clouds, and right up to the tarmac of a nameless spaceport. There were people standing in four rows—what appeared to be a rectangular formation. They were of generally young age, both genders, and varying ethnicities. They stared straight ahead of them, chins out and eyes steely. One by one their civilian clothes were computer morphed into uniforms not too different from the one I'd seen the recruiter wearing at school earlier in the day.

"Pilots, technicians, computer programmers, military police, infantry, armament and weapons specialists, they're all needed, and the Fleet needs you to do your part for humanity's future."

It felt as if I was sitting directly in the midst of the formation with them. The sun was bright, and I could hear a seagull crying in the distance. From where the view had dropped down from orbit, I guessed that this particular spaceport was supposed to be on the California coast?

The image of the people standing in formation grew still, while a menu popped up. The menu listed dozens and dozens of different kinds of jobs.

I hit the first one that looked interesting to me: weapons maintainer.

One of the people standing in formation stepped out of line and smiled at me, saying, "Good choice! Come on, I'll show you what I do!"

And suddenly I was being given a five-minute guided tour of that particular Fleet troop's responsibilities and assignments. I was shown the tools she used, the programs she had to know, the kinds of weapons she worked with, how long the training would be, what kinds of opportunities there were in the Fleet for people in her occupational slot, and so forth. All of it as real as could be, rendered through the TES's ultra-immersive VR environment.

One by one, I started swiping and selecting, letting the different virtual troops take me on tours of their jobs.

Much of it looked potentially interesting. Even the more macho stuff like infantry, gunnery, and flying. Which was a bit outside my particular taste, since until that afternoon I'd not seriously given the military—Fleet, or otherwise—any serious consideration.

But the recruiting program did have a point: if the mantis aliens were as dangerous as they seemed, who was going to protect the rest of us? What was it going to take, on the part of ordinary soon-to-be HS grads like me, to ensure that the Earth remained relatively safe?

Suddenly the program prematurely terminated, and the hatch to the TES popped open.

I was so jarred, I gave off a little yelp.

My dad leaned his head in.

"You know you're not supposed to be using this thing when your mother and I aren't home, right?"

"Yeah," I said. "But there's a good reason."

"I already know the reason," my dad said, tapping the silver recruiter's card on the edge of the hatch.

"Out," he said. "Let's talk about this."

I climbed through the hatch, suddenly grateful to be free of the small space. I'd been in there much longer than I'd initially thought. I stretched and bent my back from side to side, yawning.

"Come on," my dad said.

I followed him into the kitchen where my mom had already started up the dining computer station which was rapidly taking the raw contents of that day's grocery shopping and whipping them into something edible. I wasn't sure what menu choice my mom had selected. I could only see the little robotic waldos inside the machine moving about rapidly, making shadow-box silhouettes on the unit's frosted glass window.

"Recruiters are really pressing hard these days," my mom said. "Frankly, Harrison, I was surprised to see that you'd actually talked to one of them. You never told your father or I that you had any interest in the military."

"It's just a recruiting thing," I told them. "Me and my friends all got a card today. I figured it couldn't hurt to examine my options. I mean, I *am* going to graduate next month."

"And your grades are good enough to get you into a college," my dad said firmly. "This whole Fleet thing . . . it seems like a good option for kids who don't really have a lot of options. But you, Harry? You've got to think bigger than this."

I felt my back starting to go up. Here it came again. The grand lecture.

"Dad—" I started, perhaps a bit more petulantly than I'd intended.

"Don't," he said, putting a hand firmly on my arm. "We've been over this and over this, and we'll keep going over this until we're clear. You're only going to be eighteen once. The decisions you make in the next few months are going to resonate throughout your entire life. Don't be impulsive. Think about the path you want to take. Think about the kind of life you want to live."

"You mean, the life *you* want me to live," I said to him.

"Now, Harry," my mom said, "that's not fair to your father, or to me either. We're still your parents. We want you to be happy."

"Do you really?" I said, my irritation growing every second that this too-familiar conversation carried on. "Because what it often seems like to me is that you're more interested in me living the kind of life that will make *you* happy. Something nice, and plain, and ordinary."

Dad's grip on my arm tightened.

"Do you have any idea how much hard work it takes to build and maintain the sort of life we all enjoy here, in this house? Do you? No, of course you don't. Which is really my fault. I should have made you get a job when you were old enough to work and still carry a class load. But your mother was afraid it would interfere with your studies. Now you listen to me, Harry. In this life, everything takes effort. Nothing is given to you. You look around at our life here and you think it's boring. Well, that's the opinion of a teenager. Your mother and I? We put in long hours every week to make sure it stays that way. Because you don't want to find out what a not-boring life looks like. Trust me."

I'd heard it before—just variations on a tired theme. My dad had grown up poor, the child of a single mother struggling with addiction demons. My grandmother had died before I was old enough to really remember her, but my dad always talked about his childhood being a rather barren thing, compared to mine.

"You think the only alternative to boring is recklessness," I said to him. "I don't want to be reckless. I just want... I want to find out what more *is* there in the world than here. Why is that so bad?"

His grip slowly released. His eyes—with bags under them—grew soft.

"No, that's not bad, son. I remember feeling that way when I was your age. Just... this Fleet thing, you don't really know what you'd be getting into. Nobody does."

"The mantis aliens are real," I said. "Fleet seems to be the only thing capable of doing anything about them."

"True," my mother said. "But like your father just told you, a military career is one of those choices best suited for people who don't have many options. You *do* have options."

"If I had the option I wanted," I said, "I'd sign up for one of the colony expeditions. Go to the stars."

"If you work hard and get an advanced degree," my dad said, "maybe that will be something you can look into. In time. Seems to me Fleet's just a shortcut to that goal. You've lived an easy life so far, Harry. You won't like the military. Trust me."

"How do you know, Dad? You never served."

"I know," he said, staring intently at me. "You'll hate it."

I stared right back at him, quietly fuming. Part of me wanted to go back to the cafeteria and sign up with the Fleet tomorrow, just to lock myself in and make it so that Dad couldn't say another word otherwise. I was already of age. I could make the choice for myself.

But then, a little lingering voice in the back of my mind wondered if Dad wasn't right? Maybe I would hate it? Worse yet, what if I hated it so much that I just couldn't take it, and I washed out? What kind of face would I be seeing in the mirror then?

I looked at the recruiter's card, still clutched in Dad's other hand.

"Look," I said, "it was just a thing, okay? I was curious. I didn't put my signature on any dotted lines."

"Good," my mother said. "See that you don't. You're not even out of school yet. You have to focus on these last few weeks. Now help me set the table, because dinner's going to be ready very soon."

I did as I was told, and went to bed after the late meal—still wondering about what I might do.

The next morning, during first period, class was interrupted for a breaking news bulletin. The president and the secretary of defense were both shown at the White House podium, somberly reporting that the colony of New America had also been attacked. Again, by the mantis aliens. It was unknown whether there were any human survivors. Plans for a counteroffensive in the wake of the attack on Marvelous were now being redoubled, because it was clear the entirety of human space might be under imminent threat. The secretary of defense made a plea to the people of the United States for volunteers. The Fleet needed everyone it could get. Before any more of Earth's colonies fell.

That afternoon, myself, Tia, David, Kaffy, and even Ben, stood in a long line of students at the Fleet recruiter's table. One by one, we put our names and our thumbprints on the enlistment documents. As a mass group, we took an oath in front of the U.S. flag and a Fleet flag both. None of us had much of an idea what we wanted to do, once we were in. We just knew that this was one of those moments in human history when caution was not the better part of valor.

Something had to be done. And we were the ones who were going to do it.

CHAPTER 13

IT HAD BEEN A LONG TIME SINCE I'D RIDDEN A SHUTTLE. I FORgot they don't come with gravity. I almost threw up my breakfast when we hit space. I spent the ride—to the awaiting frigate—turning several shades of green. Once on board the mothercraft I breathed a great breath of relief, then gratefully took a small hand towel from the captain and mopped the perspiration from my face.

The young marines who'd ridden up with us, they seemed to find me funny. Until they saw my expression, and my rank. They snapped to as I walked past.

I guess being Chief is good for a few things after all?

The captain—whom I'd learned to address by the last name of Adanaho—gave me twenty minutes to clean up in the frigate's cramped guest officers' quarters.

As an enlisted man, I'd only ever gotten bay accommodations. Zero privacy. My little single-man compartment seemed palatial by comparison.

The hair on my cheeks and neck came off, and a fresh undershirt and topcoat came on. Then I used the tiny computer guide in my newly-issued PDA to walk me through the frigate's innards—to the command deck, where I was to meet Adanaho's boss.

Sakumora was a short, muscular, stern-faced flag officer who neither smiled nor offered any pleasantries as I entered the room. Two lieutenants attended to his needs, while Captain Adanaho sat at his side, and two marines guarded opposite corners of the space. Against what, I had no idea. But protocol was protocol, and some things never change.

"Sir," I said, approaching his desk and saluting, "Serg-ahhh, I mean, Chief Warrant Officer Barlow, reporting as ordered."

"Sit down," was all he said.

I took a chair which had been offered to me by one of the general's attaches. For the first time, I noticed the captain's expression. Her eyes were turned down and staring at the space in front of my knees.

"I'll get to the point," said Sakumora gruffly. "We've got compelling evidence that the mantes are building strength for a renewed offensive. Everybody knows the generalities of what you did here, on this little dustball of a world. I've reviewed the records, your own file, and the reports given to me by my officers who've been to Purgatory. There was never any guarantee that the mantes would hold off on their so-called Fourth Expansion indefinitely. I'm afraid time's up."

My feet and hands went cold.

So far as I knew, we were as defenseless as ever. The mantes were a much older and technologically superior race. Human ships and weapons amounted to little against mantis shields. For the sake of morale, when the war had been hot, the Fleet hadn't broadly revealed its numerous and inevitable defeats—human colonies seized by the mantes and cleansed of all "competitive" life. Only after the armistice and the Fleet's slow return did anyone come clean about the truth.

I cleared my throat.

"What do you expect me to do about it, sir?"

"Do what you did before," he said matter-of-factly. "Get this collective of... scholars, or whatever they are, to talk to their political leadership. Stage protests. Sit-ins. *Anything* that can hold the mantes off for a few more years."

"Assuming I could do it," I said carefully, "would it make that much of a difference? I don't think we're any closer to fending them off than we were before."

The general looked over to Captain Adanaho. She raised her eyes to me. "Few people have been told this, so I'm ordering you to keep it secret, but we've managed to develop a working copy of their shielding technology—what I think you referred to in your notes as The Wall. In the process we think we've found a way to penetrate those same shields."

"Is that so?" I said, startled. "How exactly did we make this extraordinary breakthrough?"

"That's none of your concern," the general snapped, "all you're here to do is get the damned mantes to delay their attack. Until we're ready."

"Sir, what makes you think I have any more influence on the mantes than the Fleet's team of expert diplomats?" I said, throwing my hands out in exasperation. "It's not like I'm some kind of genius about this stuff. The Professor—the first mantis I dealt with, ten years ago—just happened to reveal certain information that wound up being important. And I had nothing to lose. That my bargain convinced him, and that his compatriots had the leverage and coordination to affect Mantis Quorum policy, were flukes."

"Nevertheless," said the general, "you *will* try."

"We depart in one hour," Adanaho said. "You'll have a few days to prepare, before we meet the mantis delegation."

CHAPTER 14

Earth, 2153 A.D.

THEY CALLED IT RECEPTION.

As if I'd been invited to something you do after a wedding.

Only there was no cake.

And certainly no ice cream.

Sweat gradually trickled down into the small of my back, underneath my t-shirt. My arms and shoulders were on fire from being made to hold both of my stuffed-to-the-gills travel bags, while myself and five hundred other Fleet recruits stood at the position of attention outside the main processing hall of Armstrong Field.

If there was a hottest, most-humid, least-agreeable spot in North America, Armstrong Field seemed to have been built right in the middle of it. Sol's yellow-white rays quietly baked the acres of concrete in front of the hall, and I had to grit my teeth against the heat on my brow and the agony of having stood completely still—in the exact same place—for what had seemed like thirty pointless minutes.

People patrolled the edges of the formation—each wearing green and brown pixelated camouflage uniforms and high-topped simulated brown leather boots. They answered to names like *Corporal* and *Sergeant* and they screamed at anyone who dared to address them in any other way. Literally screamed. Loud enough I was sure none of them would have a working larynx at the end of the day.

The victims—all of us gathered from across the globe—had all been rooted to the spot, immediately following our disembarkation from a flotilla of buses which had come from Armstrong's busy aerospace field.

There had been no warning. One moment we'd all been on the buses, chattering and grab-assing, the next we'd been herded off and funneled into one of several gauntlets of very angry Fleet soldiers—men and women who seemed to have raised cursing to a high art. Men and women who looked as if they might literally burn a person to the ground, just from the raw hate in their steely eyes.

We recruits were demeaned, hollered at, cuffed, slapped, and even punched until everyone was arrayed in a huge rectangle, one hundred columns wide and five rows deep. We were not allowed to drop our bags. Anyone unfortunate enough to drop his or her bags—or anything else on his or her person—was promptly surrounded by several blister-tongued Fleet soldiers who verbally pummeled the perpetrator until he or she had secured his or her things, and returned to the proper state of being scared shitless.

For the first time, I wondered if I'd made a very serious mistake.

One of the main doors to the hall popped open, and a gorilla of a man walked out. He took his time, carefully walking down the steps, the tops of his boots gleaming like mirrors in the sun, and his hat—which I would later learn was technically called a *soft cap*—perched at a crisp forward angle on top of his nearly-shaved head.

A small brim shaded his Neanderthal brow from the sun, and in the center of the hat were three chevrons perched atop three concave half-circles, with a diamond in the middle. This insignia was replicated over the man's name on his breast—KLAUSKI—and all of the other soldiers became immediately aware of his presence as he approached the mass formation.

The sergeants and corporals ceased movement, and ran to what seemed to be pre-designated positions around the outside of the rectangle of recruits.

The one named Klauski stopped dead-center before the rectangle, slowly scanned his head and eyes from left to right and back again, then clicked his heels together, raised his chin to the sky, and bellowed, "KUHMPAHNAAAAYYY!"

At once, all the other soldiers flicked their heads towards the recruits and repeated the same yell.

"AHHTEN-*SHUN!*" Klauski bawled.

The sergeants and corporals snapped rigid.

Since I and the other recruits had already been standing at the position of attention for far too long, we did nothing.

"Good morning, recruits," said the gorilla-man.

"GOOD MORNING, FIRST SERGEANT," shouted the soldiers in unison.

When we recruits said nothing—heads and eyes looking frantically up and down the rows to determine what the eff it was we were supposed to do now—Klauski cleared his throat and tried again.

"I SAID, GOOD MORNING, RECRUITS!"

As a gaggle, our rectangle blurted, "GOOSHMOURNINFUSAGNT . . ."

Several disapproving whistles and *tsk-tsks* came from the sergeants and corporals around the formation—their heads shaking knowingly.

The first sergeant's razor-straight, thin-lipped mouth curled up slightly at the corners.

"Now, recruits, that was just piss-poor. And I do mean piss, piss, piss-poor. Y'all gonna have to git' with the program around here real fast, before I have to go and dirty my nice bright boots on your stinky little asses. Now effin' sound the eff off like you mean it. *Good morning, recruits!*"

"GOOD MORNING, FIRST SERGEANT!"

"Okay, better. Can y'all hear me?"

"YESFUSAGINT . . ."

"Bull, try again. I said, *can you all hear me?*"

"*YES, FIRST SERGEANT!*"

"Right. Now that's the kind of *volume* I should hear coming out of your effin' mouths any time any noncommissioned officer is standing up in front of you like this. Doesn't matter if she's got two stripes or six. You render respect and you clear your skinny little throats with some gawtdamned articulation and uniformity. Is that understood, recruits?"

"YES, FIRST SERGEANT!"

"Good. Now, welcome to 69th Reception Battalion, Armstrong Field. Otherwise known as The Big Sixty-Nine. You all are gonna be here for the next six to eight days as we fill up in preparation for Pickup Day. During that time my NCOs and I will do everything in our power to properly prepare you for your entry into Induction Service Training, also known as Basic. But before we start I want to make something abundantly clear to you people.

"The moment you stepped on this installation, you ceased to be civilians. All those e-documents you signed with your recruiter? All that crap about standing in front of the flag before you left to come here? Well, now the rubber meets the road. You're here for a specific purpose, and there is no time for second thoughts. You are committed. Most of you should have already realized that. But if you didn't before, start thinking about that now. It will save you—and me—a lot of heartache and assache. Do I make myself clear, recruits?"

"YES, FIRST SERGEANT!"

"Your mamas and your daddies and your aunties and uncles and grampies and grannies ain't here to rescue you anymore. And I don't care if you're eighteen or thirty-eight, it's time to grow the eff up, grow an effin' pair between your legs—females too—and learn how to walk, talk, act, shoot, fight, and be a soldier in the Fleet."

"YES, FIRST SERGEANT!"

"Good. You're starting to get the beat of things, a little. And believe me, there is a beat. And a rhythm. You're gonna find that in virtually everything you do in the Fleet. Look for it. Use it. The harder you try to cling to the old you that showed up here today, the harder it's going to be. But the more you let the rhythm take you—the more you let yourself mold to and grow with the change—the easier it will become and the less stressful this is all going to seem.

"Because make no mistake, recruits, *stress* is what Induction Service Training is all about. I can see it in your faces right now. It's effin' hot. Your arms are about to fall off. Your feet and legs are starting to get numb. You're wondering why the hell you had to wait out here for so long just to listen to me jaw-jack. It's part of the program, people. Part of the program. And you can either resist the program, or git' with the program. Now what do you want to do, recruits?"

"GET WITH THE PROGRAM, FIRST SERGEANT!"

"Gawtdamn, now that's what I want to hear! Okay, enough of me running my mouth. In front of you is the building you will call home until Pickup Day. As soon as you enter that building, at no time will you leave it unless told to do so by an NCO or an officer, is that understood?"

"YES, FIRST SERGEANT!"

"You will obey every command given to you, and if you do not understand the command given to you, you will request clarification in a proper and respectful manner, is *that* understood?"

"YES, FIRST SERGEANT!"

"Are there any questions for me at this time?"

The rectangle remained silent.

"No questions then? Alright. Time to whip a little training on your asses. You are now standing in what is called a mass formation. Most of the time you'll be broken down by platoons, but once in a while it's convenient for us to line you up like this as a large group. There are certain commands you will be given—whether in mass, or in platoon—and you must follow those commands in unison. Do you understand?"

"YES, FIRST SERGEANT," shouted the formation.

The first sergeant laughed, and the other NCOs laughed with him.

"Ch'yeah right, we'll see about that. Okay, here it comes... *Companaaaayyy!*"

The NCOs surrounding the formation snapped their heads towards the recruits and repeated the preparatory command.

"Right-FACE!"

I did my best to mechanically rotate ninety degrees to starboard, bringing me face-to-face with another recruit who had turned the wrong way. An immediate chorus of hoots, catcalls, and profanity issued from the surrounding pack of NCOs, as recruits who had turned left—or not turned at all—blushed and shuffled their feet until everyone was facing in the same direction.

"Jesus H," said the first sergeant, shaking his head and smiling. "It's gonna be a *real* fun group. Real fun. File from the left... column left... MARCH!"

None of the recruits moved.

"I said *march*, gawtdammit!"

Suddenly people were bumping into people as half the formation lurched forward and the other half stayed where it was. Like buzzsaws, the surrounding NCOs descended into the throng, screaming, insulting, kicking, hitting, and knocking bags to the ground. The recruit behind me barged into my back full-force and I dropped both bags, suddenly relieved to be rid of them but then regretting it as a female corporal appeared and slapped the back of my head.

"PICK UP THOSE EFFING BAGS RIGHT NOW, RECRUIT!"

"Okay, okay, I only dropped them because—" (slap)

"SHUT YOUR HOLE, RECRUIT, IS THAT HOW YOU SPEAK TO A NONCOMMISSIONED OFFICER?"

"No, ma'am, I—" (slap)

"*MA'AM?* MY HELL, RECRUIT, YOU'VE BEEN HERE LESS THAN ONE EARTH HOUR AND YOU'RE ALREADY EFFED UP BEYOND BELIEF!"

"Yes, ma—errr, yes, Corporal. I mean, *no, Corporal!*"

"I'M WAITING, RECRUIT! PICK UP YOUR BAGS AND GET BACK IN FORMATION!"

I quickly retrieved my bags—happy to not receive a fourth whack on the back of the head, and got back in line while others did likewise. In two minutes the entire mass formation was once again standing at attention, facing the first sergeant, who no longer seemed to be smiling.

"Wow," he said. "That was just effin' ugly. Y'all act like you just got out of the nursery. Am I gonna have to come around every day and wipe ass on y'all? Am I?"

"NO, FIRST SERGEANT!"

"I hope not, because from what I've seen in the last five minutes *none of you* has what it takes to ship out on Pickup Day. To be Fleet you have to *think*. And right now I can tell that not a gawtdamned single one of you is doing any thinking. You're all just going along and pretending to do whatever the eff it seems like you're supposed to do, and hoping nobody gets up in your ass about it. Listen, Fleet doesn't want dummies in its ranks. I'm not a dummy, and none of these other NCOs is a dummy. Dummies get people killed, even in training. Or should I say, *especially* in training. We don't need dummies. So I might as well just outprocess the whole effin' five hundred of yah and put your butts back on the runway, right?"

"NO, FIRST SERGEANT!"

"Prove it. Someone raise their gawtdamned hand and tell me what was the first thing you all did wrong just now."

A hand went up meekly, fifty down and third rank.

"You," said the first sergeant.

"We didn't follow the command correctly?"

A corporal stepped up to the recruit with the raised hand and began bawling the recruit out for not beginning and ending his sentence with "First Sergeant."

"Wrong," said Klauski. "Someone else?"

Another hand went up. "First Sergeant, we ran into each other, First Sergeant."

"Wrong."

"First Sergeant, the people up front didn't know what to do, First Sergeant."

"Wrong."

". . . not in unison!"

"Wrong . . . wrong . . . wrong."

The first sergeant put a palm up to his face and wiped it across his mouth in exasperation.

I finally raised my hand high.

"You," said the first sergeant.

"First Sergeant, we didn't ask for an explanation of the command, First Sergeant," I said as loudly and with as much gusto as I could muster.

He snapped his finger and stepped forward.

"Abso-effin-lutely *correct,* Recruit. Did everyone hear that? Finally, someone is paying attention to what I first told you. You *never* follow a command that you don't *understand* first. *Two times* I stood up here and gave a command that more than half of you didn't know what the eff to do with. At least one of you should have stuck a paw in the air and respectfully requested clarification on 'right-face' and 'file from the left column left,' but you didn't do it. Maybe 'cause you're scared, or maybe 'cause you're just stupid, I don't know. But get it through your skulls, recruits. Whether you're stupid or scared. You have to understand what the eff it is that you're doing, or you're going to fail. And when people in uniform fail, it usually means people in uniform die.

"Now, I hope this little object lesson has sunk in. Ready to try it again?"

"YES, FIRST SERGEANT," shouted the formation.

"Are you sure?"

"YES, FIRST SERGEANT!"

A hand went up. This time, not mine.

"What is it, Recruit?"

"First Sergeant, uhhhh, respectfully request—"

"*Who* respectfully requests?"

"Uhh, First Sergeant, I respectfully—"

An NCO jumped into the speaking recruit's face and barked about the proper way to self-reference during IST.

"One more time, Recruit," Klauski said.

"First Sergeant, Recruit Trucco requests clarification on 'right face' and 'file from the left column left,' First Sergeant."

"Beautiful, Recruit Trucco."

The first sergeant proceeded to explain: posting NCO demonstrators in order to properly display facing movements and the somewhat more complicated columnar split-off movement known as *file-from-the-left-column-left.* After which he called the formation once again to attention—the sunlight slamming down on us as Sol rose higher into the blue sky—and repeated his first two commands.

Right-face went much more smoothly, with only a few people messing it up.

Filing was more problematic, but after the left-most column—which had been the first row prior to facing right—stumbled through it, the other columns got the idea, and one by one they broke off and filed up the steps and into the reception center.

CHAPTER 15

THE *CALYSTA* WAS MUCH MORE SPACIOUS THAN I REMEMBERED Fleet ships being when I'd first signed up. She had wider corridors. Larger compartments. Not nearly as much exposed wiring and piping. Brighter lamps in the ceiling, all spaced at closer intervals. And so on, and so forth. They even had several flavors of ice cream in the galley's little dessert bar.

I stared at the brightly-colored frozen dessert food, and wondered how long it'd been since I'd treated myself to such a delicacy.

"Life's a little easier up here this time, isn't it?" Captain Adanaho said to me as she sat down at my table, watching me take slow, deliberate spoonfuls of Neopolitan into my mouth.

I swallowed—savoring the taste of the vanilla mixed with strawberry mixed with chocolate—and aimed my empty spoon at her.

"You could say that, yes, ma'am," I said.

"Helps that the Fleet has had much more time to refine its various starship designs," she said, poking at her own tray with a pair of chopsticks. It seemed she had rice and teriyaki beef, plus a vegetable side that looked suspiciously like some form of seaweed.

"A lot's changed since I first went to space," I said. "All of this would have seemed like decadent extravagance in the wake of New America being attacked. Earth was really scrambling then. Can I admit to being relieved that the designers thought to put a few creature comforts into these new ships?"

"It's part of Fleet's long-term plan," she said. "When the armistice stabilized the situation with the mantes, Fleet turned its focus from rapid counterattack and repulsion, to a more permanent security mission designed to protect both those colonies which had escaped being molested during the war, and those colonies which had been ceded back to us by the mantis Quorum. You can't keep people in space forever, and expect morale to remain decent, when the living conditions are too Spartan. So, Fleet's civilian contractors started getting creative with the amenities. Now life aboard ship for long durations is tolerable."

"When you've just come from the conditions I've lived in for the last few years," I said, "this is more than tolerable. It's practically paradise. I really should see if it's possible to import a few of these goodies down to Purgatory's surface, once we get back."

"Yes," Adanaho said, her eyes losing focus. "Once we get back."

I stopped, a fresh spoonful of ice cream halfway to my lips. "You've got doubts?" I said.

"Yes, and no," she said, looking around her quickly, to be sure nobody was sitting within earshot of us. "I don't like talking about it out in the open like this, but if you'd seen some of the information I've seen, you'd realize that things aren't looking so good. Yes, the armistice is intact. For the moment. But there are strong signs that the mantes are preparing for something. All our data points to that. And we're not sure if or when the fragile truce is going to break."

"I'm going to assume you're speaking as a strategist who has to plan for worst-case scenarios," I said to her, putting my spoon down.

"That's true," she said.

"But me being here is cause for hope?"

"Also true."

"So what does your gut tell you? Which way is it going to go?"

Adanaho closed her eyes and ran a hand over her forehead, rubbing softly. "I just don't know, Chief. I think that's the part which is driving me nuts right now. The lack of knowing what the future might hold. What can be planned for, and what's unknown. I mean, how did you do it, during your years of captivity? How did you know when to relax and just live your life?"

I chuckled bleakly.

"I'm not really sure it was anything like a conscious decision," I said. "We all just kind of went from day to day at the start. Nobody knew anything. We had no contact with the rest of the Fleet. We were beaten, and we knew it, and so far as we could tell, death was going to visit us any day. It got a little easier when

The Wall went up. Then it became clear our incarceration was going to be more long term. Which is why news of The Wall's gradual contraction hit us in the face like a brick. Our hope for a future—any kind of future—crumbled."

"That's what I am afraid of now," she admitted, continuing to poke at her meal without showing much enthusiasm.

"You know," I said, "has anyone in Fleet ever considered the idea that the way to beat the mantes for good is not to entrench ourselves and hold, but to pull up our stakes and run?"

She stared at me.

"There's no way Earth's sixteen *billion* people could ever possibly hope to run," she said.

"I know that," I said. "But the galaxy is a big place. The mantes don't control the whole thing. Hell, they don't even control a small fraction of it, despite their reach. There is plenty of room for humanity to get lost in. Find new worlds, far, far away from the mantis threat. Put down and settle in. Go dark, maybe. Just kind of fade off the face of the universe. Nobody to bother us if we don't bother them first. Keep quiet."

"If it comes down to it, yes," she said. "The Fleet is prepared to bundle as many colonists as it can into emergency departure flotillas, and head for unknown territory. But who is to say we won't just find something or someone even worse than the mantes?"

"A distinct possibility," I said, leaning back in my seat and resting my hands across my full belly.

"Don't you have family back home?" She asked. "I'm surprised you'd even consider running if you've got people you care about back on Earth."

"My mother and father are still on Earth. At least as far as I know."

"Don't you ever send them messages? Why didn't you go back to see them after it became possible again?"

"I don't really know," I said, frowning. "Mom and Dad... they kind of took it hard when I told them I'd signed up. They weren't there to see me off to IST. Dad especially thought I was making a huge mistake. Me, and all my friends."

"What about them?" she said. "Your friends?"

"Not sure," I said. "None of us were sent to the same IST installations. After graduating high school, we scattered. And once I got stuck on Purgatory, things just kind of went into bizarro mode for me."

"What does that mean?"

"You've no idea what it was like, existing with the mantis threat all around you every day. Caged. With only enough land under your feet to scratch a minimal living out of. My life back on Earth, before the war . . . it quickly got far away, and faded out of my thoughts. There were immediate concerns always in my face, every minute of every day. Including my promise to Chaplain Thomas. It took all I had to build the chapel, and by then, I was building new relationships with new friends, and before long, we all had new lives. Not great lives. Not lives I'd recommend to anyone in your position. But lives just the same. Earth . . . became a bit of a fairy tale for me. And when the armistice happened, I didn't have a huge desire to go back. What would I do? Where would I go? Would my parents be glad to see me, or would they slam the door in my face?"

She ate in silence for several minutes.

"You must feel very, very lonely," she said, not looking up.

"I have people back on Purgatory," I said.

"That's not what I mean," she said.

I thought about it for a second, then sat up.

"If you mean lonely for a wife or girlfriend, yeah, you could say that."

"Was there ever anybody? Someone you wanted to make a family with?"

"The chapel became my home and the congregation became my family. But there was one person. We called her the Deacon. A former gunner."

"So what happened to her?"

"Well, we were good friends, but when the armistice became a reality, she fled back to Earth the second she could catch a ride to orbit. I never saw her again, and never heard from her again either. As much as I hated life on Purgatory during our stint as POWs, I think she hated it even more. I suspect she probably considers me to be part of a long and uncomfortable set of memories she'd just as soon forget."

"A shame," Adanaho said.

"Maybe," I said. "But what's *your* excuse, ma'am?"

"I'm still under thirty," she said, cracking a little grin at me.

For the first time since boarding the ship, I belted out a genuine laugh.

CHAPTER 16

Earth, 2153 A.D.

THE REST OF THE MORNING WAS A COMPLETE BLUR FOR ME.

Immediately inside the reception center, each recruit had a number stamped to the back of his or her hand, with an accompanying barcode. Depending on that number, each recruit was broken off and directed into a different, gymnasium-sized room, where more NCOs waited.

When about forty people had filed into the room where I once again stood at attention, we were ordered to drop our bags—at last!—and then wait while an NCO came around to each of us and proceeded to dump everything out of our bags into piles on the floor in front of us.

Then the NCOs proceeded to paw through the piles.

Almost everything was deemed contraband. Phones, media players, computer pads, hardcopy books and magazines, civilian clothing... it was all unceremoniously shoved back into whatever luggage we recruits had brought with us, then each bag was closed shut with a zip tie to which a tag—with the respective recruit's number and barcode on it—was attached. The bags were then stacked on several carts, and the carts were wheeled out. No explanation given, other than that the recruits would be seeing their bags again when they left Armstrong Field for Advanced Technical School—or washed out.

Food and drink of any sort was trashed.

I grunted at my wasted effort. I had tried to travel light, bringing only those things which had been on the packing list that my recruiter had given me. But I found out quickly that the packing list was next to worthless. Virtually everything I'd carried with me was being taken away, save for a small toiletries satchel and a neutral-colored towel.

But I was lucky. Some of the other recruits were literally in tears, watching their toys and their games and their Most Favorite Of All Things taken from them and hauled off.

When the shakedown was complete, numerous recruits appeared to have been hollowed out. And that was just the first personally-invasive violation of the day.

Next came medical, where males and females were split off into separate lines and funneled into locker rooms where they were ordered to strip to the skin. I deposited both shoes and clothing into a plastic bag, which was zip-tied and tagged just like my luggage—presumably to be disappeared off to wherever it was they were keeping everyone's stuff.

Nude, cringing, and clutching my hygiene satchel, I went with the rest of the males—more variously-shaped naked bodies than I had ever seen in one place in my entire life—into a second room that appeared as if it might double as a torture chamber.

Eyes. Ears. Nose. Mouth. And apertures too sensitive to mention. It all got checked and rechecked by a busy-bodied horde of Fleet personnel in medical scrubs, some of them wielding arcane and sometimes ferocious-looking medical equipment. Beeps and boops from the med computers told the med personnel yay or nay, and a few people had to be directed off to yet another room for a full physician's inspection.

Everyone else—myself included—processed through with as much dignity as could be salvaged, right before getting hit with several injector guns that left swelling welts on our thighs, biceps, and butt cheeks.

Then came the barber.

One by one, each of us lay down on what looked like a massage table, while an automated hood closed over our scalps. A violent sucking sound, followed by devilish whirring and snipping, and each male emerged with approximately one *millimeter* of hair on his head.

I forlornly rubbed at my stubbly scalp while the uniform sizer's lasers did a quick sweep of my body, and the computer chirped at me that the recruit in question had been correctly measured, and would he please move along and make room for the next person.

It occurred to me that I was on an assembly line, with people as the product. We were never allowed to stand in one place for too long. The indignity of the process might have been tremendously upsetting to me were it not for the fact that everyone else was going through the exact same form of humiliation. Somehow that made it all right. Though I could tell my sentiment on the matter was far from universal.

Grown men—with bodies like linebackers—appeared to be on the verge of tears.

I put their pain out of my mind and tried to pay attention to the next task at hand.

Past the sizer was a long, windowless and doorless hallway, behind the walls of which could be heard a great deal of automated machinery. At the hallway's end there was a huge duffel waiting for each man—with a printed number and barcode on it identical to that which had been stamped on our hands. Each man hefted each duffel—some of us staggering to do so—and then we were herded into yet another locker room where a male NCO stood on a stool and ordered us all to ground our duffels and take a seat on the benches.

"I don't want to hear any complaining," said the sergeant, whose name tape read FUJIMORA. "So far today you've each received several thousand international dollars worth of clothing and medical attention. And you've not even *done* anything yet. So be grateful for the free stuff, and get ready for what comes next.

"I can tell that some of you feel like crying. That needs to stop right now. You're going to be with us in Reception for several more days. Use that time to toughen up and grow some thicker skin. It gets worse from here on out, not better. But for those of you willing to put in the effort, it will be more than worth it. Earth needs you. The colonies need you. Fleet is the *only* thing standing between your families, and the mantis threat. We can't afford to fail. Winning is all we care about. Winning is all you will be trained to do. Do I make myself clear?"

I was one of the loudest when the room yelled, "YES, SERGEANT!"

"Good. Now, let me introduce you to some of the uniforms you'll be wearing during IST. Everything you have in your duffel is what's called your Entry Kit. It includes five sets of uniforms that you'll be using during physical fitness training, and five sets of uniforms that you'll use during your daily routine. The proper wear and display of each of these things is part of your transformation from civilian to soldier, so pay attention and don't be afraid to ask questions..."

We were all back in our original rooms where they'd first dumped our bags, males and females remixed together. Everyone's scalp had been buzzed—even the girls'—so that everyone looked equally unfortunate as a result.

But the uniforms did look good, I had to admit. The Garrison and Field Fatigue, which everyone came to know as the GFF, was a wash-and-wear synthetic fiber outfit identical to that which we'd seen on the first sergeant and the other NCOs we'd encountered that day. Pants, topcoats, boots, even the undershirt and underpants—granny panties, one female recruit groused—fit nicely, per the computerized sizer's instructions, as relayed to the automated tailor that had lived behind the walls of the hallway.

With duffels over shoulders, we recruits were hustled into platoon formation, four ranks of ten each, then filed out of the room and directed up several flights of stairs to the barracks level.

The walls were brick, and covered in a thick layer of slate-gray semi-gloss paint. The floor was covered in brightly-shining institutional tile—white, with little speckles in it—and at the edges there was black rubber molding. The whole place stank of disinfectant, mixed with an artificial pine aroma; both of which might have been better suited to a pet morgue than any place humans might want to inhabit. These smells grew especially intense any time I walked past the door to a bathroom—what the NCOs kept referring to as the *head*.

Corporals with e-pads and barcode readers came around and began directing males to their bays, and females to their bays. When I got to my designated bay—essentially a large, open room with bunk beds and lockers around the perimeter—I was surprised to see other recruits already there.

When one of the corporals noticed the questioning expression on my face, the corporal said, "Barlow, you're with holdovers."

"Corporal, what's a *holdover,* Corporal?"

"People who didn't ship during last Pickup Day. Various problems."

I looked at the holdovers, who were all doing their best to ignore the new bodies trudging in, and I felt my stomach turn over.

Bunks and lockers were divided up by name, and I got stuck sharing with one of the holdovers, who didn't so much as say hello to me as I grunted and shoved my duffel up onto the top bunk, and waited for the corporal to come around and give further instructions.

"You new people," said the corporal, "need to understand that even though this is temporary lodging, you're expected to keep it as immaculate as it is now. Cleaning and watch duty rosters will be made up before the end of the day, and everyone will be instructed on how to make and keep their bunk, their locker, and their common area. Much of that's going to be a team effort. I feel compelled to remind you that arguing and fighting is only going to get everyone in trouble. Work well as a team, and the next few days will go smoothly. Work badly as a team . . . Well, we'll just have to find a way to fix it."

The holdovers snickered among themselves, and I had a suspicious feeling about the hidden meaning behind the word *fix*.

"Recruit Thukhan," said the corporal to the holdover that was bunked with me, "is the bay sergeant. You go through him before you go through me or any of the other NCOs. Chain of command is very important. If you come to me or another NCO and we find out you *didn't* go through Thukhan first, you're wrong. And we will make that point abundantly clear. Understood?"

As a bay, "YES, CORPORAL!"

"Thukhan, you know the drill. Help these new recruits get unpacked, draw linen, and fill their names in for duties."

"Corporal, yes, Corporal," said Thukhan.

"Any questions?"

When nobody raised a hand, the corporal pivoted on a heel and walked out of the bay, leaving myself and the new recruit males to mill about and begin talking to each other for the first time since we'd gotten off the buses in the dark at three in the morning. I felt my stomach growl, and wondered why at this time of the day we'd not had lunch.

I turned to the Thukhan to ask about it.

"They don't feed you the first twenty-four hours," Thukhan said. "There's more medical stuff tomorrow and they want you to fast before they draw blood. Don't worry, you won't be doing any PT until the third day here."

"What's PT?"

"Physical fitness. Ass on the grass."

"Oh."

I waited for Thukhan to say something else, but Thukhan just turned away and went to the back of the bay where the other holdovers were occupying several bottom bunks and conversing amongst themselves. I waited for a few moments, looking around the bay, and went to my locker. Opening it, I found a top shelf, a bar for hangers, and a cabinet with three drawers, all empty. It seemed like a waste to have to unpack and arrange everything when we were just going to have to repack and carry everything off again the following week, but the rules were the rules, and I went hesitantly to speak to the holdovers while the other new recruits broke off into pairs or trios, sitting on the bottom bunks and gabbing about everything which had happened to them up to that point.

"What do you want, Barlow?" said one of the holdovers, a pug-faced little man whose name tape read GORANA.

"Corporal says we should unpack and get bedding and stuff, and Thukhan is supposed to help us with that."

Gorana sniffed and pointed at me ironically. "Newbie."

The Holdovers laughed, and I felt my cheeks begin to burn. Angry—but determined to not make a fight about it—I turned to Thukhan, who still acted as if I wasn't worth noticing.

"Where do we go to get blankets?"

"I'll show you when I'm ready, Barlow. Shit, you've got all effing day to take care of things. Just relax and don't worry about it."

I looked back at the room full of men—boys, mostly, and all of us entirely too eager to kick back—and decided I needed to press my case.

"I don't think it's a good idea if we wait. What if the corporal comes back and finds us all just sitting around like this. Won't he be pissed?"

"So what if he is?" Gorana snorted. "Limp-dicked little effer isn't my problem. I'm out of here in thirty days, and I'm not lifting a finger for any of you chumps."

Laughter from all of the holdovers.

I turned my attention strictly on Thukhan.

"Can I talk to you for a minute?"

The bay sergeant sighed. "You already are. Too much, in fact. What now?"

"I mean privately, please."

Gorana and a couple of others snickered loudly, and seemed to think that I made for great comedy. When I didn't sulk away as expected, Thukhan stood up irritably and stalked towards the back of the bay. "In my office, Barlow!"

I followed, walking through a swinging door into what was, apparently, the bay's head.

Thukhan spun and faced me, arms crossed over chest.

"What is it?"

"First of all, I'm Harry," I said, holding out my hand.

The bay sergeant looked at my hand, and didn't respond for several tell-tale moments. Then he reluctantly put out his own hand—dead-fishing me—and said, "Batbayar."

"Batbayar. That's . . . Mongolian?"

"Can we just cut the crap, Barlow? In case you haven't noticed, none of us holdovers is particularly thrilled to be here. Maybe you're still feeling all special about yourself for having volunteered, but for some of us it's either this, or prison. Think I'm happy to be here instead of jail? No, I'm not. This is just jail of another sort. You're new so you don't know what it's like, but you'll learn. So go back to your bunk and lay down and chill until I'm ready. Do you understand?"

"I think so," I said.

"Good. Now stop bothering me,"

Thukhan turned and walked out of the head before I could get in another word.

CHAPTER 17

WE MET THE MANTES IN ORBIT AROUND A NAMELESS TERRESTRIAL planet, far from the boundaries of human space. The mantis ships were shaped like mammoth footballs, their surfaces studded with sensors and weaponry. I watched the alien vessels through the portholes of the Fleet frigate, *Calysta*. We'd brought some big stuff too. Opposite the cluster of mantis vessels—across the black expanse of space—was a squadron of Earth dreadnoughts unlike anything I'd ever seen before. Not that size and armament would do a lick of good if those new ships couldn't break through the mantis shields, as Adanaho had suggested. Hopefully we wouldn't have to find out, though I still wasn't sure anything I did or said could make a difference otherwise.

I looked over to Captain Adanaho, who had followed me to the observation deck.

"Fifteen minutes," she said.

"That means the general wants us there in five," I said.

She smirked at me.

"Always arrive ten minutes before you've been told," I said with a slight smile, "and then it's hurry-up-and-wait."

"The years on Purgatory haven't completely dulled your memory," she said. "Though it's obvious you're not happy about your current position."

I looked down at my uniform.

"No, ma'am, not really. I was nineteen when I signed up. The Fleet tried to take Purgatory a couple of years later, and then I spent the rest of my time either as a prisoner, or trying to follow through on a promise I made to my old boss before he died."

"It must have been an important promise," she said.

"I thought so," I said.

"But didn't you consider that promise fulfilled, once the armistice was reached?"

"Not really, because by then the Professor and his school kids were showing up all the time. Plus, I had more human customers coming in the door than I'd ever had before. People seemed to think the chapel was special. Significant. It grew to be a landmark in the valley. *Somebody* had to stick around and sweep up. And it's not like I had anything more important to do. Maybe if the Fleet had returned right away, I'd have jumped at a chance to go home. But when a couple of years went by and it was obvious that Fleet wasn't coming back to Purgatory any time soon, I decided to make my plans for the chapel into long-term plans."

"And yet our research shows that you don't hold services there," she said, raising an eyebrow.

"Like I said, I'm not a chaplain. I'm just the assistant. This little silver bar you guys put on my collar, it doesn't make me a chaplain either."

"Would you like to be?"

I thought about it, still looking outside into deep space. Something I had not seen in many years.

"No," I said, slipping my hands into my pants pockets. Like having facial hair, hands in pockets was also against regulation. But screw it, certain rules are made to be broken.

"Why not?" she asked.

"I'm not a preacher," I admitted. "I'm also not a theologian."

"So why even become an assistant? Of all the jobs in the Fleet available to you?"

"Seemed like the best fit," I said. "I'm not a tactical guy, and I'm not that great with equipment either. But people? I like people. When hostilities with the mantes broke out, some of my friends signed up immediately. I kind of went along for the ride. It was a chance to go to space. What kid doesn't dream about that? But I didn't want to kill stuff nor fix stuff nor do a lot of the other work on the list the recruiter showed me."

She shook her head.

"And yet you were the one who managed to use the single piece of leverage we needed to stop the mantes."

"Yeah," I said, "dumb luck, that."

She checked her watch.

"Well, it's time to see if you can't scare up a little more, Padre."

We walked from the porthole to the nearest lift car, went down three decks, and wound our way to the frigate's largish main conference room. Marines in freshly pressed uniforms guarded the hatches, with rifles at port arms. There were some mantis guards as well, their lower thoraxes submerged into the biomechanical "saddles" of their hovering, saucer-shaped discs.

Every mantis I'd ever seen was technically a cyborg. Their upper halves were insectoid—complete with bug eyes, fearsome beaks, antennae, wings, and serrated-chitin forelimbs. Their lower halves were integrated into their mobile, floating saucers. It was the saucers—the computers and equipment in them—which allowed the mantes to speak to humans, and have our own speech translated back into their language, among many other things.

The mantis guards all raised forelimbs in my direction as we approached, though they seemed to be ignoring the captain.

I blushed in spite of myself, and raised a hand in return.

Was I *that* well known among the aliens?

We entered the conference room, and I stopped short.

There was the Professor—whom I considered a friend, and whom I'd not seen in a long time—and a larger, much older-looking mantis on whom all human eyes were focused.

The human contingent was arrayed around a half-moon table with chairs and computers and various recording devices.

The two mantes merely floated in the air, about waist high.

I smiled, and in spite of protocol, walked quickly up to the Professor.

"Hello," I said. "I wasn't sure if I'd ever get to see you again."

"You would have not, Harry," said the Professor, "had circumstances evolved differently."

If the Professor had a name, it was unpronounceable for humans. The skitter-scratch mandible-against-mandible language of the aliens was incomprehensible for us. And he'd always been addressed by title, even though he'd asked permission to be on a first-name basis with me.

A familiar throat was cleared to my rear.

I turned to Adanaho, whose expression told me I was erring without knowing it. Behind her sat the general—staring hard.

"Sorry, sir," I said, then nodded knowingly to the Professor, and walked quickly to a seat that was offered to me. The captain sat down at my side, and after the general gave me one last lingering look, he ordered the doors closed, leaving us alone with our guests.

I checked my PDA. The captain and I were as early as we'd planned to be. Yet it appeared things were already well in motion.

Not good.

"Well," the general said, "he's here now. Since nothing I or my staff say seems to be worth anything to you, maybe you'll listen to *him*."

The old mantis behind the Professor floated forward.

"Padre," it said to me, its vocoded speaker-box voice coming from the grill on the front of its disc. The creature's beak did not move. The translator was tied directly into the mantis's nervous system.

"That is what some call me," I said. "May I ask who you are?"

"This is the Queen Mother," said the Professor, his manner deferential as he introduced her. "She is the highest of the Select who rule our people. Her voice carries supreme authority within the Quorum of the Select."

"She is your sovereign," I said.

"Yes and no," said the Professor. "She is elected, but she also shares a tremendous lineage, biologically. Her genetics run through countless mantes, over many of your generations."

In other words, she was fecund, in addition to being old.

I sat up a little straighter.

"Ma'am," I said to the Queen Mother, "of what service can I be to you?"

The Queen Mother floated forward a bit more, while the Professor floated back.

"Your name is spoken in my Quorum," she said. "It is the only human name that has ever reached such height. When the one you call the Professor first came before me, many of our cycles ago, and petitioned for us to halt our Fourth Expansion, I considered him obtuse. Your superstition is of no consequence to me, nor do I have any use for it. And yet, the Professor had convinced a good many of his contemporaries that the elimination of your species—of your numerous modes of religion—would be detrimental to the advancement of mantis knowledge. And his colleagues had convinced many on the Quorum. Rather than force a contentious vote on the issue, I acquiesced, believing that the merit of the Professor's proposed observation and research would become obvious in time. Even if I could see no value in it in the moment."

She let a tiny silence hang in the air.

"I no longer feel the need for such forbearance."

The room was dead silent, but the Queen Mother's words had hit me like a thunderclap. It was one thing to hear the captain talk about a possible end to the peace. It was quite another to have the nominal leader of the *enemy* in front of me declaring that she was going to drop the hammer. I felt a slithering surety in my heart: the Queen Mother would not bluff.

I cleared my throat experimentally, trying to shake off the dread I felt. The eyes of the officers behind me began to drill virtual holes in my back as I left my seat. The Queen Mother remained where she was.

"I have to think," I said, voice shaking just a bit, "that your mind isn't entirely made up. Otherwise why agree to this meeting at all? You could just as easily declare the cease-fire dead, launch your war armada, and have done with it."

"There are still some," she said, her triangular insect's head tilting back in the Professor's direction, "who petition me for further amity. I am not a hasty being. I listen to my intellectuals. If they say there is additional merit in long-term conciliation between our races, I am habitually obliged to entertain the notion—whether I agree with it or not. So rather than send a delegate, I came here myself. To meet the one human who has managed to alter the inevitable course of my empire. I had expected someone more impressive."

"My apologies," I said, "if my presence does not meet that expectation. As for what I can say or do to change your mind, I am not sure I can offer you much more than what I've already been able to offer to the Professor and his students. I am the chaplain's assistant. I've counseled the Professor that he'd do well to seek out a bona fide *chaplain*. Or, if a military man is not in order, then there are the finest theologians, scholars, religious teachers, and clergymen Earth has to offer. If I have failed to provide enlightenment, surely someone else might be better suited."

"Enlightenment," the Queen Mother said, her mouth hinged open and her serrated, vicious teeth vibrating—the mantis display of annoyance. "This is a phrase that I find utterly preposterous. I have studied what little of your planet's history is available to me and determined that we mantes were building starships when humans were still scuttling about in caves. Enlightenment. Ridiculous. Does the larva *enlighten* the adult?"

I'd learned from the Professor that the mantes had two stages in their life cycle. Upon hatching from their eggs, they were mindless herbivores, consuming vegetable matter over a period of months until entering their transformative pupa stage. Only upon emergence from the chrysalis did a newly-carnivorous mantis achieve actual sapience. Prior to that, the larval mantis was about as intelligent as a box of rocks.

"Nobody questions your technological prowess," I said, choosing my words carefully. I looked quickly behind the Queen Mother to see the Professor floating dead still, his gaze locked on her.

"When the Professor and I first met, it was shocking to discover that you mantes cared anything at all about how or what a human believed. I didn't think it was possible. I'd only ever seen your people maiming and killing my people. And yet, the Professor showed me you are a complex race. Old and powerful, but also with a history of patient curiosity. Such that on prior occasions—when you've let your thirst for expansion overrule your prudence—you've genuinely regretted those choices."

"Some of us have," said the Queen Mother, her beak snapping shut. "But not all."

"What would be gained," I said, "by throwing away the armistice? It's been a long time since humans shed mantis blood, and vice versa. I think the cease-fire is pretty good evidence that our two societies can learn to share the galaxy. Sometimes, we may even share the same planet, if after a fashion."

Purgatory was still technically mantis property. Myself and the few hundred humans who'd stuck around after the return of the Earth ships, had more or less managed to stay out from under mantis feet. It wasn't an equal partnership. More like, *keep the noise down so the landlords don't show up with artillery.* But it was a persistent peace, and the more time I'd spent around the Professor—and later, his students—the more I'd become convinced that humans and the mantes had more in common than either they or we suspected.

I waited while the Queen Mother's antennae wove a thoughtful pattern in the air.

"You are dangerous to us," she said. "Or is the squadron of warships that greeted my delegation your idea of a friendly gesture?"

I looked behind me: at the general, and the captain.

"She has a point, sir, and ma'am," I said.

"I'm not a fool," Sakumora retorted sourly. He looked past me to the Queen Mother, and his tone got sharper when next he spoke. "Who is more threatening to whom? What are my staff and I supposed to think about those battle exercises your ships have been conducting? For the first time in several years, eh?"

The Professor seemed to visibly shrink in on himself.

I guessed that even the mantes never spoke that way to their leader. Much less a human. The Queen Mother's posture was erect, and motionless. For an instant I recalled visceral memories of mantis troops striking with lightning lethality, carving into human flesh. I raised my hands instinctively in the air between the two leaders, trying to physically damp down the mood, which had grown dangerously electric.

"You both asked me to come here," I said, swiveling my head from one party to the next, and back again. "But if both of you are determined to see evil in the actions of the other, no matter what I say, there really isn't anything I can do. A new war is inevitable."

"A war we would absolutely win," the Queen Mother said.

"Are you that sure?" the general replied.

"Stupid human, you would do no better against us than you did the first time."

Now it was Sakumora who remained motionless. He seemed to be deciding something. I stared at him, feeling altogether uncomfortable. Before I could shout for him to stop, his left hand reached out and tapped a single button on the keyboard in front of him. The lights in the chamber dimmed, and went orange, battle klaxons suddenly ringing through the space.

Outside the doors, automatic gunfire roared. I knew the sound. It wasn't the sound of mantis weaponry.

"What have you done?" I said to the general.

Both he and his staff—all save the captain, who simply sat with her mouth half open—stood up and removed overly-large pistols from under the table. Pistols, hell, they looked like sawed-off shotguns, with magazines attached. Sakumora and his people aimed their weapons at the Professor and the Queen Mother.

"We weren't ready for you the first time," Sakumora said, his demeanor become icily calm now that he no longer teetered on the knife edge of an uneasy truce. "Part of me hoped this wouldn't be necessary. But part of me also knew that things couldn't end any other way."

The Queen Mother's wings unfolded and fluttered loudly.

Extreme amusement.

I'd also learned enough about mantis body language to know that the Professor's mood was utterly crushed. He shrank back from all of us, his floating disc nearly bumping the far bulkhead.

"You've made it too easy," said the Queen Mother.

The pitch of the frigate's ambient engine noise shifted upward, just prior to the room being rocked by what sounded like rolling thunder.

"I've signaled my subordinates to destroy your entire squadron," said the Queen Mother. "This ship and everyone on it will be the first to fall. The Fourth Expansion begins today!"

She looked triumphant.

I stared at the Professor, who appeared ill.

The room rocked again—with more loud rumbling.

The general tapped the large green communications key. "Damage report?" he said.

"The deflection system is holding," replied a young voice through a small speaker on the desk.

Sakumora smiled wickedly, his pistol aimed squarely at the Queen Mother's bug-eyed head.

"We adapt and learn quickly," said the general. "I don't think we'll be the pushovers that you were expecting. Though I have to admit I admire your willingness to sacrifice yourself in order to commit your people to the battle. Had our positions been reversed, I think I might have done the same."

The Queen Mother's body language had changed. Like that of the Professor, she began to slowly shrink in on herself. I guessed that she'd not expected to survive past this point. Had the general and his Fleet engineers not found the secret to The Wall, it's probable we'd have all been atomized already.

"So it's war," I said. "Only now neither side wins?"

"Shut up, Chief," said the general, in irritation. "Your job here is done. Unless you're ready to pick up a weapon for humanity, you're not much use to us."

I looked from the general's face—set in an expression of grim and determined calculation—to the captain's. Adanaho's mouth still hung half open and her eyes were wide, the whites like bright circles of ivory. She closed her mouth and swallowed once.

A small mechanical sound alerted me to our danger, but only just in time.

While the Professor's disc had never been armed—armament being unseemly for a scholar—there'd been no thought given to the Queen Mother. Weapons, previously hidden within her disc, suddenly bristled.

I tackled Adanaho to the deck just as the shooting started.

CHAPTER 18

Earth, 2153 A.D.

THUKHAN TURNED OUT TO BE PARTIALLY RIGHT. NO NCO CAME back into the bay for over an hour. The holdovers kept themselves on one end of the bay, and us new recruits kept ourselves on the other side. I couldn't bring myself to relax, so I explored the bay. The end opposite the head had several locked doors that were unmarked, while the head itself was populated by eight toilet stalls, eight shower stalls, and eight sinks on a bar countertop in front of a single, long mirror.

I looked again at the head. Then I went back out and did a quick headcount in the bay proper.

There were approximately ten bodies for every toilet, shower, or sink. It was going to be a fiasco churning every recruit in the bay through the head in a limited amount of time.

A rectangle of tiles in the center of the bay was a different color of ugly from the other tiles at the perimeter. The rectangle was highly polished and gleamed in the overhead fluorescents. A single locker stood by itself in the middle of the polished tile, as did a single-occupant bunk which was immaculately made. I stepped towards it and heard one of the holdovers—Gorana again—yell, "Get out of the Dead Zone, you idiot!"

"What?" I said.

"The Dead Zone," said Gorana. "Nobody steps foot into that area."

"Why?"

"I dunno, but they will smoke us if they see any scuffing on that wax."

"Smoke? What does that mean?"

The holdovers just laughed, as if my question merited derision, and I had to resist the urge to tell the lot of them to eff the hell off. Could I help it if nobody had told any of us new recruits very much? I glared at Thukhan's back, which was perpetually faced away, and wished the so-called bay sergeant would get off his ass and maybe clue the rest of us in on things like the so-called Dead Zone.

As for whatever "smoke" meant, I inferred it obviously wasn't good.

The entire bay found that out ten minutes later when a corporal—a different corporal—wandered in and found half the room lying on their bunks, mouths gaping and drool running down their cheeks.

"GET UP! GET UP! GET UP! GET UP!" yelled the corporal, stomping around the bay. Men attempted to comply, rolling out of their beds onto the hard floor, or sitting up and pranging their foreheads on the bars of the bunks above them.

"Everyone in the front-leaning rest!" the corporal ordered.

The holdovers—perhaps sensing what was coming—were already there. We new recruits, looking at the holdovers, all quickly assumed a more or less push-up position, with arms extended and locked and bodies made as rigid as possible—which in the case of some of the softer-seeming males, wasn't very rigid.

"An absolute disgrace," said the corporal, who patrolled the edge of the Dead Zone like a shark. "You're here not even one full day and you're already acting like it's time to kick back and party. Okay, fine, no problem, we can fix that. DOWN!"

The holdovers lowered their bodies until their chests brushed the floor. Myself and the other new recruits watched and mimicked.

"UP!"

The holdovers came back to an arms-rigid posture. I and the rest did as well.

"DOWN!"

Everyone back down to the floor.

"UP!"

Everyone back up.

After five repetitions, some of the other recruits were groaning.

At ten repetitions, some of our arms were shaking and a great many of us were bowed in the middle.

At fifteen repetitions half the recruits' legs and abdomens were resting on the floor.

"Effing Lord above," said the corporal. "What kind of garbage are the recruiters sending us these days? You all are so *soft*, I could put my boot through the ass of three of you and not even feel it. This is just effing beautiful."

The corporal looked at his chronometer on his wrist.

"Bay Sergeant Thukhan, you have fifteen mikes to square these new people away. I want bunks made to standard and everything put away correctly in lockers. I am going to stand right here while you make it happen, and if it doesn't happen, we'll do a little more *fixing* until it does. MOVE!"

"Corporal, yes Corporal," Thukhan said, and ran—not walked—down one side of the bay to one of the unmarked doors at the back. He put a palm on the print lock and it opened, revealing a large closet with shelf after shelf of pillows and sheets and fuzzy, gray blankets.

"Line up!" Thukhan yelled. We new recruits stumbled to comply.

Thukhan proceeded to hurl pillows and blankets at people, yelling at them to vacate the entry to the closet as soon as they'd received their bedding.

I looked at my wrist—a black plastic digital watch being one of the very few things I'd been allowed to keep from civilian life—and realized that it had already been five minutes. Not even half the men had been helped yet. Those that had, hauled their stuff back to their bunks and dumped it, looking about dumbly for instructions. Several of them raised their hands, looking directly at the corporal, but he just ignored them and kept his arms folded, a finger tapping his bicep while he occasionally looked down at his own watch.

"We're not going to make it," I said under my breath. The man ahead of me grunted in agreement.

At ten minutes I finally collected my allotment—two white flat sheets, two folded gray blankets, something like a fitted sheet, a pillow and a pillow case. I went back to my bunk—me on the top, Thukhan on the bottom—and stared at the bay sergeant's already-made bunk, wondering how the neat and tidy arrangement had been put together. I dumped my stuff onto the already-made bunk and flipped out my sheets, pulling the fitted sheet up to my eyes and discovering it wasn't fitted at all. It was like a giant sack. What the hell?

I looked around the bay and saw other men trying to figure out what in the world the sack was for, some of them stealing glances down the bay at the holdover bunks. People began to make their bunks in a ramshackle riot of different manners, until suddenly the corporal looked up from his watch and yelled, "Front-leaning rest position, MOVE!"

The holdovers and half the new recruits—including myself—dropped onto our hands and toes, right where we were. The other men continued to attempt to make their bunks.

"I SAID FRONT-LEANING REST POSITION, NOW!"

The other men complied out of pure shock at the immense volume of the corporal's voice.

"This is just sad," said the corporal, resuming his patrol around the edge of the Dead zone while he spoke. "You had plenty of time, and you wasted it."

Someone down the bay muttered, "Enough time, my ass..."

The corporal whirled in that person's direction and stomped down towards him, adroitly avoiding the splayed hands of those straining to keep their chests in line with their legs.

"SHUT YOUR EFFING MOUTH, RECRUIT!" the corporal screamed. "BY MY WATCH IT'S BEEN OVER AN HOUR AND A HALF SINCE YOU WERE BROUGHT IN HERE AND ISSUED INSTRUCTIONS!"

The entire bay remained silent after that, save for gasps and the shuffling of feet and hands as people struggled to stay in position. The holdovers had all arched their backs and put their butts into the air, and I did likewise, discovering that it made for a slightly less painful experience while I remained facing the floor.

"Bay Sergeant Thukhan," said the corporal. "What were your orders when these men were placed in your charge?"

"Corporal," Thukhan grunted, "the instructions were to draw linen, get the lockers ready, and fill the roster, Corporal."

"Did you not understand these instructions?" said the corporal.

"Corporal, no, Corporal, Recruit Thukhan understood the instructions."

"How can that be if, when an NCO comes back in here after so much time, nothing has been done? Either you're lying and you didn't in fact understand the instructions, or you just didn't give an eff and decided to make the entire bay pay for your stupidity."

Thukhan stayed silent.

"No explanation, Recruit?" said the corporal.

"Corporal—" Thukhan began.

"Shut up," the corporal said, cutting Thukhan off, "I don't want to hear it anyway. Okay, recruits, since your bay sergeant decided to waste both his time and yours, now you're on *my* time, and we're going to give you an advanced introduction to what the Fleet calls *corrective training.* I can see that some of you are having a tough time staying in the front-leaning rest. No problem. Roll over on your backs and get your heels in the air."

The bay complied—with much shuffling, sighing, grunting, and moaning.

"*Not* with your heels to the sky!" the corporal barked when he saw several men with their boots straight up towards the ceiling. "Heels *fifteen centimeters off the floor.* Legs straight out. Stick your palms under your butts if you have to, to support yourselves. Make it happen."

The corporal waited, and waited, and waited.

My thighs and stomach quivered, and I felt my heels dropping irresistibly towards the floor. I grunted and strained to force my legs back up, only to feel them drop again.

The corporal waited, and waited, and waited.

The room was soon filled with quiet whimpering, cursing, and groans.

"Front-leaning rest," said the corporal. Everyone rolled over.

"DOWN!" Everyone went to the floor.

"UP!" Everyone went back to arms rigid—many shaking.

"DOWN! UP! DOWN! UP! DOWN..."

Thirty minutes later, after repeated cycles between front and back, the entire bay was toast. Men—even the ones who'd come to Reception in fair shape—were in such pain, and so thoroughly exhausted, that tears leaked silently from the corners of their eyes.

The corporal watched it all unsympathetically.

"Not even really here yet," the corporal said, shaking his head, "and you're already *done.* I should just go tell the Top that Male Bay Five is worthless, and have him outprocess the entire bunch of you. It would save your drill sergeants a lot of time not having to deal with any of you losers in IST.

"But I'm not going to do that. Not yet. Armstrong Field is a learning center, and while I am convinced that each of you is presently worthless, I'm not yet convinced that some of you can't *learn* to be worth something. Eventually. So here is what's going to happen. Bay Sergeant Thukhan is fired"—I stole a glance in

Batbayar's direction, and saw him smiling broadly—"and I'm putting Thukhan's bunk mate in charge, as the new bay sergeant. Who is Thukhan's bunk mate? Sound off."

"Corporal, here, Corporal," I said.

"Here who, Recruit?"

"Corporal, Recruit Barlow, Corporal."

"Barlow, right. Your job is to fix this mess. The entire bay has linens. Nobody has unpacked anything yet—DAMMIT, NOBODY SHOULD BE LYING ON THE FLOOR, GET YOUR ASSES BACK UP—so, Barlow, your orders are to make sure every bunk in this bay is made, and made tight, and that all uniforms and issued items are properly secured in lockers."

"Corporal, yes, Corporal," I said.

He let us hang in pain for a few more seconds, then said, "Bay, position of attention, MOVE!"

The holdovers jumped to their feet. The newbies did likewise.

The corporal strode towards the closed locker in the center of the room—ignoring the highly-polished wax on the Dead Zone tile—and opened the doors.

"This is your static display," said the corporal. "You can look at it as an example of how your lockers will look. But do not step into this Dead Zone for any reason, do you understand, recruits?"

As a bay, "CORPORAL, YES, CORPORAL!"

"Bay Sergeant Barlow, the bunks should all look exactly like this bunk"—the corporal indicated the perfectly-taut bunk next to the static display locker—"but you'll need some help. Each of these holdovers has been instructed in the fine Fleet art of bunk-making. Several times. So you're to assign one of them to help several other new people. And they *will* help, is that understood, holdovers?"

"CORPORAL, YES, CORPORAL!"

"Make it happen, Barlow. You've got sixty minutes." The corporal clicked a button on his chronometer, and strode swiftly from the bay, not looking back.

Everyone broke from rigid position and the bay filled with cursing, moans, complaints, and more cursing.

I marched up to Thukhan and, just centimeters from his face, said, "You effed us over on *purpose,* didn't you?"

He smiled coolly. "Welcome to your first command, Bay Sergeant."

"You could have just told us all what to do to begin with and nobody would have gotten in trouble," I spat.

"You think you're tough enough to bring it, Barlow? C'mon, I dare you. You don't look like the kind of guy who has what it takes to handle a real man like me. I wasn't kidding when I told you some of us are here instead of prison. If you want to make it easy, just throw the first punch. *Cunt.*"

I felt my right hand curl into a tight ball. The other holdovers had formed a half-moon at the back of Thukhan, who waited patiently while I glared at him, and the rest of the bay quickly grew silent. Many of the new recruits walked up to stand behind me, each of them glaring angrily at the holdovers.

"There are seventy of us and ten of you," I said. "And right now, seventy of us would like to bitch-slap the ten of you."

Loud murmurs of agreement.

Thukhan looked around at the bay, the bravado in his posture faltering, if ever so slightly.

He laughed harshly to cover up for that fact.

"Whatever," Thukhan said. "Do you know what happens to a recruit who strikes another recruit? Mandatory stockade time. Docked pay."

"Sounds like you have some experience with that," I said.

"Maybe."

"I don't know why you did what you did," I said, "but we're all stuck here, and we don't have time for your crap." I looked behind Thukhan to the other holdovers, not all of whom appeared as ready to throw down as the former bay sergeant. In fact, three of them seemed almost embarrassed. I pointed at those three. "You, you, and you, will you help the rest of us?"

Those three looked at Thukhan and the other holdovers—who had turned to look at them—then looked at the rest of the bay.

Silently, my chosen three nodded their assent.

"Good," I said. "Start showing people how to make bunks. When those bunks get made, the people whose bunks were made need to go help *more* people, and then those people need to help still *more* people, everyone understand?"

The bay said that it did—except for Thukhan, Gorana, and the five other holdovers who didn't seem to give a damn what was happening.

I looked at my watch. "We've only got fifty-two minutes left. Let's get moving. You three holdovers—Cho, Capacha, Jackson—come with me. I'm going to show you who you're helping first."

CHAPTER 19

GUNS BLAZED. HUMAN GUNS. MANTIS GUNS.

The room rocked again from the concussion of enemy fire outside the frigate.

My ears were ringing when the captain and I both looked up to see the general and all of his people sprawled bloodily across their side of the room. The Queen Mother had peppered them with projectiles, their bodies pulped and grotesque. Though it seemed the Queen Mother had fared little better. She was down. Or, rather, her disc was down. Sparks spat from numerous holes in the disc's armored surface. *Sabot rounds,* I thought. The Queen Mother's forelimbs scraped and scratched futilely at the deck, her triangular head cocked in my direction and her mouth half open, the teeth looking wicked and deadly.

Her mandibles chattered ferociously, but the disc made no sound. Its translator was rendered useless, along with its weapons.

The Professor—unharmed—floated forward from his previous spot near the far wall, then stopped as the doors were cast open and armed marines flooded in. The instant they saw the general lying dead, they raised their rifles to fire—having previously dispatched the Queen's guards, per Sakumora's plan.

Seeing this, Captain Adanaho shrugged me off of her and stood up, shouting, "Cease fire!"

The marines hesitated.

"That's a direct order," she said for emphasis.

The room rolled with concussive grumbling.

Lights flickered.

"General Sakumora, sir," said an alarmed voice through the speaker on the general's table, "there's a feedback loop in the deflection matrix. We're absorbing hits, but we can't say for how much longer."

The captain stared at me for an instant, then she looked to the Professor, whose forelimbs dangled dejectedly in front of him.

"I'm assuming you didn't know the Queen Mother's plan either," she said.

"That is correct," said the Professor. "Though I knew as well as you that the situation was unstable. Had I known the Queen Mother intended to incite conflict, to force us to war, I'd never have come."

More thunder, more flickering lights.

"Then it seems you're destined to die with the rest of us," I said, feeling the cold, dull ache of certain doom closing around my throat. I instantly rued the day Adanaho had entered my chapel.

But then again, was it better to die on Purgatory, alone, or on a Fleet warship among my own kind? Was either of these options preferable to the other? I tried to remember what Chaplain Thomas had once told me, about keeping a stiff upper lip in the face of death, and discovered I couldn't quite remember his exact words.

The Queen Mother continued to scrape and scratch frantically at the deck, her disc become worthless. It seemed suddenly that the mantes—even this, the greatest of her kind—weren't all that terrible once you took away their technological advantage. Without the disc, she was as mortal as any man. With the frigate bucking beneath us and the captain and I struggling to keep our feet, I almost laughed as I watched the supreme leader of the enemy struggle helplessly.

Now you know how we felt!

I wasn't sure if I'd merely thought it, or shouted it.

The captain and every other human were looking at me.

That's when true disaster struck.

Kakraoooummmmmmm!

The lights vanished entirely as the room tilted ninety degrees and hurled us to the port bulkhead, then back across the space to the starboard bulkhead, before leaving us floating free. Orange emergency lamps snapped on and I fought a savagely instinctual desire to vomit—zero gee proving to be every bit as terrible in the bowels of the *Calysta* as it had been onboard the shuttle.

Marines flailed and then lapsed into their microgravity training. It had been too long for me, so I kept flailing, eventually feeling Adanaho's grip on my left ankle. She levered herself up into my face and shouted, "The deflection matrix is falling apart! We've got to get to a lifeboat!"

"How?" I said, almost spewing my last meal into her face.

She turned her head, seeing that the marines were way ahead of her. They'd instinctually latched onto and levered each other like extension ladders, until one of them could get a grip on something solid, thus bringing them all into contact with the walls or floor or ceiling.

"We just need to get outside!" she said loudly.

Almost at once, the Professor was there.

His disc moved effortlessly, seemingly unaffected by microgravity.

"Grab on," he said, a forelimb stretched in our direction. I reached for it and took it, while Adanaho stayed attached to me, and the Queen Mother stayed attached to the Professor's other forelimb. Her disc trailed drops of mechanical fluid as the Professor began to tow all of us for the nearest open exit. If the marines desired to fire, nobody pulled a trigger. Perhaps because there was no way to shoot without killing both the captain and myself—fratricide being frowned upon, especially when superior officers are involved.

We emerged into the corridor beyond. The gore of dead mantes was everywhere. The marines had done their work well. I suddenly felt embarrassed and mournful. The Queen's guards had saluted me as I entered, then paid with their lives for that trust. I gaped at the nearest of them, his young face split in two and his insect's brain oozing out.

That did it.

I turned from Adanaho and emptied the contents of my stomach, which spluttered away from us in a thick, chunky stream.

"Where?" the Professor said sharply to the captain.

Emergency bells were chiming, and an automated vocal warning was issuing from every speaker.

HULL BREACH. VACUUM CONDITIONS ON MULTIPLE DECKS. PROCEED TO YOUR NEAREST SAFE DUTY STATION. REPEAT, HULL BREACH…

"There!" Adanaho said, almost climbing up my back so that she could point over the Professor's shoulder.

A row of hexagonal hatches had opened along the walls, much further down the corridor. Personnel were piling into them. Each hatch was ringed with yellow and black caution striping, with tiny beacon lights spinning rapidly at the corners.

"Find one of those," Adanaho said.

Though the ones closest to us appeared positively choked with people, all clamoring for escape.

Grrrrakkkkaaaaanngggggkt!

The guttural grinding sound of metal announced to even my inexperienced naval ears that the *Calysta's* remaining moments were few. A wind had picked up in the corridor—air bleeding out into space. Men and women screamed, redoubling their efforts to seek escape.

For a brief instant, the Queen Mother and I locked eyes—hers as alien as the Professor's had ever been—while we clung to the Professor's separate forelimbs. I could not detect emotion behind her alien, multifaceted gaze, but her contorted body posture spoke of both fear and pain, while her mouth gaped in a show of murderous rage. I'd have let go of the Professor in terror—at the sight of those tractoring incisors—if I didn't feel sure that the Professor, and the mobility of his functional disc, were the only hope I had.

And besides, there was the captain to think of. She clung to my back like a bear cub.

Suddenly the Professor moved in a new direction. Opposite the way we'd all been looking. We shot down the corridor, headed aft, bumping aside crew and marines alike. A few gunshots rang after us, but in the panic of the moment they went wide, embedding themselves into the bulkheads.

The wind spiraled up to become a gale-force howl.

Now, humans no longer floated or pulled themselves along the corridor. They were vacuumed away, shrieking.

My ears suddenly began to hurt.

I wanted to yell at the Professor—to ask where he thought he was going—but then I saw it: an open emergency hatch, unblocked.

The Professor's disc moved toward it at best possible speed.

We passed through the doorway and the captain had the good sense to reach out and slap the panel just inside the threshold. The doors to the emergency exit snapped shut with a loud *clang.* Suddenly we were all flattened against the hatch as the lifeboat spat through the disintegrating interior of the *Calysta,* following a predesignated route. Rapid egress shafts honeycombed the ship—as with all Earth war vessels—such that it took only moments for the lifeboat to be disgorged into the emptiness of space.

We floated free as the force of our acceleration ebbed. I found myself at a small porthole, catching a glimpse of the *Calysta* as she spun away—from my point of view—from us. There were huge wounds in her belly, punctuated by the gradual fragmenting of her exposed bones as new missiles from the mantis armada continued to home in on and decimate the frigate.

Then the *Calysta* flashed. Her reactors going up.

I jerked away from the porthole, having been strobed almost to blindness. There was a human coughing sound behind me, and the additional noise of mandibles skittering and scratching out the mantis native language.

I rubbed my lidded eyes and then opened them, seeing through purple spots that it was only the captain, myself, the Professor, and the Queen Mother aboard.

We were alone.

CHAPTER 20

Earth, 2153 A.D.

MY TIME IN RECEPTION PASSED QUICKLY, THOUGH I RAPIDLY came to understand why Thukhan had been so eager to be out of a job. The bay sergeant occupied a more or less powerless, thankless position where he was punished for everyone else's mistakes as much as he was punished for his own. Thus I became well acquainted with the various and devilish forms of so-called corrective training that the NCOs could dish out. This punishment went by names such as The Chair, The Plank, The Flutter Kick, The Cherry Picker, and on and on. Almost none of it hurt if you only did it for a few seconds. All of it was agony after fifteen minutes—though I considered myself lucky if they let me off in that short a time. And the corporals seemed to delight in initiating multiple twenty- and thirty-minute punishment sessions *per day*, for the smallest of infractions.

By the time Pickup Day arrived, I was positive that every muscle in my body had become a purple lump of overstressed, tenderized gelatin.

But I'd managed to avoid any further confrontations with Thukhan. In spite of the fact that I slept over the bastard every night. Mostly we didn't talk to each other and we worked to keep out of each other's way. Ergo, if I was brushing my teeth in one sink during morning prep, Thukhan was brushing his teeth in the sink farthest opposite me. And vice versa.

Those holdovers who seemed loyal to Thukhan—such as the always-grumpy Gorana—didn't speak to me either. Though I was pleased to see that Cho, Capacha, and Jackson seemed to have turned it around.

All three of them had had some disciplinary dust-ups with the corporals, which had previously caused them to be held back for reevaluation. Through them I learned that, aside from the regular IST battalions, there was a special, supposedly "hardcore" training battalion where the truly hopeless cases would be sent. The corporals called it Alcatraz, and being sent to Alcatraz was a threat held over the head of every recruit—even the ones like me, who did their best to get things right.

Of course, no recruit could ever be right. About anything.

Most of the punishment was conducted *en masse*, with the entire bay on its face or rolling over on its back, legs scissoring and quad and abdominal muscles screaming, the corporal in charge counting off the strokes, "One, two, three," while the bay had to reply back with the repetition count, "ONE"!

"One, two, three—"

"TWO!"

"One, two, three—"

"THREE!"

And so on, and so forth, until the NCO was satisfied that the recruits had been properly and judiciously pulverized.

It occurred to me—once, during a particularly brutal evening session—that none of us recruits *had* to perform the exercise. There was no gun to our heads, and even though I'd seen and been the recipient of an NCO slapping, cuffing, and even hitting a recruit who got too far out of line, nobody was being threatened under penalty of death. There was only the threat of Alcatraz, and, failing that, being sent home with a dishonorable service letter sealed permanently into our citizen files.

These twined threats—combined with the perpetual smoking—served to more or less keep everyone in line.

Through more medical testing and hole-poking.

Through hellish mornings and afternoons spent on the infernal cement in front of the hall, practicing the basics of marching, columnar movement, and facing movement.

Through quiet hours spent awake in the middle of the night, pulling seemingly pointless guard duty at exits and doors, everyone rotating on and off shift according to a roster that I'd had to fill that first day.

There was also cleaning. Endless, endless cleaning. Cleaning things that were already clean. Cleaning things that probably should have been cleaned a long time ago, and somehow weren't. Toilets. Showers. Sinks. Under the bunks. Under the lockers. Between the lockers. Up and down the stairs. Up and down the hallways between the bays, and the gyms where we did daily PT, and the massive chow hall where we ate.

Meals. Now, that was a whole project unto itself.

For whatever reasons, the Fleet seemed to think it important that every recruit learn to function as a mess peon. Something—we were all told—which would continue long after reception.

So once a morning, several dozen people were selected from all of the male and female bays, and were sent down to work in the kitchen. It was work that on many worlds was ordinarily handled by machinery, but at Armstrong Field, it was done by hand. Either because of budget cuts or, as I suspected, just because the NCOs liked to see recruits worked until they dropped.

And drop we did. Lots of people had to make multiple trips to the triage and infirmary center. For blisters. Cuts. Dehydration and heat injury. Broken bones. And the mysterious plague of so-called Barracks Crud that seemed to have invaded our ranks.

On Pickup Day almost half of the group I was with were coughing, sneezing, and wiping their noses. Some people looked pale and about near to passing out. Nobody dared go see the doc, though, because it was rumored that anyone who went on sick call on Pickup Day would be left behind, thus becoming a holdover, and nobody wanted that.

I kept looking at the slowly-vanishing bruises on my thighs where the injector guns had struck, and wondered if there wasn't a correlation between whatever inoculations we'd been given, and half the bunch of us winding up dead-dog sick.

Still, the air on Pickup Day was somewhat electric. Everyone had secured their gear in their duffels, turned in their linen, and given the bay one final, superb cleaning before shuffling out onto the cement in front of the reception hall—just as the sun was starting to peek up over the horizon. Those who would be held over had already been sorted from the press—and sent sulkily and sometimes indignantly—back to the building, while everyone else—including Thukhan—was outside.

There were three *thousand* of us now, a number which I couldn't believe had been crammed into the reception center—and we had been lined up alphabetically by last name in a gargantuan mass formation one hundred columns wide and thirty ranks deep. Each of us stood at attention in front of our duffels, the bottom of the duffel facing upward while we each secured the duffel by its shoulder straps—to keep it from falling.

Corporals and sergeants with e-pads and huge wax pencils walked down each of the ranks, double checking the name on the breast of the recruit in question before tapping on the e-pad a few times and quickly marking a cryptic series of letters and numbers on the bottom of each of the duffels.

When the sergeant for my column got to me, he wrote the letter C and the numbers 414 on my duffel, then moved on without a word. I looked to my left and right, and didn't see anyone with the same letter or numbers. Which was fine. During my time as bay sergeant I'd not been able to really get to know anybody, mostly because I was so busy acting as abuse-interlocutor between the corporals and the rest of the bay. So I was glad to have been relieved of duty, during a ceremony which amounted to nothing more than someone with stripes saying to me the words, "You're fired."

Now I could try to—hopefully—find out how the blissfully anonymous half lived.

Droves of familiar buses—which we'd not seen since coming to Armstrong Field the first day—rolled up.

Men and women stepped off the buses. Unlike the reception NCOs, these men and women all wore sunglasses and were dressed in the ultra-sharp-looking uniform known as Dress, Type 2. Their black shoes were similar to flat business loafers, but shined like patent leather. Gray slacks were pressed, with the seams razor sharp. Similarly pressed, white, short-sleeved shirts all had closed collars. Over the obligatory Fleet emblem on each soldier's chest—the emblem now reduced to a smaller brooch-type color pin, instead of the subdued, sewn-in version on the GFF—there was a crazy pastiche of badges and rectangular ribbons.

Each of the NCOs was at least a sergeant and several were staff sergeants or sergeants first class. Instead of soft caps on their heads—like reception NCOs—they wore a curious sort of black, round-brimmed and bevel-topped hat that leaned at a ferocious angle over their eyes; the hat's rear strap seeming to be the only thing that kept the odd headgear from blowing away in the light morning breeze.

First Sergeant Klauski appeared and went out to shake some of the staff sergeants' and sergeants first class's hands. Then he went to stand up in front of the mass formation, and—this time with megaphone to his lips—hollered, "BRIGADE, AHTEN-*SHUN!*"

All three thousand of us snapped rigid.

"Okay, recruits," Klauski said, the megaphone blasting his already massive voice across the formation, "I am happy to say that each and every one of you standing here today proved me wrong. I said that none of you—not a single damned one of you—had what it took to be in the Fleet. Well, look at you now. You're standing tall, and looking good. You're alert, and a titch leaner than when you first got to Armstrong Field. Doesn't take long, does it, recruits? I look in some of your eyes and I can already see the change happening.

"Today is Pickup Day, when you pass out of my old hands and into the care of these fine drill sergeants from some of Armstrong Field's finest IST battalions. These men and women are unlike any human beings you have ever known in your lives. They are harder than steel, sharper than razors, and they will not quit, nor will they compromise. Nor will they—I should add—expect anything less from all of you."

Klauski stuck out a paw and swept his thick, pointed index finger across the mass formation for emphasis.

"Everything up until now has been rehearsal. An attempt to prepare you for your journey ahead. Induction Service Training is the crucible through which you will be taken and hardened into a new kind of being. The kind of being that is capable of defending our planets and our race. If you survive IST you will be passing into a new fighting community with new history. Fleet doesn't just defend a single country. Fleet is truly international. Fleet defends both the Earth and her colonies, and is peopled by the finest soldiers you could ask for. From every walk of life, every ethnic background, every belief and creed.

"Good luck, recruits. As your first sergeant, I wish each and every one of you the best possible outcome. It's all up to you now."

One of the round-brimmed sergeants first class stepped over to Klauski, the two saluted, and Klauski handed him the megaphone before stepping away. The sergeant first class spun and put the megaphone to his mouth.

"It begins now, recruits," the sergeant first class said.

"Each of these buses out here has a letter and a number on it, and each of these buses has a team of Fleet's finest NCOs waiting to take you aboard. When I give you a right-face you will conduct a right-face, and you will wait for the drill sergeant at the head of your column to give you the signal. When you have been given the signal you will run—not walk, run—to one of the designated buses. Show some motivation, recruits, otherwise it's gonna be a long damned day."

The sergeant first class scanned down to the right of the mass formation and waited until other NCOs with round-brimmed hats, e-pads and megaphones had taken their places.

I suddenly felt like a racehorse in the starting gate. I itched to move.

The sergeant first class, satisfied that his people were where they needed to be, went rigid and put the megaphone back to his mouth.

"BRIGADE . . . RIGHT-*FACE!*"

Then he looked down to the heads of the columns.

"Drill sergeants, take charge of your columns and move 'em out."

Immediately, each of the thirty drill sergeants—one at the head of each column—began to bark names. As a name was barked, the drill sergeants would point to one of the many, many buses, and the recruit at the head of the column would bolt off towards the vehicle.

Some people were a little too amped up, and tripped somewhere along the way, or dropped their very heavy duffels. They got back up, however, scrapes and bruises aside, and charged onward. As each column moved forward, I could feel the familiar sweat moving down into the small of my back, the sun gaining in the blue sky and the heat beginning to build. It didn't matter, though, because I felt like I'd survived the first test. For one whole week—seemingly the longest I'd yet experienced in my young life—I'd managed to hang on to my sanity, and was now being ushered off to the next, toughest challenge.

By the time I was at the front, I was practically jumping up and down with anxious tension. The drill sergeant looked at me, the number on my bag, and punched something on his e-pad, then pointed to one of the buses with a line of recruits filing on, and shouted, "BARLOW, CHARLIE FOUR-ONE-FOUR, BUS NUMBER TWENTY-EIGHT, GO!"

I took off.

Ten steps out, I tripped and did a faceplant as my duffel swung wildly.

I was up in an instant—ignoring the pain in both hands—grabbing the shoulder straps of the duffel and hefting it onto place on my back, then running—well, slow jogging really—over to the bus with the large orange 28 on it. I was soaked with sweat when I got there, and felt it sting my raw palms. Two drill sergeants flanked the doors of the bus and were screaming at each recruit as he or she approached.

"DUFFELS ON THE FRONT, RECRUITS! DUFFELS ON THE FRONT!"

One of the drill sergeants had to yank a small female out of line and manhandle her duffel off her back and put it on her front-wise, so that it stuck up so far she had to crane her head around the side in order to see. She shakily grabbed the handrails on the bus and started up the stairs to where rowed seating awaited. I promptly took my duffel off and slung it around front, straps over the backs of my shoulders in the same fashion, eyes just able to peek over the duffel's top. One of the drill sergeants yelled, "THERE YOU GO, GOOD JOB, RECRUIT," as I stepped onto the stairs and began to go up.

For some reason, I felt a tiny spark of pride. Compliments from the NCOs had been practically nonexistent until now.

More drill sergeants hollered for the oncoming recruits to move to the back and take a seat. I did as ordered, not seeing the faces or identities of any of the others, stopping only when I noticed that I was the last one at the middle of the aisle, standing. I turned and slumped into the bench seat, huffing and breathing heavily.

When enough recruits had boarded and sat, one of the two drill sergeants onboard stepped over to the pilot's chair and began warming up the engine. The bus was a multi-wheeled, multi-axled affair with an enormous motor, and I felt the hum and rumble through the seat of my GFF trousers while the drill sergeant who was still standing ordered us to observe absolute silence.

"Noise discipline," she had called it.

No problem, I thought. I had no idea what I'd say anyway.

Then I turned to my right, to examine the face of the person sitting next to me.

The corner of Thukhan's mouth curled upward ever so slightly.

"Eff me," I breathed.

CHAPTER 21

THIS FAR NORTH OF THE EQUATOR, THE NAMELESS PLANET WAS arid and unremarkable—with barely enough oxygen and nitrogen to support a grown man.

A heck of a lot like home, I thought bitterly.

Hours after our ejection from the dying *Calysta,* our lifeboat had plummeted into the atmosphere. There'd been no sense trying to figure out who was winning or who was losing. The lifeboat had no tactical data nor any theater sensors with which to ascertain the progress of the battle. Every once in a while lights in the sky would sparkle and flash—ships exploding in the emptiness of space, their fantastic vanishings observable even in the daylight. Human. Mantis. All perishing together in one pent-up orgasm of long-delayed, hateful fury.

Death.

That was the thought that most concerned me as I trudged back up the broken-scree slope upon which the lifeboat had come to rest. The lifeboat's yellow-and-orange-striped parachutes drifted and fluttered on a cold breeze, their cords stretched out across the crumbled and rocky bluff. My old survival training told me I'd best collect the chutes and tuck them away. But now it didn't much matter. Human or mantis, whoever found us, there'd be hell to pay.

I climbed up the side of the lifeboat and dropped in through the top hatch, closing it behind me so as to preserve the batteries that were keeping the interior warm. The captain sat with her arms folded tightly across her stomach—back hunched and head down.

The Queen Mother was still helpless, her disc a dead weight while the Professor attended her with the gentleness and focus of a lover. Had they, I wondered, ever mixed seed? He the drone and she the recipient of his genetic lineage? There was still so much about the mantes' culture and society of which I could only guess.

The Professor and the Queen Mother were engaged in gentle conversation, her mandibles clicking and chittering while he held one of her forelimbs in both of his. I'd once asked him to try to teach me their alien tongue. It had proven to be an almost impossible task.

"How is she?" I asked.

"Not good," the Professor said, his disc rotating so that he could face me. "The internal systems of her carriage have all failed. If we do not get her to a mantis physician soon, it's probable that she will pass from life."

"She's not bleeding," I said. "Internal injuries?"

"I do not think you understand," the Professor said, his mechanized voice only hinting at the emotion that seemed to hover beneath the surface of his chitinous skin. I'd spent enough time around mantes—and this mantis in particular—to know his body language. The Professor's agitation was plainly spoken in the way he moved his forelimbs and rapidly swiveled his wedgelike head from side to side.

"No," I said, "I guess I don't. Unless she's been hit somewhere I can't see, I don't understand what's the matter with her."

"Our carriages, or discs as you commonly call them, are integral to us from the moment we achieve consciousness. No mantis lives without one. They protect us and provide us with mobility, allow us to work and manipulate the world around us, they expand our senses as well as our consciousness, and without them we are worse than helpless. The mantis and the carriage are *one*."

"Okay," I said carefully. "But this can't be the first time an adult has had her disc—her *carriage*—shot out from under her, right?"

"Of course not," said the Professor. "But in those instances, death has either come quickly or medical aid has always been ready at hand."

"So we can't just pull her out of it?" I asked.

The Professor's antennae shot upward, waved a bit, then curled into an expression of pronounced shock.

"That would surely prove lethal," he said, acting as if I'd suggested the worst sort of obscenity.

"But you just told me leaving her in the dead disc is bad too," I said, growing frustrated.

The Professor seemed to want to respond, but let his antennae fall to either side of his head, and turned back to speak to the Queen Mother in the indecipherable native language of the mantes. A language no human had ever learned, because no mantis had ever thought to teach it to us. Easier to use the translator and speaker in every disc.

Now it was the Queen Mother whose antennae gave a sign of shock. She stared intently at me—multi-faceted eyes cold and alien without the vocoder of her disc to give words to her thoughts—then she yammered something at the Professor in a rather rushed fashion, and slumped back into the center of her ruined disc.

"She says that while she was prepared to die in battle for our people, to commit helpless suicide in front of you humans is not to her liking."

"If the Fleet finds us," said Adanaho, surprising everyone as she finally looked up at us—her eyes puffy and red, "then the Queen Mother faces much worse than suicide. I'm with Intelligence and you can be certain that, with hostilities renewed, my comrades will spare no effort picking both of you apart in their quest for tactical and strategic information."

"You assume humans will outlast the Queen Mother's armada and reach our lifeboat first," said the Professor, his wings rustling slightly with grim amusement. "Did not your warship fall before our own, despite your best attempt to replicate our defensive technology?"

"The flashes we've been seeing in the sky since planetfall tell me not everything has gone your way," the captain said, also grimly. "The fighting continues. General Sakumora was rash and quick to shed blood, but he was also well-prepared. Our dreadnoughts are the finest in all of human space. Built using every lesson taught to us during the first war."

I waved a finger in front of me, not looking at anyone in particular.

"The new war's a nonstarter if the Queen Mother can convince the mantes to cease offensive operations," I said.

More fluttering of wings.

"And why would she do that," asked the Professor, "assuming she could regain contact with our forces?"

"Because Captain Adanaho saved both your lives when it would have been more expedient to let our marines fill you each full of bullets."

The Professor had no answer to that. The Queen Mother snapped and chattered at him. He relayed to her what he'd heard. They proceeded to engage in a quick series of mantis exchanges.

"She says," the Professor said delicately, "that the mercy shown by a single human does not translate to good will on the part of all humans. In fact, while we remain stranded here, events are doubtless in motion that are beyond recall for either side. If what the Queen Mother has told me is correct, her return to the armada was not expected—all they awaited was her signal, at which point the war plans would be put into effect. She is officially considered a casualty. And a successor has already been prepared to lead in her place. Doubtless our couriers are speeding back to join the rest of our ships, eager to relay news of this—and of the renewed offensive. Human planets will be under siege in a matter of weeks, if not days."

"I don't doubt it," I said. "But assuming we could contact the mantis hierarchy—prove that the Queen Mother, *our* Queen Mother, was alive—could she broker a cease-fire on your side of the battle lines?"

The Professor communicated my question to the Queen Mother, who stared at me a moment, then replied.

"Yes," said the Professor. "It might be possible."

"Then what are we waiting for?" I said. "We've got to find a way to get her back in touch with your people."

"Chief Barlow," Captain Adanaho said, "I appreciate that you might still feel obligated to accomplish the mission, as originally assigned. But events have clearly wiped all previous considerations off the table. Our first objective is to alert Fleet to our presence. Intelligence will want otherwise, but I can argue from historical precedent that the Professor and the Queen Mother should be processed as *prisoners of war.* As such, they'd each be entitled to certain rights. Perhaps with her safely in our custody—unharmed and unmolested—we can bargain our way to a new armistice?"

"You sound too much like your old boss," I said. Then thought better of my tone and added a respectful, "ma'am."

Adanaho raised an eyebrow.

"Believe me, Chief," she said, "I didn't intend for any of this to happen, either. Nobody wanted a war."

"But the Fleet bosses were obviously prepared for it," I snapped.

"And why not?" she said. "your own records from the original armistice state the matter plainly—the Fourth Expansion would have wiped humanity from the face of the galaxy. We were up against the wall, one way or another. It would have been foolish to count on the cease-fire to last indefinitely. Even though you and the Professor had managed to achieve some measure of mutual understanding."

A digital chime suddenly sounded through the speakers in the lifeboat.

Adanaho got up and checked the lifeboat's computer.

"Our emergency beacon's been spotted," she said. "We're getting telemetry from a Fleet rescue team in orbit. Looks like they'll be here in a few hours, once they've picked up other survivors."

"Do they know we have the Queen Mother with us?" I said, alarmed.

"If they knew," the captain said, "we'd be their topmost priority. That we're not tells me they think we're just another lifeboat filled with survivors—one of many, from the looks of it."

I would have been lying if I said I didn't feel some degree of satisfaction in that news. A human rescue team meant that not only were we holding our own against the mantes, we were doing well enough to be able to afford search missions for the retrieval of survivors from lost ships. Not exactly the actions of an overwhelmed and beaten species.

The Professor shrank in on himself, just as he had while aboard the *Calysta*.

"Prisoners of war," he said. And none too happily.

"It could be worse," I said to my old friend. "I survived the experience for years. You will too, if Captain Adanaho is right about being able to secure your POW status under Fleet protocol."

He chitter-scratched with the Queen Mother, whose deflated body language grew even more so.

"Of course," I said, thinking pessimistically, "if the captain *can't* secure your status as POWs, then you're meat—subject to the total spectrum of our interrogation techniques."

Adanaho didn't meet my gaze as I looked at her.

I snapped my fingers, then turned to face the Professor.

"Tell the Queen Mother that if she can promise us safety among the mantes, we'll help her escape."

Adanaho opened her mouth to object, but I held up a hand, not wanting to get into an argument with my superior—at least not yet.

"Impossible," said the Professor. "With her carriage nonfunctional the Queen Mother is trapped here."

"This is ridiculous," I said. "There's *no* contingency mode?"

The Professor hesitated, then he and the Queen Mother conversed for several minutes, their heads shifting back and forth and their mandibles rattling, clacking, snapping and stuttering. If Adanaho picked up on the fact that the Professor was straining to remain respectfully persistent, she didn't show it. But I could see what he was trying to do. Doubtless, like me, he was required to display deference to a superior, lest he forfeit his position. Or worse. But in the Queen Mother's current state, she was dependent on him totally. And might be forced to acquiesce to whatever he suggested.

"The carriage's engineering has changed little in hundreds of your years," the Professor said. "It is one of the all-time outstanding technical achievements of the great forbearers of mantis civilization—the first ones to meld mantis biology with mantis cyber-technology. There is an emergency release procedure, though it is seldom used. And I have never seen it done."

"Good," I said. "The sooner she's out of that thing, the sooner we can get moving. No doubt your own carriage has been sending out coded mantis distress signals, ever since we landed."

"You guess correctly," the Professor said.

"Then it's a race against time—the further we are from humans, the safer we'll be. We'll have to hope that your people have started dispatching rescue missions of their own."

"But where will we go?" the Professor asked.

"Anywhere but here," I said, raising my arms out and indicating the walls of the lifeboat with my open palms.

"Very well," said the Professor. "But you and the female must wait outside. The extraction from the carriage will be even more humiliating for the Queen Mother than remaining bound to it. This is not a thing for human eyes to see. Gather your human survival equipment and supplies and be gone. We will come out in time."

The captain and I quietly collected what we could, slung the frames of the emergency packs on our backs, and climbed out of the lifeboat and walked up to the top of the bluff, pebbles and sand swamping over the tops of our boots with each step.

"You realize I could order us all to stay put," she said, her short-cropped hair ruffling slightly in the cool, dry breeze. The sun—a star smaller and yet brighter than that which Purgatory circled—was still high up in the sky, but sinking almost imperceptibly towards the horizon.

"Ma'am," I said, "if you meant it when you told me you didn't want a war, then there's no way you can turn these two over to Fleet in their present circumstances. We might as well stuff apples in their mouths and shove them into the oven. They'll be picked apart like frogs in a biology class. First their minds, then their bodies."

"Are you forgetting that you have a duty, Chief?" she said sternly, turning to face me fully, with hands clutching the straps of her pack, elbows thrust just slightly out.

Our uniforms were barely keeping the cold at bay, and I suspected we'd have to use the emergency jackets in our packs if we didn't start hiking soon.

"What good's that duty going to do if we still lose? C'mon, Captain, you know the odds. The mantes own thousands of planets, and even with the years of the armistice taken into consideration, I can't believe humanity has caught up much. Have those colonies crucified in the first war even fully recovered yet? What about Earth? No, ma'am, if the mantes want us dead, it will happen eventually. The only difference now is we can actually put up a fight, whereas last time they cut us down like lambs."

My superior officer didn't appear convinced.

"When you got deployed against Purgatory, you lost," Adanaho said. "No doubt that's left a big, wide scar on your faith in the ability of the Fleet to effectively prosecute a war, or erect an effective defense. Believe me when I tell you, we've come a *long* way since you were taken prisoner. You talk as if we've already lost, when the fact is, we've got a new roll of the dice, Chief. A new chance to prevail."

I opened my mouth to speak, then shut it. Maybe she was right. I'd spent so long living under mantis rule, maybe I'd unconsciously absorbed the idea that once beaten, humanity would always be beaten.

Still, the fresh fighting seemed atrociously unnecessary. Not when there were people like the Professor who could call on the better angels of mantis nature. Especially if the Queen Mother could be made to serve as the Professor's surrogate in this regard. Otherwise, even if humanity did stand a better chance, was the ensuing bloodshed worth our pride in the matter? How many worlds might be gained or lost for the sake of ego?

I breathed deeply, collected my thoughts, and spoke again.

"Look, I've never been a great one for protocol and going along with orders at all costs. In some ways, the absence of Fleet rules and regulations from Purgatory life was the best thing that ever happened to me, because it made me realize what kind of man I am. I'm not a very good soldier. I don't like being told what to do. And if I'd had a choice in the matter I'd have thrown my nonstandard commission back in Fleet's face.

"Chaplain Thomas gave me a job once, and I did all I could to carry it out. For his sake. Now I have a new job, and until that job's been done—the resumption of peace between the mantes' race and our own—I won't rest."

The captain considered at great length, her eyes evaluating my expression while her mind evaluated the wisdom of my plea. It hadn't been a very persuasive one, but it was the only one I had to make. Either she went with it, or I'd be forced to mutiny. Definitely not something I'd prefer doing. But I'd do it just the same. And I think she knew it too.

Adanaho drew in a long, gradual breath through her nostrils, then let it out just as gradually, tilting her head to one side.

"You're right," she said. "You're not a very good soldier. You've been two steps from dereliction ever since I met you. But you've got guts, Padre. And I respect that. Okay, just so things are official, I am *ordering* us to escort the Professor and the Queen Mother until we can make contact with mantis forces, at which time we will parlay for a cease-fire, and pray that things get rolling positively from there."

"And if the Fleet finds us before the mantes do?"

"Then let me do the talking, while you do the praying."

There was a noise behind us. We turned to see the Professor slowly levitating upward, out of the lifeboat's hatch. He had the Queen Mother balanced on the front of his disc—his forelimbs wrapped under her insectlike shoulder joints while the rest of her body rested on the front of the disc proper. Her lower thorax was pale and shone with dampness, its chitin looking soft, and mantis blood trailing from several holes.

Adanaho and I rushed over to them.

"Does she need first aid?" I asked.

"What can be done, I have done," said the Professor, who seemed visibly shaken by what had just transpired inside. "She will heal. In time. The Queen Mother is severed from her carriage, and I do not know if she can ever be mated to another—such things being almost unheard of among adults of her great age. Her pain is terrible, but she is conscious, and she bade me tell you that we are in your care now. I have no weapons—as you well know—and would not use them to coerce you, even if I did. The Queen Mother rides with me, and I will follow wherever you choose to go. I can signal for mantis help with my own carriage—for several of your months, depending on how long my carriage's fuel cells last."

"May fortune favor the foolish," I said.

The Professor's antennae made a questioning expression.

"Old Earth literature," the captain said, in reply. "Come on, let's go. Padre? Since this is your idea, you're on point."

"Roger that, ma'am," I said, tugging down on the straps of my pack to tighten them into my shoulders.

CHAPTER 22

Earth, 2153 A.D.

THE FIRST DAY OF ACTUAL INDUCTION SERVICE TRAINING TURNED out to be little different from the first day of Reception. Screaming and profanity from the drill sergeants was had by the bucketful. Everyone's carefully packed duffels were upended and dumped onto the cement—despite the fact that virtually everything that could be taken as contraband had already been taken. Each recruit was personally insulted, demeaned, or otherwise cut down by a sprinkler system of sarcastic comments, and there was far too little time given in which to get far too many things done, which resulted in a lot of smoking, which resulted in some very tired recruits at the end of the night.

I lay in my new bunk—identical to the old one, save for the fact that I was on the bottom now, and not the top—and stared into the relative dark. Gentle snoring around the bay—which was also identical to the one which I'd just departed, save for the new motivational mosaic in the Dead Zone—told me that I ought to be asleep. Only, I couldn't. My body was hurting, my mind was hurting, and I couldn't relax enough to drift off. Because not only had Batbayar Thukhan been assigned to the same IST company as me, he'd even wound up in the same platoon.

I turned on my side and stared down the rows of bunks to where I knew Thukhan was. The dim glow from the emergency exit sign illuminated my enemy's face just enough for me to see that he was staring right back at me. I quickly flipped over to the other side, and shivered. We'd barely interacted with one another since that initial showdown in Reception, but I had a sure feeling that Thukhan was always watching me. Closely. The glance across the bay seemed to confirm that. It made me nervous, though I couldn't be sure why. I'd been fairly sure at the time of the initial showdown that Batbayar was a talker, not a fighter. But the way in which the man had switched from hot to cold—like a machine—left me particularly unsettled.

And now we'd be dealing with each other for fourteen Earth weeks.

Whether I liked it or not.

Morning wakeup was the usual shuffle for sinks and toilets, and since only a handful of the men in the male bay knew each other from their first bay in reception, people had to work out a system all over again. Which didn't always go smoothly. There was bumping and jostling and a few harsh words between particularly stubborn recruits. But with so little time, nobody could spare more than a curse and a hard glance before moving on to the next hurried task.

We missed the time hack for accountability, of course.

Three men were still in the head when the drill sergeants—a PT-uniformed trio composed of two males and one female—popped on the lights.

Those of us who'd managed to toe the line around the Dead Zone groaned audibly as one of the drill sergeants—the woman, named Schmetkin—looked at her chronometer and began to *tsk-tsk-tsk* in a tell-tale way that made it clear we were all in for some early-morning hurt. I was just glad we were already in our PT uniforms, because the sweat we worked out in the bay would simply be added to the sweat we worked out on the PT field.

By the time the three offending recruits had rushed to their lockers, thrown their hygiene supplies into drawers and slammed their lockers closed, the drill sergeants were smiling evilly.

"Don't hurry on our account," said one of the male drill sergeants—a black-skinned sergeant named Davis.

"They're on their own schedule," said Drill Sergeant Malvino, the only staff sergeant of the three. "Looks like we're gonna get the PT started a little early today."

Myself and the other males spent ten minutes on our backs and faces, alternating between push-ups and flutter kicks. By the time we'd actually collected our rolled foam PT mats and were shuffling down the stairs to the open-air expanse of concrete beneath the bay, half the male recruits' PT tops had been soaked dark with perspiration.

Waiting on the concrete—and also showing signs of having had some early PT of their own—were the rest of Charlie Company. Already lined up, according to platoon. All of us from my bay broke off and ran to our respective platoons and squads. For me, that meant second squad of second platoon, or 2/2. Thukhan was in fourth squad of second platoon—known as 4/2—and I could feel Thukhan's eyes on me as I fell in at the position of parade rest, feet shoulder-width apart, eyes forward, hands overlapped at the small of my back.

Drill Sergeant Malvino—the nominal senior drill sergeant for second—took his place at the center head position, facing the recruits. His face was blank while his head slowly turned back and forth, eyes swiveling. Me and the others had learned previously that any movement on our part—even accidental—would earn us a huge ass-chewing from the drill sergeants, so we remained as still as we could, our rolled PT mats aligned uniformly next to our right legs.

Behind second platoon was fourth, and behind fourth was sixth, and to the left were first, third and fifth platoons, respectively.

Together we made up Charlie Company, Four-Fourteenth IST Battalion.

The double doors in the brick wall in front of Charlie Company's common area slammed open, and Charlie's first sergeant stalked out. Her name tape read CHAU, and she was all of five feet tall, and looked like she could bench-press a grown man. Her brownish hair was shaved close to the head and hidden beneath her soft cap—she did not wear a black campaign hat like the drill sergeants—and her face seemed permanently frozen in a sour scowl.

All six platoons' posted DSs spun smoothly on their heels to face the Top, while the remaining DSs fell into a line at the back of the company.

"*Companeeeee,*" Chau yelled in a piercing soprano, failing to draw out the *ayyy* sound as had been the custom of the first sergeant from Reception.

Each of the six posted DSs went to the position of attention and swiveled their heads to the right, shouting, "Platoon!"

Chau finished: "Ahh-ten-*SHIN!*"

All six platoons—composed of roughly two hundred recruits—went rigid.

"Drill sah-*jeens*," Chau barked in an accent I wasn't sure I'd ever heard before, "take accountability of your platoons and prepare to deliver report!"

Malvino spun back around and, head turned towards the rightmost man in first squad, ordered, "Report."

Each of second platoon's squads had been given a squad leader the day before, and each of those squad leaders had supposedly been instructed during Reception on how to take accountability—*before* it came time to report to the platoon sergeant. First squad's squad leader suddenly blushed and leaned his head forward, looking to his left so that he could see down the rank. His mouth moved silently as he counted, and Malvino's face darkened with frustration.

"First Squad Leader," Malvino said angrily, "do you have accountability of your squad or not?"

"Hold on a sec—" first squad's squad leader began.

"Shut up," Malvino said. "First Squad Leader, front-leaning rest. Second Squad Leader, report!"

When the second squad leader failed to promptly give accountability, she was in the front-leaning rest.

Swiveling my eyes, I could see peripherally that a similar scenario was being played out across the common area, with multiple recruits going down to their hands and their toes.

Second's fourth squad leader had fair warning, so he got it right. But that left the squad leaders for first, second, and third on the cement, with Malvino looking like he was going to explode.

The tirade from Malvino began.

"First of all, this is not gawtdamned lollygagging Reception anymore, recruits. You should know this already. We shouldn't have to be reminding you of how this works. We have more important things to do than to dick around with you at morning formation, to say nothing of getting your stupid asses out of the head on time to toe the line up in those bays. It's a bad start to the day, recruits. A very bad start. I'm already in a very bad mood, and it's not even breakfast yet. In IST we hit the ground running every single gawtdamned day. No excuses. No time to relax. You get up out of that bunk and you vacate your bowels, scrub your grills, scrape your necks and your pink little cheeks, and you report on-time and ready to train. We're already well behind schedule, and do you know what that means? Less time for you. Less time for hygiene after PT, less time to take care of all the little crap I know you didn't take care of before the lights went on."

Malvino stopped, though it seemed he had a lot more on his mind that he wanted to say. He extended his palm like a meat-cleaver and rapidly "chopped" his way down the platoon, counting columns of heads. When he was satisfied he had a number, he ordered, "Recover, squad leaders," then spun around and faced to the front. First, second and third's squad leaders quickly got back to their feet, and I waited silently, glad that I hadn't been stuck with any kind of recruit "authority," as had happened in Reception.

First platoon's platoon sergeant sounded off with their accountability, saluted the first sergeant, and then the first sergeant's head turned towards Malvino, who shouted while saluting, "Second platoon, thirty-four recruits assigned, thirty-four recruits present for training," then dropped the salute after the first sergeant had dropped hers.

When all of the platoons had performed this ritual, the first sergeant looked at her chronometer and gave Charlie Company an at-ease.

"Oh-kay, Chah-lee," Chau said, "let's rub sleepee sand from eyes and wake up. Yesterday was day zee-roh, and today it's gonna be on. You know what I mean?"

As a company, Charlie weakly sounded, "YES, FIRST SERGEANT!"

Boos and hisses from the line of drill sergeants in the back.

"Wow," Chau said, taken aback, "that was really half-ass, Chah-lee. Makes me think I should have gone on sick call, not come out here to be with you. 'Cause if you no wanna be here, I no wanna be here. You wanna be here?"

Company: "YES, FIRST SERGEANT!"

"You mean it?"

"YES, FIRST SERGEANT!"

"'Cause I don't believe you, recruits. We are soooo fah behin' schedule today. So fah. So fah I don' even wanna talk about it. You gonna learn, recruits, the longer you in *my* company, the tighter I expect you to be. Time hacks especially. You gotta be on time *every* time, because as some of my drill sah-jeens already say, we have a lot to do, and if we get behind schedule, we gonna take it out of *your* time, recruits. Not ours. And not mine. Is that understood?"

"YES, FIRST SERGEANT!"

"Oh-kay . . . Companeeeee!"

"—Platoon!"

"Ah-ten-*SHIN!* Drill sah-jeens, take charge of da platoons and move 'em out for physical fitness training."

The six platoon sergeants saluted, while the Top saluted back, then she dropped her salute, spun, and marched back through the double doors.

Platoon sergeants spun—Malvino looking particularly murderous—and began snapping commands. Before long I was trailing off in-file with the other recruits, out from underneath the overhead cover afforded by the stacked-block structure of the bays—each of which radiated out from the battalion's administrative core building, like spokes on a bicycle wheel. Off in the distance Charlie Company could see several of the other companies already arrayed on the massive expanse of grass—acres upon acres—that fell back from Charlie's east side. Beyond that were the towers, cranes, and skyscraperlike hangars and buildings of Armstrong Field's tremendous aerospace works. All of which appeared as black silhouettes against the early morning sky, which was now beginning to color.

Sweat came instantly. I gritted my teeth.

Technically, this was the Midwestern portion of North America. Not the Mississippi Delta. But the air was already uncomfortably moist, as well as warm. Despite the early hour. I suspected there would be no relief in store for me, as the sky continued to brighten towards actual daybreak. Once the sun was fully up, things would get even more hot, and more humid.

Charlie eventually arrayed itself around a cement platform in the middle of the gargantuan grass field—Alpha and Bravo companies already sounding off as they entered their warm-ups—with all six platoons in a circle facing inwards towards the platform. Several of Charlie's DSs—Malvino among them—mounted the platform and began to call off additional commands. As in Reception, you couldn't just blow right into PT, they thought someone might get hurt that way. So once each platoon had been broadened and extended—to give each recruit some real-estate on which to ponder his or her own personal physical suffering—the drill sergeants ran us through stretches, followed by in-place calisthenics.

The grass was mildly damp, and our shoes had become wet. The cloying air smelled of lawn clippings.

We unrolled our mats next. Each recruit's mat had to remain on his or her right, and each recruit's mat had to line up more or less with the mat of the person on his or her right. Canteens—large, pliable, liter-sized squares with shoulder straps on them—came off and were placed in the upper right corner of each mat, stenciled name tape facing up. Before the drill sergeants on the platform went any further, the other drill sergeants quickly made their way down each rank, picking up and hefting each canteen.

"Where is the rest of your water, Recruit Gerome?" said Drill Sergeant Schmetkin as she picked up the canteen of the male directly to my front. "Were you not instructed to completely fill your canteen prior to morning accountability?"

"Drill Sergeant," Gerome sputtered, "I wanted to fill my canteen, but—"

"But nothing, Recruit Gerome."

Schmetkin stepped up to Gerome's face and, one-handedly unscrewing the cap on the canteen, used the other hand to upend the canteen over Gerome's head. His mouth hung open in shock as the water flooded across his face and down his chest and back. She slapped the dripping canteen to his chest and said, "You have sixty seconds to run back to the company common area and fill your canteen, then be right back here. Sixty, fifty-nine, fifty-eight..."

I resisted the urge to watch as Gerome fled, though I could see many other recruits from the other platoons doing the same. I stood still while the platform and the drill sergeants on the ground waited. And waited.

There wasn't enough time. There *never* was enough time.

When all of the now-wet and terribly flustered recruits returned to the PT formation, the drill sergeant leading from the platform ordered everyone into the front-leaving rest, and our PT session for the day officially began.

I couldn't really tell the difference between morning PT and a good smoking. The commands were the same, some of the exercises were the same, and everyone felt brutalized by the time it was over. Whatever comfort the PT mat was supposed to provide was quickly lost to the fact that centimeter-thick foam could not prevent lumps in the grass from inevitably sticking into a recruit's butt and back. When it was over, we were each drenched from head to toe, our canteens drained to within a gulp, and the sun was obscured by gathering clouds—the first threat of rain I had seen since arriving at Armstrong Field.

Warm-down was a repeat of warm-up, then we rolled our mats and trooped in-file back up to the company common area, where we again formed by platoons, again took accountability, and then were dismissed up the stairs for what should have been twenty minutes of shower time—now reduced to five, because of all that morning's screw-ups.

CHAPTER 23

WE WALKED.

On rock, when we could find it. The sand and pebbles proving to be a lot of work despite our best efforts. I envied the Professor with his disc, floating effortlessly above the ground. Occasionally I dropped back to talk to him as he kept the Queen Mother securely held.

"Will you be able to sense it?" I asked. "If we get near any other mantis troops or equipment?"

"Yes," said the Professor. "Though I must warn you that my connection to my people has been nonexistent since our landing. I am beginning not to trust my own machinery. Perhaps there has been damage I cannot ascertain? Or perhaps your military has devised some way of blanketing or cloaking mantis communications—such a thing would prove very useful against us, in a pitched battle. Our coordination is our greatest strength. Forced to fight singly, we might not be nearly as effective."

"If we did have such a weapon," the captain said, overhearing, "I am sure I'd have known about it."

"I think we'll have to trust that your readings are accurate," I said to the Professor. "Meanwhile, we will go south, and hope that both terrain and climate are favorable."

It seemed like a vain hope. All I could see on the horizon were rocks, more stony, broken bluffs, and sand dunes. Not a tree nor a bush in any direction. Nothing running, flying, squirming, or jumping. It occurred to me that when we'd entered orbit, the seas of the planet had appeared small, and tinted green. Local evolution might not have gotten much beyond the microscopic level, and then only in the shallow oceans. Enough photosynthesis to turn the sky a pale blue.

Which was both good and bad. Stranded for too long without rescue, we'd starve. Or die of thirst. Purgatory suddenly seemed a lot more homey.

We plodded, and I stretched out the distance between myself and our little group. I scanned relentlessly for gullies or creek beds—any sign of fresh water. Adanaho and I only had enough for a few days, even with rationing.

A wind began to whip. The captain jogged to catch up with me.

"I do not like this," she said. "I feel a sandstorm is coming."

"How do you know?" I asked.

"I grew up part of the time in North Africa," she said. "I can tell."

"Look!" said the Professor, his speaker grill yelling the word.

We stopped and turned. An ominous, dark wall of billowing dust was moving rapidly upon us from the rear. It seemed to stretch into the sky for a kilometer or more. I swallowed hard, then began to frantically search for shelter. The captain pointed, and we ran for a nearby hill with a small overhang. When we got there we discovered a water-worn hollow at the hill's base. We pushed ourselves into it, huddling together, emergency jackets pulled tightly over our heads. The Professor landed his disc and used both the disc and his body to shield the Queen Mother.

If it was possible for a mantis to look more pathetic, I wasn't sure how. Her limbs were curled tightly against her body and dried blood dribbled away from the fresh scabs where her lower thorax had formerly interfaced with her disc. Her lower limbs were small and feeble looking, compared to the impressive forelimbs, and I wondered just how long it had been since *any* mantis had walked under its own power.

Without her carriage, the Queen Mother had been made small.

I experienced a moment of unexpected pity. Then the rushing cloud of detritus swept over us. I closed my jacket across my face as tightly as I could make it, listening to the muffled howling of the wind as it broke across the top of the hill.

CHAPTER 24

Earth, 2153 A.D.

BY THE SECOND WEEK OF IST, THE MORNING ROUTINE HAD straightened itself out. Nobody was late getting out of the head anymore, and we'd had enough individual and group smokings over the details of accountability formation that the squad leaders—two of whom had already been fired and replaced—knew their lines. Second platoon's drill sergeants—Malvino, Davis, and Schmetkin—weren't bellowing as much as they had the first week, and I and the others were beginning to find the "beat," as Top had called it, back in Reception.

Training was hard, of course. Week one focused almost entirely on immersive drill and ceremony, where we marched as squads and as a platoon, around and around and around the huge grass field. Column-right, column-left, right-flank, left-flank, rear-march, and so on and so forth, until we'd all begun to respond to the commands with an almost subliminal quickness. Otherwise, the DSs PT'd us to death, and we drew additional training equipment in between numerous and mindlessly boring briefings about military protocol, aspects of Fleet's complex, internationally-oriented military justice code, and a weekend computer exam on same.

Which surprised me. Book work? In Basic? But book work there was, and a surprisingly large amount of it, too. In addition to helmets and body armor and field packs, each recruit was given a use-worn e-pad with a built-in library of Fleet manuals, pamphlets, regulations, and so forth. Including an all-in-one quick guide to IST, which I found myself referencing quite often for general orders and reminders on Fleet jargon, in addition to bits of recent history about the Fleet, and the war with the mantis aliens.

All of us recruits were required to carry the e-pad on our person—as part of our uniform—and if at any point the platoon was stopped for any moment, be it waiting in line for chow or waiting out on the field as the DSs switched out for the afternoon, we were to pull out the e-pad and study. Study, study, study. Which made even my eyes glaze over—and I'd been pretty good in school. But I'd never had to read and memorize while functioning on this little sleep and doing this much daily physical work.

Of course the e-pad became an easy thing to lose, too. And it was apparent that losing anything became a guaranteed ticket to discipline. Our names were on every scrap of clothing and piece of equipment. If ever a DS found anything with your name on it not secured in your locker or on your person, you were suddenly in a personal world of hurt.

On three separate occasions, I ran across e-pads which had been left in the head, left on the floor, or in one case, left on one of the bench seats in the cafeterialike mess hall where we ate three times a day. Rather than stare dumbly at the things, I scooped them up each time and surreptitiously sleuthed out the owners.

"Thanks," said one of the other platoon's troops, named Zaratanski, when I found her one afternoon while we filed up the stairs to our separate bays. The e-pad passed quickly between us. "I was almost sick thinking about where I could have put it. I appreciate you getting it back to me."

"No problem," I said, smiling. "If we don't look out for each other, who will, right?"

She smiled back at me, and I knew I'd made an instant friend.

Before I headed into the bay, I thought I caught DS Schmetkin watching me out of the corner of her eye. Had she seen what I'd just done? If she had, she gave no hint that it mattered to her.

Going into week two we each had a heavy batch of required reading to prepare for the next exam. So much so that most of us stole an hour or more after lights-out, our heads and e-pads carefully concealed beneath our blankets while we caught up on all the crap that we hadn't been able to get to during the day.

Which was pretty much Standard Operating Procedure—SOP—for the third week as well. Never enough time. Never, ever enough. The single hour at night—the hour the recruiters had promised us would be for personal business—was gone. It invariably wound up being the only time some of us could reasonably find to thoroughly shower and get the salt, oil, and dirt out of the cracks of our bodies, not to mention prepping equipment for the next day's training.

The e-pads were equipped to send and receive monitored e-mail once an evening through the battalion centralized wireless server, but I only had enough time to jot my mother a quick hello, letting her know I'd arrived and was up to my eyebrows in training, before I was either studying for the exams or doing something else that I'd rather not have to be doing.

Meanwhile I kept feeling Thukhan's eyes on me. During odd moments, when I thought nobody in the bay or in the platoon could possibly care enough to pay attention to me. I'd look up, and there Batbayar would be, watching without saying anything, and I would just turn away and silently feel angry that I was letting the asshole psych me out.

After ten days of such mind games, I decided I'd had enough.

It was our first visit to the armory, and as the platoon filed up onto some bleachers for our initial introduction to our assigned weapons, I deliberately sat next to Thukhan.

Batbayar looked at me, but I deliberately didn't look back. I stared straight ahead as one of the range cadre—sergeants without campaign hats, and remarkably nice people, too—began to explain the functions of the R77A5 automatic rifle.

"Each of you," said the cadre member, a female sergeant first class named Secce, "will become intimately familiar with this weapon."

Secce held it up: a longish metal tube with an attached fiberglass stock.

"The first thing you need to remember is that while you might not always have ammunition for this rifle on your person, the rifle itself *will* be on your person for the rest of the time you're in Induction Service Training. Your rifle will go with you when you go to sleep. Your rifle will be with you when you go to PT in the morning. Your rifle will be with you as you train each and every day. Your rifle is the thing that makes you valuable as a fighter in the modern arena of battle.

"Some of you may have already had experience with firearms, especially pistols, but you'll notice that nobody in IST ever carries a pistol. The reason for that is because the pistol is a very specialized weapon that is practically useless in open terrain, or across long distances. A pistol lacks the power of a rifle cartridge—the ability to hit and knock a mantis out of the fight—and this is what learning to handle and use the R77A5 is all about."

I felt Thukhan's eyes on me, but ignored him and kept watching SFC Secce.

"If you've done your homework," said Secce, "then you should already know a lot about this weapon, even before you've handled it. Unlike some other kinds of rifles you might have fired, this one is built to operate aboard spacecraft. It uses *caseless* ammunition, which does not employ traditional powder explosives, but rather a split mixture of chemical propellant. This propellant is not active until the round has been discharged in the rifle's firing chamber. Which means the ammunition is extremely resistant to heat and moisture, and will seldom cook off or prematurely fire under adverse conditions."

Secce held up an example of the caseless round, and stepped to the foot of the bleachers. She told the nearest recruit to look at it, then pass the round along.

"Also, because this round is not powder-based, there is far less carbon to foul the breach and barrel, meaning longer duration between mandatory cleaning, and less chance of a jam or a malfunction. Likewise there is no spent casing—no brass—for you to hassle with, which means less work for you when you come off the ranges, but more importantly, when you get out into the Fleet and have to do real fighting, less dead weight, and more room for you to carry more ammo."

"What do you want?" Thukhan finally growled at me, as he passed the round to me. I ignored him long enough to hold the single piece of ammunition up to my eyes. The e-pad specs said that the bullet itself was ten millimeters wide, but the actual *cartridge*—which felt a little bit like soft plastic, and was transparent so that I could see the bullet and the two differently-colored liquid chemicals behind it—was much wider, and many times longer. According to the operational guide, when the trigger on the rifle was pulled, the firing pin would plunge into the back of the cartridge, puncturing the internal wall that kept the chemicals separate, thus causing an instant reaction that vaporized both the chemicals and the rubbery plastic shell, expelling it all as hot gas behind the bullet, which would be forced down the length of the barrel and out the muzzle at approximately one thousand meters per second.

"I want you to either tell me what your effing problem is," I said to Thukhan, continuing to examine the round, "or get off my case and quit acting like I don't know you're trying to eff with me."

I turned to him and held the round up between us, looking Batbayar square in the face and using the round for a point of emphasis.

"Here," I said, handing it back to him.

"This round is also vacuum-proof," said Secce to the platoon, "which you will find comes in very handy later in IST when you get to your orbital combat training phase. It can even be fired in water, in fully oxygen-depleted gaseous environments, and will not rust or corrode, nor does it require any oil."

"I don't know what you're talking about," Batbayar said, grasping the round in his hand, his eyes still locked on mine.

"Bullshit," I breathed.

Secce continued, "As a result of all these wonderful abilities that modern weapons technology has given us, the round for the R77A5 is *very* expensive—as is the R77A5 itself.

"On the table in front of me you can see approximately sixty-seven different accessories for this weapon, making the R77A5 highly mission-flexible, with a variety of stock and grip options, scoping and sighting options, and load-bearing options which will make the weapon both easier to hump and easier to shoot than a traditional sport rifle.

"But, for the purposes of IST, you will not being seeing most of these specialized pieces of equipment. You will instead be using the R77A5 in its factory-issued mode: fixed shoulder stock, flat forward grip on the barrel, twenty-round magazine, and basic three-power scope with manual zeroing studs and flip-cap aperture protection."

The corner of Batbayar's lip curled, just as it had on the bus on Pickup Day.

"It's not my fault if you're nervous, cunt."

"Eff you," I growled.

I felt my fists closing up into balls, and suddenly there was a peculiar silence.

"Do we have a problem, recruits?"

I broke eye contact with Thukhan and realized that SFC Secce—and the rest of the platoon—were staring at me. I blushed and sat up, facing forward.

"Negative, Sergeant," I said. "Recruit Barlow does not have a problem, Sergeant."

"You?" Secce said, raising an eyebrow at Thukhan.

Batbayar repeated what I had said.

"Very well then," Secce said, continuing the lecture.

"Just stay the hell away from me," I said in a rasp, through clenched teeth.

Thukhan said nothing, but I was pretty sure the corner of Batbayar's mouth resumed its disquieting curl.

One hour later, each recruit in second platoon was holding his or her own R77A5. None of the weapons looked nearly as new as the one Secce had shown us, but all the weapons were clean, and all of them had been issued as promised: factory spec, nothing less and nothing more. It was a much lighter than it looked, and I felt both excited and intimidated.

No rounds had been issued, as the platoon was still at least one full week away from going anywhere near a range. But we were instructed strictly in the proper carry of the weapon while in cantonment, as well as in the field. Which basically meant that at no time would the barrel of the weapon ever rise towards or aim at another human being. Such an action—which Secce called "flagging"—was a serious violation and could be grounds for administrative punishment, in addition to corrective training. Repeated flagging would result in potential recycle—being sent back to Reception as a holdover and then placed into a new batch at a different IST battalion—or expulsion to the dreaded and mythic Alcatraz battalion.

I found myself quickly emulating Secce and the other cadre, who demonstrated what they called a practical carry, with the rifle's single shoulder strap hooked over my elbow while I held the rifle's handle—located behind the trigger and trigger guard—in my right hand, barrel towards the ground, the straight forward grip in my left.

The platoon was also trained in integrating the rifle into the drill and ceremony movements we'd learned the previous week, with additional movements performed strictly from the position of attention, such as order-arms, right- and left-shoulder arms, and so forth. I managed to stay fairly well away from Thukhan through most of it, and actually enjoyed the instruction and training—which was given while out from under the baleful eye of the DSs, who had quietly been banished during armory cadre instruction.

But the joy did not last. As chow time approached, the drill sergeants reappeared, and the platoon was hustled back into platoon formation for several minutes of hard marching around the PT field before being marched back up to the Charlie Company common area, in prep for chow.

While we waited, huffing and puffing, to take our turn rotating through the limited space of the chow hall, Drill Sergeant Malvino taught us the meaning of "stack arms"—all the rifles being quickly and uniformly pitched into cones, or "teepees," which would remain outside with a watch detail, rather than be carried into the chow hall, which was verboten. He also spent a significant amount of time warning us about the dire consequences of losing or misplacing our rifles. If losing an e-pad was bad, losing a rifle was about a thousand times worse.

"That weapon is a part of you now," Malvino said, walking up and down the ranks. "Treat it as such. You don't forget your feet or your hands or your mouth when you go somewhere or wake up in the morning, so you shouldn't forget your weapon either. Unless your weapon has been secured and is under guard—during chow and a few select other times—your weapon will be on you at all times. Is that understood?"

Second platoon, "YES, DRILL SERGEANT!"

"Have you been told what will happen if you are caught flagging?"

"YES, DRILL SERGEANT!"

"Good, 'cause let me remind you again. We will smoke you so hard you will throw up. You haven't seen the kind of smoking we'll give you if you're stupid enough to leave that weapon, or flag another troop, or an NCO. We'll smoke you up one side of the bay, and back down the other side. We'll smoke you clear across the PT field and back, then do it again just to see you cry. We'll smoke you until you literally don't have a damn piece of yourself left for us to smoke, and then we'll smoke you some more.

"And then," Malvino said, not smiling at all, "we'll take your pay, we'll take your privileges, and if necessary we'll take you all the way back to square one. And that means recycle, or Alcatraz. And you all know and we all know that nobody wants that to happen. Do you want that to happen, recruits?"

"NO, DRILL SERGEANT!"

"Do any of you want to recycle or be sent to Alcatraz, recruits?"

"NO, DRILL SERGEANT!!"

"Good. See that it doesn't."

After chow and after training, when we males and the fewer-in-number females had been sent to our respective bays, maneuvering with the R77A5 proved a challenge. With the full stock and standard barrel, the rifle wasn't exactly friendly in close quarters. There was also the issue of taking the weapon into the head—which, like taking the weapon into the chow hall—was a no-no. Weapons had to be left in the care of other recruits—volunteers, or those unfortunate enough to be pressed into the job—while people bathed and used the toilet.

I waited until the very end of the hour to nab a shower. With so much reading to do, and not wanting to endure the ass-tastic, full-court-press of bodies that queued up at the beginning of the hour, a last-minute rinse would have to suffice.

By the time I was in my flip-flop slippers and PT shorts and T-shirt, there was only five minutes to spare before the DSs came in for the final accountability check of the day, followed by lights out.

I found the latest rifle-guard-slash-victim standing dumbly by a bunk piled with several weapons. I thanked the poor soul for helping out, he grunted at me, and I added my rifle to the pile, and went to do my business.

Thankfully the barracks had a near-endless supply of hot water from the high-efficiency all-points heating system. I momentarily luxuriated in the feel of the near-scalding fluid as it flowed over my skin, washing away that day's layer of grit and filth. Soap, suds, rinse, and I was padding back into the bay with ninety seconds to spare—pure eternity.

The recruit watching the rifles was not the same recruit I had seen when I'd gone into the head.

I checked the bunk for my weapon—each of them having been stickered on the shoulder stock with a number and barcode identical to that which had been stamped on our hands in Reception, and printed onto our duffels—and could not find it.

Sudden, cold panic overtook me.

"Where's my rifle?" I asked.

The male recruit just shrugged. "I dunno."

"Weren't you *watching* while you stood here?"

"Look, people come and go, taking and leaving weapons, I don't know whose is whose."

I rechecked the pile. And rechecked again. The last people exited the head and collected their weapons from the bunk, leaving it empty.

The recruit guarding them just shrugged at me, and walked away, his own weapon in his hands.

The cold panic had become a maw of icelike fangs, closing on my heart.

The bay had begun to line up around the edge of the Dead Zone, each man in his flip-flop slippers, PT shorts, and PT shirt tucked in, rifle butt on the ground at the order-arms position.

I frantically ran up one side of the bay and down the other, praying that someone happened to have two rifles. I scanned the bunks, and the lockers, and the spaces between the bunks and lockers, and saw nothing. My eyes darted from face to face, finding indifference—or occasional sympathy.

"Has anyone seen my effing rifle??" I finally begged, to which the other men just shook their heads and shrugged their shoulders.

Nearly-blinded by desperation, I ran into the head and banged open all the toilet stalls and went through all the shower stalls, madly hoping that somehow I'd forgotten to put the weapon on the bed, but had instead left it hanging on a hook or leaning up in a corner.

Suddenly, the communal cry of "DRILL SERGEANT ON THE FLOOR!" went up from the bay—somewhat muffled by the head doors—and I knew I was doomed.

Going out there to toe the line—more naked without my rifle than I would have been if I'd actually *been* naked but *had* my rifle—was a thought almost too horrible to bear. I remained frozen at the threshold of the head, my mind and heart spinning wildly. Then I dumbly pushed open the door and walked out into the suddenly harsh and unyielding light of the bay.

"Nice of you to join us, Recruit Barlow," said Drill Sergeant

Davis. "You've still got ten seconds left to find you a spot on the line."

I walked to the nearest spot and pushed between two men, not bothering to say excuse me or look at their faces.

Davis pulled out his e-pad from under his arm and began to tap a few items on its screen, then suddenly froze, his head coming back up slowly until he was staring straight at me.

The DS placed his e-pad back under an arm and walked slowly and deliberately across the Dead Zone until he was standing directly in front of me, so close that I could feel and smell his breath beating hotly down on me.

"Where is your weapon, Recruit Barlow?"

He'd said it at almost a whisper, calmly and slowly.

I felt my lip begin to quiver.

"I asked you a question, Recruit. Where is your R77A5 rifle?"

I willed my lip under control, only to feel my stomach rebel. If the man hadn't been standing directly in front of me, I'm sure I'd have thrown up.

"Drill Sergeant, I don't know, Drill Sergeant." I said, croaking the words.

"I'm sorry, Recruit?" Davis said, still speaking in a low whisper. "I want to make sure I heard that correctly. Did you say that you *don't know* where your weapon is?"

"Drill Sergeant," I said, still croaking, "that is correct, Drill Sergeant."

Davis's breathing seemed to halt for a moment, his eyes like hot drills on my head as I couldn't bring herself to meet his gaze, lest I lose it completely.

Then Drill Sergeant Davis drew a deep, long breath, and clenching the e-pad in his hand so tightly the tendons stood out, screamed, "WHAT DO YOU MEAN YOU *DON'T KNOW* WHERE YOUR WEAPON IS?"

My legs and arms began to physically shake.

Davis continued, at full blast.

"SENIOR DRILL SERGEANT TOLD YOU WHAT WOULD HAPPEN IF YOU LOST YOUR WEAPON, DID HE NOT? YOU'RE AWARE, IN FACT, THAT THERE IS PRACTICALLY NO WORSE THING YOU CAN DO IN THIS BATTALION THAN LOSE YOUR WEAPON."

Davis didn't even wait for me to stutter replies.

"RECRUIT BARLOW, YOUR FILE FROM RECEPTION WAS A RATHER GOOD ONE. THEY SAID YOU DID WELL AS BAY SERGEANT. THAT YOU WERE DETAIL-ORIENTED AND COULD GET THINGS DONE. WELL, I GUESS RECEPTION LIED. YOU'RE A MISERABLE PIECE OF FORGETFUL GARBAGE, BARLOW, AND I WANT TO KNOW HOW YOU COULD POSSIBLY LOSE YOUR WEAPON IN THE FEW HOURS SINCE IT WAS GIVEN TO YOU?"

"Drill Sergeant, I—"

"EFF THE FORMALITIES, JUST TALK!"

"I had it with me right up until I took a shower," I said, my voice wavering.

"And what happened then?"

"I gave it to the weapons guard at the head door."

"And what happened after that?"

"I came out, and none of the rifles left was mine."

"So you're the only one in the whole gawtdamned bay without a weapon?"

"Yes, Drill Sergeant."

"And who is this person that was guarding the weapons?"

I pointed at the recruit I'd seen guarding the pile when I exited the shower. The recruit's face lit up with fear, and his mouth hung open as if to plead innocence.

Davis spun on the open-mouthed man. "WHERE IS RECRUIT BARLOW'S RIFLE?"

"Drill Sergeant, I don't know, I . . . I was just covering for someone else."

Davis grabbed me by the bicep and dragged me across the Dead Zone to stand in front of the hapless recruit that I had fingered.

"Recruit Barlow, is this the troop you surrendered your weapon to upon entering the head?"

"No," I said. "When I came out, this is the recruit who had taken over."

"Then who is the one you gave your weapon to?"

I turned and scanned, then pointed. "Him. Recruit Webber."

Now it was Webber's turn to protest his innocence.

"Drill Sergeant, I just had to take a quick—"

But Webber's plea fell on deaf ears.

Davis dragged me, Webber, and the second guard—Recruit Ajala—into the center of the Dead Zone.

"I want to know one good reason why I shouldn't send all three of you to effing Alcatraz for this. One good gawtdamned reason."

I stared dumbly into space, unable to come up with a sufficient response.

"Do you know how much that rifle costs? Do you? Well, guess what happens now, recruits. I have to call Drill Sergeant Malvino, and tell him a weapon is missing. And then he has to inform the first sergeant, who then informs the captain, who then informs the colonel, and then the colonel is going to put the entire gawtdamned effing *battalion* on lockdown until that weapon is recovered. We will go through every locker, every bunk, look in every closet, every stall, crawl up every last asshole, until we find it. We'll be up all night doing it, if necessary. All of us. You, me, and every other living soul in the battalion."

Ajala and Webber appeared nearly as ill as I felt.

Someone suddenly shouted, "Drill Sergeant, what's that over there under that bunk?"

Davis spun and marched across the Dead Zone—recruits making a hole for him without being asked—and got down on his hands and knees, coming back up with an R77A5 in his hands. He flipped it over and examined the sticker on the stock.

"Recruit Barlow, did you memorize your serial number as instructed?"

"Drill Sergeant, yes, Drill Sergeant," I said, amazed and immediately angry to see the rifle—which had been under all their noses the whole time, yet nobody had had the effing decency to help me check for it. They'd just stood on the line and waited for the shit to come down.

"What is it?" Davis asked.

"Seven zero delta zero zero niner foxtrot one eight one zero," I said.

Davis marched back into the Dead Zone and thrust the weapon into my hands.

"Here's your effing rifle, Recruit. All three of you, get back on the line. *Now.*"

The three of us scattered, taking up spaces where we could find them at the edge of the Dead Zone.

Davis glared around the entire bay, making eye contact with each of us as he went.

"All of you, get in the front-leaning rest," he said. His voice not even raised. But it was as loud as a firecracker in my ears. I dropped where I was, my palms out to either side of my shoulders and my back straight, toes on the tile below. My rifle balanced across the tops of my hands.

"This shouldn't have happened," Drill Sergeant Davis said, his voice made sandpapery from his previous hyperbolic outburst. "You aren't individuals anymore. You're a *team.* A team that's expected to work together. You're only as strong or as weak as you make yourselves. You're going to learn that it's not enough to just keep your own ass clean. If you think your shit is straight, and you're just standing there thinking that's enough, you are wrong. Wrong, wrong, wrong. Recruit Barlow trusted Recruit Webber to watch the weapons, and Recruit Webber trusted Recruit Ajala to watch the weapons, but in the process, all three of them forgot the purpose of that exercise.

"It's not just because these rifles are expensive and we don't want to lose an expensive item. It's because in garrison and in combat you will only have each other to stand by. And if you're all wandering through this thing like it's just you by yourselves and you don't really have to give an eff about someone else when the fuel hits the afterburner, then none of you is going to make it until graduation. You will all wash out. The Fleet doesn't tolerate individuals who think like individuals. The Fleet is a team that thinks like a team. Works like a team. And tonight this bay showed absolutely no teamwork. None.

"I could smoke you, but I'm so tired of hearing myself talk, I'm not going to bother. It's too late in the damned day for this crap. So I'm gonna let you have this one—and only one—freebie. Mess up like this again, and it's no mercy. Do I make myself absolutely and one hundred percent clear, recruits?"

Bay, together and straining, "YES, DRILL SERGEANT!!"

"I said is that one *thousand* percent burned into your little minds, recruits?"

"YES, DRILL SERGEANT!"

"Good. Now get to the position of attention and stay on the line while I check your miserable names off."

We got back to our feet. Most of us sweating.

I stood where I was, face slowly drying in the gentle air from the overhead ducts. My heart rate slowly began to slow. The awful feeling in my stomach subsiding. For many seconds I had been positive that ultimate extinction was falling down on my head, and I had been powerless to prevent it. Now...?

Now, I flicked my eyes around the rectangle, checking blank—and mostly relieved—faces, for signs of culpability or guilt. Webber and Ajala looked ashamed, and wouldn't meet my gaze, but I couldn't bring myself to blame them because I knew they weren't the ones at fault.

I rapid-scanned until I found the one person I suddenly was sure in my bones had been behind it.

Thukhan wouldn't meet my gaze either, even though I glared at Batbayar with enough seething rage to melt holes in a tank's hull.

He just stood there, as if oblivious to the whole thing.

Only, a little curl crept up at the corner of his mouth.

And I suddenly wished very much for a magazine of live ammunition.

CHAPTER 25

SOMETHING NUDGED ME AWAKE.

I slowly pulled the jacket off of my head. There was a sensation of fine grit in every pore and crevice of my skin. My lips were dry and my throat parched.

It was dusk, or getting on towards it. The storm had passed, and the air was clear. So clear, in fact, that I could see the stars, sharp and precise in the purpling sky.

I saw the captain's pack in front of me, but no Adanaho.

The Professor hovered nearby.

"Is everyone okay?" I asked, my tongue rubbery. Saliva flowed into my mouth, and I spit several times to get the dust out—though I still felt it on my teeth. My eyes were crusted and I wiped at them with hands that felt caked in powder.

"Yes," said the Professor.

I slowly stood up, yawning and stretching my back. There were wind storms on Purgatory too, but in the valley where my chapel was built, things had been more or less protected.

Not so, here. Though the hill had done us good. I couldn't begin to guess what might have happened if we'd been caught out in the open with nowhere to run and nothing to hide behind. There weren't any mountains on this world, from what I could see. No recent or ongoing geologic activity. Everything had been slowly worn flat by wind and occasional water. It was probable we'd see several more sandstorms before our journey was over.

My bowels suddenly told me it was time to do God's work.

"Excuse me," I said. And began walking away from our hill, looking for something farther and smaller—just big enough to crouch behind and relieve myself.

When I was done I made my way back. The far horizon still glowed with the setting sun. I stopped short, seeing two silhouettes at the top of our hill: one human, distinctly female, and the other mantis. I observed them for a time. They were both facing into the setting sun, their heads erect and their eyes forward. I thought I could just barely hear the sound of Adanaho's voice.

Coming back to the makeshift camp in the hollow at the base of the hill, I quietly spoke to the Professor.

"What are they doing?" I asked.

"When the storm lifted, your Captain was the first to rouse. She checked the status of myself and the Queen Mother, then she shed her equipment and went to the top of the hill to survey the surround. When we heard her voice coming softly down to us, the Queen Mother asked me what your Captain was saying. I told the Queen Mother that it sounded like prayer."

Prayer.

I was surprised, though I don't know why. I'd not known the captain long enough to inquire as to her upbringing or spiritual affiliation. If any. Was she Muslim? She had mentioned North Africa.

"So how did the Queen Mother get up there?"

"I carried her," said the Professor. "She was curious. She'd never seen a human engaged in religious rite. Of any sort. Your captain did not seem to mind. The Queen Mother asked that she be left alone with your captain, and I have done this. I suggest you do it too."

"It sounds to me like Adanaho is still talking," I said. "She has to know that the Queen Mother isn't able to understand."

"Perhaps her words are not for the Queen Mother?" the Professor said.

Yes, perhaps.

I sat down in the hollow and retrieved some water and a concentrated food bar from my pack, drinking and eating in slow, deliberate portions. The Professor softly landed his disc next to me, and I felt his alien eyes studying me as I stared at the gravel in front of my toes.

"You are a curiosity," he said.

"Oh?"

"Yes, assistant-to-the-chaplain. In all the time we have known each other—through all of the work that you have performed in my presence, as a religious human—I have never known you to be overt about your feelings in the way other humans are overt."

I felt my face get warm.

He was treading in uncomfortable territory.

"I don't believe it's my place to be showy," I said. "It might make some of the chapel's attendees think I was playing favorites. In terms of which 'flavor' I subscribe to."

"But we are not in your chapel," said the Professor. "And there are no other humans around us to see you, save your Captain. Who is now occupied. Our circumstances are dire. I know from studying the human history of belief that this is the ideal time for supplication. Harry, why do you not pray?"

The warm feeling in my face grew more intense.

"I don't know," I said. He was asking me questions I didn't dare ask *myself.*

"You built a holy house with your own hands, and you maintain this house for use by any human who comes through your door. You do this out of loyalty to your deceased chaplain. Yet, you do not perform services in your chapel. Never have you offered a sermon. You do not pray, nor have I ever known you to habitually carry out any religious ritual of any sort—save for demonstration purposes, for the educational benefit of myself and my students."

"Stop," I said. Though perhaps too quietly. It was a plea, not a command. My eyes were closed, but that didn't prevent the tears.

"My apologies," said the Professor, when he noticed the muddy streaks on my cheeks. "It was not my intent to cause you grief. I was merely curious. It seems to me a very large irony that you of all humans should be a non-believer. Yet this has been my slow, hesitant conclusion. After spending many years away from you, during which I was able to further digest our mutual experiences. You support and feed the belief of others. You have made it your mission in life. Yet you cannot partake of that which you give."

"I'm . . . I'm not sure *what* I goddamned believe," I said, though perhaps too loudly. The gentle, whispery sound of Adanaho's voice had ceased. And suddenly the clicky-clacky speech of the Queen Mother replaced it. The Professor listened intently for a few moments, then looked down at me—his body and disc just faint outlines in the near darkness.

"I must go. The Queen Mother wishes me to translate."

He left me there, feeling embarrassed and miserable.

I put away my food and water and rewrapped myself in my jacket. Nights in the desert—any desert—tend to be cold. Though I didn't think the chill was entirely physical.

CHAPTER 26

Earth, 2153 A.D.

I WAITED SIX DAYS.

Acting any sooner would have been a mistake. With the situation between Thukhan and I coming to a head, any immediate action on my part would have been expected, or even planned for, by him. So I hid my rage behind a mask, and plowed through the immersive marksmanship training, to include simulator exercises prior to the following week's live-fire trips to the open-air range.

I also redoubled my efforts to find excuses to demonstrate through action what the DS had been screaming about the night my weapon went temporarily missing. It didn't take much. Notice someone struggling to get his bunk made on time? Help him make his bunk. Spot someone's uniform out of whack? Walk up and straighten things out for her. See an error of any sort? Correct it before the DSs did. And so on, and so forth. To the point that I got to know a goodly number of my fellow bay inmates, and a few more people around the company as well. Simply by making an extra effort to notice things, and help a brother or sister out. Usually earning me a smile, or an embarrassed thank you, or a fist bump.

Before too long, the trick caught on. Spontaneously. Just little things, here and there. A locker left open would magically find itself locked. A latrine kit, accidentally abandoned in the head, would be secured for later return to its owner when the DSs weren't looking. Boots and shoes not aligned properly under bunks became mysteriously aligned. Until it seemed as if the bay, and the platoon, and indeed the whole company, began to think and act on a different, almost subliminal level.

The smokings and the chew-outs predictably dwindled in number as well as intensity. Which meant more time to actually focus on training, and less time spent locked up at the position of attention or parade rest, wondering what kind of terrible punishment was going to be dished out.

In the back of my mind, I relaxed and waited. Just long enough for Thukhan's eyes to begin wandering elsewhere.

I knew I had my chance when Batbayar drew night watch assignment: midnight to three in the morning. When the bay was full of sleeping recruits and the only other person awake would be Thukhan's assigned double on duty.

They each took an end of the bay, per longstanding instruction from the DSs. I'd pulled a few shifts already. I knew the routine. Everybody did.

Sweat coated my skin as I lay in my bunk, awake with nervous energy. I'm not a violent person. But even I knew that someone with Thukhan's mentality wouldn't stop until something drastic was done. I didn't want to wait to find out what a man like Thukhan would do with a live weapon in his hands. Maybe the DSs didn't have the time or the energy to see it yet, but I knew in my heart that Thukhan was going to hurt someone. If not me, it would be someone else. And in this environment there were plenty of ways for a person with ill intent to ruin someone else's whole life.

Which is why at 2:08 AM, when I saw Thukhan walking back to the head doors at the rear of the bay—far from his counterpart, who sat yawning sleepily at the other end—I became almost spastic with anxiety. If I was successful, it would get Thukhan out of the bay and out of the platoon. Perhaps even out of IST altogether? Failure would leave me more wide open than ever to Thukhan's depredations, and I had no doubt that once he'd been openly retaliated against, Thukhan would let nothing stand between himself and his vengeance.

At 2:13 AM, I finally forced myself out of my bunk. Thukhan was clearly distracted or otherwise occupied, and the recruit on watch at the other end of the bay had his chin on his chest while a quiet snore issued from his throat.

I padded silently down the side of the Dead Zone—bare feet being forbidden in the bay, but in this instance they were essential—until

I was leaning an ear against the head door. There was no sound coming from inside that I could hear. Had Thukhan fallen asleep on the pot? Was he pulling on his pud, PT shorts around his ankles? He'd be in a for a very rude surprise, if so.

I clenched my rifle in my hand.

In addition to shooting, we'd been practicing man-to-man contact maneuvers with our weapons as blunt instruments. Not that these moves would work against a mantis, but there were some military traditions that simply refused to die. Tonight I hoped my training would serve me well enough to put Thukhan out of the picture for keeps.

"Don't do it, man," said a whisper to my left.

I nearly jumped off the floor.

The shape in the darkness was impossible to make out. I couldn't tell which recruit had spoken. So far I'd pretty much kept to myself, and while I'd managed to get along with most people, I'd not exactly become friends with any of them either.

The interloper was unwelcome.

"This is none of your business," I hissed.

"Eff that," he said. "You think we're all blind? You and Thukhan have been spoiling for a fight ever since we got here. You think the DSs don't know it too? What happens when they find the body? Who do you think they'll point the finger at?"

"I don't want to kill him," I said.

"Then what?"

Our hushed whispering seemed overly loud in my ears. I craned my head over my shoulder to be sure the night watch at the end of the bay was still snoozing. Which he was. Then I turned back to my nameless interrogator.

"I just want him gone," I said. "A broken arm or leg should do it. Knock him unconscious. Say he slipped on the wet floor, or something? That way he's recycled, at best, and I don't have to deal with him anymore."

"Naw, man, Thukhan is from the street. You're not from the street. You've learned a little bit about fighting from the cadre, but that doesn't mean you know how to close with a man and put him down. Not yet. Maybe not ever. You don't seem like the kind of guy who wants blood on his hands."

I was sweating profusely at this point, despite the cool air from the ventilators.

"I don't," I said, swallowing hard.

"Then let it go, bro."

"He's going to hurt someone if he's not stopped."

"You mean he's going to hurt *you*."

"And someone else after me, and someone else again after them, and so forth. Look, who the eff are you anyway? And why do you care?"

"I'm just someone who thinks you're about to make a big mistake."

I had no reply. I simply stared at the dark silhouette to my side, trying to make up my mind whether or not to go through with my plan.

"Look," said the shape, "you do whatever you want, I can't stop you. Just don't say you weren't warned."

"So if I do nothing, Thukhan gets to keep on being an asshole?"

"Maybe," said the shape. "Or maybe assholes have a way of weeding themselves out? So far, Thukhan has been a loner. You haven't. You're making friends. He's not. By doing this you're letting your focus on him distract you from gaining allies elsewhere."

"Are you my ally?" I asked honestly.

There was a brief moment of silence.

"Yeah," said the voice. "Maybe I am."

More silence.

Then the tell-tale sound of a plastic toilet seat dropping onto its ceramic bowl, followed by the gurgling growl of flushing water.

Without even thinking about it, I hotfooted my way back up the bay and slid into my bunk, the springs bouncing just slightly as I hurriedly covered myself up.

Thukhan emerged from the head a moment later.

If he'd heard either myself or the nameless recruit talking, he didn't seem to show it. He simply sauntered up the bay, nudged his partner awake, then went back to take a seat for the remainder of his shift.

I stared at the springs to the bunk above me.

When I joined up with the Fleet, I'd simply wanted to do what my friends were doing: get away from home, and go to space. To see the stars. For real. Help the human race survive. Beyond that... I'd not put much thought into it. What kind of plan did I have for myself, or my future?

Lying there in my bunk I considered the fact that I'd been

on the brink of trying to really hurt another human being—and possibly hurting myself worse in the process. My interrogator was right. I wasn't from the street. I was from the suburbs in Colorado. Had grown up and been raised by a mother and father who, while firm, had never put a hand to my face in anger.

What did I know about taking anyone to the woodshed—whether they deserved it or not?

With my rifle securely tucked beside me under my blanket, I felt a wave of quick exhaustion sweep over me. With a little luck, I'd still get three hours sleep, before morning reveille started the regimented madness of IST all over again.

CHAPTER 27

CAPTAIN ADANAHO WOKE ME.

"Chief," she said in a whisper.

"Hmmm?"

"Sun's coming up. We need to get moving."

I slowly uncurled—stiff and cold.

At least on Purgatory there had been something akin to trees from which we'd harvested firewood. On this nameless sphere there wasn't so much as a tumbleweed to burn. I shakily fished some food and water from my pack, the captain and I ate in silence while the mantes watched dispassionately, then we began trudging into the brightening dawn.

The labor of the march warmed me up soon enough, and before long I felt myself sweating as the bright, alien star climbed steadily into the sky.

This time it was the Professor who led. He claimed to have felt the ghost of a flicker of a mantis signal due roughly southwest, and he stretched out a large distance between himself—with the Queen Mother riding on the front of his disc—and Adanaho and I as we walked side by side in their wake.

"Is it true?" she said to me as I put one boot stubbornly in front of the other—we were going too fast; there'd be blisters at this rate.

I yelled for the Professor to slow it up, then asked, "Is what true?"

"That you're not really a religious person."

"That was a private conversation," I snapped.

"The mantis voice system doesn't do whispers. I heard everything the Professor said."

I didn't respond right away. Just kept walking.

"Let me put it this way," I said, letting my words roll around in my brain a few moments before they came off my tongue, "in my time as an assistant in the Chaplains Corps I've been exposed to virtually every systematized form of human religion in existence, and a great many examples of nonsystematized faith—either the do-it-yourself smorgasbord variety, or the deeply personalized, individual one-of-a-kind variety.

"Almost everyone claims to have discovered some unique or otherwise 'true' path to God, or the Goddess, or at least to a deep connection with the Cosmic. The more I saw all of it, together, and heard all the insights and the prejudices and could observe the blind eyes being turned to this or that inconsistency or hypocrisy, the more convinced I became that we're probably just fooling ourselves."

"So if it's all a load of shit," she said, "why didn't you quit and do something else?"

"I never said it's a load of shit," I replied, my eyes still on the gravel two meters in front of me. "I told you before: I like people. And many people on Purgatory would have withered and died if they'd not had their beliefs to hold on to. Just because I don't necessarily believe in any of it doesn't mean I have to doubt or deride its value for other people. That's one of the problems with our modern society. General Sakumora had it in his eyes and in his voice: obvious contempt."

"You noticed, huh?"

"How could I not?" I said, throwing my arms out in exasperation. "It practically oozed off the man. He thought I was nuts."

"And yet you are closer to his view than he ever suspected," she said, a tiny smirk on her lips.

"No," I corrected her. "Disbelieving and being openly scornful of belief are not the same thing. I don't begrudge those with faith. In fact, I admire it. I admire it a great deal. All those people who walked into my chapel all of those years while we were imprisoned? I thought they were impressive. I think one of the reasons why I stuck with my job was because I wanted to find out what made those people tick—how they managed."

The captain didn't say anything after that, for several minutes.

"So," I said, clearing my throat and spitting the grit from my tongue, "what conversation did you and the Queen Mother have? Any groundbreaking heart-to-hearts?"

"I don't think she understood a word I said," Adanaho replied.

"The Professor told me it sounded like you were praying. I didn't ask before, but I want to ask now: are you a Muslim?"

"No," she said. "Copt."

I stopped short.

After the purges in Africa in the twenty-first and early twenty-second centuries, many religious scholars doubted that the Coptic Christian religion had survived at all—that any modern Copts extant were "revivalists" trying to reinvent the faith following its literal extinction.

As if reading my thoughts, the captain chuckled.

"Oh, we managed," she said. "On the down-low, of course. Family legend has it that my ancestors fled North Africa, and went to Australia. Succeeding generations then went to Southeast Asia, then South America, then North America, and finally back to North Africa as part of the resettlement agreement with the Brotherhood. Once the war with the mantes began, our enemies among the Muslims had a new devil to hate, so they left us alone. For a change."

"Do *you* believe?" I said. "Are you a Copt in your heart, as well as by birth?"

"I didn't used to be," she said as we started up walking again.

"What happened?" I asked.

"You," she said.

I stopped short for the second time.

"Me?"

"Yes."

"Whatever could I have done that reignited your belief?"

I felt my face growing warm again, and not from exercise.

"When I got out of officer school and went to the Intelligence branch, I began studying the roots of the armistice. I read all of your depositions and your final summary. It wasn't scholarly writing by any stretch of the imagination. But I agreed with you then: the cease-fire was a practical miracle, achieved against all odds. Without it, humanity would have ceased to exist. The mantes had every intention of doing to us what they'd done to previous intelligent competitors in the galaxy. That they did not, and that they did not for the sake of something so utterly beyond their understanding and experience, as religion, spoke to me of a higher power at work."

"Yeah, well..."

"You are a modest man, Padre," she said. "I know you try not to take too much credit. I personally believe you were a tool. And I don't mean that in the pejorative sense."

"Others have said as much, before," I admitted.

"You are uncomfortable with this."

"Of course I am uncomfortable with it!" I said, almost shouting. "Do you know how many human pilgrims have passed through my chapel in the last decade? All of them wanting to sit at my feet like I'm some kind of effing Buddha? An enlightened one? A *savior?*"

"To their minds, that's not far-fetched."

"No doubt!" I said, facing her directly. We were deep into the weeds of the discussion now, and there was no holding back. "But do you have any kind of idea how much *pressure* that put on me? How badly I felt when these people—from all over human space—came to my chapel and sat in my pews, and expected some kind of transfiguring or overwhelming experience, and didn't get it? I saw it in their eyes when they left. Every time: confusion and disappointment. I never wanted to be anyone's damned prophet. I was never good at preaching. I was never good at teaching. All I was ever trying to do was provide people with a quiet, clean, calming space where they could come and find their own answers. For themselves."

"Because you made a promise to your Chaplain Thomas," she said.

"Yes," I said, breathing heavily.

The Professor had stopped too. Had the mantes overheard? He was chattering for the Queen Mother's benefit; she seemed intensely interested. I suddenly felt a sharp desire to melt into the ground. Some messiah I'd turned out to be. I'd only delayed the war, not averted it. Things seemed to be more pointless than ever before. I'd have quit right then if I'd not still felt deep down that there was a chance—if only we could get the Queen Mother back to her people, she could make them listen.

"Okay," I said, waving all three of them off. "Let's get moving again."

The Professor and the Queen Mother floated off without protest. The captain resumed her place at my side.

"Thanks, Chief," she said.

"For what?" I asked, embarrassed.

"I think I'm finally starting to understand you."

I grunted, and didn't say anything more.

We kept walking.

CHAPTER 28

Earth, 2153 A.D.

RANGE FIRING AND SIMULATOR TRAINING PROVED TO BE TWO entirely different things.

For starters, we didn't have to hike to reach the simulator.

Each morning we were out of our bunks an hour earlier than usual, followed by a four-kilometer tactical march across Armstrong Field to the hills on the southwest side.

Along the way I was able to do plenty of rubbernecking. The Fleet spacecraft landing at and taking off from Armstrong every day were the most advanced, finest pieces of military machinery ever created: sleek aerospace fighters and bulky gunships, as well as wide-body troop carriers and the overly massive destroyers with their missile bays levered open and nuclear-tipped death rockets being carefully fed into the destroyers' magazines.

Humanity had only been at war with the mantes for a handful of years. Fleet was very proud of the fact that peacetime designs and production had been so thoroughly and quickly converted over to wartime use. The military-contracted starship yards in orbit had run nonstop for the entirety of the conflict, twenty-four hours a day. On the ground, it was much the same. One whole sector of Armstrong was dedicated strictly to a series of kilometer-tall and kilometer-wide Fleet assembly hangars, where the arsenal of Earth was cobbled together in whatever shape and form Fleet desired.

I'd seen still-life pictures of some of Earth's world wars of the past. Armstrong Field reminded me of the Atlantic and Pacific naval yards of North America in 1943: forever crowded and buzzing with soldiers and civilian workers, all churning out ship after ship for the war effort.

It was a sight to make any recruit proud.

But once we got to the range, business was business. And for some, business was brutal.

Plinking pop cans with a squirrel rifle wasn't the same as trying to put holes in a mantis warrior who was moving at speed across broken terrain. Each of the mantis silhouettes was in fact a plate-steel cutout attached to a micro-sized version of the same motors that boosted ships into space. The motors would hiss and zip across the firing lanes, spewing vapor as they burned fuel. Each was controlled from a large houselike control center on top of a five-story tower that overlooked the entire range complex.

When you hit a mantis, the silhouette flipped back and the motor grounded. Until that particular firing sequence was complete, scores were tallied, and the silhouettes were flipped back into place and their motors restarted.

I discovered that the ability to traverse and elevate quickly enough to sight in on and hit targets was not a talent given to all.

With twenty different mantes presenting themselves during a two-minute window, there wasn't a lot of time to sit back and take stock of the situation. You had to look, aim, and shoot. The men and women with good reflexes and keen eyes did well. The men and women with middling to poor reflexes and bad eyes . . . well, they did what they could to compensate. But by the end of the first day the range cadre had sent some of us back to the re-zero.

Not me specifically. I had qualified early, and grown bored with waiting for the rest to finish. So I volunteered to be somebody's buddy.

Drill Sergeant Davis shook his head at us as we lay on our stomachs, elbows propped on elbow pads while I sighted through my binoculars, and my struggling partner sighted through his rifle's scope at the static target twenty-five meters away, and tried to tighten his shot group.

Pang, pang, pang, pang.

Secce had been right. There was precious little fouling. The R77A5 could fire almost endlessly without jamming. But the chemical stench of the vaporized propellant was pungent in the air. Enough so that I began to wonder about any potentially deleterious effects on any recruit who breathed in too much of the stuff.

"Damned shame to see a recruit wash out because he can't hit his twenty required targets on the silhouette range," Davis said to my partner, a now beleaguered and nervous Recruit Sanchala.

Like all of us recruits on the range, the DSs wore their body armor jackets and helmets, though each helmet had a bright band of orange reflector tape around the brim. Snap-down eye protection, from inside the helmet itself, kept any dust or kickback particles from causing us grief. And the lenses themselves were light-activated such that the glare of the afternoon sun wasn't overly bothersome.

Sanchala simply couldn't swing his rifle back and forth in time to hit more than twelve or thirteen of the moving silhouettes, regardless of how well he'd re-zeroed his weapon.

Davis continued to shake his head.

I didn't want to think about the expressions on the faces of the range cadre to our rear. Three different NCOs had been called down from the tower to help Sanchala specifically, and in each case I'd done my best to be a cheerleader and fellow troop, assisting Sanchala to implement the advice given. But what sounded like easy work during bull sessions with the cadre, proved to be entirely more difficult once it was just Sanchala out there on the silhouette range, four sandbags at his disposal for support, and two fifteen-round magazines slipped into the pouches on his vest.

Pang, pang, pang, pang.

Sanchala slipped the empty magazine out of the shoulder stock of the rifle—the R77A5 having been configured in what one of the range cadre had called bullpup style—and stood up, to walk down to his target with Drill Sergeant Davis in the lead. I followed obediently. When we got there Davis examined Sanchala's shot group—four holes neatly contained within a constricted circular space the range cadre had already deemed adequate—and *tsked* at Sanchala.

"Boy, if the mantes stood still and didn't move, you'd be a crack troop. Unfortunately for you those sumbitches *move,* and move fast. I hate to say it, but because Fleet needs all the able hands it can get, we've been dumbing these ranges down about as far as we dare. So that even someone as clumsy as you can pass, Sanchala. But there's no doubt about it: you can't shoot for shit, son."

"Drill Sergeant," Sanchala said, "what happens to me if I can't pass the range, Drill Sergeant?"

"What happens if you can't pass any other test in IST: you're a no-go, Recruit," he said, matter-of-fact. "Doesn't matter what Fleet job they select you for, in the end, if you can't shoot, you can't shoot. You'll be dumped back out into the civilian world with a section forty-six-dash-bee in your file. Failure to achieve minimal military competency. You seem to get the fundamentals of most everything else we've shown you so far. What the eff is your problem now?"

Sanchala didn't have an answer to that.

Again, sniping at aluminum with a relative's .22 was a lot different from trying to place head shots on simulated aliens as they bore down on your hasty fighting position—at ranges anywhere between twenty-five meters, all the way out to four hundred fifty meters.

Always, Sanchala was just a touch too slow. And the bullet would go high, or wide, or spit up dirt and grass as it ate the turf where the motorized silhouette had just been a split second earlier. I looked at Sanchala's despairing expression, and tried to figure out how I could possibly help. I'd more or less been telling Sanchala the same things the cadre had been telling him, and it wasn't doing much good.

We trudged back to where we'd been laying on the ground, and as Sanchala readied himself to make another go at the next shot group, Davis stared down at us. I looked at the target, then at Sanchala, and back at the target, then held a palm up for Davis to see.

"Hold up," Davis said, raising a paddle into the air. One side was red and the other white. The red side, when waived at the tower, indicated that the NCO on the ground had noticed a problem.

The tower acknowledged, and waited for the paddle to be white.

"What's the issue, Recruit Barlow?" Davis asked.

"Drill Sergeant, I want to try something, Drill Sergeant," I said. Then I snuggled right up against Sanchala and spoke low and clear.

"You right-handed?" I asked.

"Yes."

"You ever shoot with your left?"

"I don't think so."

"Without corrective lenses, it shouldn't really matter, but at this point anything's worth trying. Swap over to left shoulder and let's re-zero your scope."

"But that will just take more time."

"As if you've got anything to lose now? Just try it."

"Okay," Sanchala said.

And I explained the plan to Davis, who simply nodded his approval.

Sanchala did as instructed, with Davis leaning down and fiddling with the manual studs on Sanchala's weapon's scope as I awkwardly helped Sanchala move the rifle butt to his left shoulder.

Of course, the first two groupings were way off.

But the third grouping was better and, with a bit more tweaking of the scope, Sanchala achieved two final groupings that were tighter than any he had done at any earlier time in the day.

"Alright," Davis said, slapping the back of Sanchala's vest as he pulled down Sanchala's static target and handed it to me to go present to the range cadre. "Let's get your clumsy ass back to the silhouette range and do this thing."

If Davis had been ferocious at other times, strangely, he was practically human now. Not that either myself or Sanchala made the mistake of getting lax in our formality. But for once, the senior drill sergeant wasn't half scaring the piss out of us. He was almost friendly.

With muzzle aimed at the dirt and no magazine in the breach, Sanchala walked with Davis and me back three hundred meters to the silhouette range, where a few strugglers like Sanchala were still going through their next iteration. The muffled popping of the rifles was dampened by my helmet's ear protection; which also contained speakers for the wireless communication network that tied us together by squads or platoons for group battle-rush exercises. Of which we'd done several, while waiting for rotation through the silhouette range.

I waited with Sanchala for his turn in line, then proceeded with him up to the base of the tower where two recruits—sharpshooting early range grads, who'd been rewarded for their steely prowess by being assigned the inglorious task of ammo detail—slapped fresh magazines into Sanchala's hands.

One of Sanchala's other problems, besides having trouble getting his rifle on-target in time to make his shots, had been ammunition depletion. The rules of the range were simple: thirty mantis enemies, and thirty rounds with which to hit and take out no less than twenty of the enemy. On paper, back in the simulator, it had seemed like cake. Who didn't love a good first-person shooter VR game? But on the live-fire range, once your magazine was empty, it was empty, and you had only so much time in which to load a new magazine. To say nothing of trying to conserve your shots for those moments when you might stand the best chance of hitting.

I took the magazines for Sanchala as we both began walking to our assigned lane, and noted the weight of the fifteen rounds in each container, testing the top round with my thumb, so that the rounds slid up and down easily on the spring inside. Then we reached Sanchala's designated fighting position where he placed the barrel of his rifle into a vee-notch cut in the top of a colored yellow stake driven into the earth.

I stood there, half-zoning while the tower called out requisite and familiar safety guidance, then I got down into the prone position next to Sanchala. Securing his weapon from the stake, he loaded his first magazine and charged his rifle: a sliding handle on the top of the stock snapping back and forth so that a round was taken off the top of the magazine and chambered for firing.

The tower announced that the mantis invasion of the range had begun, and I put my binoculars to my eyes, scanning the space in front of us.

There, a mantis appeared from behind a berm.

Pang. Dead on. Sanchala got that one. A good start. But only two or three would be that easy.

I kept scanning.

There, a mantis far off, zipping across the lane from one berm to the next.

Pang. Miss. *Pang.* The target was gone. And I could feel Sanchala begin to deflate. Two misses and one hit out of three rounds so far, and still eighteen total targets to go.

Three more mantis shock troops hit the lane simultaneously.

Sanchala got one of them. Out of five tries. The odds weren't looking good.

There, another close one. *Pang.*

Got it.

There, about middle distance. Moving slow. *Pang.*

Four down. But I could tell Sanchala had lost count of how many rounds he had left, and there was no getting around the fact that he'd yet to see the very-far-distance silhouettes make an appearance.

Pang... Pang... Pang... Pang... Pang.

Per instruction, Sanchala tried to be methodical in selection and rate of fire. But some of the last few targets had been moving so quickly, I wondered if he should not have just let them go and saved ammo for something a little easier to hit?

There, coming right up the middle. Full charge.

Click, click.

Sanchala was out of rounds.

He grasped the shrouded rifle barrel in his left hand and flipped it over, depressing the magazine ejection button with his right thumb. The empty magazine came free and I handed him his second magazine, which he slapped into place, feeling it click, then worked the charging mechanism and got back down in the prone just in time to see a mantis silhouette flee out of sight, unharmed.

There was no way. He'd missed too many.

Emptying his second magazine went quickly.

Sanchala cursed in Spanish, then flipped the selector lever to SAFE mode, removed the second magazine and slipped it back into my hands next to its empty brother. He put his rifle into the vee-notch stake, and stood up. The tower waited until exactly two minutes had passed—and all sixteen of us on the line, eight shooters and eight helpers, had cleared and safed our weapons—before ordering us to retrieve our rifles and report back behind the range line for review of our scores.

Drill Sergeant Davis waited. He was not smiling.

"Fifteen," was all he said to us we walked up to him, Sanchala's barrel aimed at the dirt.

Sanchala's cheeks reddened.

"But you're already better than you were on the right shoulder. Go back in line, Recruit Sanchala. All you need to do is execute to standard. Give it another go. Copy?"

"Yes, Drill Sergeant," Sanchala said, and walked slowly back to where a final six shooters now stood, waiting for the next iteration. I went with him, not saying much. With the sun waning in the sky, I feared that we might not get too many more chances to qualify. And if we couldn't make it, even with all the corrective training and counseling and the many, many chances he'd had to get it right, would it even matter if they gave Sanchala a second day? Or a third?

I felt a touch of despair on my heart as I proceeded with my buddy to the base of the tower, we collected his magazines, and went to his fighting position like before. This time it was one of the spots closer to the tower, where more recruits had been firing more often all day.

As I got down on my knees I noticed several unspent rounds laying in the dirt.

That was against protocol. Any whole rounds cleared out of rifles during misfires were to be picked up directly and given back to the ammo detail at the tower—for turn in to the range cadre. And the rules specifically called for no more than thirty rounds per recruit, per iteration.

I opened my mouth to shout something to one of the NCOs who stood behind us with their paddles in their hands, then shut my mouth.

Were those rounds *really* defective?

I stared at them for a moment. They seemed fine.

Looking to my left and right I saw the other recruits positioning their sandbags and checking their rifles, their helpers offering whatever lame duck advice could be given. They were oblivious to me, though Sanchala seemed to have detected that something was up, and watched me closely.

Then I looked up at the tower itself. And considered.

Eff it.

I scooped up the unspent rounds, wiped dust from them with my thumb and forefinger, and guided them into the top of the first magazine. At only fifteen rounds per box, there was room to spare. Three unspent rounds went into the first magazine, and two went into the second.

"What are you doing?" Sanchala hissed.

"Giving you an edge," I said quietly.

"But it's against the rules," he said.

"You think when it's us against the mantis aliens there will be rules? You shoot everything you have. I've noticed something about your tendency to hesitate, Sanchala. I think you're spending too much time worried about conserving rounds, but you end up wasting them when you try to keep your attention on a number, and not on finding and hitting targets. Now you've got a little breathing room. And I don't think anybody's going to give a crap or notice if you actually shoot more than thirty shots. Not with eight of you all popping at targets simultaneously. So don't worry about it. Okay?"

Sanchala smiled slightly.

I reached out my fist. He bumped it with enthusiasm. Then we both got down in the prone and he went to work when the tower called its instructions.

Pang... Pang... Pang... Pang...

Good. He was slow-breathing. Nothing hurried.

"Ignore the very-far targets," I said between shots. "And ignore the ones moving too quickly over too short of a distance. Don't worry about ammo. Just shoot what you know you can hit."

I watched every shot through the binoculars.

When his first magazine was empty, I handed him the second, which he quick-snapped into place, and kept going.

Two minutes elapsed, and we stood up. Having no idea how he'd done. Because I'd lost count of how many targets he'd knocked down. It had seemed like enough. But would it be?

Myself and the other helpers waited while our charges collected their weapons and filed back past the tower, dropping empty magazines into the hands of the recruits on the ammo detail.

Davis waited for us as we walked up to him.

"Twenty-four," he said, still not smiling.

Sanchala blinked in astonishment.

"Twenty-four, Drill Sergeant?"

"Yup," Davis said. "You made it. Good work. Now get off the firing line."

Sanchala almost ran, his teeth bared in a bona-fide grin, pumping his weapon over his head several times before one of the cadre yelled at Sanchala to face the muzzle back into the dirt.

I smiled, and started to follow.

"Hold it," Davis said, sticking a hand out to block me.

I waited, my heart suddenly sinking.

"Funny how Sanchala suddenly did so much better. And not just because of switching shoulders. I wonder why that was? Seemed like he only had his usual thirty rounds. Or was it more?"

Davis waited, staring at me.

"Drill Sergeant," I said, "he used the magazines the ammo detail gave to us, Drill Sergeant. Maybe they lost count and Sanchala got an extra round or two."

"Yeah," Davis said, still staring at me. "That must have been it."

But his hand still blocked my way.

I said nothing, and just looked into his eyes, as he looked into mine.

Finally he said, "You'll clear your ass off the range before I decide to report your little trick to the tower. I see everything you think I don't see, Recruit Barlow. Believe it."

I swallowed hard and said. "Yes, Drill Sergeant."

His hand dropped out of my way.

As I moved to shuffle past him, his opposite hand slapped me on the back. Not hard. But friendly-like. Enough to send an altogether different message than his mouth had been sending in the moment before.

And from that point forward, I decided that Davis wasn't nearly the ogre most of us had assumed him to be.

CHAPTER 29

ON THE THIRD DAY AFTER LANDING, A RAINSTORM BLEW IN.

I wasn't sure whether to be happy or scared. The wind was ferocious, whipping my poncho about and driving the water into me sideways. It was cold water too, and before long the captain and I realized we'd be in danger of hypothermia. Unlike when the sandstorm hit, there were no hills or outcroppings of rock to hide behind. We simply had to sit down on a raised mound of half-buried boulders and do the best we could.

If the storm bothered the Professor, he didn't show it. The Queen Mother looked perfectly miserable.

After an hour, things calmed down enough for me to get up and walk over to where the Professor was hovering over the Queen Mother, doing his best to protect her from the elements. My hands were shaking and my teeth chattered as I spoke.

"Is she in danger?"

"Yes," the Professor said, matter-of-factly.

"She can have my poncho if it will help," I said. "Though I can't say it's done me much good. The captain and I are both soaked to the bone."

I removed my poncho and went to place it over the Queen Mother, who had curled up tightly on the rock, when I felt a sudden wave of delicious warmth on the top of my hand.

It was coming from the bottom of the Professor's disc.

The mantes may have been insectlike, but they were as warm-blooded as humans, varying only by a few degrees. I realized that the Professor had to be burning a lot of power to keep both himself and the Queen Mother warm.

"How long can you keep it up?" I asked.

"I do not know for certain," he said. "I can shut down various functions to compensate for the raw energy expenditure, but if these sorts of storms are the norm for this planet, and not the exception, it will dramatically reduce my carriage's longevity."

"Do you mind if the captain and I try to share the heat? We can't make a fire, and our uniforms aren't designed for warmth when wet."

"Proceed," he said.

I beckoned the captain over, and her face went from an expression of utter misery to utter amazement as she put her hands into the zone of pleasant heat directly below the Professor's disc.

We quickly huddled up close and stuck both arms and legs under the shadow of the disc, our ponchos over our heads and backs while our rear ends remained cold and soggy on the damp stone.

For a while, I dozed. Between the lack of adequate food and walking many kilometers every day, I was definitely feeling the physical toll. Eventually I felt the captain slump against me, and I allowed myself to do likewise, my head balanced on top of hers, a little patch of protected warmth growing between us. I closed my eyes.

They didn't come open again until hours later.

The storm had passed, and the sun was out again: still brighter and cooler than either Purgatory's star, or Earth's own Sol, but a welcome sight just the same. It was midday, and there was a bit of a breeze, which meant the captain and I might be able to dry our clothes out—essential, if we were going to survive the night without further draining the Professor's energy reserves.

The Queen Mother had drawn herself out from under the Professor's disc and was perched on a boulder a few meters away. Her wings were spread widely and she appeared almost frozen in place, forelimbs outstretched and her head tilted back. She seemed to be soaking in every last ray she could get.

The sound of running water nearby reminded me that we'd best replenish our own water supply while we had the opportunity. I regretfully roused the captain, who jumped at the chance to refill our bottles. We located a formerly dry creek bed—now swollen with slowly running, very soiled water—and began to fill up. The mouth of each bottle had a micro filter on it that screened out the bulk of the soil. Leaving only the thinnest of hazes. Unsure of the bacterial hazard, we unscrewed the filters and dropped survival tabs into each bottle—the tabs made the water taste chemically nasty, but it would be safe to drink.

Returning to where the Professor kept watch on the Queen Mother, the captain and I each did an about-face and stripped to the skin. Our emergency packs had one-piece smocks in them, which we quickly donned, then we laid our uniforms, underwear, boots, and socks out on the rocks as best we could, hoping that the strong daylight and fresh breeze would be enough to dry things out. The smocks weren't nearly as sturdy as we needed them to be, and the slip-on shoes that came with them would quickly disintegrate on this planet's rough, unforgiving terrain.

With nothing better to do, Adanaho and I ate a little, drank a little more, went and did our business as far away from each other as possible, then returned and stared at the Queen Mother—who'd remained motionless as a statue the whole time.

I did notice that her lower limbs—which had seemed almost useless when the Professor had first removed her from her disc—appeared to be getting stronger. She was balanced on them now, with just a hand's width of space between her belly and the stone on which she perched.

"How is she doing?" I asked the Professor.

"I do not know," he said. "She has not spoken to me since the storm passed. I am suspecting that she is manifesting an instinctual behavior of our species, from the time before we had carriages to provide for our needs."

"What about food?" I said.

"The carriage provides that too, though we can ingest nourishment with our mouths for the pleasure of it."

I shuddered a bit, remembering mantis warriors devouring human flesh during the initial fighting on Purgatory.

"Can the Queen Mother eat our food?" the captain asked.

"I do not think it wise," the Professor said. "Our nutritional requirements are not the same as yours. Besides, we have the ability to store a reserve—naturally—which should suffice for the Queen Mother's needs for some time yet. Assuming she gets water."

"She should go drink while the drinking's good," I said, pointing back to the creek bed, the water in which had begun to wane as the sun gradually began to drop towards the western horizon.

"I have already purified a supply for her," the Professor said. "For now, I simply watch, and wait. The Queen Mother's behavior is unusual and fascinating. I have never seen any of my people forced to live without a carriage. The Queen Mother's actions speak to me of how my people must have lived, eons ago in the distant past, before we ourselves even had fire, or tools. Before we took to the stars."

As the angle of the sun's light shifted, so did the Queen Mother. Like a solar panel, she made sure her wings caught the maximum amount of direct light.

Occasionally the captain or I would get up to go check on our clothes, flapping them vigorously to try and get out every drop of remaining moisture. When evening came and the sun began to dip into the far horizon, we pulled out our emergency sleeping bags and prepared to make do on the hard stone.

"I'll be back," Adanaho said.

"Nature calls?" I replied.

"No."

"Oh . . . well, find privacy and peace then."

To my surprise, she went to join the Queen Mother, who'd folded up her wings, but remained staring in the direction of the setting sun.

Adanaho sat cross-legged and appeared to hold something in her hands as she bowed her head. The Queen Mother's own head tilted just a little, her antennae moving ever so slowly, as if entranced by the captain's soft, slow words of supplication. The Professor was listening too—I could see him alert. Like before, I was too far away to make out what was being said. And, I suddenly realized, I was a little bit jealous that the captain felt perfectly fine sharing her prayer with the mantes, but not with me. A tiny spark of anger flared, and quickly died as I realized that maybe she was just doing what I'd done with the Professor many times: giving the mantes a demonstration, so that maybe the Queen Mother might enjoy a degree of understanding.

Though I couldn't be sure what progress Adanaho hoped to make, which I hadn't been able to make with the Professor or his students in all the years of trying back on Purgatory.

Eventually the sky faded from blue to purple, and from purple to black. Adanaho returned, and I was already in my bag, my one-piece rolled up under my head for a pillow. I averted my eyes as the captain stripped, rolled her one-piece up for a pillow, then slipped into her own bag.

I didn't stay awake long enough to see what arrangements the Professor and the Queen Mother had made between them.

Sometime in the night I felt a hand nudging my shoulder.

"What's happening?" I said. "Is something wrong?"

"I can't sleep, Chief," Adanaho said. "There's a hole in my bag and it got damp inside, and I am freezing."

My eyes popped open. I could barely make out the black silhouette of her shoulders and head against the perfect expanse of stars that stretched across the night sky. Clear sky meant frigid temperatures, and I could feel the cold night air on my face. I reached out and felt Adanaho's hand in mine. Her fingers were icy.

Not even thinking about it, I unzipped my bag and beckoned her in. She slid down beside me and zipped the bag up to our chins. Not designed for comfort, as an emergency bag it could hold two in a pinch—and I certainly was glad for it, as the captain felt dangerously cold, her body shuddering next to me.

"Ma'am," I said, "why didn't you come earlier? You're a popsicle."

"I feel like a popsicle," she said, her nose stuffed.

"Here," I said, and closed my arms around her. Despite the frigidity of her skin, it was smooth, and womanly, and all of a sudden I realized I hadn't lain in bed with a girl since shortly after IST, and that had been a long, long time ago.

"You'll have to forgive me," I said, clearing my throat.

"For what?" She said. And then, because of the impossibly close quarters of the bag, she said, "Oh. I get it."

I felt a rush of blood to my face.

"It's okay, Chief," she said, sensing my mortal embarrassment.

"I hope you're not married," I said. "Explaining to your husband how you spent the night naked in a sleeping bag with another man who was unable to contain his . . . ahhh, *excitement*, could be problematic."

"No, I am not married," she said, laughing a bit. Then began to cough.

I suddenly realized that pneumonia could kill as easily as low temperatures, and held her tighter. She squirmed in my grasp and was suddenly face to face with me, her nose like a cold, damp button in the nape of my neck. She coughed a few more times, snuffling, and clung tightly to me. I rubbed my hands vigorously along her bare back to try and accelerate the process of warming. Gradually, her body relaxed. I then heard a small, quiet snore.

I shifted and repositioned my rolled-up smock so that her head rested on it, not mine, crooked an elbow up to my ear, kept my other arm wrapped tightly around her, and let myself drift off.

CHAPTER 30

Earth, 2153 A.D.

THE COLA HIT MY THROAT LIKE A COLD WAVE. I SAVORED ITS chilled, fizzy, delightful sweetness, and took another long chug on my bottle, before resting the bottle lightly on the table in front of me.

It was Halfway Day. The official midpoint of IST.

Every recruit in Charlie Company *not* on corrective detail was given an entire Sunday afternoon with a base pass: as long as we didn't attempt to leave Armstrong Field, we could either walk or catch a bus to the half dozen exchanges and vendor malls that serviced the massive military installation.

Dismissed at 1400, our return formation was at 1900.

It felt like we had all the time in the world.

"Enjoy that while it lasts, Recruit Barlow," said the recruit directly across from me, a female by the name of Cortez. She tipped her own bottle at me and swigged down a healthy draft, then did a long, drawn out, theatrical "*ahhh*," while wiping the condensation-frosted bottle across her sweat-beaded brow.

The outdoor pavilion was jammed with recruits. Ours was not the only company at Halfway Day. Since none of us had been able to even look at a soft drink—nor anything else sugary—for almost two months, we were making the most of our limited parole.

"And here I was trying to lose a few pounds in the military," said recruit Handley, who upended his own bottle. At twenty-nine he was one of the older guys in second platoon. Married, with a child on the way, he'd been one of the first people I'd truly befriended. I sometimes wondered if he had been the one who'd stopped me from trying to hurt Thukhan that one night.

I'd not asked anyone about the incident, nor had anyone come forward and offered to identify himself. Because we'd been mostly whispering at the time, I couldn't identify the culprit by voice. Hence the event had become something of a very curious mystery to me.

Which was not to say I hadn't taken the anonymous recruit's advice.

The truth was, that night had scared the dickens out of me.

I'd let Batbayar get so far under my skin with his head games, I'd almost gone and done something incredibly stupid. But after that night, I'd made a point of warming up to the people who seemed worth warming up to, and together we'd formed a nice little nugget of camaraderie through the following weeks of rifle and marksmanship training.

It hadn't stopped Thukhan from trying to mess with me, but it had blunted much of the resulting emotional trauma. Now that I didn't feel so alone against him, it was easier to endure the insults and the petty attacks. Such as the time he got ahold of my laundry bag and filled it full of shaving gel, or swapped my duty boots with someone else's boots on the other side of the bay, so that each of us was sent scrambling to identify who had the size eights, and who had the size tens, and *could I please have my boots back, oh yes, here's yours, thanks so much,* followed by a lot of under-the-breath cursing.

With Thukhan not around, and no DSs in sight, I realized that the pavilion was the closest I'd come to experiencing real freedom in a long time.

Recruits Kealoha and Sembeke were the other two in my group. The former female, and the latter male. They each had their mouths full of hamburgers and fries from the pavilion grill.

Only two of us were north American by birth, and only three of us spoke the military's version of common English as a first language. But we'd gravitated to each other for one reason or another. As the recruits who seemed destined for everything and anything other than an infantry or armor assignment.

"So what do you think?" I said to Cortez, who didn't need to inquire as to the context of my question. Now that we were on the downhill slope to graduation, one thing was increasingly on everyone's mind.

"Starship mechanic," she said, wiping her mouth on the back of a fist.

"You got pre-existing training for that?" Handley said.

"No, but I got this," Cortez said, tapping the side of her head. "You think they let dummies play with the drive cores on the big capital vessels? Nope. As soon as I graduate out of this hole, I'm going to Fleet engineering school. No more DSs. The cadre aren't NCOs, but officers with degrees in their subject matter."

"You gonna go *ossifer* too?" I said, deliberately slurring the word.

"Maybe," Cortez said. "I can think of worse ways to spend a war."

"Me too," Handley said. "It's why I'm hoping for transport pilot."

Kealoha and Sembeke stopped chewing, and stared at the older recruit.

"For serious," he said, looking at all our raised eyebrows. "When I got out of high school I put some money into getting a private pilot's license. I haven't had the chance to use it much since Kelli and I got married, but it's in my personnel file. They'd be stupid to ignore it. Like the lovely Recruit Cortez here, I hope to go far away from this place, to a training station where everyone speaks to me in respectful tones and nobody is trying to blow my ears off with sheer screaming."

"...and the skies are blue all day, it's never hot outside, and they leave chocolates on your pillow after making your bunk for you in the morning!"

Kealoha had said it through a grinning mouthful, and we all laughed uncontrollably for several seconds.

"How about you?" Sembeke said, wiping his mouth with a napkin and pointing a long, bony, coal-black finger in my direction.

"Deck swabber," Cortez said, grinning wickedly.

"Toilet-scrubber Second Mate," Handley said, also grinning.

"Yeah, well," I said, chuckling, "like Cortez says, there are worse ways of spending the war."

"It would have been nice if they'd let us have a sure choice," Kealoha said. Like me, she was a volunteer. But not everyone in Charlie Company could say the same. There were the hard cases—like Thukhan—and there were the draftees. Young men and women from all over the world, between the ages of seventeen and twenty-five. Plucked from their ordinary lives by their respective governments and pressed into Fleet service. Whether they liked the idea, or not.

And whether we'd volunteered or been drummed into uniform, none of us had been told upon reporting to Reception what our final destinations would be, in our newfound military careers. We were allowed to pick two options upon filling out our sign-up sheets, but everyone had noticed that there was a third option—always check-boxed and always grayed out—that simply said RECRUIT'S FINAL OCCUPATIONAL SPECIALTY TO BE DESIGNATED PER NEEDS OF THE FLEET.

Theoretically, Fleet had a massive semi-intelligent database that constantly tracked all available Fleet slots and attempted to match Fleet strengths and weaknesses with recruit preferences and aptitudes. Though this was mostly recruit scuttlebutt. I knew for a fact that two of my older friends who'd gotten good grades in school, had been sent directly into marine training out of IST; though both of them had also been on the football team too. Did that have anything to do with anything? I'd not heard from them in the two years since they'd left Earth.

As a matter of fact, none of us who had friends or relatives in Fleet service had heard from *anybody*, once they went to space.

Which I found just a little unsettling. But this was neither the time nor the place to speak of such things. Today was a day for merrymaking.

"So who's going to get laid?" I said, picking up my cola and tipping it to my lips.

Handley laughed so hard he half-spit out a mouthful of his own drink.

"In just the short amount of time they've given us?" Sembeke said. "I think maybe you're a little too eager, Barlow. Besides, they put chemicals in the food that suppress our libidos."

"That's a lot of crap," Cortez said. "My grandfather was in the military and he said the same spook story was circulating when he was in Basic, all those years ago. God knows nothing is suppressing *my* libido."

"So you would be the lucky one getting her rocks off, then?" I said, raising my bottle in her direction. "I salute you, madam."

She reached across and slugged me in the arm.

I almost dropped my drink.

"If I was," she said, "I certainly wouldn't be doing it with any lousy recruit!"

"You wound me," I said.

She raised the same fist she'd punched me with, and erected her middle finger.

I laughed, remembering Tia doing the same to me many months earlier. Through the haze of the past two months, it seemed like another lifetime.

Our eyes flicked to Handley.

"Don't look at me," he said. "Kelli and I already took care of business. We had one final night together, after I signed up."

"Must have been a good one," Kealoha said.

"Simply the best," Handley replied, grinning.

I smiled, and finished the last of my drink.

"I honestly don't care if I'm mopping the head," I said. "As long as Fleet lets me go stare out the window once in a while, it's all good with me."

"A stargazer," Sembeke said, smiling. "Me too."

"Me *all* of us," Cortez said. "Who hasn't dreamed about going to space? Maybe touring some of the colonies? None of us could have hoped to afford it on our own, and most of the colonial missions were either closed-shop operations, or had application criteria so severe, you had to be a super-genius or a genetically healthy freak to get onboard. Now look at us. Future spacers, all! In one form or another."

"You're mighty right," I said.

Five fists went into the center of the table and touched, followed by five hands that opened—palms wide, fingers splayed—before withdrawing: *blow it up!*

On our way back to Charlie Company, the base shuttle stopped at a little concrete building with a tall spire at one end. A meager handful of recruits slowly stepped aboard. Each of them clutching a small book in his or her hand. They stared at the rest of us as we made jokes and laughed loudly, then they decided to stay up front—apart from us.

"What's their problem?" I asked quietly.

"Church boys," Cortez said, snickering loudly.

"It *is* Sunday," Handley said. "Didn't you ever go to service when you were a kid?"

"No," I said. "My parents aren't religious."

"And yours were?" Sembeke asked Handley.

"My mom kinda was," he said. "Lutheran. I think? Though I only went for a little while when I was very young. I remember the meeting house being a very empty place."

"Looks like that post chapel back there was mostly empty too," I said as the base shuttle pulled away and resumed its route.

"Why do you say that?" Sembeke asked.

"Look how few there were," I said, pointing to the five boys and two girls who'd boarded. Their backs were turned and they faced straight ahead, not saying anything as the shuttle rumbled along the road.

"Service runs all day," Handley said. "Maybe people attend piecemeal? Or didn't you look at the chapel hours in the IST manual on your e-pad?"

"I hadn't noticed," I said. "Why would anyone go waste their time sitting in an empty building on a day when they could be out having fun?"

Cortez loudly voiced her agreement.

One of the recruits up front turned, looking hard at us, and then got up and walked back to where we were sitting. We shut up and stared at him as he came up to us, his hands resting on the backs of the bench seats in front of our group.

"It might seem like a waste to you," he said, "but there are still a few of us who like to go to chapel on the Lord's Day. Please, we're only going to get a few more minutes of peace and quiet before the shuttle drops us off at Delta Company. Do you mind not making fun of us?"

"Sorry," I said, feeling somewhat sheepish.

He went back and sat down.

I was quiet all the way back to the company area. As we climbed off the shuttle Cortez poked me in the ribs.

"Church boy put you in your place," she said.

"Yeah," I said, not smiling.

"Did that bother you as much as it seems like it did?" she asked.

"I guess so," I said. "I wasn't trying to hurt his feelings. I just don't get why anyone goes to church in the first place. My family never did. My mom and dad never expected me to. I mean, people can believe whatever they want, but this is the twenty-second century. Church . . . that's in the past. Haven't we kinda left that behind us? We're traveling the stars now!"

Sembeke put a hand on my shoulder.

"You Americans enjoy a lot of material luxuries. You have your nice safe houses with your modern machinery and your VR and you don't think much about what some of the rest of us out in the other parts of the world think about. I am not religious either, but I grew up around religious people. This thing you say you do not understand... it *matters* to them. I feel that perhaps we were disrespectful in our boisterousness."

Cortez snorted.

"We have to be quiet on the shuttle just because they went to service?"

"No," Sembeke said, "we don't *have* to. But we probably *ought* to. In the future, at least."

I looked at Sembeke, and slowly nodded my head. He'd definitely given me something to ponder, as we moved into our second half of training.

CHAPTER 31

I WOKE EARLY.

The Captain was still snoring softly, so I slid out of the bag as slowly and as stealthily as I could, letting my superior curl the fabric around herself and bury her face deeper into my jumper. The sun wasn't yet up, but I could see well enough. Being both naked and cold, now seemed as good a time as any to go see if my uniform had dried. But first, business. I spied a low mound of split rock not too far off, and headed directly for it.

The Professor caught me halfway back.

I felt a bit awkward over my nudity, then decided it was silly to be modest in front of the alien. Though I also thought this is how the Queen Mother must have felt when she was forced to disengage from her disc.

"Good morning," the Professor said.

"Hello," I replied.

"The female still sleeps?"

"For the moment."

"Did you mate with her?"

I sputtered a quietly exclamatory denial. Then asked, "Whatever gave you that idea?"

"On Purgatory you once told me that when male and female humans wish to copulate, they will share the same bed."

"On Purgatory, sure, and then only if the male and the female know each other well enough and have agreed to have that kind of relationship."

"It is not an automatic biological function?"

"No," I said firmly. "Is it for you mantes?"

The Professor considered, a forelimb gently running along the edge of his disc.

"In some ways, yes. The egg-laying females—like the Queen Mother—when they enter what you would call estrus, they exude a pheromone that is both sexually rapturous and psychologically debilitating for males. Any male within reach of the pheromone becomes somewhat mindless in his pursuit of intercourse. The only way to avoid it is to avoid being where the pheromone can get to you."

"But once you get a whiff—"

"Then the male is in for a delightfully stupid time of physical pleasure, followed by a lengthy period of slumber."

"Well," I said, smiling, "at least *one* thing is shared between human males and mantis males."

"Still," said the Professor, "with Adanaho, if she is available to you and there is the possibility of sex, are you not . . . desiring?"

"Of course I'm desiring," I snapped. Then apologized for being harsh. "It's been at least a dozen or more years since I had a woman in my arms like that. But when a human male gets excited, he's still in full command of his faculties. He can still choose. Or at least he's expected to behave as if he has a choice. Personally, I think it's one of the few things that actually makes us different from mere animals. We can deny our lusts, even during moments of opportunity."

"So you chose to abstain."

"Yes."

"Is she not attractive?"

"Yes, she's attractive."

"Forgive me, Harry, I am still struggling to understand."

"Look," I said, my hands on my hips as I walked slowly over to the rocks where my uniform and boots were spread out, "attraction is only part of it. There's other factors too. Like, she's too young. Much younger than I am. I'd feel like I was taking advantage of her. Plus, she's my superior officer in the Fleet. It's against the rules for a superior and a subordinate to engage in sexual congress."

"Why?"

"Bad for discipline in the chain-of-command, among other things."

"And that's all?"

"No," I said, testing the fabric between my fingers. It felt dry enough. I started to put my undergarments on. "The male and the female should really love each other first, before they have sex. When sex happens before love, or without love, it gets . . . complicated."

"Also immoral," said the Professor.

"If the man and the woman subscribe to certain 'flavors' of religious or moral tradition, yes. That too. Though most religious proscriptions surrounding intercourse simply involve matrimony, not love. A few centuries ago, before humanity went into space, it was quite common for young men and women to be married off by their families. For political and social reasons, among other things. Love didn't really enter into it."

"Fascinating," said the Professor. "Among my people we mate for genetic enhancement and advantage. Many, many males. A few females. In the far distant past males engaged in mortal combat to determine which ones would mate during a given cycle of estrus. Now we select for genetic traits we consider positive and bar those who don't meet the standards. Those of us who meet the standards are then chosen via lottery to attend to the females when they are ready. I have copulated six times in my life. I am considered somewhat fortunate in this regard."

"Because you're smart?" I said, sliding on pants, then socks, then boots.

"Intelligence is key," he said. "But chance rules the final selection process, yes."

"Assuming you win the lottery," I asked while buttoning up my topcoat, "do you choose the females or do the females choose you?"

"The females choose us," he said. "In descending order of matriarchal seniority."

"Did you ever mate with the Queen Mother?"

The Professor paused. A small flush of color along the semi-soft portions of his chitin told me I had embarrassed him.

"No."

"I'm sorry if I intruded into a private area where I should not have," I said honestly.

"No, Harry, it is I who began this conversation. The discomfort comes from knowing that no female of the Queen Mother's stature has ever selected a scholar for mating. They prefer warriors to thinkers."

"The more things change, the more they stay the same."

"What does that mean?"

"Never mind," I said.

The sun's first rays peaked over the horizon.

I observed the Queen Mother's silhouette in the distance. Just like the day before. She was immobile, faced directly into the growing light as it slowly bathed the landscape. The Professor and I watched her for a time, then I asked, "Penny for her thoughts."

"If by that you mean to say you wonder what's in her mind at this time, I wish I knew. I have inquired, and she will not tell me. I sense in conversation with her that the Queen Mother is both fascinated and troubled by her experience living without the disc."

A rustling to our left told me the captain was arising.

"Clothes are dry," I called, deliberately loud.

"Roger that," she said, her nose sounding stuffed up.

I walked away from the rocks where her uniform still lay, and kept my back turned while she shuffled up and slowly put on her uniform in silence.

"Okay," she said.

I turned around.

"You look like shit, ma'am," I said.

"I feel sick," she admitted. Wiping her nose on her sleeve.

"We should have checked your bag sooner. We'll have to let it dry out before nightfall if we don't want a repeat of last night. Meanwhile, perhaps the Professor can spare room on the back of his disc for you while we travel today."

"I'd be grateful for that," she said, eyes drawn and puffy-looking.

"It could be managed," the Professor said, after looking down at the captain—his antennae moving thoughtfully.

The captain and I did what we could with the ration bars still in our packs, chewing because we needed the fuel, not because it tasted good. I'd never been a heavy chap. I realized that too much time on this nameless world would thin me down even more.

When we'd collected our gear and secured our packs, I helped Adanaho climb onto the back of the Professor's disc—following his having helped the Queen Mother climb onto the front. The Queen Mother and Adanaho both seemed unusually quiet this morning, and I shouldered my burden wondering what the day would bring. The captain had taken some pills from her pack's emergency medical kit, and wrapped her sleeping bag around herself inside-out so as to let the liner properly dry. Her belt had been looped into a small cleat on the back of the disc so that she wouldn't slide off.

A cool breeze started up.

We moved out, due southwest in the direction of the hinted-at mantis signals the Professor had previously detected.

Plodding through the gravel and sand I thought about the one time I'd been to the Mojave, back on Earth. At least there, I'd had some mountains to look at in the distance, along with a few Joshua trees, and the occasional rattlesnake. On this world, everything had been worn flat and made unremarkable. Without the Professor's telemetry to guide us, I suspected it would have been supremely easy to wind up meandering in circles. One dune or low bluff looked like the next.

After a while I noticed that the captain's eyes had closed. She was slumped against the Professor's back. If either she or he were bothered by such close contact, neither of them showed it.

"Military is as military does," I said under my breath. Sleep anywhere you can, when you can.

Good for her.

I kept walking.

CHAPTER 32

Earth, 2153 A.D.

MICROGRAVITY TRAINING WAS A COMPLETE HORROR SHOW.

No baby steps in jets performing parabolas, like in the old astronaut times. We took a straight shot to orbit, all of us in Charlie Company packed into a single company-sized assault carrier. If at first it had seemed like a whale of an amusement ride, the fun stopped for me once the falling sensation became ever-present.

"You're going pale on me," Cortez said. Like me, she was in her training-issue combat vacuum armor suit. We were strapped into opposing benches that ran up and down the length of the carrier's main troop deck. Our helmets were strapped down in our laps, and for good reason too. Next to each helmet was a plastic bag into which we could hurl the contents of our stomachs, if the need so arose.

And it arose.

Again, and again, and again.

After several minutes of anguished upchucking, I pulled the opening of my bag away from my face and chanced a look around the immediate area. To my relief, I wasn't the only one who'd tossed his cookies. Though I could see from the evil smirks on the faces of our DSs that certain people were enjoying the show just a little too much.

"You gonna feel a lot worse if even one piece o' bahf touch the inside o' my carrier," the first sergeant said. "Some of you act like you never been to space before. You mean nobody take a transcontinental flight? Not even once? My drill sah-jeens gonna enjoy watching you all get sick over the next two weeks. We have four more flights coming and those of you who can't adapt, you're out. Grounded. You'll be stuck scrubbing gah-bage cans at a Fleet mess facility."

Right about then I think I'd have been perfectly happy to see the business end of a mess hall trash barrel. It certainly couldn't get any greener nor smell any worse than I did.

A few seats away, a male recruit who'd been playing tough guy let loose. No bag on his mouth. The female recruit across from him shrieked as she took the blast full force.

A collective cry of, *"Eeewwww,"* went up from Charlie Company.

Second platoon's trio of DSs were all doing their best to suppress laughter, and failing. Then they put on their helmets—something we recruits had been strictly forbidden to do during this first flight. With faces and noses safely behind transparent faceplates, Senior Drill Sergeant Malvino, Drill Sergeant Davis, and Drill Sergeant Schmetkin all began to shake with mirth. I guessed that they'd seen and experienced this many times. I guessed also that once a man got used to microgravity, such scenes could become funny. In a gallows humor sort of way.

More stomachs were emptied around the deck. Some people were smart enough to employ bags. Some were not. Fluid and bits of half-digested food began to float freely.

After we landed—just one orbit on the initial run—it took all six platoons working in shifts *two whole days* to get all of the gack off our suits, out of the cracks and crevices of the equipment, and out of the carrier's ventilation system; to say nothing of cleaning and disinfecting the troop deck proper.

Ample incentive to develop an iron digestive system—for those who'd not had the sense to use their bags as intended.

The next orbital sortie was longer in duration, resulting in fewer sick cases, and had absolutely zero projectile events.

After the second orbit—when the DSs were convinced that all of us who could get sick, had sufficiently emptied ourselves—we were ordered to go vacuum tight. Which meant helmets on, and sealed. Having spent many days on the ground going through the complexities of our armored space suits, their computer systems and oxygen generators, CO_2 filters, hoses, emergency patches, etc., now was our chance to put that knowledge to the test.

The first sergeant's voice was patched into our helmet speakers via the Charlie Company wireless, and we listened as she instructed one of the fifth platoon DSs to activate the lock cycle that would evacuate the entire troop deck's atmosphere, and clamshell-open the massive troop deck bay doors at the tail end of the carrier.

There was an extremely loud hiss—which died quickly.

In my helmet's virtual display I saw the atmosphere bar rapidly drop from green, to yellow, to orange, to red, and then blink an angry crimson at me.

Still strapped to our benches, we all craned our necks as best we could to get a glimpse out the back of the carrier as the doors gradually opened, and revealed a rather spectacular view of the Earth.

At several hundred kilometers altitude, all of humanity's worldly achievements were dissolved into the swirling natural blues, browns, greens, and whites of land, air, and sea.

A collective exclamation went up from the lot of us, even the ones like me who were still wrestling with the silent physical terror of weightlessness.

"That's right," First Sergeant Chau said. "Take a good look, Chah-lee. Our home. Yours and mine. Only it might not be for much longer if we don't do the job Fleet asks us to do. The mantes *aren't* human. They don't think human. They don't feel human. They don't care human. All they want is to see humans *die*. Are we gonna let that happen, Chah-lee?"

As a company: "NO, FIRST SERGEANT!"

"Are we gonna let the insects take our home, or our colonies?"

"NO, FIRST SERGEANT!"

"That's damned good, Chah-lee! We are what stands between the mantes and Earth's destruction. You are all training to be part of humanity's first, best defense against the mantis threat. Up until now you've spent most of your time on the ground, learning how to so-jah the way so-jahs have learned for hundreds of years. Now we gonna teach you to fight twenty-second-century style. Drill sah-jeens, prepare for EVA!"

My heart leapt in my throat.

There'd been nothing on the company white board that said anything about us actually going *outside* on this trip. Just a longer case of up-and-back. Not so long that I thought I couldn't hold it together until we landed. But the idea of actually getting up off the bench and floating free, much less going beyond the confines of the troop deck, seemed like a unique kind of torture.

Senior Drill Sergeant Malvino was up and out of his seat, the bottoms of his boots magnetically locked to the deck. He began shouting at us to hook our tie lines to the cables that ran up and down the length of the troop deck. We'd move aft in an orderly fashion—pulling ourselves along the backs of the benches by the railings we found there. One squad at a time, in sequence.

As with everything else we'd experienced in space to date, much ground practice had gone into this moment. Rehearsals which had looked rather comical when performed on the PT field now came back to us as we mimicked our ground training.

At the end of the cable we began to daisychain ourselves in a human strand: each squad stretched out with troops hooked to troops, which in turn formed spokes off of platoons, and the platoons spoked off of the company proper. All of us spread out to the limits of our tethers. Tiny reaction control thrusters in each suit allowing us a limited amount of extravehicular maneuverability.

I found I did best by *not* looking down.

Some astronauts and supersonic skydivers have reported no fear, upon stepping into the void of space. Because the ground is so impossibly far away, falling towards it feels abstract and unreal.

I, on the other hand, found it excruciating. So I faced away, into the blackness of interplanetary space, and focused on my breathing, trying to pay attention to the commands being given on the squad, platoon, and company wireless networks.

By the fifth sortie, I'd gotten used to it. Not immune. Just... used to it.

And we were practicing limited EVA squad tactics using individual maneuvering units, as well as squad-level "pushers" which were basically automobile-sized devices that allowed eight to twenty people to clamp on, latch on, or grab hold, and zoom around in microgravity.

The assault carrier's troop deck was stocked with a maze of temporary barriers, where we practiced mock shipboarding, our R77A5s outfitted with small lasers that activated upon trigger-pull. The training-issue armor suits would blip at you when you got hit. Depending on where you got hit, the suit would relay your injury information back to the DSs running the mock fight. Torso shots were often judged to be fatal—making some of us wonder what was the point in wearing extra-bulky space armor if said armor was not, in fact, capable of absorbing and deflecting rounds. But an extremity shot was deemed survivable. In the event that the armor was punctured, sealant gel would pour from a liner in the outer layer and into the hole, while a specialized non-toxic, anesthetic, blood-clotting foam would fill around the arm or leg from the inner layer, causing the affected area to stiffen and immobilize, like a cast.

For our purposes the sealant and the foam were kept dormant. The DSs would yell out that your left or right arm was officially useless, and if you got caught using it during the fight your name went onto the punishment detail roster. Something many of us had experienced, more times than we cared to admit, so we tried to err on the side of caution, going limp as dish rags any time we got tagged by a rival squad's or platoon's laser beams.

"Live fire is for the LCX," Drill Sergeant Schmetkin said to me as she worked with my squad, marshaling us through exterior hull movement drills—the bottoms of our boots *clomping* across the heat-absorbing tiles that covered the entire assault carrier. Magnetism in our boot soles was just strong enough to keep us glued to the exterior, assuming we didn't jump or push off too hard.

The LCX was the Lunar Combat Exercise: a twelve-day final trial wherein all of us who'd survived IST thus far would take everything we'd learned about soldiering and put it to the test—on the surface of the Moon. When I'd first heard about the LCX it had sounded like a blast. But now that we were coming up on it, I realized that it was going to be a combination of tedium and frenzy. Four days to reach the Moon, four days to bust our butts taking and holding a mock mantis outpost, then four days back. All carried out under as real of conditions as could be managed. Which, in space, where even tiny mistakes could be fatal, was pretty damned real.

Following hull drills, and after we'd all clambered back inside and resumed our seats on our respective benches, I wondered just how the LCX would compare to an actual combat assault. Assuming such things were even conducted? So much of what we'd been doing and training for seemed theoretical. Centuries of infantry tactics and knowledge adapted to conditions and terrain where no human soldier had ever soldiered before. Would we be any good at it, when the situation mattered? Or were we just fooling ourselves?

I chose to keep such wonderings to myself.

CHAPTER 33

AFTERNOON BROUGHT US TO THE EDGE OF A NARROW, DEEP canyon. A small river wound its way across the bottom headed northwest to southeast. The water tumbled and rushed against the rocks below, and a rumbling echo drifted out of the canyon as the Professor and I considered our options. I reluctantly woke the captain, helping her down off the back of the Professor's disc, while he helped the Queen Mother down too. The two aliens spoke briefly in their insect language, then she scurried off to the Canyon's edge, peering out over it while the captain and I counseled with the Professor.

"Have you detected any further signs of mantis signals or technology?" Adanaho asked. She didn't sound as stuffed up as she had in the morning, and her eyes looked somewhat better too. I was encouraged by this. Maybe the extra sleep had done her good.

"No," said the Professor. "But, given our new geographical impediment, I do not think it would matter even if I had."

"Can't your disc take us over?" I asked.

"The carriage is not an aircraft," the Professor said. "Its impellers operate according to proximity with solid and semi-solid mass, not gravity per se. I would sink like a stone until I'd reached a point within a few of your meters above the canyon floor."

"If we can find a way down," I said, "maybe we can rig up a method of traveling on the river current. Plus, we'd have fresh water any time we wanted it. I bet that flood creek we filled our canteens in is a tributary to this drainage. If we follow it far enough, we might reach a lake or something larger. What's your hunch, Professor? Would your people prefer such a location for setting up a temporary base of operations?"

"I believe that is a logical assumption," said the Professor.

"How about it, ma'am?" I asked, looking at my superior.

"It's as good a plan as any we've had so far," she said. "We'll have to make sure and get the Queen Mother's opin—OH MY GOD!"

I froze, watching the captain's arm shoot out with an index finger pointed behind me to the canyon's edge.

I turned just in time to see the Queen Mother's body drop over the side. The Professor nearly bowled me over as his disc shot after her, then he too was over the side. The captain and I rushed to the edge and flopped onto our bellies, sliding across the last few inches of sand before putting our chins at the lip, hands clawed across the precipice.

What we saw was the most improbably beautiful thing I'd witnessed since going to space with the Fleet as an older teenager.

The Queen Mother circled lazily around and around in the air, slowly spiraling with her wings spread to their maximum width, each beating in concert with the others, and together making a low rhythm that sounded not too dissimilar from a helicopter. She obviously weighed too much and her wings were too small for sustained flight, but while she flew—her body extended and piercing the air like a javelin, her beak aimed directly forward and her legs and forelimbs folded up tightly against her body—she was magnificent.

The Professor's disc fell straight down the wall of the Canyon. The speaker grill on the disc's front was blaring amplified mantis speech. Which the Queen Mother appeared to happily ignore.

"She's beautiful," the captain whispered.

"I didn't know they could fly," I said, still astonished.

After a couple of seconds, Adanaho's lips peeled back from her teeth in a wide, genuine smile. "I don't think the Queen Mother knew either. Until now."

We watched as the Queen Mother continued her slow descent, until at last she lightly touched down on a wide sand bar in the middle of the river. Walking to the edge, she lowered her mouth to the water and began taking in copious amounts of fluid. The

Professor zoomed up to her, his disc's motors making funny shapes in the surface of the water as he moved across it. The Queen Mother appeared to ignore him for a few more moments as he hovered directly next to her, animatedly talking with his mandibles.

Finally she looked up at him. She said something.

The Professor backed away from her and went across the water to the canyon wall directly beneath us. I gauged the distance to be two hundred meters down. Now he really did look like a bug. Smaller than my thumb.

"We are committed," he said, his speaker grill turned up to maximum. His vocoder-voice echoed long and far, up and down the canyon.

"We can't climb down at this point," the captain yelled, then began coughing.

"Let us travel downriver until there is a place where you can join us," replied the Professor.

"Agreed," I called at the top of my lungs. Then I stood up and retrieved my load from where I'd dumped it on the ground. The captain stood up too. She trudged over to me.

"Sorry ma'am," I said. "Looks like you're hoofing it again."

"It's okay," she said. "I need to work the knots out of my muscles. Here, give me the pack; I will carry it."

I eyed her, but decided to follow orders. She took the pack without complaint, and off we went, staying close enough to the canyon edge that we could see down to the Professor and the Queen Mother, but not so close as to give either of us vertigo. Afterimages of the Queen Mother's sudden, elegant, altogether astounding flight ran across my vision as we walked. Until that time I'd still considered the mantes to be an ugly race. They were also vicious and brutal in combat. But for a minute or two, I'd seen a mantis take flight—soaring and spectacular.

"What a story you'll have for the intel people," I said as we walked.

"What a story," the captain agreed. "Nobody's going to believe this. I wish I'd had a camera or a recorder on me to get evidence. She looked as natural as can be. Free as a bird, one might say."

"Amazing that her instincts were that good," I said. "She jumped off that cliff purely on faith, apparently."

"Apparently," said the captain.

I sensed something else from her, though she didn't speak for several more minutes.

"Chief," she finally said.

"Yes, ma'am?"

"Is it true what you said?"

"About what?"

"About you not having had a woman in your arms for a dozen years?"

"You were eavesdropping again," I chided her.

"I have good ears," she said. "So, it's really true?"

"Uhh, yes, ma'am."

"How come?"

"Beg your pardon?"

"How come you didn't have a lover on Purgatory? That Deacon person you talked about, back aboard ship. Wasn't she interested?"

"That's a good question. I'm not really sure. Granted, I am not the world's most handsome fellow, but that didn't stop a lot of the other prisoners from getting the attention of the opposite sex. I think once I built the chapel and took over where Chaplain Thomas left off, people viewed me like I'd been set apart. The chapel and I became synonymous."

"That's too bad," she said. "It must have been hard."

"Yes, it was," I admitted.

It took a couple of seconds for the unintended double entendre of my reply to sink in, then she and I both burst out laughing.

For a moment we stopped and doubled over, until our diaphragms hurt. Then we got back to walking, the laughter dying to giggles, and then spastic coughing on Adanaho's part.

She drank water while I waited, then we started out again.

"Sorry," I said. "Didn't mean to make you gag up a lung."

"I think it's allergies," she said. "Something here—in the dirt, on the dust of the wind—is rubbing me wrong. I'll be okay. FIDO."

"Fuck it, drive on," I said, smirking. The motto had been around in one form or another for as long as men and women had saluted and marched. Contrary to my first impression, as an intel officer the captain didn't seem averse to physical challenges. In fact, the longer we walked and the more I watched her, the more I came to believe she actually relished the effort. Every stride was a statement. Her back held straight and her head up, swiveling occasionally so that her eyes could take in the landscape.

"Ma'am," I said.

"Yes, Chief?"

"What have you and the Queen Mother *really* been discussing the last couple of nights?"

"Like I said, it's hard to discuss anything with someone who doesn't speak our language," she said.

"I've been thinking about that, and I've decided I'm wrong. They may not be able to speak as we do, but they can hear us just fine. You don't have to be able to speak a language to hear it, or understand what's been said. I'm now wagering that the Queen Mother understood every word out of your mouth. Back on the *Calysta* she stated that our beliefs and rituals were of no interest to her. Why's she suddenly become curious now?"

Adanaho knit her brow while she considered my words.

"I can only speculate," she said.

"Speculation's better than nothing," I replied.

"I believe the Queen Mother is in a state of flux. Pulling her out of her disc terrified her almost to the brink of insanity. But in the days since we left the escape pod, her perceptions have been pure. Unadulterated."

"Unadulterated?" I said, somewhat incredulous. "You make it sound like her disc was an impediment, rather an advantage. Five will get you ten the Fleet would kill to replicate a functional disc. That's a nifty piece of the mantis puzzle we've still been unable to unravel. Imagine that kind of advanced technology adapted for human use."

"I can," she said, with a slightly sour expression. "But we're already so dependent on our own technology—for what we eat, how we travel, how we live, even how we play, and for what we *think* and *how* we think it—that we forget what it was like before computers, spacecraft, faster-than-light travel—"

"Do I detect the sensibility of a Luddite?" I said archly.

"I do *not* hate technology," she replied. "I simply think we've gotten lazy. Did you know that the bulk of our major scientific discoveries came to us without the aid of modern equipment? Hell, Chief, they built the first atomic weapons using long math and vacuum tube processing power. The first true spaceplane, the X-15? Also built using nothing but slide rules and a lot of shrewd paper-and-pencil figuring. Then came the Information Age, and suddenly anyone could know anything via Internet search engines.

Why waste time memorizing or synthesizing? Click, the info's at your fingertips. Entertainment too. The immersive games became addictive. People forget about the danger of VR."

"Nobody's forgotten about *that,*" I said. "There are boatloads of Americans back home who were going through therapy and rehabilitation when I joined the Fleet."

"Not just in America, Chief," she said, stopping in her tracks and facing me. Her eyes had begun to sparkle keenly. I could tell from her posture that we'd hit a sore point.

"There are whole generations of people addicted to VR. Why come out and face the real world when make-believe is so much nicer?"

"Plenty of people recovered when the mantes attacked," I said.

"Sure, when we were forced to, we snapped out of it. Sort of. But if the mantes never existed and we'd been left to just toodle along the path of least resistance . . . I am not sure any force could have reversed the trend. We built ships in virtual bottles, then climbed in after the ships and pulled the corks tight behind us."

I couldn't deny the ferocity or facts of her argument. Just about every American knew somebody who'd become addicted to VR. Minds lost to imaginary spaces existing purely inside the global information networks. Each man or woman become a fairy king or cyber queen, a god or goddess of his or her own private electronic realm. Wealth, luxury, power, all limitless and beyond belief. Sit down, plug in, turn on, and tune out. An infinity of sweetly alluring lies.

I shuddered.

"So how does the VR addiction epidemic tie back to the Queen Mother?"

"Have you ever seen the bad cases? The ones who went into VR as kids only to come out as adults? Everything you and I take for granted, even eating and drinking and shitting, is an alien experience for them. They don't remember the real world, and because there are no rules in VR there's no need to bother with the mundane functions of ordinary existence. Most of those recoveries take years, and the patients hate it.

"But a very few of them delight in escaping. Like being reborn. They can't get enough of the *real* around them. Every morning they wake up is a chance to feel real hot and cold water from a real tap, running through their real fingers. To hear real music played on real instruments with their own real ears. To see a really blue sky with real clouds and a real sun with real warmth on your face when you..."

She trailed off. I stared at her as she walked. Her eyes were looking straight ahead, but she was clearly lost in reverie.

Instantly, I intuited the truth.

"You were one of them, weren't you?" I said.

She looked over her shoulder at me.

"Yes, I was."

"How young were you when you went in?"

"Six."

"Jesus, your parents let you get on VR at that age?"

"It's the world's most amazing babysitter."

I swallowed hard.

"How old were you when you came out?"

"Fifteen," she said. "The war was hurting us. The government began cutting off and rationing resources. My parents unplugged me and sent me to a state rehab school for VR kids. When I was sixteen, they said I was well enough to go stay with my mother's sister in North Africa, since my parents were denied custody. Auntie hated VR, considered it a tool of the devil, and took me in like the daughter she never had. When I was eighteen I joined the Fleet through an ROTC scholarship. When I was twenty-two I went to space, and never looked back."

I didn't say anything for a long time. The captain's revelation had turned the mood stone-cold sober.

"I think the Queen Mother is going through something similar to what I went through," Adanaho finally said. "After living her entire life through the technological lens of her disc, she's suddenly experiencing reality on *its* terms. I think she's finding the experience to be revelatory. Old instincts, long suppressed, are coming to the surface. Abilities. Perceptions. A whole new way of seeing and interpreting the world."

"That's a hell of a speculation," I said, shaking my head. "No disrespect, ma'am, but can you be sure you're not just projecting?"

She was silent for a time. Then she reluctantly said, "No."

We took a few more steps.

"But can you offer any other explanation as to why she'd suddenly leap off a cliff, relying on wings she's never used to prevent her from falling directly to a gruesome death?"

"No," I admitted.

"You said it yourself, Chief. It took a leap of faith."

Again, I had no answer.

Finally we came to a crumbling break in the canyon's edge. The canyon itself grew wider and the sides less steep. It appeared to me that we could make our way down, provided we took our time. The Professor must have seen this too, because he and the Queen Mother had stopped and were looking up at us expectantly. Waiting.

It took the captain and me the rest of the day to make our way down. When we reached the bottom, the entire canyon was in shadow and the air had begun to chill. I wished hard for a clutch of driftwood and some matches to light a fire. None appeared.

While Adanaho set about preparing our camp for the night, I noticed that the Queen Mother kept apart from the Professor. She stayed near the water's edge, gazing into the swirls and eddies that marked the surface. The water was mostly clear, all the way to the bottom. If I'd thought there might be trout, I'd have rigged a pole and a line. But the Professor's sensors and my own water test kit revealed the depressing truth: the river was as lifeless as the surface through which it had carved its course. There would be nothing fresh to eat for dinner.

I pulled the Professor aside before we all went to sleep for the night.

"I've been wondering," I said, "about what you told me."

"Specifically?" he asked.

"Sex. You said the males of your species are in a sexual stupor until they've mated with the female producing the pheromone."

"That's a close enough description, yes."

"How in the hell do you mate when you're still attached to the discs?"

He looked at me, unmoving.

"Very carefully," was his only reply.

I didn't have the heart to pester him further.

In the morning we renewed our journey. Whatever I'd thought about building a raft, we simply didn't have the resources to do it. The emergency inflatable life preservers in our packs might have kept us face up in the river, but the water was so frigid we'd have been risking hypothermia as a result.

So we walked all day, following the river's edge along the

bottom of the canyon. More and more, the Queen Mother tested the strength of her small lower legs. Every time we stopped. She also tested her flight capabilities, flitting from rock to sand bar to the far side of the river, and back again. Whether it was instinct or learned skill, or both, she appeared to be getting distinctly comfortable in that mode.

Every night, the Queen Mother and the captain sought solitude together, while the Professor and I just sat by the water and wondered between us what was happening with our women.

CHAPTER 34

Earth, 2153 A.D.

THE NIGHT BEFORE THE LCX, IT WAS TOUGH TO GET SLEEP.

Everyone was up late checking their armor suits, rifles, and other equipment, as well as going over the final squad and platoon ops planning which the DSs had been drilling into us for the past two weeks. Recruit leadership had been divvied up—with NCO and officer slots having been pinned on both the ambitious and the unlucky. In some instances, the assignment had seemed every inch a punishment. As in Thukhan's case, since he'd lately been letting his mouth run too loudly within earshot of the DSs, and was thus consistently on corrective detail.

Now he was recruit platoon sergeant for second platoon, and even surlier and more nasty than the DSs. Who had, in fact, begun to mellow out on us during the lead-up to the LCX. For reasons I only began to understand long after graduation.

Mercifully, I'd not drawn any short straws. I was just another rifleman, nestled in amongst the crowd.

Lying in my bunk and listening to the little fidgets, clinks, and whispers that were going on after lights-out, I thought about Senior DS Malvino's threat that anyone found wanting on the LCX would be summarily drummed out, or kicked planetside for a landlocked tour. Which had, to be honest—and after so many weeks of space training—appeared to offer advantages. After all, I didn't actually *want* to see the stars run with blood. That wasn't why I'd signed on specifically. And I'd definitely proven throughout training that I was nobody's idea of a steel-and-guts hero. I didn't have the reflexes nor the tactical mind for it. I could perform drill and ceremony with crispness, ensure my bunk and locker were squared away to perfection, but during battle drills and combat-applicable training, I was average at best. Never quite bad enough to get kicked out, but never good enough to rank with the more razor-edged go-getters who were obviously spoiling for a stand-up fight with the mantes. In whatever form that happened to take: ground, orbital, ship-to-ship, and so forth.

Could I lurk my way through the LCX? How many of the rest of us had the same game plan? Quite a few, I reckoned.

I must have dozed off, because suddenly I felt a fist slug me in the shoulder.

I popped my eyes open to see a shape looming in the semi-dark of the bay.

"Up, cunt," Thukhan said in his usual tone. "You should have been on watch five mikes ago."

"Roger that," I said, realizing that in the commotion of pre-LCX prep I'd forgotten to set my e-pad alarm for night watch duty—in my case, the dreaded midnight to three AM slot that kept a man from getting anything even approaching decent sleep.

I struggled up and put my flip-flops on my feet, securing my weapon and trudging for the chair where I'd be forced to sit awake—or at least semi-awake—for the next three hours.

Thukhan stopped me halfway.

"In my office," he said. Pointing.

I shrugged and we went into the head, leaving my chair empty.

"What's the issue?" I asked, remembering that the last time I'd considered going into the head alone, with Thukhan, I'd been contemplating doing a fair amount of evil to the man. He'd had me spooked halfway out of my mind. Now I merely felt a spongy kind of buffered contempt. We'd both made it through IST so far, for different reasons, and the rigor and grind had helped me focus on things other than my foe.

Which was not to say the man didn't still piss me off. I considered Thukhan to be a menace. But he was a *managed* menace. Someone I could compartmentalize, and push out of my lane of consciousness whenever I wanted or needed to.

Until tonight.

"Malvino says there's one slot on the Charlie Company LCX duty roster that's been left open, and someone from second platoon's gotta fill it. I didn't find out until tonight, and I have to have the roster ready in the morning when we roll for the flight line. So you're my pick."

"What's the detail?" I asked.

"Not a detail. A role. You know anything about effing church?"

I blinked, remembering the day when the recruits from the chapel had climbed aboard the base shuttle.

"Not a thing," I said honestly.

"Good, because you're the recruit chaplain now. Congratulations. That means you get to play ossifer like the other cunts. I even have to call you *sir.*"

"Well, I could say thank you," I said. "But then I have to wonder why you didn't volunteer for the job, since as far as I know a chaplain does zip-diddly-squat during live-fire exercises. It's your big chance to sit on your ass and waste time."

"Listen, Barlow," Thukhan said, leaning in close. "I never liked you. From the moment you came sauntering into the bay back in Reception. You looked soft, you talked soft, and you *are* soft. They told me I don't have the option of getting out of recruit platoon sergeant. So as long as I have to run this stupid platoon during the LCX, I want as few headaches as possible. Which means getting you the hell out of my way."

The insult was clear. He considered me dead weight. And if I'd not already gauged myself to be about as useful in a real fight as boxing gloves on an eighty-year-old, I might have wanted to argue the point. As it was I was too tired, and too ready to just get the LCX over with, to care. I mock saluted and snapped the heels of my flip-flops together.

"I'm honored to have been promoted to the position of recruit chaplain. And now, if you'll excuse me, Recruit Platoon Overlord, I have to go sit in my chair like a good peon and ponder what the hell I'm going to do with myself for the next twelve days."

"Read," he said. "The DSs will push a bunch of files at you in the morning before we move out."

I spun around, then went out the head door.

Come morning, there was no chow.

We fell out of our bunks, stripped them of bedding, dumped the bedding into huge sacks bound for Armstrong Field's central laundry facility, and did some last-second tidying of the bay, before the recruit squad leaders and recruit platoon sergeants—not the

DSs—filed us downstairs into the company common area with our space-duty uniforms on our bodies and our space duffels on our backs. The armor suits in the duffels wouldn't be worn until we'd actually reached the preflight formation zone which lay in the shadow of our assault carrier on the flight line. Putting them on now would be like walking a mile in the sun with an arctic coldsuit on. And the armor was going to wind up chafing and stinking enough without each of us filling ours with a gallon of perspiration—before we'd even reached the edge of the atmosphere.

Huge cargo trucks—not buses—waited for us when we route-stepped from the Charlie Company barracks, across the PT field, to the edge of the tarmac. We filed up into them, jostling until we'd packed ourselves in like hot dogs, then the doors on the trailers were slammed and we waited several long minutes as the trucks drove us across the long, wide flight line to our intended destination.

When we got there the recruit leadership—not the DSs—filed us off and formed us up again by platoon, for total company-level accountability and last-minute equipment inventory. With the sun still behind the horizon we all had to walk and work by muscle memory, as much as by sight. And because we'd rehearsed the whole routine during the five previous spaceflights aboard the assault carrier, there was no first-flight baloney about people missing equipment or not having their crap in order.

Accountability was crisp, efficiently called, and by the numbers.

Standing at the position of attention and scanning my eyes about, it occurred to me that we'd actually gotten the trick of it all. The protocols. The *beat.* Without a single prompting from our DSs, who hung back away from the formation a fair distance, each of them toting a space duffel of his or her own.

Charlie Company was moving and talking and executing like a real-live unit of real-live effing *soldiers.*

As had occasionally happened before, I suddenly felt a quiet surge of near-euphoric pride. Sure, the training wheels might be coming off soon. But we were ready. By hell!

A crew chief from the assault carrier trotted down one of the long ramps that emptied out of the side of the ship. He approached the recruit officer leadership at the rear of the formation and had a conversation with the recruit captain. Since I'd been assigned as recruit chaplain, I now fell in with this bunch, and listened intently as the crew chief told the captain that we'd be a good forty-five minutes on the ground, still, as he and the others in the ship took care of a few preflight checks on the computers and engines.

This information was relayed to the recruit lieutenants, who relayed it to the recruit platoon sergeants, and so on and so forth. With the recruit first sergeant barking orders, all of the platoons dropped their duffels in-place, where we were ordered to prep for donning of armor. Otherwise, stand fast and await further orders.

I unloaded myself and extracted the pieces of my suit from my bag, laying them out on the ground in sequence. The space-duty uniform was like a set of long underwear, only with a series of fluid-filled cooling tubes skeined throughout the fabric, and an extra tube sealed onto the business end of a man's penis. All of which would be hooked into the suit's internals once it came time to put the armor on.

And if the dick-tube had seemed at first to be embarrassing and uncomfortable for the men, we didn't complain. The women had it much worse.

As in all things IST, you learned to get over it.

I sat down on my duffel—now mostly empty—and pulled out my abused e-reader.

Thukhan was right. They'd pushed me some files.

With the sun and the heat coming up, I tried to ignore the prickling sensation of sweat breaking out all over my body, and focus on what I'd been given to read. Of all the things I could have potentially been assigned, either in training or in reality, chaplain definitely seemed the most unlikely. Didn't you have to have a degree as a minister or a priest or something?

"Recruit Barlow?" said a woman's voice.

I reflexively stood up and faced in the direction the voice had come from.

An older Fleet officer, with the color of steel in her hair and a lieutenant colonel's tabs on her GFF, approached me.

"Ma'am," I said, snapping a crisp salute, which she returned.

Her name tape said JICERSKI.

"You can call me Chaplain J," she said with a slight smile.

"Yes, ma'am," I said. It was rather unheard of for a lowly recruit to be addressing or dealing with someone of such high rank.

"At ease, at ease," she said.

"Yes, ma'am," I said, snapping to parade rest.

"No, I mean *relax,* kid. Relax. I need to talk to you for a minute and I'd like to do it without you leaving a brick in your undershorts. Can we do that?"

"Yes, ma'am. I mean, uhhh, sure."

I let my arms hang at my sides.

"First Sergeant Chau tells me you drew this cycle's straw as the recruit chaplain. Is that right?"

"Correct, ma'am," I said.

"Know anything about the job?"

"Not really, ma'am."

"Have you been attending service while you're in IST?"

"Uhhh, no ma'am."

"Figures. Every cycle they find a way to pin the job on someone who's not interested. Just once, Lord, I'd like to see them find a recruit who's actually requested Chaplain's Assistant on the entry form. Okay, Barlow, let's you and I sit down for a minute."

She sat down cross-legged on the tarmac, and I followed suit. She took her soft cap off and dropped it in her lap—unusual, in that the GFF was strictly forbidden to be worn outdoors without the soft cap. Did the rules get bent for chaplains?

"During this training exercise," Chaplain J said, "you're going to be acting the role I'd occupy if this were an actual battle deployment. Have you had a chance to read any of the literature I sent Drill Sergeant Malvino?"

"I was just about to," I said.

"Good. That will help. In your civilian life, do you go to church or synagogue or mosque or temple?"

"No," I said. "Never."

"Is the idea of God utterly foreign to you? Are you not a believer in Him?"

"Beg your pardon, ma'am?"

"Do you believe in a higher power? A supreme being? Or anything along those lines."

I had to think about it for a minute. Spiritual questions had been about as far from my mind as possible during IST. It wasn't exactly an environment that fostered deep contemplation. I stared at her eyes and saw crow's feet at the corners. This was a woman who was used to smiling a lot. I decided that I liked her.

"I'm not sure if I believe, or if I don't," I said. "In my family, church wasn't on anyone's priority list. My mom and dad were busy with other stuff, and liked to sleep in on the weekends."

"Seems sometimes like it's not on *anybody's* priority list these days," Chaplain J said. "But the war's changing this, I think. People are remembering the value of spirituality—at a time when so much else seems uncertain. And frightening. Tell me, Barlow, why did you sign up with the Fleet?"

"My friends and I, we sort of had this deal between us. That, and I really wanted to go to space. Plus when New America got attacked, well . . . I didn't want to be the only guy I knew who wasn't doing his part for the war effort. Even though my parents thought it was a big mistake."

"You've done a brave thing, Barlow. I hope your parents realize that some day. What do you hope they slot you for when you graduate IST?"

"I didn't pick anything in particular. I left the lines blank. I figured the Fleet would find a job for me, in whatever capacity I was needed. Beyond that, I didn't have much preference. I just want to see the stars, and to serve."

"Not a bad way to go, son, but now I'm going to ask you to get a little more serious, okay? Being the chaplain, for any unit of any size, is a pretty serious responsibility. You're sort of expected to be part pastor, part counselor, and part bartender."

"Bartender?" I said, startled.

"A soldier will tell the barkeep stuff she'd never tell her priest," Chaplain J said. "And let me tell you, when you're a chaplain, you get to hear it all. The good, the bad, and the ugly."

"I'm going to have to listen to the other recruits tell me their woes?" I asked.

"No, hopefully not," she said, chuckling. "I'm just trying to let you know what your job is. There are numerous ways to soldier in the Fleet. Everyone has a role, and everyone has to know that role and execute to standard. Some people make great marines. Some people make great pilots. Some people make great technicians, or great administrators. And once in a while, some people make good clergy."

"What will I be doing throughout the LCX?" I asked.

"I'll nurse you through it," she said.

"You're coming along?"

"I have to. It's required by regulation."

"Why?"

She looked around pensively, then leaned in closely.

"Recruits occasionally die during LCX. Not often. Not many. But it does happen. This will be a live-fire exercise on the Moon, after all. Not exactly the safest thing a person can be doing. In the event that someone gets hurt or killed, they like to have at least one chaplain around."

"So why do they assign a recruit to do it, when one of you comes up on the LCX anyway?"

"The LCX regulations require that all trainee officer and NCO positions be filled with recruits. And in the case of the chaplain, that's you. Don't sweat it, Barlow, you and I are going to make this the quickest twelve days of your entire IST. Drill Sergeant Davis said you're a mature troop who tries hard. He also said something else that I thought was important."

"What's that, ma'am?"

"He said you like to help."

"Ma'am?"

"He said he's noticed you're usually helping people. Other recruits. In big ways, and small."

"Isn't that the whole point?" I said. "For us to all work as a team?"

"Some people work as a team better than others," she replied. "Malvino and Davis both think you're easier-going than most. And I like that. It tells me you're a people person. Someone who can go along to get along. That too is essential for a chaplain. We carry officer rank, but we don't boss people the way your company captain or battalion colonel boss people."

I nodded my head, genuinely intrigued. "Sounds cool."

"It can be," she said. Then her gaze went far away. "And then there are times when it's not."

She came back to the present when she noticed me silently staring at her.

"Sorry," she said. "Just stick with me, Barlow, and it'll be a snap."

She held out a hand—which I hesitantly took, and shook.

Smiling, she pointed to my e-reader.

"Open the files," she said. "Let's use the time on the ground while we have it."

Chaplain J was right. The time in transit to the Moon passed much more quickly than I'd anticipated it would. I followed her around in "no recruit country" up on the assault carrier's crew decks, and she gave me the low-down on what the chaplain's job entailed. And while I was a little reluctant to dive deeply into the nature and meaning of some of the religious rituals—it turned out that Chaplain J had a masters degree, and was a former instructor at a religious college—I warmed to the idea of the chaplain serving as a shoulder for Fleet troops to cry on.

Lord knows I'd already seen a hot mess of troubled souls during IST. Many people barely holding it together under duress. Their carefully-crafted shells of control occasionally leaking bits and pieces of truer vulnerability when they hit their max stress points.

Sometimes talking was the best medicine. A friendly conversation, about something other than the immediate task thrust in front of your face.

When we reached lunar orbit and I was ordered back down to the troop deck to suit up and prepare for vacuum-pressure operations, I was feeling so good about things that I almost dropped my formality in front of DS Schmetkin, who coldly reminded me in no uncertain terms that I'd not gawtdamned graduated yet, so I'd better get myself right and stay right for the rest of the LCX, otherwise she was going to wash me out.

With the assault carrier going in "simulated hot" I sat on the bench next to the other recruit officers—our helmets on and our suits gradually reducing the internal pressure while elevating the oxygen percentage in our air—and contemplated dealing with simulated casualties. Could I give simulated Last Rites? Offer a simulated prayer? Chaplain J hadn't yet covered it, but as the assault carrier began to jink and swerve, throwing us this way and that as it "dodged" simulated missiles, I felt a little tickle of excitement in my stomach.

LCX might actually be fun.

CHAPTER 35

"WE HAVE TO GET UP AND GO. NOW." IT WAS ADANAHO'S VOICE.

"Why?" I said, suddenly coming up off the sand, despite the aching stiffness in my joints. We were two weeks from landing, our food stores almost gone, but still no closer to finding a mantis base than we'd been before. We'd stayed in the canyon for the water supply, yes, but also to give us shelter from the sand storms that hit every third or fourth day.

I'd grown to like the canyon, despite the gnawing in my belly. Sleep came easily with the sound of the river droning in my ears.

Tonight, my rest was interrupted. Or was it morning? The faintest hint of light was growing above the canyon rim to the east.

"A vehicle has landed. Not far from here. The Professor says it's not a mantis craft. They will be searching for us, and they will have marines with them."

She already had her pack snugly slung over both shoulders.

The Professor held the Queen Mother securely aboard his disc.

"We can't move quickly on foot," I said.

"This I know," said the Professor. "Which is why you must ride with me."

"Can the disc—your carriage—handle all three passengers?"

"I do not know. But we must try."

The Professor offered a forelimb.

I helped the captain climb up onto the back of the disc. She hugged her arms around the Professor's upper thorax, then I climbed aboard too. The disc's motors whined with additional strain, and for a moment we were all deathly still—waiting for any sound to tell us we'd been noticed. When none came, we began to slowly float forward.

"How did our people find us?" I asked Adanaho in her ear.

She leaned over and spoke into mine.

"Fleet's been quietly reverse-engineering a lot of different stuff during the years of the cease-fire. I've only been involved in some of that. It's probable they've discovered a way to home in on the signals from the Professor's disc, even if they can't reverse-engineer the disc itself."

"Please tell me you can switch off whatever it is that's not been switched off?" I said to the Professor.

"We are now running silent," he said, not looking at me.

The Professor scooted along, his disc become sluggish—this time not nearly as high off the ground as before, and complaining in an audible fashion.

The dark landscape of the canyon passed by us in a blur. There were no moons. Only stars in the purpled sky. The Professor could see, though, if one could call his mechanical-cyborg senses sight. What was it like to "look" with Doppler sonar or radar? What images or pictures were in the Professor's head as he steered us through the canyon?

Suddenly the Professor halted.

A trio of spotlights illuminated us from overhead. The loud purring of VTOL fans told me the gig was up. Those were human machines in the air, not mantis.

I suddenly had the desire to lie on the ground, face-down, and put my hands behind my head.

Busted!

"MANTIS SOLDIER," a booming human's voice commanded through an electronic bullhorn, "RELEASE YOUR HUMAN PRISONERS OR WE WILL DESTROY YOU."

Frantic skitter-scratching from the Queen Mother.

"We cannot allow ourselves to be taken," the Professor translated.

But what could we do? The captain and I both put our hands up to shield our eyes against the harsh light. I felt my heart begin to beat double-time. On the one hand, being discovered by Fleet meant our famished sojourn in the alien wilderness had been cut short. On the other hand, it was probable my friend was going to wind up as an *hors d' oeuvre* on some Fleet Intelligence geek's interrogation menu.

"Ma'am," I said. "You'd better be damned right about being able to push the POW angle."

"Set us down, Professor," she said. "I swear on my honor as a Fleet officer that I won't let them hurt you, or the Queen Mother."

There was a moment of agonizing hesitation as the Professor's head tilted this way and that, his antennae waving frantically as he tried to quickly deduce the best course of action: were there any escape routes, and if escape was impossible, could Adanaho be trusted to fulfill her promise?

The canyon suddenly took on an air of claustrophobia.

Slowly, the disc settled to the ground.

The Queen Mother shoved herself off of the disc and began to skitter away—her stubby lower legs moving rapidly on the rock and sand. The Professor's mandibles clacked and chattered violently. I guessed that he was yelling at her? But it did no good.

More spotlights appeared, this time from the ground.

Wheeled trucks roared around a bend in the canyon ahead and squads of human troops began to pile out, quickly surrounding us.

The captain and I both stepped off the Professor's disc, our hands held up.

"I claim these creatures as prisoners of war!" Adanaho shouted at the top of her vocal range. The marines approached us hesitantly, rifles at their shoulders.

"Don't hurt them," I yelled. "They're under our protection."

One of the marines lowered her rifle and walked out of the pack. It was difficult to see her rank in the blinding glare of the spotlights, and the blowing dust from the VTOL fans that kept the gunships aloft.

"Ma'am," the female marine said as she approached us, saluting Adanaho. Then she saw me, and added a quick, "Sir."

The captain and I both reflexively saluted, then dropped our arms.

"Sergeant," the captain said in a trained tone of authority, "I'm giving you a direct order to stand down. Neither of these mantes are armed. They're not a threat to you or your marines. As an officer in Fleet Intelligence, I claim them as POWs."

"Mantis prisoners?" the NCO said, sounding doubtful. She

watched as the Queen Mother continued to scramble, and the Professor's antennae drooped, his body language expressing utter defeat.

"Yes," Adanaho said. "We took them from the *Calysta* before she was destroyed. It's essential that we get these POWs off this planet and into safe keeping. They are vital to the war effort."

"We've got orders to frag every mantis we come across," said the marine. "No exceptions. Hundreds of lifeboats came down all across this world. It's been a hell of a job policing up survivors. Especially with so many mantis patrols running interception."

"Who has orbital space superiority?" the captain asked.

"We do, for the moment," said the NCO. "But that may not last. There's no time to waste, ma'am, sir, we have to get you out of here. And I'm not authorized to bring back any mantis carcasses."

The NCO signaled with a gloved hand and the marines moved in, separating us from the Professor and the Queen Mother—who'd given up escaping, and simply lay prone on the dirt at the Professor's side, exhausted as well as defeated.

A dozen muzzles were trained on them both, and I distinctly heard safeties clicking off.

"NO!" the captain and I both shouted together. We pushed our way through the marines to stand in front of the Professor and the Queen Mother.

"How much more clearly do I have to give a direct order, Sergeant?" Adanaho commanded sternly. "In fact, if I don't see people standing down by the time I get to three, there's going to be hell to pay. One . . . Two . . ."

The squad looked confused. Eyes—covered by goggles—darted from Adanaho's young but determined face, to their squad leader's. The female NCO looked angry, but she wasn't about to ignore the captain.

"At ease," the NCO finally said, slowly pushing a palm down towards the ground. "If she's Fleet Intel like she says she is, we'll let her bosses figure it out. Get the heavy-lift transport in here and we'll evac the lot of them to orbit."

Several *roger that*s echoed around the group, then some of the marines trotted back to their trucks while others remained to guard the mantes. The troops stood close enough to keep the mantes under watchful eyes, but not so close as to be within reach of a swiping forelimb. As I watched their young faces I realized that none of them—save for the squad leader herself—were old enough to have fought in the first war. All they'd ever heard about mantes had come to them from training VR. They stared at the Professor and the Queen Mother the way children might stare at a pair of freshly-landed sharks.

Dangerous monsters.

There was a deafening shriek in the air, and the landscape around us instantly lit as one of the gunships overhead burst into flame.

Other shrieks announced themselves, and suddenly all three of the gunships were coming down in pieces, the wreckage scattering while it burned brightly.

"INCOMING!" the marines yelled collectively.

I scanned the constricted strip of orange-to-purple sky over our heads.

Several swift, lethal-looking shapes swooped over us, their engines sounding distinctly different from those used by humans.

The mantis cavalry had arrived.

PART THREE

The Chaplain's War

CHAPTER 36

Earth (the Moon), 2153 A.D.

WE BOILED FROM THE ASSAULT CARRIER LIKE A SWARM OF ANTS, all of us bounding across the regolith in carefully orchestrated formations that were broken down by platoon and squad. As part of the rear detachment of the command party that was officially detailed to "support" the mock offensive, I hung back with a few other recruit officers and observed the lot of us leapfrogging over the lunar surface: weapons at the ready, arms pantomiming signals as the Charlie Company wireless came alive with the excited but controlled chatter of recruit leadership directing their different elements forward.

In the far distance was a lumpy white and gray mountain. Supposedly that mountain was crawling with mantes. Why we'd not landed closer—or even right smack on top of it—was a mystery to me. Why waste time and potential lives crossing the distance when we could have just pancaked down on them, and gone for the throat?

Chaplain J informed me that simulated anti-ship missile fire from the mountain had necessitated our grounding well short of the objective. Now it would be up to the recruits to go in "old school," using infantry tactics and techniques which had not changed much in hundreds of years. I loped quietly forward with my little group and looked on as our overwatch elements suddenly became pinned down by hostile fire.

In the middle distance, the silhouettes of mantis warriors—not too different from the ones we'd shot at on the qualification ranges—were maneuvering against us in defensive bundles that were not unlike Charlie Company's groups. It occurred to me that we were training against human-controlled, simulated aliens—which were going to fight us like *humans* would. Didn't anybody think that was a bad idea? Wasn't there any record of prior Fleet battles with the mantes, from which to draw sufficient analysis?

Again, Chaplain J filled me in: nobody was entirely sure *how* the mantis infantry fought. But training against something was better than training against nothing.

I voiced my hesitant agreement as Charlie Company began to take casualties.

Recruits tagged by the enemy training lasers were given a warning gong in their speakers, followed by red lights on their helmets coming alive, at which point said recruits were expected to fall in place. Those few who did not fall in place and kept maneuvering were screamed at over the wireless by the DSs, and threatened with punishment detail when we got back to Earth. Presently, everyone with red lights on his or her helmet, flopped immediately into the lunar dust.

"Okay, here we go," Chaplain J said.

I followed her as we broke from the rear and began our own bounding maneuver, with four armed guards as our guides. Occasionally one of them raised a weapon and popped off a shot down range: towards the mantes and their mountain fortress. It occurred to me that our own people were shooting over the heads of our own people, and I remembered how Chaplain J had said Fleet occasionally lost recruits during live-fire exercises.

Once in a while, a mantis silhouette flipped over. Simulated dead. One less bad guy to molest us during the fight.

Chaplain J and I arrived at a squad of recruits from sixth platoon. They'd bunched up behind a small boulder just big enough to protect them from the enemy lasers. Two of the squad had red lights illuminated.

"Dead, or hurt?" I asked.

"Dead," one of them said, while the other said, "hurt."

One of the DSs cut in over the wireless, "Badly wounded, both."

My instinct was to call for the medic and an evac, but then I realized there would be no medic nor any evac. The assault carrier had lifted into the blackness of the sky and was slowly maneuvering away from us, out of the fight. We'd been summarily dumped into the situational meat grinder, and there would be no do-overs now.

I looked at Chaplain J.

"I can't give aid through the suit," I said.

"No, you can't," she said. "If these were real hits, the suit would be doing that automatically. You have to assume these two are severely hurt and your job is to offer comfort."

I looked at the unlucky victims, who merely looked back at me. Their faces were vaguely familiar. People I'd passed in the chow line or on one of the endless number of details to which I'd been assigned.

"Uh, how do I tell their affiliation? I can't even see their ID tags."

"Ask," she said firmly.

"Uhh, right. Guys, do either of you, uhhh, you know, belong to a church?"

They each cracked grins and seemed to find me supremely funny.

"Eff this," I said under my breath. "It's stupid."

Chaplain J cuffed the side of my helmet.

"Nothing stupid about it, recruits," she said to all of us on the squad wireless. "You two wouldn't be laughing if you had holes in your torsos and were slowly bleeding out. Now answer the Recruit Chaplain's question before I put all of you on the detail list."

Their smiles disappeared.

"Catholic," one of them said.

"Nothing," said the other.

"Atheist?" I said.

"Uhhh, no, just, well, hell, Rastafarian."

"I didn't bring you any weed," I said.

"Eff you," the joker replied.

I turned to the Catholic. At least here there was something I could work with. I'd done enough reading to understand that for Catholics, there was a last rite involved. I tapped a couple of small keys on the left wrist of my suit and called up the block of text I'd preloaded into the suit's memory. The text hovered in my helmet display: a glowing sequence of words preserved in my field of vision.

Mumbling my way through it, I felt fantastically uncomfortable. When I was done, the recruit—Jones—had a surprised look on his face.

"That's not in the reading I gave you," Chaplain J said.

"I looked it up online while we were en route," I replied.

"Problem is, you're not an ordained priest in the Catholic church."

"Does it matter?" I asked.

"It might matter to *him,*" she said, pointing at Jones.

He smiled at me. "Thanks anyway, bro. My mom would have liked that. Priest or no priest."

I chanced a look around me—at the tense faces of those squad members who were still fighting—and wondered why God would even care whether or not I was a Catholic, assuming Jones were in fact dying. I decided for the purposes of the LCX any kind of effort on my part was better than no effort at all. So I refocused my attention on the joker.

"Seriously," I said. "No affiliation?"

"Nothing," he replied.

"Nothing at all?"

"Nope."

"Okay then. Well, you and, uhhh, Jones here, are both hurt plenty bad. And I don't know if you're gonna make it. But I'll stay right here until we either get an evac, or until, uhhh, well, you know, uh—"

"Right," he said.

I reflexively grabbed his hand through his suit's gauntlet.

We each squeezed tightly.

And we stayed that way, just looking at each other, until forty-five seconds later the lights on his helmet went from red to blue.

"Recruit Sungh, KIA," said a DS over the wireless. "Don't move a muscle, and enjoy the rest of the show."

Sungh let his hand fall to his side.

He smiled up at me and tried to speak, but I suddenly discovered I couldn't hear him.

Oh yes, I'd forgotten. Killed-In-Action troops were cut out of the wireless entirely—so as to make them as dead as could be to those of us around them.

I tipped my finger to my helmet and dropped it in his direction. Sungh nodded at me and laid back calmly, staring up into space.

Jones was still red.

I held his hand for a good three minutes before his lights went blue.

"Recruit Jones, KIA," said the same DS.

I imagined that the DSs were keeping tabs on all the Charlie Company casualties via computer roster. I wondered how many we'd lost, or were losing. Were things going well? Since arriving at this particular squad's position I'd dropped out of the recruit command wireless entirely.

Tapping more keys on my suit's wrist, I plugged back in.

Recruit command wireless was frazzled. People were dropping orders over the top of other people. Frago this and frago that. So many fragmentary orders at once, I couldn't tell what the hell was going on. Suddenly a couple of mantis dummies appeared over the top of the rock I was crouched behind.

The entire squad screamed in unison—a very real sound—and opened up with their rifles. Rounds—also very real—chewed into the steel mantis silhouettes, which flipped backwards and drifted to the soil. Their maneuvering units automatically grounded.

In prep for the LCX we'd all done practice maneuvers using "rubber duck" weapons equipped with CO_2 canisters and firing semi-hard pellets filled with red jelly. Those pellets had hurt like the dickens. So that we'd all learned fairly quickly that carelessness with friendly fire was a good way to bruise up your buddies. Which might lead to a bruising of a different kind if certain people didn't watch their sectors of fire, and use discretion.

Now, things had gotten serious. About as serious as they were liable to get, short of an actual combat action.

I stared at the bullet holes in the mantis silhouettes and imagined what a real mantis might look like. Were they green and disgusting on the inside, like when I'd stepped on a grasshopper back home? Or did they have blood the way we humans have blood? Was it warm?

Suddenly the squad was up and moving. Me and mine just sat and watched them go. I was still hearing the chaos of the command wireless, but apparently that particular squad had been ordered forward.

I waved goodbye to Sungh and Jones—who looked halfway to falling asleep as they lay in the boulder's protective shade—and followed Chaplain J out into the hard sunlight. Our face shields immediately deployed. Their one-way mirrored surfaces would protect us from going blind or getting burned by the sun's intense rays. Without atmosphere or an ozone layer, the sunshine on the Moon could get mighty hot and dangerous.

There, another squad clustered around a couple of wounded—taking refuge behind another small boulder.

Again, I asked the requisite questions. This time, I found a Buddhist and an agnostic.

I had to ask, "What's the difference?"

The Buddhist rolled her eyes at me while the agnostic laughed.

I held their hands and scoured my mind for words of comfort, forcing them out hesitantly and with no small degree of embarrassment. Eventually their helmet lights turned blue, they were ordered to lie still, and I could no longer hear them as they were cut out of the wireless.

Their squad also advanced, leaving me to look at Chaplain J as she looked over the top of the boulder at the simulated battle going on beyond.

"One person couldn't possibly keep up with it all," I said.

"Pardon?" she said, coming back from her far-gazing reverie.

"One chaplain," I said. "If the casualties were piling up fast, no single chaplain could handle everyone all at once."

"In a real fight," Chaplain J said, "you wouldn't be the only one. Though the chances of you finding each of the casualties still conscious, or even living, wouldn't be as good as it is for us today. You'd be finding corpses, not wounded. Perhaps seven times out of ten. Even given how advanced these armor suits are, the weaponry of the enemy is very efficient. And space is very deadly, even when we're not getting shot at. Most of the time you'd be getting to the dead long after the fact. Or hauling the less critically wounded back to the rear, with the medical people."

Which is precisely what I wound up doing a few minutes later.

Some of the recruit medics—assigned to their roles, like all of us—had set up a makeshift aid station to the rear of the fight. When next Chaplain J and I bounded out to check on a squad with recruits who had red lights, those lights were flickering between red and yellow, back and forth. Hit, but not doomed. Not yet. And someone had to help get them back to where they could maybe have more done for them? Whatever that might be. Without a vacuum shelter there was no way to peel a person out of his or her armor without sentencing the troop to instant death.

But the red-yellows couldn't move on their own.

So I wound up doing stretcher duty—thankful for the low gravity, and resentful of the bulkiness and clumsiness of the armor suit.

DSs—also in armor suits—had clustered near the ad hoc aid station, and were seemingly making remarks to each other on the secure cadre wireless while half a dozen medics were putting hole patches on suits or inflating balloon bandages around limbs too imaginarily mangled for hole patches. The vital signs monitors on each of the wounded were carefully checked and integrated into a closed medical wireless loop, to which I was summarily added without my consent. Suddenly eight different waving sets of vitals appeared in my field of vision, each with a name next to it.

I noted that one of the wounded was a recruit platoon sergeant from fifth platoon.

"Are we winning?" I asked her as I pulled out a patch, per the DS nearest her pointing at her leg and informing us she had a hole in it.

"Can't quite tell," she said. "Fifth platoon was split and I was trying to get us formed up on our weapons squad when a fat wad of mantes came over the top of a low rise and creamed us. Most of my squad were blue-lined immediately. The rest grabbed me and hauled it for the back of the battle. And dropped me here."

I looked around and noticed more red-yellows being dropped off.

"How many casualties in all?" I asked the recruit platoon sergeant.

"Uhhh," she said, tapping keys on her suit's wrist while I applied the patch to the imaginary hole where the drill sergeant had pointed.

"Sixty-eight," she said.

"Dead?" I said.

"Not all. Command stats wireless shows twenty-one wounded, the rest permanently out of action."

Heavy casualties, considering the fact that the fight was only about twenty minutes old. Charlie Company was down roughly a quarter of its total strength.

I keyed my way back into the command wireless. Things still seemed chaotic.

Once I was convinced my patch job would hold, I slapped the recruit platoon sergeant on her shoulder and went to work on others.

Then I was summarily called away as a squad from first platoon began howling for medical support.

I bounded behind the two medics who went with me, Chaplain J, and our four assigned guards.

One of whom became a blue-liner along the way. One more was blue-lined on the way back. For the sake of three more simulated wounded.

Back and forth. Forward, and out.

I found blue-liners and red-yellows and reds-soon-to-be-blue. When the cluster of casualties at the aid station had passed thirty, I was sweating profusely and growing quite exhausted. Even in the weak lunar gravity, carrying someone—or assisting someone in the process of being carried—was strenuous work. Such that by the time the fight was over an hour old, I was trudging my way forward, not always looking where I was going, and allowing myself to be led by Chaplain J, who exhorted me forward with every new call for help.

"Might as well be a corpsman," I said, huffing.

"We do a lot of that," Chaplain J said, bouncing her way in front of me. "Since chaplains don't carry weapons—we have chaplains' assistants for that—we pretty much try to find ways to keep ourselves useful. One thing we didn't do back on the carrier was have a pre-battle service."

"What's that?" I asked.

"If there had been time, and if we'd have been headed for a real fight, I'd have spared time to set up something on one of the assault carrier decks—where people could come and get a last dose of spiritual pick-me-up. Even offer confession, if I were ordained and authorized to hear it."

"Confession?"

"Catholic stuff. Didn't you look that up too?"

"No," I admitted.

"Anyway, as the chaplain you don't send your flock into battle without a last bit of hope and a prayer. Doesn't matter whether those who come to hear it are truly believers, or just the kinds of atheists and agnostics who temporarily find faith when it suits them. The Fleet chaplain's job is to support the spiritual well-being of the Fleet soldiers. Before, during, and after the battle."

"I doubt I'll have any energy left over, even to tend to my own bladder," I said, becoming annoyed by the fact that any sweat that ran into my eyes could not be wiped away—with my hand hitting the transparency of my helmet's face plate.

"Just be glad these wounded and dead are all simulated," she said. "If they were real..."

She didn't finish her thought.

CHAPTER 37

MY HEART RATE WENT TO TRIPLE-TIME.

The war—humans versus the mantes, round two—had suddenly become real again.

The burning remnants of human aircraft lay scattered across the canyon, or steaming in the river itself. Marines were firing their rifles indiscriminately into the air. Whatever had attacked and destroyed the gunships was momentarily gone. Though I suspected they would return, probably with drop pods loaded with mantis shock troops. I'd seen such in action on Purgatory. The canyon was about to become a slaughterhouse.

I saw the Professor with the Queen Mother half aboard his disc. They'd been pushed far out into the river by a trio of marines who were shouting at them, rifles raised and aimed dead-center.

Captain Adanaho was between the marines and the Professor, water up to her waist. She'd pulled out her sidearm and pointed it at the marines.

Humans hurled incomprehensible commands at each other.

One of the rifles went off.

Captain Adanaho was pitched backwards into the water.

Alien jets howled down on us. The water around the trio of marines suddenly erupted with hundreds of little fountains. What was left of the trio began to drift down stream.

Not caring whether I was next to be fragged, I plunged into the river and strove mightily to reach the captain. Her body was limply drifting with the current, and the Professor stared dumbly at it as it passed both him and the Queen Mother, who also stared dumbly.

I threw myself forward and began to breaststroke, the water chill and electric on my skin. My hand finally hit something soft. I knotted my fist into the fabric of the captain's uniform and began to beat back towards the shore.

When I came out, my chest heaved for air.

I dragged the captain's limp body onto the sand at the river's edge.

Turning her over, I observed the bloody hole in the front of her uniform. A liver shot? Warm blackness flooded from the wound and the captain's eyes blinked furiously as she tried to draw breath. Whispered gasps were all she could manage.

"Oh God, no," I said, wishing madly for one of the med kits in our packs. Which were who knew how far away. The current had taken us downriver too quickly for me to correctly reckon where camp might be. And there was still shooting happening, though from whom and towards whom I could not be certain. Lacking a better idea, I pressed my hand hard on the wound and willed the bleeding to stop.

The captain groaned loudly and clutched at my arm with both hands. Her eyes were wide and she stared up at me.

"Chief," she spat. I read her lips more than I heard her.

"Ma'am," I said, trying to sound calm, "you're hurt bad, and I have to stop the bleeding."

"Chief," she said again, our eyes locked. I quickly lowered my ear to her face. Her voice rasped and sputtered.

"The Queen Mother," Adanaho said, "you've got to protect her. She is the key, Chief. She has been . . . chosen. Like you. Padre . . ."

I started to blubber my incomprehension, then looked up to see the Professor hovering almost directly above us. The Queen Mother slid off the front of his disc and came to Adanaho's side—her forelimbs framed Adanaho's young face as the captain fought to draw additional breath, but could not.

I pressed harder, to combat the gushing blood, but felt in my heart that it was no use.

"We must flee!" The Professor commanded. "Caught in the crossfire, we will all die."

"We can't move the captain!" I hollered, looking up at my friend with a sense of panicked helplessness ripping me up inside.

A trail of bullets spattered across the sand near us.

The Professor spun on his vertical axis to face the four marines who advanced with rifles up. I couldn't see them, but I could hear them splashing through the river shallows. Automatic fire stuttered and suddenly I was flattened across Adanaho's body as the Professor lowered his disc right down on top of us: me, the captain, and the Queen Mother.

"My friend," the Professor said, "I regret to inform you that—"

He never finished his sentence. Bullets *pinged* and *panged* off his disc. Some tore through chitin, slicing mantis organs and soft tissue. The Professor's disc moved forward three meters, then gouged its bow into the wet sand—the disc proper tilting up like a shield. I looked up to see the silhouette of his thorax and limbs flailing around the disc's black edge, bits and pieces of him coming off and mantis blood splattering.

Then I put my head down as a concentrated series of bursts from the advancing marines shredded the Professor's disc completely.

It split in two and burst into flame, sparks and electrical arcing lighting up the horrific scene of the Professor's dismantled body.

The sky roared. Mantis fighters overhead. Making a third sweep of the canyon. The marines in the shallows vanished in a blinding display of pinpoint antipersonnel rocketry.

I flattened across Adanaho's body. Long moments of silence followed.

The Professor's disc slowly smoldered, so close I could smell the cooking flesh. I turned my eyes back to Adanaho's face. She stared up at me unblinking, her mouth half open but not drawing breath.

I began to hurl obscenities at the cosmos. Towards any deity or deities that would listen. I damned the Professor. I damned the Queen Mother, and the mantes, and the marines, and the awful stupidity of precious lives cut short. I damned Earth. I damned the Fleet. I even damned Adanaho for being young and idealistic and coming to me as if I had some power over circumstances; enough to alter the course of history. Such idealism had gotten her killed, and all I could do was sit there, soaked and cold and clutching the captain's lifeless hand in my own.

A slow build of tortured sobs burst out of me as I lowered my forehead to Adanaho's chest and shook with grief. For her. For my alien friend. For the fate of two species apparently committed to annihilation.

After a few moments I heard the Queen Mother suddenly rise up, her wings unfolding and extending to maximum width. I opened my eyes and looked. Enough light was coming down into the Canyon now that I could see her clearly. She watched the sky.

A loud, thunderous, mechanized whining to my rear me told me that the drop pods had finally come. Multiple buzzing sounds told me the shock troops—their armored discs studded with a variety of lethal weapons—were on top of us.

Perhaps it was for the best. To end things in this manner. I wasn't sure I wanted to live to see the mantis war machine slowly grind the planets of human space to powder. Instead of a quick termination, now there would be a long, drawn-out, dreadful fistfight as the Fleet contracted and toughened its defensive circle. World after world would be *cleansed* of humanity. Until at last Earth would fall under mantis crosshairs.

The final stand.

And then . . . humanity would join the handful of other extinct races in the mantis archives. A dead people, wiped from the face of the galaxy by a species determined to have the stars to itself.

I kept my eyes closed and held the captain's hand tight.

The buzzing was loud now. They had to be just meters away.

A sharp hissing cut through the mechanized sound. It was a shrill, painful sound, almost like fingernails on a chalkboard. I reflexively looked up to see the source, and saw the Queen Mother hovering over myself and Adanaho, her wings fluttering and beating the air ferociously. Her mouth was open as wide as possible and her tractor teeth were vibrating so quickly they were a blur. It must have taken an astounding effort for her manage the display, but it had gotten the attention of her subordinates.

Several dozen mantis soldiers surrounded us, looking unsure of what to do. Those in the front rank were recoiling at the sight of the Queen Mother: a mantis without her carriage, unchained, feral, her insect eyes adamant.

Her hiss slowly died in her throat, followed by a rapid series of clicks and clacks as she spoke to her people in their own language. I couldn't be sure what she was saying, but their reaction was immediate. A path opened through the mass of soldiers allowing four other mantes to maneuver forward. I didn't see weapons on their discs. In fact, their discs seemed like the Professor's.

Were these medics? I could only guess.

Two of them converged on the remains of the Professor. The other two on the Queen Mother herself, who settled onto her small lower legs and began to instruct the lot of them, her forelimbs waving and pointing with the distinct authority of one bred to rule.

None of them touched me. Nor the body of the captain. The troops moved back, then began to disperse. Securing the area, no doubt.

I slowly sat up, tears and mucus down the front of my wet uniform, and glared at the Queen Mother. She sat on the sand, her wings folded tightly and her beak shut. She glared right back, her eyes alien but her posture erect and dignified.

Eventually the medics returned with what appeared to be a small disc—a carriage without an owner. Though I guessed by size that it was only temporary, for the Queen Mother's benefit. She looked at me for a long while, not saying anything, and me not saying anything to her. Then she slowly climbed aboard the disc and settled into the saddle. A series of squeaking and mechanical snapping sounds told me she was being re-integrated. She shuddered once and her mouth opened in irritation, then the disc rose off the ground.

Hovering over to myself and the body of the captain, the Queen Mother announced, "Pick up your captain. There is a transport waiting for us. I have a truce to call!"

CHAPTER 38

Earth (the Moon), 2153 A.D.

WE DIDN'T TAKE THE ENTIRE MOUNTAIN UNTIL THE MIDDLE OF the following day. At which point none of us had gotten any sleep, and Charlie Company had amassed sixty-three percent casualties. Positive devastation, for any line unit. At least according to Fleet doctrine. But lucky for us we were "reinforced" by a second "company" which had extracted from an imaginary nearby objective. In other words, the wounded and the dead were magically resurrected, putting us back at full strength for the remainder of the LCX.

Inside the mountain we found vacuum-tight compartments and quarters, hideously painted and festooned with alien-looking props. Almost like the set of a horror movie.

"The hive," Malvino called it, looking proud.

I guessed that he and the other DSs had put in a lot of labor on the thing. Again, without knowing what the inside of a mantis installation really looked like, they were guessing—and channeling a lot of Hollywood in the process. Right down to the smell. Which seemed to be a vague mixture of rotting pig carcass and dog dung.

"Ya ain't gotta like it," said Schmetkin when she noticed my wrinkled nose the first time I pulled off my helmet. "But as long as your suit says it's safe to breathe, it's safe to breathe. You'll be lucky if things are this posh out on one of the mantis worlds. Be happy you get to lie down for a couple of hours."

And I was. Oh yes, I was.

Since the former wounded and dead had been more or less lying about for the past thirty-six hours, they were immediately put on task reworking the defenses of the objective and prepping for a presumed immediate counterstrike by the simulated mantes. The rest of us were allowed to use the heads—plenty of those in this supposedly alien warren—and grab a quick bite of food. Cold rations. The kind you wouldn't touch under normal circumstances, but will wolf down with delight when it's been at least a day since you had anything proper to eat.

We couldn't exactly take our armor off. But we dressed down as far as we dared, with only an occasional growl from a DS, and tried to find quiet corners in which to curl up and grab a few winks.

One thing about the many weeks of training: they had forced me to learn the trick of falling asleep quickly, at any time, anywhere. I was reasonably certain my brain was off before my skull touched the rolled-up rations sack I'd elected to use as a pillow. My brain stayed off when the various jostlings and mutterings of the similarly-incapacitated souls around me formed a dull, monotonous background noise for dreams.

Strange dreams. Of never being in the Fleet. Of going back to my civilian life as if I'd never walked over to that recruiter's table with my friends. As if there was no war presently happening, far out on the frontiers of human settlement in the galaxy.

Wishful thinking, I suppose?

I eventually came around when a persistent hand kept nudging me.

"Barlow, Barlow," said the female voice.

I groaned and sat up.

Cortez looked at me, a small smile on her face.

"You're back on-line in thirty minutes," she said.

"How long was I out? And where the hell have you been all this time?"

"Four hours, give or take. Me? I was lucky in that I got shot within the first ten minutes of the offensive. Had a nice, leisurely nap out there on the surface. Regolith is soft as a pillow, did you notice? Anyway, we're nearing the end of LCX Day Two and the cadre wants every recruit on the line at dusk."

"Does the Moon even have dusk?" I said.

"Stand to," she said.

"Oh, right."

Another remnant of infantry eras past. In theory, the brief periods of semi-light right before true dawn and right before actual night were the best periods to attack. When would-be defenders would be hardest pressed to notice bad guys slithering up to the line and/or would be most disoriented in the event of a counterattack. Not that anyone had consulted the mantis playbook. Especially not here on the Moon, where conventional Earth notions of day and night were on holiday.

But some traditions never die.

I collected myself, got to my feet, ran for the nearest head, then returned presently and allowed myself to be lead away to the windows. How or why mantes would install square windows in an underground installation was beyond me. But there they were. Row after row of them. Recruits clustered closely together while DSs roamed around behind, like sharks. Watching, listening, and waiting.

I found my command group, but no Chaplain J. Odd, that. Was I going to be flying solo for the second round?

The chatter indicated that enemy action was expected any minute. The recruit captain and lieutenants were poring over a digital projection map displayed on one wall, which had been cleared of "eggs" and other pseudo-alien debris. Half the weapons squads had been hunkered down in fighting positions equidistant around the mountain, while the other half were detailed to a single mobile body being held in reserve: for instant reaction towards whichever side of the mountain got hit.

Standard squads had been placed out at listening posts far down on the plains, at least one to two kilometers from the mountain's base. Supposedly satellite and Fleet orbital watch were being "jammed," so it was up to human eyes to do what machines would normally be useful for. Which made me wonder for the umpteenth time why Charlie Company was not working alongside or in support of heavier armor elements. The Fleet arsenal included an array of tanks and fighting personnel movers, in addition to different kinds of gunships and other air-to-ground support vehicles that could effectively eliminate the need for a foot fight.

"If you make it to marine training," one DS snarled at me as I dared to voice these questions aloud, "you'll get to play with the heavy stuff. For now, shut up and run the defense of this position like you've been taught. You'll notice that none of the mantis troops you've faced have had tanks or gunships either. So why are you bitching?"

Which was good enough for me—point taken.

With recruit command relying on wireless communications for all relevant updates, they were glued to the map, making constant, fidgeting changes—with occasional input from this or that cadre member who just happened to walk by when the recruit captain and recruit lieutenants were hashing things out with the recruit first sergeant and the recruit platoon sergeants.

I specifically avoided Thukhan's gaze. I didn't have the will or the energy to deal with him at the moment. Mostly I was hoping that the talk of an imminent counterstrike was bogus, so that maybe we could back off the line a bit—and I could go steal a few more minutes of sleep.

My hope was short-lived as the command wireless began to light up with reports of mantis troops closing in on several of the furthest scout squads, lying in wait for just such contact with enemy forces.

"Here we go," the recruit captain said.

People began to scatter. Squads and platoons formed up near the airlocks and began to cycle through. Without Chaplain J to lead the way, I cast about until I located the medic team, and hung with them. Most of whom had been rotated out of their jobs in favor of fresh blood—no pun—who hadn't had to carry the load during the first assault. So that it was me who wound up explaining to them how things would more or less work, once the casualties began to stack up.

And stack up they did.

Once it became apparent that the simulated mantes were attacking the mountain with an even larger force than the one which had first defended it, I guessed that Charlie Company was in for its George Armstrong Custer moment. No doubt this was some kind of object lesson to all of us about the need to stand fast and hold our ground despite overwhelming odds.

Bounding up and down the mountain chasing wounded proved to be even more of a workout than it had on the first day.

This time, however, there was literally no possible way of keeping up. There were just too many. All of the forward elements were wiped out simultaneously, indicating that a "noose" of mantes was constricting around the mountain. I helped gather wounded back to the aid area, went back for more, and each time found our perimeter foreshortened by at least a quarter of a kilometer.

The cooling system in my armor suit was working overtime, trying to keep pace with the tremendous amount of exertion I was making. I had put my actions on autopilot. Almost relishing the idea of getting lasered into inactivity, such that I could make myself a bed in the regolith and catch my breath.

That's when the call came in. Not a standard training casualty call. But a frantic, desperate-sounding cry of alarm.

Somebody had actually been hurt.

I was pouncing across the Moon's surface with three other medics—hearts thudding in our chests—when I saw a moon car with Fleet colors zoom over the tops of our heads. Presently, I arrived to find several cadre working over the prone body of a recruit who was covered in regolith dust up to his helmet. They'd slapped an inflatable bandage around one leg and were trying to get a hole patch sealed over the lower left side of the recruit's stomach.

The cadre picked the recruit up and gently carried him to the bed of the lunar car, then one of them turned and looked at me and said, "You, into the back. Put your hands *here* and don't move. He's bleeding heavily."

I spared only a momentary glance for the recruit hunched at the car's side, her R77A5 hanging limply from one hand. I couldn't see her face due to her sun shield being down, but I intuited that whatever had happened to the poor fool in the car's bed, it had been her fault.

The car lifted and was suddenly zooming back towards the mountain. I kept my wits about me and pressed both hands over the patch on the recruit's stomach. He lay limply, and I suddenly realized I knew him.

CAPACHA was stenciled along the collar of his helmet.

"Christ," I muttered to no one in particular. "What happened?"

"Friendly fire," one of the two cadre said. "You're a recruit medic?"

"Recruit chaplain," I said.

That I hadn't added the requisite *Drill Sergeant,* and that the cadre person hadn't chewed me out for failing to properly address her, told me all I needed to know about the seriousness of the situation. We overshot the entrances to the mock mantis base and flew to the very crown of the mountain, where a large set of double doors were hanging open, and the car glided in.

The cadre hopped out and suddenly I found that they and two other cadre were bodily lifting both myself and Capacha out of the car—the stretcher below us having been invisible to me as I'd clambered aboard and focused all of my attention on the wounded recruit. We were hustled into an airlock, which cycled quickly, then rushed into a larger interior room—no mock mantis paraphernalia this time—which was home to a pair of real Fleet medics and what appeared to be a real fleet physician to boot.

My suit told me that pressure was green safe, but I kept my hands on the patch until one of the medics shooed me off, and I stood up and backed away, dumbly looking down at Capacha as they pulled his helmet and gloves off with the emergency-release toggles.

He looked pale.

But his eyes fluttered and came to focus on me.

He raised an arm weakly in my direction as the medics began to split the top of his suit off of him, exposing the pink-and-red lumpy foam that had discharged into the suit the second the bullet had struck Capacha's stomach.

I pulled my helmet off and threw it down as the medics continued to work.

"The torso's fine," one of them said, "it's the leg artery that's the problem."

Capacha kept his arm stretched out to me. I knelt down next to him, trying to stay out of the way. If the cadre or medics were upset with me, they didn't show it.

Pulling my gauntlets off, I grabbed Capacha's hand in mine, my knees at his left ear as we looked at each other.

"Barlow," he said in a whisper.

"The pros have got you now," I said, forcing a smile. "Must hurt like a sunuvabitch, but you're gonna be okay."

"You're a bad liar," Capacha said, forcing a smile of his own. Then he began to cough, which appeared to agonize him as the medics and, now, the doctor, worked furiously on his leg.

"Almost time to graduate," Capacha said. "Aren't you glad you took my advice?"

I must have looked baffled because he began to laugh, and wound up coughing again for his trouble.

"You don't remember, do you?"

"Remember what?" I asked.

"Back in reception, I was one of the holdovers. I was also the guy who caught you that night, walking towards the head with your weapon, ready to butt-stroke Thukhan. Remember what I said to you then? You took my advice."

Suddenly it dawned on me.

And suddenly I had to know.

"Why did you help me?" I asked. "We haven't said more than four sentences to each other this whole time."

"Because you helped me," he said.

"How?"

"Little things... here and there. Mainly you were the first person I ever saw in Reception who wanted to take this shit seriously. And after the way Thukhan... got himself out of work, I... started to think. That... maybe it was time to straighten my act out."

Capacha's armor was now entirely off his body and the foam that had encased his wounded leg looked dangerously soaked with thick, dark blood.

I could tell in his eyes—he was losing the battle.

One of the medics checked Capacha's tags and then rushed to a nearby cart for two bags: one clear saline, the other filled with bright red, oxygenated blood. An IV went into each arm and the volume drip spigots were opened all the way. One of the medics began to massage the blood bag, seeing as how the Moon's gravity made the flow sluggish. I offered to take over that chore, which the medic gratefully let me do so that she and the other medic, and the doc, could try to hit the leg wound.

"Hell of a way to earn your first medal," I half-joked as I gently ran my hands along the sides of the blood pouch, pushing the red fluid down through the IV tube with as much force as I dared.

"As if they give... medals for dying... while being stupid."

"Not your fault, man," I said. "You can't help it if someone else got careless."

"No," Capacha said. "It was... me. *I was careless.* Didn't break contact when I was... ordered to do it. Got left... behind. Tried to... catch up. Made it through a bunch of... mantes. Wound up in the middle. Tried to wave my arms. But it was... too late. When the... mantes got hit, I... got hit too."

Capacha craned his head back to look at one of the cadre.

"My fault," Capacha said, gritting his teeth.

"Mine . . ." he said.

Then his eyes dropped closed.

I stopped massaging the bag and took up Capacha's hand as it lay on the floor. I explored his wrist and felt his pulse—weak, tenuous—gradually slow, and stop.

"Shit," I said, and instinctively dropped his hand, putting my legs over his torso and bracing myself on his sternum with my fingers laced together to form a double fist on his sternum. I shoved down as hard as I could five times, then leaned down and put a cheek to Capacha's mouth, which hung half open.

There was no reassuring warmth nor moisture of breath.

I put my mouth fully over his and blew hard, feeling my own ribs complain. Five more quick compressions on his chest. A breath. Five more quick compressions on his chest. A breath. Just like they'd taught us. Just like I'd memorized.

And after ten iterations, there was nothing. No response.

I kept going.

After twenty iterations, I was shaking badly, and still nothing.

One of the medics put his hand gently on my quivering shoulder.

"You can stop now, kid," the sergeant said gently. "Bullet tore right through the femoral. Once we opened the foam around the wound there was no way to stop the bleeding in time. Maybe if he'd not already lost so much, in getting to us . . . but it's over."

I wanted to scream at the medic, but held my tongue.

I sat up—lungs heaving—and stared down at the slack, pale face of the man who had quite probably done me one of the biggest favors anyone had ever done me in my short life. He'd been right, about me wanting to take out Thukhan. About me not having the lethal edge it took to go in and cut a man down in cold blood. I'd turned a decisive corner that night, and all because a stranger had been kind enough to talk me out of a stupid choice.

And now he was dead.

The two medics helped me to my feet, which almost came out from under me. I stumbled away from Capacha's body and thumped my left shoulder against a wall, and slowly slid down to a sitting position, my knees curled up to my chin. I hugged my lower legs and clenched my eyes closed, willing the tears to retreat. Which they did not. I could feel them sprouting from the edges of my eyelids and running scalding-hot down my face.

The mantis threat was light-years away, and already, people were dying.

I remotely heard the medics take Capacha away, as well as a detail that came to clean up the blood. If the cadre cared that I was ignoring everyone and everything around me, they didn't say anything. They simply went back through the airlock, took the moon car, and left.

I let my forehead rest on my knees.

Exhaustion seemed to sweep me back to the same place I'd been before: to the vision of myself and my former life, free of the Fleet and free of the training hell of IST. It seemed an altogether surreal life, where a man could eat as he pleased, drink as he pleased, wake up and go to sleep when he pleased...

"Barlow, Barlow," said a female voice.

Only this time it wasn't Cortez.

I picked my head up and looked into the eyes of Chaplain J.

"Are you okay?" she asked.

I simply shook my head from side to side.

"Come on, kid," she said, getting up off one knee and offering me both hands. Like me, she was still in her armor suit, but with helmet and gauntlets off. Her legs were coated in lunar dust. She'd been traipsing about *somewhere,* even if it hadn't been in the immediate AO.

I weakly put my hands out, grasped her hands, and let her pull me up to a standing position. She pressed a thermos mug of something warm into my hands. I put the spigot to my lips and sucked. Deliciously hot chocolate flowed across my tongue. I swallowed hard, took another mouthful, and swallowed hard again.

"What's happening with the others?" I asked.

"The battle is over. The mantes retook their mountain," she said.

"I figured as much. The odds were badly against us."

"On purpose."

"Yup, I figured that too. Did anyone else get hurt?"

"A few sprains and strains, and a few bumps and bruises, but no, nobody else got shot."

"What happens to the recruit who gunned down Capacha?"

"Cadre say that the victim says it was his fault. There will be an official investigation. They'll gather audio and video and eyewitness accounts. To determine if anyone should be punished. Meanwhile Charlie Company's actual commander and actual first sergeant are going to have to write Private Capacha's family a couple of very sorry letters."

"*Private* Capacha?"

"Worst way I know of getting promoted. But Fleet figures that any recruit who dies on the job ought to deserve full membership honors. To include burial at a Fleet cemetery back on Earth if the Capacha family so desires it. Did you know him well?"

"Not hardly," I said. "But he was the best friend I had."

She gave me an ironic look.

At which point she guided me to a bench along one of the walls, and I told her the whole story—in between gulps of near-scalding cocoa.

"I guess I ought to be getting back," I finally said.

"Don't worry about it, kid," Chaplain J said. "You were with me on the way up, you'll be with me on the way back. At this point nobody from cadre is going to question it if I keep you under my wing. Besides, I want to talk to you about something."

I looked at her.

"What's that, ma'am?"

"You've got heart, Barlow. A good one. The Fleet needs that. Unless you're dramatically opposed, I'm going to send some e-mails when we get back to Earth and have you put directly into Chaplain's Assistant training."

"Just like that? What about graduation?"

"Oh, you'll still do the parade field routine like everyone else. Clean out your locker and kick off a final, high salute to your drill sergeants. But the Fleet needs you. You haven't been told this, but things on the frontier may not be going exactly as well as everyone believes. Some big offensive missions are being put together. World-walloping stuff. I've got friends in the Chaplains Corps going out on some of those missions. They will need a smart, sensitive guy like you. You game?"

I numbly thought about the offer. I'd made a pretty piss-poor chaplain. But as I sat there staring at the floor, one of Chaplain J's kind arms draped comfortingly around my shoulder, I suddenly realized that I probably didn't have anything to lose.

"Sure thing," I finally said. "Sounds like a plan."

CHAPTER 39

THE MANTIS DROP POD CARRIER WAS VOLUMINOUS BY FLEET standards.

With no benches, seats, nor chairs of human description, I simply sat on the carrier's bare deck with Captain Adanaho's head resting in my lap. I'd retrieved my pack and spread my emergency sleeping bag over her body. Disinfectant wipes from the med kit had allowed me to clean away the water, sand, and blood from her face. I'd closed her eyelids and given her as much dignity as I was able at the moment. Having no idea where my final destination might be, I was hoping there would be better means with which to properly care for the body.

There were four mantis troops in the compartment with me. Once upon a time I'd have been mortally afraid of them. Now?

I wasn't terribly sure I cared what would happen. If the Queen Mother was as good as her word, she'd attempt to stop the fighting. Assuming she could regain control of her own forces first. For myself I felt only guilt over the passing of the officer—the young woman—in front of me. She'd come to me on Purgatory, filled with hope. She'd believed I was special. That I could make a difference. And it had ultimately cost her her life.

I'd also lost a good friend. The Professor had given his life for the Queen Mother—primarily—but I believed he'd given it for the captain and me as well. He'd wanted to preserve the peace—just like Adanaho—and he'd been willing to risk and lose his life in the process. When he'd first appeared in my chapel those many years ago, I'd thought him no different than the warriors who guarded the carrier deck on which I now sat. I'd learned otherwise.

The mantes could be as individual as any human. And he had been exceptional in so many ways. With him gone, would the Queen Mother be the single voice of peace among her people?

A slight rumble told me we'd gone transonic prior to boosting into orbit. I readied myself for the sickening sensation of micro-gravity. When it never came I was both confused and relieved. But then it occurred to me that the mantes had had much more time than humanity to refine their engineering—that they could build artificial gravity cells small enough to fit on a craft the size of the carrier was not that much of a surprise.

I waited and wondered what life might be like on one of their bigger ships. So far as I knew I was going to be the first human to ever board one. At least of my own free will. During the first war there had been rumors of mantis ships ramming human vessels, the mantis shock troops storming into the besieged human ships and "harvesting" human crews. Whether or not those rumors were actually true had never been determined. After I met the Professor, and the armistice was secured, I chalked those rumors up to creative propaganda.

Now, though, I felt a tickle of cold unease—as the minutes went by before docking.

A few more rumbles, followed by occasional mild lurches, and suddenly the main deck ramp was unsealing with a hiss. My ears felt the pressure differential. I forced a yawn and worked my jaw side to side in an attempt to pop my ears while I watched the ramp lower down to a different, much larger deck entirely. Six mantis soldiers floated up the ramp to where I held the captain's body. One of them towed a flat sled which appeared to function in the same manner as the discs themselves.

"You will place the female on the transport," one of them ordered.

"No," said another mantis voice.

The Queen Mother hovered up behind them on her temporary disc.

"He is a guest," she said. "Not a prisoner. We will show respect."

The six troops said nothing, though they retreated from me by half a meter or so. I looked at them—each in turn—then slowly bent to the deck. It took considerable strength to get her up onto the sled. I moved as carefully as I could, treating her gently. Anything less would have seemed unkind. I'd had to help with the wounded and the dead before. We'd buried countless people on Purgatory—after our failed invasion.

As I looked at Adanaho's slack features, I remembered Capacha's face too.

"What are your wishes for the captain's remains?" the Queen Mother asked.

"On a human ship she'd be taken to the morgue," I said.

"Cold storage?"

"More or less."

"For what purpose?"

"Depending on the circumstances, she might be transported home for burial according to the wishes of her next of kin. Under combat conditions she'd be given Fleet rites in accordance with protocol, and the body jettisoned into the nearest available star."

"It would seem there is no precedent in our case."

"Then cold storage is fine for now."

"We have something better. We use stasis technology to preserve various foods and other organic materials without resorting to reduced temperatures. This will keep her body in the condition it is now until a permanent choice can be made."

"Okay," I said. "Do that."

The Queen Mother relayed her instructions in mantis speech to the six troops, who quickly maneuvered down the ramp again. I watched Adanaho go—with a unique and dreadful hollowness in my chest. She might have lived to have a husband, children, grandchildren . . .

"Come," said the Queen Mother. "There is much we must discuss."

I slowly walked down the ramp.

The docking bay of the mantis ship wasn't all that different from that of an Earth-built craft. Contrary to the many imaginings of us humans, the interior of the mantis craft was not a nest nor a lair of any sort. No goo dripping from ceilings. No webs nor cocoons nor other organic grotesqueness. It was made of metal, plastic, and other materials which seemed familiar. Labels and signage were in the fascinatingly different script of the mantes—a semi-spiraling assortment of slashes and dots in an endless number of configurations. A linguist might have understood it. Maybe even Adanaho, who'd doubtless had some exposure during her training. I'd had some too, thanks to the Professor's teaching during our years shared on Purgatory. But he'd been primarily interested in what I had to teach *him,* so the cross-transfer of knowledge had been limited. He could read the human script far more easily than I could write in the mantis version, just as he could speak my language whereas I would never speak his.

I saw several other drop pod carriers arrayed in neat patterns, with hundreds of mantes—soldiers and unarmed workers alike—moving to and fro. They were conducting inspections, performing maintenance, loading and unloading equipment and munitions . . . all as would be expected with a human warship of similar size and function. Which somehow comforted me in a way I'd not expected. I'd been bracing for a scene that might be utterly alien. That it was in fact rather mundane spoke to me again of human-mantis similarity versus difference.

"What's going to happen now?" I asked the Queen Mother.

"I have ordered a conference with the ship's top officer, who I have learned is in fact the flotilla commander for this particular star system. We have lost many vessels, as it appears your Fleet has too. The planet we were formerly on is still contested territory. I will order all mantis vessels, troops, and craft to reassemble and withdraw. At which time we will depart for one of the many star systems serving as staging areas for the Fourth Expansion. From there I will dispatch couriers to the various fleets tasked with engaging human space. Hopefully the Fourth Expansion can be recalled before the damage is irreparable."

"Purgatory?" I said. "What's happened there?"

"I was not privy to every detail of the Expansion plan. I left much to the individual creativity and initiative of my top warriors."

"And what about Earth? Surely you must know if Earth is under attack?"

"That I think unlikely. There has not been enough time. The overall battle strategy was to engage your colonies closest to mantis space first—siphoning away as much of your Fleet strength as possible to the front—then decimating your Fleet prior to fanning out into human space proper."

"Will your top warriors be willing to disengage?" I asked.

"Much depends on whether or not they accept my authority according to my former rank. Now that I am not dead, my successor and the Quorum have a conundrum to solve. It's been rare in our history for any Queen Mother, once departed, to then attempt a return to office. If my successor does not demur, and demands that the war effort continue, then I will be more or less stripped of authority. Unless or until that happens, though, on this ship at least

I am still the Queen Mother. No mantis here would dare oppose me. We will know more when we reach the first staging system."

I looked around at the docking bay and its busy goings-on, and I suddenly realized I was going to have a lot of time on my hands in a very unfamiliar and not necessarily hospitable environment.

"What will you do with me?" I asked.

"As I told my soldiers," she said. "You are our guest."

"Do you have shipboard accommodations friendly to humans? A bed, a sink, a toilet?"

"Such things can be created. I will summon the ship's engineers to work with you on this. It will take time, but they will do their utmost to see that you are made comfortable."

"Thank you," I said.

We waited silently as a score of mantis troops glided up on their discs. One of them hailed the Queen Mother with a raised forelimb. They did not speak. I sensed that whatever information was being relayed was being done disc-to-disc. On Purgatory the Professor had instructed his students to avoid this practice when possible. He'd considered it a matter of transparency; a way to earn human trust. I suddenly felt wary of being excluded from the conversation, and looked to the Queen Mother as my only source of protection in this environment.

Unnerving, at best. Not long ago she'd gleefully tried to sacrifice herself aboard the *Calysta* so as to ensure that the Fourth Expansion could be launched under a pretext guaranteeing full commitment. Over the days on the planet below I'd watched her pass through an experience unlike anything any mantis had endured in hundreds or possibly even thousands of Earth years. Maybe *tens* of thousands? I didn't know. Whatever had happened, it had affected the Queen Mother such that she was now having a genuine change of heart.

I just wasn't sure if I could trust her entirely. Would she *re*change her mind?

I thought of all the humans on Purgatory who'd found God—or at least religion of one form or another—once we'd been sealed behind The Wall. And especially in those dreadful days when The Wall had been closing in and we'd all thought death was certain. It had been easy for people to turn over a new leaf. What other choice had they had? But then when The Wall fell and safety was more or less assured, many people drifted away. Returned to old habits. The attendance at my chapel dwindled. Not back to its prearmistice levels per se, but dwindled just the same. And how many of those people had, upon leaving Purgatory, gone back to their old lives and their old ways of thinking altogether?

For me, the experience on Purgatory left permanent marks. The Queen Mother had only lived without her disc for a few days. Captain Adanaho had speculated that the Queen Mother's perceptions—indeed, her attitudes based on those perceptions—would be in flux. I wondered if old patterns of thinking—and of seeing the universe—might reemerge now that the Queen Mother was among her own kind again, with all the familiar trappings of mantis technology.

I swallowed hard. From the frying pan into the fire?

"Do not fear," said the Queen Mother.

She'd disengaged from conversation with her subordinate, who seemed to wait patiently while the Queen Mother floated over to me. The Professor had been adept at sensing my moods. Mainly through smell. I guessed that the Queen Mother was little different in this regard.

"You'll have to forgive my distrust," I said. "I am the only human, alone among a sea of mantes. Humans and mantes are still at war until proven otherwise. I want to believe that the situation can be remedied. But I have no guarantees. Therefore I am rather nervous."

"Understandable," the Queen Mother said. "If the situation were different I might consider finding a way to return you to your people. But I need you now, assistant-to-the-chaplain. With your captain dead, there are no more human officers to vouch for my intentions. When the time comes to—I think the Professor told me the correct phrase among humans is *extend an olive branch*—your services will be vital."

I voiced my understanding, but I wasn't exactly sure that a single Chief Warrant Officer would count for much if Fleet Command was bound and determined to continue the fighting. They'd be damned fools to do it, but then they'd sent General Sakumora to handle the original negotiations. And he'd clearly been swayed to the side of war long before the meeting with the Queen Mother.

If a majority of Fleet Command believed as he did...

I suddenly felt an overwhelming wave of fatigue sweep me.

"You appear exhausted," the Queen Mother said.

"And you're not?" I replied, half-incredulous.

"Deprivation has weakened me, but mantis females are able to survive such things without a significant erosion of our faculties. A biological legacy, from a time when females would be left alone to guard both eggs and larva until pupation. It was the task of the males to provide food, and if the males were killed or delayed in returning . . . but I repeat academic trivia. Assistant-to-the-chaplain, you are spent. I will instruct some of the available ship's technicians to take you immediately to a space where you can rest."

I tensed.

"How do I know one of them doesn't hold a grudge against humans?"

She considered this question for a moment.

"There are quarters being prepared for me as well. This vessel is now my flagship. I will designate that your quarters be located directly next to mine. You are the only human aboard, and I will *know* if you have been molested in any way. No sane mantis would dare harm you."

"And what about the not-so-sane?"

She hovered over to me, her forelimbs gently stroking the edge of her temporary disc in a fashion I'd often seen the Professor emulate.

"Assistant-to-the-chaplain—*Padre*—there was a time not long ago when I was forced to abandon my carriage and place myself almost entirely in your hands. I understand your misgivings. I can only ask you to trust me in the same manner that I was once asked to trust you—and your dead captain. You have returned me to my people as promised, despite the loss of your captain's life. I would honor her commitment to duty by ensuring that you also are returned to your people. On my own life and as the Queen Mother, I swear an oath to it."

I felt myself nodding as she said these things. Had she been a human, I'd have put my hand out to shake hers.

"Very well," I said. "I will hold you to that oath. And I apologize for my behavior. You're right, I am tired. And the grief I feel at the deaths of both the Professor and the captain is deep."

"Go now," she said. "My people will take care of you."

A trio of unarmed mantes floated up to us.

"We are ready to receive the human guest," said the leader.

I allowed myself to be led away, my head growing ever more foggy and my legs feeling like lead.

CHAPTER 40

Earth orbit, 2155 A.D.

EIGHTEEN MONTHS AFTER I WATCHED PRIVATE CAPACHA DIE, I reported to my billet just down the corridor from the quarters of Major Thomas, an ordained Baptist minister who hailed from West Virginia. He was roughly Chaplain J's age. I apparently came to him with Chaplain J's hearty recommendation. Which was both good and bad. Having endured the much less harsh—compared to IST—rigors of the Chaplain's Assistant specialty school, I still wasn't feeling too confident in myself, or my new role. I didn't fancy myself a spiritual person per se, and while the school had dramatically improved my comprehension and understanding of many of Earth's larger religious groups—their doctrines and beliefs, their histories—I wasn't exactly feeling "in the swing of things," as I later learned Chaplain Thomas liked to say.

"Come," he said through the speaker at his cabin door.

It opened, and I walked in, presented a salute, and said, "Specialist Barlow reporting as ordered, sir."

"Ah good," Thomas said. He had a jolly mustache that was just on the edge of being too bushy for regulation, and he wore a tiny silver cross on his uniform—something Chaplain J had not done. The rules for this weren't precisely clear. It seemed to be a matter of taste among the individual chaplains in the Chaplains Corps.

When I didn't relax right away, Thomas waved a hand at me.

"Relax, young man, relax. Three weeks out of school and they've still got you scared stiff, eh? That's no way to approach the world. From this point forward you can all me Chaplain Tom. Or Major Tom, if you like."

"Major Tom," I said, testing it out.

"It's a joke from my grad school days," he said. "Something to do with an old pop song from a long time ago. Anyway, the point is, I expect no formality of the sort drummed into you up to this point. Respect, absolutely. But as you've no doubt discovered in your brief time in the Fleet, plenty of people render formalities without giving an inch of respect. Yes?"

I raised an eyebrow, and nodded my agreement. Chaplain Tom was an astute fellow. I let my saluting hand fall to my side, then settled into a very relaxed at-ease.

"Is there anything I can do to help?" I asked, noting that Chaplain Tom still had an unpacked duffel on his bunk.

"No, I'm fine, thanks. This is my fourth ship in as many months. They're moving a lot of us around as Fleet gears up for the big offensives. I've learned to travel light, and pack and unpack quickly."

"Have you heard anything more about that?" I asked.

"About what?"

"The missions."

"Just that Fleet has identified five different systems it wants to evict the mantes from. Places of some strategic importance, I gather. Probably because they've each got Earth-similar worlds in them, and Fleet can do much more with an Earth-type planet than it can with any other sort. We'll know more when we'll know more, you know? So, for now, try to put that worry out of your head, son. Or shall I call you Harry?"

He shocked me with my first name. Not even Chaplain J had used it.

"Uhh," I said, "Specialist Barlow is fine, sir."

He looked at me, broke into a grin, and shook his head.

"Right," was all he said.

I looked around his quarters—somewhat larger than a breadbox. But because he was solitary, whereas I shared an eight-man room, his quarters seemed positively decadent.

"Church much?" he asked me as he sat on the edge of his bunk.

"Not before—uh, no, sir." I said.

"No problem. You could be a thoroughgoing atheist for all I care. Tammy said in her e-mail to me that you were a hard worker and that you like to help people. And that's good enough for me. Because helping people is the name of the game. Fleet poses one of the most rigid, uncompromising, otherwise inhospitable environments a working man or woman can know. My job—and now your job, too—is to help these men and women *cope.* Officers. Enlisted. Doesn't matter. Everybody has a snapping point. And if you've just come from school, on the heels of IST, you know what I mean when I say *snap.*"

"Yes, sir," I said.

"Good. So, I want you glued to me whenever you're not required to be partaking in priority training. It'll be weeks or months to get anywhere, even after this ship gets specific orders for a specific destination. Lots of time during which Fleet's going to try to keep everyone on board as busy as possible. So that we stay sharp. Motivated. Ready. Problem is, this puts us at or near 'snap point' and our job—yours and mine—is to see if we can't help the rest of these people see past the grind of their schedule. And the worry about combat to come—which nobody on this boat has seen, I might add. Not even the woman commanding it. We're all 'green' as far as that goes. Which means there's no reason not to have a mutual sense of humility and understanding. Right?"

"Right, sir."

He looked at me, still smiling, and sighed.

"Well, you take your time getting into the flow of things. I'm counting on the fact that Tammy didn't sell me a lemon—and it would shock me to death if she did. The rest is up to the Lord."

"Yessir, thank you. I do have one question, sir."

"Okay, shoot."

"Do you mind if I, ummm, ask you about that from time to time?"

"About what?"

"The Lord. God. Church. Things like that."

"I'd be delighted," he said.

"Just please don't turn me into a project," I said, noting his sudden enthusiasm.

"I wouldn't think of it, Specialist Barlow. A chaplain's job is not to go around pushing faith down peoples' throats. A chaplain's job is to help foster what faith may already be there—in whatever supply or form it happens to exist. Beyond that, I try to keep my views and opinions close to my vest. Understand?"

"Yessir," I said.

"Now, if we're done here, I think I need a quick nap before I walk up a few decks and join the muckety-muck meeting with all the other ship's officers. Can you come beep my door again at 1445 hours?"

"Yessir, I can do that."

"Good. Thanks. Sounds like we're going to get along just fine."

I snapped my heels together, and began to offer a salute, when he waved me off for the second time in ten minutes.

"Specialist, you're dismissed. Go get some lunch or something. Just knock off all that spit-and-polish crap. It scares me. Jeez."

I smiled despite myself, turned, and went back out the way I'd come in.

CHAPTER 41

THE COMPARTMENT WAS BARREN, BUT THEY'D MOVED IN A SECtion of pliable material not too different from memory foam. I tested it with my hands and was delighted at its softness. After spending so many days sleeping on sand and gravel, the thought of lying on an actual *bed* suddenly became irresistible.

Blankets and sheets there were none, though the mantis engineers quickly fashioned a smaller piece of the foam for a man-sized pillow. They also produced both my pack and the captain's pack, along with all of the contents thereof.

I pulled out the captain's emergency sleeping bag and fluffed it out over the bed, noticing the dust that came off—laundry concerns could wait.

My bladder and colon could not.

The three technicians conferred at length.

"We are unfamiliar with this biological function," one of them said. "But we realize that humans are too primitive to have carriages. We will bring a storage container into which you may deposit your waste. We will also bring a different storage container with fresh water for your consumption and hygiene."

"Heated?" I asked.

They conferred at length again.

"This should be feasible."

They left the compartment to retrieve what they needed, and I slumped onto the foam.

It molded deliciously to my body.

Sleep tugged at my brain like the suction of a whirlpool.

The technicians returned more quickly than expected. They had several sleds similar to the ones used to remove the body of Captain Adanaho. On each sled had been stacked numerous pieces of equipment, tools, raw parts, as well as the bulk containers they'd spoken of earlier. For several minutes I went back and forth with them explaining the rudimentary basics of what a toilet looked like and how it worked, as well as a wash basin. I also told them I'd eventually like to have a shower stall built or even—Lord, please—a bathtub. Though that would wait until I wasn't semi-dead from lack of proper sleep and nourishment.

"Food," said one of the technicians, "may prove to be the biggest problem. We do not know which of our foodstuffs will be palatable to you, and there is no way for us to procure foodstuffs from a human vessel at this time. Do you have anything you could give to us which we might take to our refectory and examine in detail? So that we might learn your basic nutritional requirements?"

I rummaged through the captain's pack.

She still had a ration bar.

"Here," I said. "These will keep a human alive. They've got everything I need. Except variety."

The lead technician's antennae made a questioning expression.

"Humans cannot eat the same exact food over and over again before it becomes sickening to them. We require variety. At least as much as can be provided."

"It will be a process," said the lead technician. "We may have to go through many iterations before we present you with something tolerable."

I supposed that would just have to be good enough, so I thanked them for making the effort and sat on my mantis foam mattress while the technicians went to work fashioning my toilet and sink. They did it all mechanically. Each of their discs had slots from which manipulator arms and tools extended. The air smelled of adhesive and welded metal as they worked. Occasionally they asked me a question. I found myself tapping my teeth together impatiently. It had been hours since I'd been able to relieve myself.

Finally, they had the job done.

I tested the two spigots on the hexagonal wash basin—hot and cold water—and the circular toilet seat was the right size, with a sealable cover so that I wouldn't have to smell my own piss and shit all night and day.

"Close enough for government work," I said, slapping my hands together and rubbing them eagerly.

"Then it is . . . sufficient?" said the lead technician.

"It is," I said. "And now I would ask for some extended privacy."

"We understand," they said.

I ushered them out.

Ten minutes later I was stripped to my skin, my bowels happily empty. Using the water from the basin and sanitary wipes from the emergency packs, I gave myself an overlong version of a soldier's bath. Occasionally rinsing the wipes in the basin, I noted the sound of the waste water tumbling into the container beneath it. I estimated I had about two hundred liters before the waste water tank would need to be dumped. Roughly as much for the loo, too. Though I'd be wanting to get both of them emptied well before hitting the limit.

With skin tingling—the compartment's ventilation blew gently across my face—I lay on the mattress and pulled the sleeping bag up around my waist. They'd put in a small control box near the bed's head, with touch displays on it for temperature and light control. I dialed the temp down a few degrees, and turned the light off.

For a moment, I missed seeing the stars.

But the ship had a low mechanical hum that was as pleasantly hypnotic—as the river in the canyon had been—and I quickly faded into deep sleep.

My dreams were violently lurid.

Over and over again, I pressed my hand to the gushing wound in Captain Adanaho's torso. Which suddenly became Capacha's torso, back during LCX at the end of IST.

Over and over again, they both died.

At one point the repetition became so horrible I swam up out of sleep with a start. Fumbling for the control box, I dialed up the light and kicked off the sleeping bag. I rinsed my face and head in the basin—cold water this time—then used the toilet again, prior to getting back on the mattress. Which was still delightfully soft.

I was hesitant to let myself go back to sleep if that's the kind of nightmare I was going to be greeted with.

To distract myself I remembered the interior of my chapel back on Purgatory. I mentally took myself through my old routine: lighting the oil lamps, going up and down the rows of roughly-cut stone pews, collecting bits of debris and making sure everything was neat and orderly. In my imaginary version of the chapel, I sat on the stool to the left of the altar where the symbols of human faith were normally displayed. It occurred to me that the chapel—indeed, everything in the entire mountain valley—might have been razed to the ground in the Fourth Expansion.

Memories might be all I had from now on. It had not been a comfortable life, living in that little place. But it had been a life of purpose. I vowed to myself that if ever I made it back, I would rebuild.

"No, it's not that, Specialist. See, a few hundred years ago there was this kid—not much younger than you are—named Joseph Smith. He thought he could talk to God, and he thought God told him to go start a new church. Which he did. The poor fool. He got killed for it. But the church is what we now call the Church of Jesus Christ of Latter-Day Saints. It's outlived its founder by centuries."

"If that's their name, sir," I said, "then how come they're not Christian?"

"It's complicated, son," he said.

From my standpoint, the only complication appeared to exist in Chaplain Thomas's mind. But I let it pass. The man was old enough to be my father, and I'd already learned from cross-examining some of his statements that if I pushed too hard on any given point, he got frustrated with me and sent me away to work on something for him.

"Are they a good church?" I asked.

Chaplain Tom just stared at me.

"How do you define 'good' in this context, Specialist?"

"Oh, I dunno, what do you think of them?"

"Absolutely fine men and women," he said, slapping a hand on his thigh. "Whatever their doctrinal differences are with true Christianity, I can't fault the folk. Leastways not the ones *I* know. They work hard, they tithe, they tend to be honest, and they do seem to love the Lord."

"So what's the issue, if you don't mind my asking, sir? The marines down in the hangar, they said they were going to make fun of the book."

"And that I can't countenance," he said with a sour frown. "Mormons have been getting run off and run out of everywhere for a long time. Some of it maybe they deserved, but most of it? Hell no. Excuse my language. That's no way to treat people, even if they do have some odd ideas about things. I'll say this, they stick to their guns. Find me a devout Mormon and I will show you a man who has absolute faith in his doctrine. Enough to outlast most arguers. Even me."

His face had flushed, but just slightly.

I gathered that in his civilian ministry days, he'd gone around the barn a time or two with his Mormon peers.

"Anyway," Chaplain Tom said, handing the book back to me, "if you want to know what makes a Mormon tick, it's all in there.

Like I said, I wasn't aware we had any aboard, but then we've got so many people crammed together from all over creation, I've not had time to work with the ship's chaplaincy to figure out percentages and statistics. Like everyone else in the world, the Mormons are signing up with Fleet to defend the human race. As is proper. And the Jews, and the Hindus, and the Muslims too. Now, those Muslims, they're a double-edged sword. Many of them joined Fleet to kill mantes, only because some mullah or other told them that the only thing God loves more than a dead Jew or a dead Christian is a dead mantis. Seems the more militant Muslims have decided to call a truce with the rest of us. At least until we've beat off the mantis horde, and can go back to hating each other like men again."

Chaplain Thomas's words sounded gradually more frustrated and tired as he said the last part.

I'd not thought much about the state of affairs back on Earth when I'd joined the Fleet. But I realized that for men older and more experienced than I was, the state of affairs now was perhaps very odd, compared to the state of affairs as it had been when they were young.

"Are the Muslims dangerous?"

"Oh goodness, Specialist, no, not all of them. A few extremists here and there. Fleet tries hard to screen for them so that we don't have really dangerous people getting their hands on Fleet weaponry that might be turned against Earth. Most Muslims in the Fleet have no love for Jews or Israelis, I can tell you that much. But then this is the way it's always been. And you're going to find, the longer you do your job, that it's not necessarily your place to try to *enlighten* some of these folks—Jew or Muslim or Mormon—to what you think is the proper attitude. As long as they can salute and march and execute to standard, that's all Fleet asks. Everything else is . . . details."

"Thank you, sir," I said, flipping pages in the book with the trumpet-playing silhouette on the front. The pages were amazingly thin, and the print very small. It was obviously a compact version, for service member use. Much like the standard twenty-second-century edition Bibles that Chaplain Thomas had me keep in boxes—for those few troops who actually came to Sunday service.

I thought it odd that the Mormons needed their own scripture, apart from that which seemed to suffice for all the other

Christian denominations. But then the Buddhists and the Hindus and the Muslims all had their own books too. Some of them overlapping in content with each other, but not always. And I figured as long as nobody was trying to beat anyone else up for it, those differences ought to be harmless.

CHAPTER 43

I AWOKE TO FIND A TRAY SITTING ON A TABLE AT THE SIDE OF the bed.

When I leaned over to see what was on it, my nose was assaulted by a most unpleasant smell.

"Oh boy," I said.

Though my stomach was a gnawing pit, I wasn't sure I could hold my nose for whatever it was the mantes had concocted for me. It was a solid square of... something. Roughly ten centimeters on a side and two centimeters thick. I couldn't tell if it was raw, nor could I tell if it was cooked, nor could I even be sure if it was animal or vegetable—or both.

I stared at it for the longest time.

After using the toilet and refreshing myself at the wash basin, I sat back down on the edge of the bed, my disgust with the square's smell competing with my body's demand for fuel. It had easily been forty-eight hours since I'd put any food in my face, and though this didn't seem the least bit appetizing, I wasn't sure I had anything better to work with—besides one or two half-eaten ration bars that may or may not have been squirreled at the bottom of the packs.

There were utensils in the pack's unused mess kit. I fished them out. Steeling myself, I stabbed into the square and forked up a sizeable hunk of what appeared to be pureed dog shit. I stuffed it into my mouth. And promptly gagged the contents back up onto the tray. At which time I retched repeatedly.

I took the tray to the toilet and upended the contents. Then I washed it, as well as my mouth, and went to the packs. I tossed out everything I could—until the packs were empty—and upended them vigorously.

A single, lonely, mostly-eaten ration bar tumbled out. Sans wrapper.

I fetched it up and plopped it into my mouth—ignoring the gritty dust that covered it as I chewed several times, then swallowed.

The door to my compartment opened, and the Queen Mother floated in. I noticed that she no longer rode the small emergency disc. This time she had a full carriage identical to the one I'd originally seen her use when I'd come to meet her aboard the *Calysta*. It was polished and sparkled in the overhead lights, though the Queen Mother's body posture indicated she was not particularly pleased.

"Good morning," I said.

"By your internal time keeping, perhaps," she said. "But not by ours. Was the meal satisfactory?"

"It was not," I admitted. "I managed just a mouthful before I threw it up. Whatever your ship's refectory thought it was creating for me, I found it entirely inedible."

"It contained all of the calories and nutrients you might need," she said. "What was the problem?"

"As I explained to the younger mantes who helped me set up this compartment with amenities comfortable for humans, there is more to human food than raw nutrients such as proteins and sugars."

"I don't understand," she said.

"It's the way in which those raw nutrients and proteins are put together. And especially the way in which the raw food is prepared. Consider a sirloin steak."

"What is that?"

"It's a choice cut of meat from a human livestock animal called a cow. Most humans would never eat a sirloin steak when raw. Even if rubbed with herbs and salt, most humans would never touch it. But take the steak and prepare it with sea salt and ground peppercorn, then broil it over the bare coals of a fire made with pine and mesquite wood, then serve it with a baked potato, fresh corn on the cob, butter, sour cream, bacon bits, chives—"

"I believe I have the idea," she said. "My refectory examined your ration bar at length and attempted to reproduce it in quantity. Perhaps they took the task too literally?"

"Yes, perhaps. What was offered to me on the tray looked very little like something I'd want to put in my mouth twice. Rather, it seemed to have more in common with what comes out the other end."

Her wings did not flutter at my joke. Was I being a bad guest?

"You are bothered," I said.

"Yes."

"I am sorry if I am being too blunt in my appraisal of the food."

"I care not for your appraisal. My technicians and the refectory have been instructed to appease your every desire, where eating and comfort are concerned. Instruct them as you will. Throw away what you do not like."

"Then what is the issue?" I asked.

"I am bothered because . . . because . . ."

Her forelimbs were tapping on the new disc she rode, while her mouth opened halfway and her tractor teeth began to vibrate in annoyance.

"Are there problems with the carriage?" I asked.

"No. The carriage is perfect. It is *I* who am the problem."

"Was the Professor right? Can you not be wholly reintegrated with a new disc, as he suspected when you were pulled out of the old one?"

"No, the issue is not physiological. Assistant-to-the-chaplain, my world has become . . . flat."

"Flat?"

"Yes, that is the best way I can put it in your language. Flat. I perceive in full the ship around me, and everyone in it, and my senses have regained the crisp articulation and range afforded by carriages for many generations of our people. And yet, the experience is . . . flat. There is a quality that is missing which I cannot precisely put into words. I have struggled with this for several of your hours, believing it was merely the new carriage's software and interfaces having to adapt to my particular biological signature. When the newly-born adult emerges from the chrysalis, it takes time for the carriage to learn its master, while the master must learn her carriage."

"So give it a few days," I said.

"No," she replied. "I detect not even a subtle change. Not in the specific way I would expect. The essence of what I saw and heard and felt while apart from my original carriage . . . it is lost.

I cannot account for this, save for the fact that some kind of permanent damage may have been done to me during the hasty egress from my ruined carriage."

I sat on the bed and thought for a moment.

"Captain Adanaho told me she suspected that life without the carriage was a significant revelation for you."

"It was."

"Then why are you surprised that upon returning to disc-integrated life, those revelations—the quality you spoke of—is gone? For many days you were forced to rely only on your own eyes, your own ears, your own nose—"

"Mantes do not have ears or a nose as you call them—"

"I know that, but consider: while you relied solely on your biological senses, your entire range of perception was significantly altered."

She still showed annoyance. So I tried a different approach.

"Consider this," I said. "It has long been noted among humans that if one of us loses a major sense—say, sight, for instance—that the other senses become more acute. Sometimes, dramatically so. Therefore the blind man may suddenly find himself tasting more subtly than ever before, his ability to perceive through touch will improve, along with his hearing, and so forth. They all become accentuated. It is the natural way in which the human body and mind compensate for the loss of a very important faculty."

"But I was not made blind, nor deaf," she said. "I could see and hear just as well without the disc, as with it."

"I would wager not," I said. "Otherwise you'd not be so perturbed now that you've regained your biomechanical augmentation. By reintegrating with a carriage you have most probably muffled your raw, instinctive senses by a significant percentage. You just never noticed before because you've never, ever lived without a disc. You said it yourself: the adult mantis never lives without a carriage."

The shape of her antennae told me I'd intrigued her, but her vibrating teeth told me she was still vexed.

"There must be a way to compensate," she said. "I cannot believe that the carriage is a limiter. We cannot survive without them. They are the foundation of our civilization."

"That may be true," I said. "But does this change the 'flatness' you perceive now? Does believing in the absolute necessity of the carriage make it any less bothersome?"

She paused a long time, then said, "No."

"Then I am afraid I don't have an answer for you," I said. "Other than to do voluntarily what you did originally out of necessity. Separate yourself from your disc. See if the *depth* you're missing returns. Perform this experiment as many times as it takes to be satisfied with an answer. Or . . . learn to live as you once did. In a 'flat' world of technologically purified perception."

Her mouth opened all the way and she almost frightened me with how much her unhappiness manifested.

She fled the room without a word.

Swallowing hard, I let the door slide shut and decided there was no sense chasing after her. She'd have to figure it out on her own one way or another. Best for me to just stay put, inventory and organize what little human equipment I still had with me, and hope that I'd get a chance to talk to the technicians about additional improvements to my quarters.

They arrived thirty minutes later.

I explained the problem with the food, and I also explained to them my desire for soap. Both for bathing, and also for washing my clothes, not to mention the sleeping bag.

"You do this by hand?" one of them asked me, his posture surprised.

"Not ideally, no," I said. "We have machines to do this work. Though I can't imagine you have a laundromat onboard, do you?"

"Describe this laundromat," they said in unison.

Which required me to explain how an electric washer and dryer worked: the filling with water, the injection of the soap, the wash cycle, the rinse cycle, drying, and fabric softener.

"Why softener?" one of them asked.

"Without it, the dried material is rough to the touch, and it does not smell so good."

"Can you provide us with examples of these things?"

"I am afraid I can't. Look, don't the mantes ever use fabric for anything?"

"For some applications, yes."

"Then there must be some way you keep such fabric clean."

"Fabric is regarded as disposable," one of them said. "We do not generally clean it."

I put my head down and puffed my cheeks out with frustration.

It was going to be a long trip.

CHAPTER 44

Target planet (Purgatory), 2155 A.D.

THE ASSAULT CARRIER'S DESCENT DURING LCX HADN'T DONE AN actual combat landing justice. The bench to which I was strapped was rattling so hard, I felt like it was going to shake my teeth out of my head. Despite the relative cushioning provided by my armor suit—new, this time, and built to the latest specs. Lighter. Supposedly tougher too.

Chaplain Thomas was in the same state next to me: rattled to distraction.

All of us on the troop deck bucked and swayed in unison as the carrier made its way pell-mell down through the atmosphere of the world we were about to take from the enemy.

My old friend nausea lurked in the center of my stomach as the rumbling and jerking of the ship threatened to turn into a full-blown carnival ride of sideways-up, downwise-side, upways-down.

I saw the looks on the faces of the marines as they hunched with their rifles and other weapons—ready to go the second the loadmaster gave the signal. Unlike during LCX, we also had tanks and mobile artillery nestled in our belly. They'd deploy almost the instant we hit the ground—growling out onto the planet's surface, and hosing down any immediate mantis threats. With automatic cannon fire and missiles.

Outside, somewhere in the stratosphere, aerospace fighters were also going in hot—their threat sensors now coming on-line after the short black-out period caused by reentry. If there were mantis fighters in the air waiting to pounce on the assault carrier, our fighters were ready and prepared to ruin the mantes' day.

Suddenly the assault carrier crashed and shook. Flashing orange alarm lights told us something had gone very wrong.

"Missile hit," I heard someone say over the wireless.

BOOM!... BOOOOOOM!

Two more, in relatively rapid succession. How effective *was* the assault carrier's armor, anyway? I suddenly realized we were all going to find out. For better, or for worse.

Slowly, the troop deck began to spin. Or, rather, I could feel that the assault carrier was revolving over onto its back—not a prescribed flight profile for the big, wallowing ship in *anybody's* anti-aircraft evasion manual.

Those few marines who'd been keeping straight faces finally broke and showed their fear. Our assault carrier was clearly in trouble, and we were nowhere close enough to the ground yet to feel like we'd made it to relative safety.

BOOOOOOOOM! Unnggggkkkkktttktktkttttt!!

"Shit," I heard Chaplain Thomas say.

The man usually worked very hard not to curse. That he'd cursed told me all I needed to know about the situation, as the sounds of ripping and tearing metal became more pronounced. For an insane instant, I recalled clearly that the prelaunch briefing had said we'd be expecting moderate resistance.

So much for that.

The prelaunch briefing had also spent far more time dwelling on perimeter security and establishing ground-based hardened defensive positions—after we landed—than it did on what to do in case the assault carrier we were riding in was being shot to pieces right beneath our feet.

We had no parachutes. Would not have tried them, even if we did. So far as we knew the assault carrier was still moving at supersonic speed high over the alien planet's desertlike terrain. Anyone fool enough to bail out in *those* conditions was signing his own death certificate, regardless of how tough the new armor suits happened to be.

Suddenly the carrier righted itself—to our relief—but then the bottom dropped out of our stomachs as we felt ourselves begin to fall precipitously.

"BRACE FOR IMPACT! BRACE FOR IMPACT!" the loadmaster began to yell on the company-wide wireless.

There was little to do but cringe and hope. Many seconds ticked by in virtual free-fall. When the crash came, it came as a whirling, end-over-end chaos of benches coming loose from the troop deck and whole squads of marines and support personnel being hurled across my field of view like rag dolls.

The collision damping system suddenly flooded the entire deck with massive jets of thick foam that began to solidify the moment it touched air. I felt myself scream as I rolled, and rolled, and rolled, and kept rolling. Until finally, I was resting upside down, my vision entirely blocked out and the company wireless hissing vacantly.

Were we down? Had we made it?

I couldn't tell. For a long time, the world around me was nothing but stiffened crash foam. Until suddenly the wireless came alive again—helmet to helmet this time, with no assistance from the shipboard system.

Things were grim. Only one hundred and five people survived, out of almost three hundred on my assault carrier. This included Chaplain Thomas, though the poor man was busted up something awful. After clawing my way out of the collision foam, I had to search far and wide across the impact zone to find him. The carrier had burst apart, its engines, flight decks, and other vital parts scattering to the wind. How or why the reactors hadn't gone up was a mystery, but I wagered we didn't have much time. So I frantically searched for survivors—many of whom were wounded—helping them to walk, or limp, or even be dragged, over to a far hill. It wasn't much, but it seemed to offer at least *some* protection from the potential blast, if or when the reactors finally melted down.

In the sky overhead, it was obvious that we—the Fleet—were getting our asses kicked. Mantis fighters zipped lithely to and fro, seemingly impervious to the missiles spat at them by the few Earth fighters that still prowled the air. Occasionally one of those Earth fighters burst in a white fireball, followed by a thunderous report. And then silence.

Our impact zone was in a wide valley dominated by several rough-rock bluffs trailing off towards what seemed to be our east.

It was difficult to tell, given the foreign sun's position overhead. We'd come in about midday, and wouldn't know true directions until much later. Assuming we lasted.

The few officers and NCOs who could stand and give orders arranged us into a hasty defensive perimeter—with the wounded in the center—while they tried to use their suit wireless to contact anyone in orbit.

Fruitless.

I gazed up into the thin air and wondered if there was anyone *left* in orbit to talk to? If my introduction to this charming little planet had gone badly, who was to say things hadn't been as bad—or worse—for the big capital ships in space?

Such thoughts depressed me as I held Chaplain Thomas's hand and tried to keep him from slipping into a coma. Our helmets were off. The air here had oxygen. If we were scared of germs, we figured it best to chance the native atmosphere—lest we rapidly deplete our own. I had Chaplain Thomas propped against a rock, at a more or less forty-five-degree angle, his legs limp from the spinal injury he'd suffered in the crash.

"Hell of way to join the fight," he said in a small, pained voice as I tried to give him water from his suit's hydration tube. He ignored the tube and simply stared past me—through me?—out to where the alien sky met the alien earth at a lumpy horizon.

"What have we got left?" the chaplain asked.

"Not much, sir," I said. "Armor assets have been totally obliterated. We've got rifles, and have a fair bit of ammo. But we're nowhere close to the planned objective—hell, we're not even sure we're on the same *continent* as the planned objective. No sign of mantis ground patrols, yet. But they've got fighters all over the air. And we can't reach orbital for a situational analysis, nor call for reinforcement or an evac."

"That's what I thought," he said. "When the carrier came apart around us, I knew we'd come to this world woefully unprepared. No doubt the enemy fortified themselves in anticipation of our arrival. I just hope the assault missions elsewhere on this planet—on *any* of the other planets—are going better than ours."

He coughed a bit, then grimaced.

"Broken ribs," he guessed.

I didn't have the heart to second-guess him. All of our medics were gone. Pulverized and strewn over the impact site like toy soldiers tossed from a car that's rolled several times on the interstate. I suddenly and intensely regretted my decision to join the Fleet. Chaplain Thomas must have read my facial expression.

"God's will," he said.

"What, sir?" I asked.

"God's will, Harrison. Try to look at it as God's will—His plan for all of us."

"This is part of God's *plan?*" I said, half-incredulous.

"Everything is part of God's plan," he said.

"Sir, I mean no disrespect, but you have to be out of your mind to think that any of this is part of *anybody's* plan, except for maybe the mantes. Their plan appears to have worked out quite well. We came here to kick them in the teeth, and instead it seems they're quite nicely effing us in the ass, sir. If there is a God, then His attention is focused very, very far away from here."

"Faith, Harry," he said to me, then began coughing and hacking.

I decided not to vent my anger any further, as his attempts to remonstrate me were simply causing him pain. I stood up from where the chaplain lay, and walked over to where some technicians from the assault carrier's crew were trying to use a big hunk of a control panel and a jury-rigged battery connection, to talk to anyone in our vicinity.

"Nothing?" I said.

One of the specialists looked up at me and shook her head.

"Figures," I said. "We're blind. Probably, Fleet doesn't even know where we are. I am surprised those mantis fighters we've been seeing haven't come down on us."

"The day is young," said a different woman—older, with plain, stern features. Her chevrons indicated a platoon sergeant.

"Forget the wireless," she said to the techs. "We've got to scrounge up an anti-air defense."

"With what, Sergeant?" one of the techs asked.

"Anything you can salvage. There were a lot of missiles in that assault carrier, and more missiles on some of the tanks. Not all of them have been destroyed. I'm taking a team back to the crash site to look for hardware that we can salvage. Get ready to move in two mikes. You too, church-boy."

"But I've got to—"

"You're a soldier first, and there's nothing you can do for

Chaplain Tom right now. We need everybody who's not pulling security to get on salvage detail. That's an order."

I did a *yessergeant* and went to tell the chaplain the plan. Unfortunately he'd already passed out from the pain. With no medics, I had no idea how we'd bring him back around now.

With rifles at the low ready and marching in a tactical column, we streamed out beyond the perimeter, around the base of the low hill, and back towards the smoldering, evil-looking furrow our carrier had dug into the planet's surface.

CHAPTER 45

IT TOOK THEM THREE DAYS TO COME UP WITH SOMETHING palatable for me to eat. At which time I was so ravenous I actually thought I might eat a plate of dog shit—just to still the hunger pangs and get rid of the headaches.

It wasn't gourmet by any means, but the engineers had managed to come up with five different "bricks" of edible material which were sufficiently non-gag-worthy that I could put them down. Each of the five pretended to represent one of the human food groups I'd explained to my hosts: meats, vegetables, grains, dairy, and fruits. None of it would have passed muster in any Fleet mess hall I knew. But I packed it away with gusto nonetheless. And was grateful to sleep with a full belly for the first time in weeks.

The problem of the clothes washer was remedied after several tries. They ultimately wired up a box with a spinning drum in it, much as I'd advised, with an attached clean water source as well as a waste water receptacle. The detergent provided was adequate for washing hands and doing the laundry alike, though there was little hope of actual fabric softener. Such a concept was simply too foreign for them to grasp, though they promised they'd keep working on it.

They also built me a chair, a desk, a small rack upon which to hang my clothes, a chest of drawers for other items from the packs, as well as a holographic stand which allowed me to fill half the room with a starlight exterior view of the ship.

"Quite a night light," I said, regarding the display.

"Is that not a contradictory purpose?" one of the technicians said.

"It's a human phrase," I said. "A night light is usually a soft, small, or dim light you leave on in a bedroom overnight. Usually for children, who are often afraid of the dark."

"Human children . . . pupa?" said one of the mantes.

"Not pupa, no," I said. "Immature adults. They can think and reason and use tools the way adults do, just not that well because their brains are not fully developed and they are much smaller, with less experience."

The three engineers seemed to consider this a remarkable piece of information.

"We had no idea," they said.

"Just what *do* you know about humans anyway?" I asked.

"You are the first live human we have come into contact with, and we know next to nothing. Save for the fact that you are the third sapient species our race has ever discovered, and that the mantis you called the Professor was instrumental in convincing the Quorum of the Select to delay exterminating you. Though it seems your ultimate destiny was only delayed, not avoided."

"There's still time to avoid it," I said, the hope in my heart making my words a bit more forceful than they'd otherwise have been. I wanted it to be true so badly—for myself, sure, but also to bring honor and purpose to the deaths of both Captain Adanaho and the Professor.

"Do you have children?" one of the technicians asked.

"No."

"Ah, you have never been fortunate enough for selection," he replied.

"No. Or perhaps yes. I tried to explain this to the Professor before he died. Human procreation doesn't work exactly the same way as mantis procreation. There are many . . . complicating factors . . . involved."

"When we have more time to query you, can you tell us of these complicating factors?" they said in unison.

"Sure," I said, suddenly feeling sheepish.

They bid me farewell and exited the compartment—my *quarters,* now that there was sufficient furniture and accoutrements.

That night I let the holographic stand fill most of the space above the bed with an image of the stars. They were smeared and shifted blue at one end, as well as smeared and shifted red at the other—relativistic effects of our faster-than-light state. I guessed that I was now farther from Earth than any human had ever been before. Plunging into the heart of enemy territory.

If I'd been afraid on the day I stepped off the drop pod carrier's ramp, that fear had slowly diminished as the Queen Mother and especially her technicians had sought to care for my needs.

But there were still so many uncertainties.

I decided the best I could do was take it day by day.

CHAPTER 46

Target planet (Purgatory), 2155 A.D.

AS IT WAS, THE MANTIS FIGHTERS LEFT US COMPLETELY ALONE.

For almost two whole days, we saw nothing. No human aerospacecraft, no mantis aerospacecraft, nor even a hint of life larger than the scraggly little insects that burrowed here and there in the sand.

The techs had managed to jury-rig the chassis of an anti-air tank that had been recovered from the rubble, and driven it slowly on its damaged tracks back to our little AO. Now its generators provided electricity and light and a potentially secure communications link to orbit. Though we still detected nothing—not the big ships, not the small ships.

The mood was grim as a result.

Like a collection of terminal cancer patients, all of us waiting for the end.

"Why don't they finish it?" one corporal said to me as I helped him fix the splint on his leg.

"Maybe they don't have to bother," I said. "Look at where we are. This is like Death Valley in the winter. Dry, almost lifeless, and not a living soul for kilometers on end. Unless we get a thunderstorm soon, we're going to be hurting for water. And without water—"

"I get it, I get it," the corporal said, shushing me.

"Sorry," I said.

"Not your fault, Barlow. It's just that..."

"What?" I asked.

"I never thought I'd go out like this. Without even firing a shot. I mean, I knew the mantes were dangerous, but that was part of the challenge. When I joined, I wanted to get a piece, if you know what I mean? Instead we got our asses handed to us before we ever touched the ground. And now it's like they're ignoring us. We're not even worth coming out to get. The assault carrier's reactors have gone cold, so they know we're finished if they just leave us alone. Some war this has turned out to be. I wanted to go down with my rifle on full auto. You know?"

I nodded my head.

Yeah, I suppose I knew.

My sense of anger and frustration was as great as anyone's. The heady days of signing up with the Fleet to see the stars had been replaced with the painful, ever-present reality of the world around us. A desolate, barren little ball of rock and sand that appeared to offer almost nothing of value to humankind. Beyond the fact that it belonged to the mantes.

Or did it?

I let myself wonder if maybe the lack of alien air patrols was a sign that our guys had slowly pruned the mantes out of the air, and that a recovery effort would soon be underway to retrieve survivors. If only the tank's damned communications equipment worked. If only the Fleet people in orbit would respond to the emergency distress calls!

One day later, we got our definitive answer.

An alien craft—far bigger than an aerospace fighter—thundered down out of the sky. It opened up with a chain gun, slicing our anti-air tank to ribbons, along with the men and women who'd rushed to hastily crew the thing. Those not killed by the blast lived to see the huge ship deploy massive ovoidal pods around our perimeter, out of which poured hundreds of alien troops.

The mantes. Face to face. At last.

Or, rather, face to beak.

They were far more hideously insectlike than their reputation made them out to be. As we'd been shown in the video footage from Marvelous, their lower halves were connected to what could only be described as miniature flying saucers: discus-shaped devices perhaps three meters in diameter, each floating above the ground by a means none of us could determine.

When the marines on the perimeter started cracking off shots, the mantis infantry went to work. It was a horrid display. Not only did each of the discs contain automatic slug-throwing weaponry similar to our R77A5s, they also contained anti-personnel rocketry and, failing that, the mantis soldiers would simply swoop in and swing at a man with one of their long, vicious-looking, serrated-chitin forelimbs.

Heads and arms popped off like corks.

Flesh was sheared and devoured in the aliens' ferociously fanged mouths, the inner teeth working like that of some Earth snakes: tractoring backward with each bite, to pull the victim—or what was left of the victim—deeper into the mantes' gullets.

I stayed near the chaplain, but kept my rifle down as the mantes demolished the perimeter and drove the survivors back into a huddled cluster around Chaplain Thomas.

"Throw down your arms," the chaplain wheezed.

"Beg pardon, sir?" one of the corporals said, his face tight and his armor covered in the blood of his comrades.

We numbered just thirty-five now, while barely a dozen of the enemy had been killed—their floating discs ruined and their corpses slowly cooking in the thin air as the discs burned.

"If they wanted us all dead, they'd have done it by now," Chaplain Thomas said with as much force as he could muster. "Obviously they have orders to disarm and detain us. Notice that nobody who hasn't fired a weapon yet has been harmed."

I remembered the LCX on Earth's Moon. The last stand. I'd been out of action when it had happened, but I'd heard about it. The simulated mantes had come in hard. Relentless. Chipping away at defenses until only a few survivors were left, and then they too were destroyed. The entirety of the company overwhelmed.

Only, now it wasn't a simulation anymore. I itched to put my rifle to my shoulder and start firing. I'd fire until I made them kill me. Better a quick death on my feet than a slow death on my knees. But Chaplain Thomas's stern hand on my wrist stopped me from committing suicide.

"No, Specialist Barlow," he said. "I will not permit it. We have been spared. For what reason I cannot yet say, but we have been spared. Do not look a gift horse in the mouth."

"They're demons," I said. "Look at them!"

"I see them," he said. "I see the visage of a people so utterly unlike us that they may very well be beyond our comprehension.

But I also see that they have stayed their hand. I beg of you, men and women of Earth, lay down your arms. To fight at this point is hopeless. We are outnumbered and outgunned. We came to this world puffed up in pride: the pride of our hearts, of ourselves, of our weaponry and our mighty Fleet, and we have been summarily defeated. We can die in pride, and be damned for it. Or we can be patient, and see what the Maker of All Things has yet in store for us."

It was the closest I'd ever heard Chaplain Thomas come to doing any bona fide fire-and-brimstone preaching. The force of his words must have hurt him terribly—to speak them while in such pain. But he'd spoken them just the same, and he'd gotten our attention. Both because he was the last officer alive, and also because I think—to this day—that each of us in that little circle desperately wished to stay alive. If only for a little while longer.

One by one, we slowly laid down our rifles. Then we put our hands and arms into the air. Not that the mantes would have any idea what that meant. Old human habits die hard.

The mantes did not speak, yet communication between them was apparent. I guessed it had something to do with those damned discs.

An armed corridor of mantes suddenly formed, aiming away towards one of the giant pods the mantis ship had deposited.

A mantis near us aimed a forelimb down the length of the corridor and then stared at us, as if to say, *go now.*

Forgetting our weapons, we stumbled forwarded.

In the chaplain's case, we had him on a stretcher—which I carried at the rear, and a burly marine carried at the front. The chaplain winced and coughed with every move we made, but before long he let himself lay still and stared up into the alien planet's dimly blue sky.

"Not like home," he said as I walked, my cheeks puffing with effort.

No, I thought, *definitely not.*

CHAPTER 47

THE NEXT MORNING THE QUEEN MOTHER MET ME AT MY DOOR.

"Come with me," she said.

Having eaten and dressed, I raised an eyebrow and followed her out of the compartment and into the corridor. Mantes passed us moving to and fro, their discs humming softly. If they thought a human remarkable aboard a mantis vessel, they didn't show it. In fact they all seemed to be making a point of ignoring me. Or was it the Queen Mother? I remembered the old Earth traditions of the monarchists. To look a king or queen in the eye had been a forbidden thing in some courts. I wondered if this was something similar?

I walked while the Queen Mother floated. We passed through numerous passageways and connecting corridors, each of them arranged in what seemed to be a very definite geometry. The ceilings were high and the bulkheads were all coated in a somewhat translucent, plasticlike substance that seemed both harder and more durable than plastic—at least when I stole a moment to rap my knuckles on it.

"Here," she finally said. We emerged into what I might best describe as an observation deck. A transparent dome in the side of the ship, into which a platform projected. I walked out onto it with the Queen Mother leading the way, and we stopped at the very end. I noted that the stars were fixed. No relativistic compression of light.

"Is there a problem? We're at sublight velocity."

"We have dropped to conventional propulsion for a routine navigational calibration. I am using the opportunity to seek your counsel. Look into the universe and tell me what you see," she said.

"I beg your pardon?"

She aimed a forelimb into the inky depths of the cosmos, pinpricked a hundred thousand times by tiny, bright stars.

"Look, and tell me the knowledge of your heart."

A very curious choice of words, I thought.

But I caught her drift. The Professor and I had played this game many times while stargazing back on Purgatory.

"If you're asking me for a metaphysical answer, I can tell you that when I view the galaxy—especially a view as magnificent as this—I am overcome with a sense of humility."

"You are humble?"

"Yes. The galaxy is vast, and yet it is only one of a countless number of galaxies spanning a virtually endless ocean of space."

"An ocean," she said somewhat dubiously.

"Not literally," I said. "It's metaphor."

"I see. So you look upon space the way your ancestors once viewed the seas of your home world. A liquid medium across which to explore and travel, seek new lands, colonize, and expand."

"You see it differently?"

"No, the traditional mantis view is much as yours. I speak to you now only of my particular struggle. When we were marooned on that nameless world onto which your human lifeboat landed, I was struck by the fact that while each of our peoples pretend to 'own' space, this ownership is an illusion. The distances between stars are immense. It would take lifetimes to travel at sublight speeds. Both our races have been primarily focused on those planets and resources concentrated nearest the stars themselves. But we know from study that there is a great deal between the stars too—planets without stars, as well as gases, whole clouds of minute rock and dust particles, all swirling in an immense gravitational dance according to the specific masses of the aggregate whole."

"Indeed," was all I said. I caught the gist of her pontification, though it seemed to me she was expressing much of it for the sake of prefacing a deeper argument.

"For perhaps the first time," she said, "I asked myself, what is it all for? The universe, I mean. If not for the boundless expansion and dominance of the mantis people, then what? Sharing this universe with humans is not merely a question of territory, Padre. A long-term peace means sharing space with humans in our collective *consciousness*. We will be admitting that we are no longer alone. That there is a type and kind of mind in the universe that is equal to our own. If not precisely in function or capacity, then at least in value."

I watched the stars intently, not looking at her as I spoke.

"On my world, many hundreds of years ago, the dominant nations faced a similar question. Indeed, we have been forced to face that question in terms of gender, in terms of ethnicity, sexuality, socioeconomics, whatever way in which one human can be different from another human, we've been forced to adapt to the fact that there are people different from ourselves, that they exist with the same rights and fundamental freedoms, and that no one human group or collection of groups has the authority to revoke those rights or freedoms. Despite the fact that values and perceptions of values continue to clash."

"I do not understand," the Queen Mother said. "Are you telling me that it is common for humans to fight *other* humans?"

"Precisely," I said. "Because the raw truth of it is that many humans cannot tolerate sharing the universe with many other humans."

"Example," she said, in a most demanding tone.

I considered for a moment.

"Consider the captain. She was of a religious order known as Copts. Not generally the same as an ethnicity, the Copts were persecuted and driven practically to extinction by the Muslims. Another religious group which believed both similarly and also very, very differently from the Copts."

"Yes," she said. "This I know of from the archives: the races we discovered previously also warred in this way. I am perhaps surprised to learn of such human conflict occurring recently."

"It's still ongoing," I said. "Before the mantis threat was discovered and the original war begun, Earth itself—and its colonies—were divided. In fact, several of the colonies were established precisely as a way for certain humans to flee the persecution they'd experienced as a result of coming into conflict with other humans."

"Remarkable," the Queen Mother said.

"Unfortunate," I added. "Had we spent the last few thousand years as a unified people—as the mantes have—I wager that when our races met, we might have been on par with yours. With an equally enlarged footprint in the galaxy proper. Instead, we were caught by surprise. And though we learn and adapt quickly, I believe very much that our ultimate fate still rests in mantis hands."

"You say this without shame," she said.

"I was ashamed once," I told her. "The Professor saw that, when he first went to Purgatory to talk to me. I was ashamed, and I was angry. At the mantes. At humanity too. So much so that I attempted to provoke the Professor on more than one occasion."

"Provoke," she said. "I can't imagine how."

"It doesn't matter. After the armistice I grew to accept the situation for what it was. To borrow terms from an ancient human game, the mantes held all the face cards. We might resist you for a while. We might put up a brave and extended fight. But there are simply too many of you, and too few of us. Sooner or later, humanity will be overwhelmed."

"Something I am afraid I was only too eager to prove," she admitted. Out of the corner of my eye I saw a flush form along the semi-soft portions of her carapace.

"You are embarrassed by the new war," I said.

"Yes. But not just that. I am growing more horrified every moment at the thought that somewhere out there right now, mantes and humans are killing each other. And I *caused* it. I prepared the way, and I started the fight. Because I had no room in my imagination for a universe with humans."

"Many humans have no room in their imaginations for a universe with mantes," I said, trying to balance the scale.

"If that is a crime," she said, "then it is a small thing compared to what I have done. Padre, what reckoning can I hope for? Even if I am able to establish an understanding with my successor, and get the Quorum to recall all of our forces . . . how can I hope to mend the damage? I cannot resurrect the many lives lost. I cannot give to the kin of the dead—to the family of Captain Adanaho—any apology sufficient to the enormity of their suffering."

Now I turned to look directly at the Queen Mother. The semi-soft portions of her carapace had become so discolored I realized I'd never seen a mantis this sorrowfully emotional before. Had she been a human, I imagine she'd have been sobbing.

"Stopping the war is all that matters now," I said.

"No," she said, her speaker box failing to translate the bulk of her distress, though it clearly showed on her. "I must find some way to mend what I have done. This war I've created—"

"You didn't create it alone," I said. "General Sakumora and the other officers of Fleet Command were also eager for the fight. Having been beaten and humiliated in the first war, they wanted a second crack at you. Though anyone with eyes and a brain could have told them it was futile."

"Pride," the Queen Mother said. "My pride. Your general's pride. And blindness. Both of us, so blind..."

Her head hung and her forelimbs lay limply on the front of her disc. I hesitantly reached out a hand and touched one of those forelimbs. The chitin was hard, but not cold. She was as warm as the Professor had been.

"What you're seeking is something we humans call absolution," I said.

"I do not understand that word."

"It means you're feeling the full weight of your...wrong choices, and you are trying to find a way to make up for them. Because it...hurts inside when you think about those wrong choices."

"Yes, yes," she said, suddenly rearing up. Her forelimbs tapped at the center of her thorax. "It hurts, Padre! *I* hurt, and the world is *flat,* and I cannot see how any of this will change!"

I suddenly remembered a midnight conversation the Professor had had in my chapel, with a couple of folk from the Church of Jesus Christ of Latter-Day saints. They'd been specifically discussing the standard Mormon practice of immersing people fully in water, prior to making them members of the church. The Professor had been engrossed in the concept, because no such concept had ever existed in mantis culture: a cleansing of the soul, for an accumulated lifetime of errors.

Had it, the Queen Mother could seek the mantis equivalent of a priest, a rabbi, a shaman, *someone* capable of understanding what she was going through, and either assign proper penance in the Catholic fashion, or perhaps give the Queen Mother a framework in which to grapple with her growing sense of self-horror.

Were it also that men of Earth's history—Stalin, Mao, Hitler, Osama Bin Laden—had found their consciences as readily as the Queen Mother had apparently found hers, perhaps there might have been a lot less blood shed during the so-called birth of the modern human age.

"I'm not sure I can do you much good," I said. "I told the Professor this again and again. I am not a chaplain, just the assistant. I do not preach nor do I pretend to hold any kind of moral or spiritual authority."

"But you must believe in something," she said. "Otherwise why did you build your chapel at all? Why did you let Captain Adanaho talk you into coming with her to the summit meeting between myself and your General Sakumora?"

Now it was my turn to flush. Dammit, why did this keep coming up? Why did things always find a way of circling back around to what *I* believed? As if what I thought was true had any bearing on this mantis or her people?

The Mormons had once told the Professor that their version of Heavenly Father was the God of all—human, mantis, and any other sapient life in the universe. The Professor had found the idea rather extraordinary. I'd thought it a gross presumption on their part. Even I would not have pretended to make such statements no matter how strongly I felt about my beliefs.

Now I actually regretted not having such faith. The Queen Mother was in pain. She needed answers. And I was ill-equipped to give them because I'd never sought out such answers in my own life—had not *demanded* them of myself. Easier to hide behind a veneer of benevolent neutrality. Play at being a facilitator for the spiritual progression of others, while ignoring my own.

I realized for the first time how much of a coward I'd been. Tears leaked down my face.

"For me?" The Queen Mother asked.

"Yes," I said. "And for myself as well. Were I a better man, I believe I could give you some of what you seek. Or at least point surely to a way of gaining clarity. But your predicament—this new war, and all that's come with it—has exposed me to the fact that I have been deluding myself."

"How?"

"It's difficult to explain. Just that Captain Adanaho and the Professor both called me on the carpet about it. You're not the only one with sins to atone for."

I wiped at my face and sniffled, trying to compose myself.

"Then we are allied in more ways than one," she said. "Padre, your Captain Adanaho once told me—by way of the Professor—that all of this was happening for a reason. She believed it firmly. Perhaps she is right. *What* that reason might be I cannot say. But you and I must work together to find solutions to our mutual problems. The question for me at this moment is: where do I start?"

I considered the question, looking at her through my unexpected tears.

"Get rid of the carriage," I said.

She backed away from me.

"Yes," I said. "That's got to be it. You said it yourself when you came to my quarters. The disc is hampering your natural perceptions in ways you didn't realize until you had to do without a disc long enough to tell the difference. I think the choice is an obvious one."

"I would be a permanent cripple," she said. "You know the carriage is part of who we are. I can no more do without it than you could do without your arms and legs."

"Then find a way to compromise," I said. "Break it up. Pare back the carriage's functions one by one until the 'flatness' fades or disappears."

She looked at me, the flush along her semi-soft chitin beginning to dissipate and her forelimbs caressing the front of her disc thoughtfully.

"Yes," she said. "Yes!"

Almost immediately, she spun on her vertical axis and shot back down the length of the platform.

"Wait!" I cried, but she was gone.

And I'd been left to find my way back to my compartment, alone.

I stayed on the observation deck for a few more minutes, then slowly walked back into the ship's interior.

CHAPTER 48

Target planet (Purgatory), 2155 A.D.

THE MANTIS CARRIER PUT DOWN IN A MOUNTAIN VALLEY. AS did over a hundred other carriers just like it. We were herded out of the pods like cattle. Thousands of us. The ragged survivors of a once-mighty human flotilla. With only the clothes on our backs, or what we'd been able to salvage in duffels, bags, packs, and satchels. Anything that wasn't obviously a weapon, but which might still offer some kind of use.

Perhaps a third of us were wounded. Some very seriously, like the chaplain.

With mantis infantry standing watch at the valley rim, we were left to figure ourselves out.

"No escape," one NCO remarked bleakly.

Chaplain Thomas was looking worse every hour.

A Fleet nurse who'd been trying to do his best to stand in for an actual physician approached me and pulled me aside.

"He's not going to last much longer."

"Tell me something I don't know," I replied tersely. "Is there anything you can do for the pain? He's hurting bad."

"I want to save the pain meds for the people I think we can save."

I wanted to retort in anger, but realized the futility of it. If we'd had the capacity to get Chaplain Thomas to a surgeon, even his present injuries—dire as they seemed—weren't life threatening. But the nearest surgery center had been back aboard the Fleet starship we'd left behind, and which had now obviously been destroyed, or tucked tail and run when the tide turned.

There would be no help for the chaplain's injuries.

He chuckled bleakly at me when I told him the bad news.

"Figured as much, all by myself," he said.

"I'm sorry," I said. "I wish there was more I could do."

"You can do something," he said.

"What?"

"When I'm gone, build me a chapel."

I stared at him.

"I am completely serious," Chaplain Thomas said. "If the mantes have let so many of us live, there's got to be a reason for it. Sounds like they're not letting anyone in or out of the valley. Which means we're prisoners of war. And that means these people—all who have survived—are going to need somewhere to come and cry out their sorrows to the Lord."

"But I don't know anything about architecture—"

"You don't have to know," he said. "Noah built an ark with nothing but the power of God to guide him. Surely you can put together something with four walls and a roof? If you want to do something for me, Harrison Barlow, you will build me a chapel. Keep it clean. Keep it neat. Make sure anyone and everyone is welcome. So that they can come in, sit down, maybe talk about their problems, and seek some peace of mind."

"I'm not convinced there will be any peace of mind for any of us," I said. In a matter of days, all our lives had been smashed to ruins. Earth was cut off from us. Our friends, our families. Gone. And we ourselves might as well have been dead, for how much optimism I saw in the expressions on the faces of the people around me. The surviving officers and Fleet NCOs were trying to rally. But the shock still hadn't worn off. People milled about in little camps and circles: hollow-eyed, flinching at even small sounds, and so very, very afraid.

My dour reverie must have been apparent.

The chaplain snapped his fingers at me.

"Yessir?" I said.

"Boy," the chaplain said to me, snagging my hand in his, and pressing his fingers into my flesh with as much strength as he could muster. "Tammy swore to me that you were a good one. The kind of fellow who could make a difference in peoples' lives. Listen to me now. Whether or not you live or die is no longer important. You hear me? Not anymore. That's completely in the Lord's hands now. Which means all you need to decide is what you want to do with yourself in the time the Lord's got left for you. Are you going to sit around and be so frightened that you can't move or breathe? Or are you going to try to make the world a better place?"

He began coughing terribly, wincing all the while. Bits of blood speckled the front of his armor suit now.

"Ripping up my own lungs," he wheezed.

"I'll go bring the nurse back," I said.

"Forget it. It's almost over. And I'm sorry, son. I truly am sorry. For me, captivity will be short-lived. I go to my reward. But for you? The Lord's got a trial in mind for you. And a work to be accomplished. You dodge that, and it will haunt you for the rest of your days. Such as they are. Don't run away from it, Harry. Time to grow up and take it by the horns. Life is filled with challenges, and you've got a big one now. Promise me you'll build the chapel? Promise me."

I looked away from him as he started coughing again. It wasn't fair. The whole thing. The decimation of the flotilla. Getting rounded up in this valley like pigs in a pen. Having everything I'd once considered dear ripped away from me and placed light-years distant. But most of all, it wasn't fair that a dying man was making me carry out his last wish.

"You know what you have to do," Chaplain Thomas said.

"Alright, dammit," I said. "You win. I promise I'll build it."

"And keep it clean, and make sure people feel welcome."

"Yes, yes."

"No one will be turned away."

"I'll see to it."

"Make it a house where the spirit can dwell."

"I don't know how."

"You will *learn* how."

And with that, he laid his head back on the stretcher, took one final, shuddering breath, and died. As if he'd chosen that moment to depart. I wanted to call him a few choice names for making me promise to do something I had no desire nor intention of doing. Instead, I simply laid a towel across his face and set about seeking the best place to bury him.

That night I found the spot. It was away from the mass grave—where most of those who'd died since our being deposited in the valley were being put. I didn't want Chaplain Thomas's remains moldering with everyone else's. He'd been a nice officer and an affectionate clergyman. It seemed wrong to just carry him to the hole and up-end him into it, with all the others. So I strapped Chaplain Thomas's body to the stretcher and began the painstaking task of hauling him towards a high, flat spot perhaps five hundred meters from where the bulk of the Fleet refugees had assembled themselves. The grumbling din of conversation fell behind me as I trudged.

Every ten minutes or so, I set the body down and let my arms rest.

To my surprise, I heard a voice call to me out of the dusk.

"Need a hand?" asked the woman.

"No," I lied.

"Seems like a big job for one specialist," she said. As she approached me I noticed she had on a somewhat grimy flight suit. Her name tape said FULBRIGHT, and the patches on her chest and shoulders indicated she'd been a gunner.

I relented, and let her pick up the other end of the stretcher.

"Someone special to you?" she asked as we walked: me in front, her in the rear.

"His name was Chaplain Thomas, and he was a good man."

"Too good to be put with the rest of the dead?"

"Look, it doesn't matter, okay? If you're going to help me, can you do it in peace?"

"Sorry. I haven't had much of a chance to talk to anyone. I came down in an escape pod after the *Seahawk* began to break up in orbit. The mantes found and picked me up earlier today."

"Did *any* of our ships make it?"

"Not sure. I was blazing away like there was no tomorrow, and none of my shells nor any of the missiles made so much as a dent in the mantis destroyers. They've got this kind of shielding that glows when you hit it. Our weapons couldn't touch them. Would have been nice to know in advance that they had *that* little trick up their buggy sleeves."

I grunted my agreement. What we hadn't known, had indeed hurt us.

When we reached the spot I'd picked—the light now all but gone from the valley—I set to work with my small hand shovel.

Gunner Fulbright got down beside me and went to work with a folding spade she'd saved from her escape pod's emergency supplies.

"Why are you helping me?" I asked.

"Because I need a friend," she said. "And there's no better way to make friends than to pick the guy who seems to be doing the most thankless work, and pitch in."

"Your attitude is far more positive than it deserves to be," I said.

She laughed at me.

"Maybe," she said. "But my mama always told me the Lord hates a coward, so I'd rather apply myself to something positive, than run around being afraid of my shadow the way a lot of these other survivors seem to be doing."

Again, I grunted my agreement.

We dug for hours. By feel. Until we were exhausted. When we slept, we slept on the dirt—something every survivor had rapidly learned to do in the wake of the Fleet's destruction on-planet.

When light peeked over the tops of the mountains that ringed the valley, we got up and carefully lowered Chaplain Thomas's remains down into the grave. Neither of us had anything particularly special or meaningful to say, so we said nothing. We simply pushed the soil and sand back over the top of the body, tenderly tamped the layer down, then levered a large oblong boulder into place as a marker.

In fact, the entire area was strewn with stone.

I considered the promise I'd made to my now-deceased boss. What passed for trees on this world wouldn't be much good for cutting timber. If anything was going to be built, it would be built out of rock and mud.

I used my heel to mark off a largish rectangle in the ground not far from where the chaplain had been buried.

"I'm hungry, and we'd better get back," Fulbright said.

"You go ahead," I said. "I want to finish this first."

"What for?" she asked.

"I made a promise," I said. "And I don't want to leave until I've left behind something permanent—which I can come back to and build on later."

"Okay then, I'll see you back down with the others."

"Hey, Gunner," I said to her as she walked away.

"Yeah?" she said over her shoulder.

"You were right," I said.

"About what?"

"About making friends. Thanks. For being mine."

She stopped. Then turned and smiled at me.

"Any time, Barlow. Any time."

CHAPTER 49

NOT KNOWING THE MANTIS SHIP'S LAYOUT, AND NOT HAVING paid attention to the way I'd come when the Queen Mother had been in the lead, I quickly got lost. Unlike before, the mantes I passed *did* notice me—which seemed to confirm my theory about underlings not meeting the eyes of their sovereign.

The longer I passed aimlessly through corridor after corridor, the more acute my disorientation became. Not to mention my sense of paranoia. The mantes weren't merely looking at me now. A solid dozen of them had stopped what they were doing so that they could follow me. At a distance, yes, but still following me. Not saying anything.

I walked faster; they simply kept pace. Until I finally turned and confronted them.

"May I help you?" I asked, trying to remain calm.

"Tell us, human," said a soldier in the lead, "by what power is it that you're able to bend the greatest among us to your will?"

"I don't understand," I said.

"The Queen Mother is dependent on you," said another soldier. "We are constrained from criticizing her openly, but amongst ourselves we note this unpleasant deference to an inferior life form, and we do not like it."

I felt a sudden chill in my chest.

The mantes slowly circled me until I was surrounded.

"I am sure the Queen Mother would be willing to assuage any misgivings you might have," I said, the sweat springing out across my body as my heart rate began to climb. Back on the planet where the lifeboat had come to rest, we'd been fleeing human troops—humans I'd at least have had a shot at dealing with. Here? On this ship? I suddenly realized that beyond the Queen Mother herself and perhaps the three technicians specifically tasked with helping me, I had no friends. To these mantes, I was not much better than vermin.

I swallowed hard.

"We are not permitted to redress such concerns directly," said the first soldier. He floated forward until he was practically on top of me.

"I have seen humans in battle. I have killed humans. I have seen mantes killed *by* humans. I want to know how it is that you have managed to force a conciliatory course on my people when we are in fact on the brink of total victory. Our scholars were befuddled by you once in the same manner. I know of the fool you called the Professor. I am pleased to learn he is no longer alive to spread his particular brand of pacifist idiocy."

"So now you intend to rid the universe of me as well?" I said.

"I desire this greatly, yes," the soldier said.

"Then why don't you do it?" I said.

Feeling the sudden courage of action that comes with disregarding all personal safety, I reached out and pulled the soldier's forelimb right up to my neck, the serrations just millimeters from my skin. In one raw stroke he could have my throat open down to the spine. It would be over. It would be quick.

I waited, almost breathless.

"You taunt me," the soldier said.

"Not at all. I am defenseless. I have no firearms nor grenades nor other killing devices with which to harm any of you. If you believe I am a threat, you must take action."

The soldier's insect eyes stared down at me. I could almost feel the longing in him—to shed my blood.

A sudden klaxon blared and the soldier dropped to the deck. Or, rather, his *disc* dropped to the deck. I jumped back, watching him and all the mantes around me drop in a similar fashion.

"What the hell—?"

Three shapes zoomed down the corridor and surrounded me: the technicians who'd been setting up my quarters next to the Queen Mother's.

"What's happened?" I asked—panting—with a finger pointed at the lead soldier, who now flopped and flailed harmlessly.

"Disciplinary override," said one of the mantes. "When the Queen Mother came to us to discuss her project for the slow dismantling of her carriage, we asked her where you were. Realizing her error, she dispatched us to find you—with her command override code at our discretion."

"What does that mean?"

"It means, assistant-to-the-chaplain, that so long as any mantis is aboard this vessel, its disc can be ordered to commit a partial shutdown. We have known since your arrival that not all mantes welcome your presence. Or your relationship with the Queen Mother. We are only fortunate that we found you in time to stop something unpleasant from happening."

I was almost delirious with adrenaline as I realized I'd been moments from certain death. How or why I'd thought it a good idea to place my head in the proverbial guillotine and shout, *bring it on,* was something I would have to ponder later.

"Thank you," I managed to say to the three technicians as they began escorting me away from the scene.

"Thank the Queen Mother," they said in unison. "Only her code has the power to do what we just did. Without it, we'd have merely been spectators."

"What will happen to them?" I asked.

"In a few more moments their discs will all come back up to full operational capability. At which point we will be far out of reach."

"Is this how the mantes maintain order in the ranks?"

"An extreme example, yes," said one of the technicians. "I am afraid your presence here has greatly disturbed the harmony that normally exists aboard a mantis vessel. We must ensure that you are never again allowed to wander unprotected."

"Yeah," I said, walking so fast I was almost running, "that's a pretty good idea."

By the time we got me back to my compartment I was shaking like a leaf.

I bade them another thankful farewell, then went to the wash basin and braced my arms on either side—muscles quivering. I splashed so much water on myself there was a huge puddle on the deck around me, and my uniform was soaked. I stripped and threw the uniform into the washer-dryer, then flopped out onto my bed and turned the lights back off.

The universe had suddenly reminded me just how hostile and unforgiving it really is. My little philosophical conversation with the Queen Mother had made me complacent. Of course these mantes were still hostile. Just because they were following orders didn't mean they wouldn't seize an opportunity to act.

I told myself I'd get my technician friends to provide me with a way to lock my compartment against outside intrusion. I suddenly felt very, very vulnerable without it.

CHAPTER 50

Target planet (Purgatory), 2155 A.D.

THE WALLS OF THE CHAPEL WERE ABOUT A METER HIGH WHEN I first noticed it: a translucent curtain that seemed to shimmer in the air right at the crests of the mountains around the valley's edge. Where once the enemy had kept companies of troops endlessly patrolling the rim, now there was simply the energy barrier.

"Remember the shields I told you about?" Fulbright said to me during one of her routine visits to the gradually-growing chapel.

"Yeah," I said, hefting another stone into place. My mortar wasn't construction-grade by any Earth standard. But it was the best I could do under the circumstances. I'd once helped my father build a river rock wall along the back edge of our property. This kind of work wasn't much different. Each day I brought several buckets of silt-laden water from the shallow creek that ran about a kilometer away, dumped pieces of clay and other appropriate-seeming soil into the buckets, then mixed until I felt I had the right consistency. Onto the existing walls went the mortar, then the new batch of rocks, and though it had taken me almost six local months, I had to admit I was proud of what I'd accomplished. Little by little, the chapel was taking shape.

With occasional help from friends like Fulbright, of course.

I stopped what I was doing and looked at the valley rim.

"Not to protect us," I said, speculating.

"No," she said. "To keep us in."

I thought about it for a moment.

"Makes sense from their point of view. Since it's obvious they've not got much interest in us, other than to keep us here. Why have troops on guard round the clock when you can just tighten the cap on the bottle, and call it good?"

Fulbright's expression was dour.

"It bothers you," I said.

"Yes," she said. "Only because of what I've seen that energy barrier do. I wonder how it works?"

"I wonder how a *lot* of their shit works," I said. "Do you ever get the feeling that we came here with sticks and bones, and found the bad guys using automatic cannon?"

"All the time," she said.

"Well, try not to let it bother you too much. Where's that enthusiasm from the first day we met?"

"Even I get tired," she said, and sat down, her head resting against one of the dry parts of the chapel wall.

I kept working for a little while, slapping on gobs of mortar, then piecing rocks together as they seemed to fit, followed by more mortar. Once I was done with that day's section, I'd go out and help forage in the foothills for food. All of us had lost an average of five to seven kilograms since our incarceration in the valley. Local food sources were few and far between, and we had no Earth seeds with which to plant gardens. What little wildlife there was had proven small, and horribly gamey when eaten. Enough so that I was seriously considering becoming a vegetarian for the first time in my life. Except there weren't many veggies on hand, either.

"How's it going around the rest of the valley?" I asked.

"It's going," she said. "You're not the only one building. People are busy. It's the only thing they have right now, to distract them from our mutual predicament. You should know that there are other chapels going up."

"Good," I said. "Because there's no way this one would be able to accommodate the thousands of people who'd potentially come. Assuming anyone does come."

"Oh, you'll get people," she said. "Word's out that you're carrying on in Chaplain Tom's name. A lot of the marines liked him. His good reputation is doing you favors. Enough so that a small bunch of them have even started talking about coming out to help you. Once there's time."

I laughed softly.

With no infrastructure and no guarantee that we'd be able to scrape up enough food for us to last the cold season that seemed to be creeping over this hemisphere of the planet, time suddenly seemed to be the one thing that was in short supply. All of us were working hard on our separate tasks. And not always with the blessing of the Fleet leadership that was trying—and, daily, failing—to maintain control in the valley. Apparently I wasn't the only one who'd allowed his military bearing to lapse in the wake of being captured. If I was going to be stuck here for a long duration, I damned well wasn't going to let myself stay locked into a military regimen. There just didn't seem to be much of a point. We had no more weapons nor any ability to fight. Nor, apparently—now that the mantes had put up the barrier at the valley rim—anyone to fight against.

We were an island colony, unto ourselves.

And I sure as hell wasn't going to worry about showing up for accountability formations. Nor did I have any interest in any of the other claptrap the Fleet had drilled into me since joining. Maybe aboard ship it had become easy to lapse into the routine. But here, now, all routine had been thrown out the window. There was simply survival. Scratch life out of the dirt—every day, all day.

I looked at Fulbright as her chin sat on her chest.

"Try not to get too down about it," I said.

She stayed silent, staring at the dirt.

A small gust of wind swept over us, tossing up dust.

"Do you think they'll send a rescue mission?" she asked.

"Fleet?" I said.

"Yes."

"I guess it all depends on whether or not they think there is anyone left alive worth rescuing, and whether or not a rescue squadron could have any better chance against the mantis defenders than we did. For all we know a rescue squadron *did* come, and got blown out of space without our even noticing."

She put her fists to her eyes and rubbed. Suddenly, I felt bad for speaking my mind.

"Sorry," I said.

"It's not your fault. I agree. But now I'm wondering, what are we being saved for?"

"The mantes, you mean?"

"Yes," she said, looking up at me with red, tear-soaked eyes. "Are they keeping us alive just because they think it's *fun?*"

I tried to remember my military history from Earth. Traditionally, military prisoners were kept for three reasons: extraction of military information, collateral for prisoner exchange, or in accordance with treaties and rules of war. In our case almost none of these situations applied. So what value were we—if any—to the mantes? Beyond objects of curiosity?

During one of Earth's worst world wars, one of the European armies had put people into extermination camps based on religious or ethnic affiliation. Many of these poor prisoners had become subjects for horrific medical experimentation. I shuddered at the thought of all of us being used as the human equivalent of lab rats or dissection frogs.

"Who knows how the mantes think," I said. "They're as different from us as we are from them. Maybe they have some kind of ethic about total annihilation being wrong?"

"Being stuck here forever doesn't seem much better than being dead," she said.

"I guess that's why Chaplain Thomas wanted me to build this," I replied, motioning with my hands to the walls I was constructing.

She pulled her knees to her chin and returned to staring at the dirt.

In the two local years that followed, the walls of the chapel got higher, and higher, until finally I was forced to contemplate a roof. Several enterprising people in the valley had built kilns, and were firing bricks as well as tiles. I bartered work for materials, and had to put in several stone-and-mortar pillars to hold the ceiling up. With rainstorms occasionally blowing through, I found out very quickly where the leaks and holes were. I also found out that my tile-laying technique needed work, such that by the warm season of the third year I'd replaced the roof almost entirely with a much more durable, long-lasting patchwork.

This had not deterred attendance. Even before the roof was on, I was getting people coming in the door. Or rather, the frame where I eventually built a door. They sat on the floor until I bartered for some roughly-quarried benches.

If ever the attendees expected any kind of sermonizing from me, they didn't show it. And I didn't offer. Chaplain Thomas had been very specific: build it, keep it clean, and welcome all who wish to enter. Which was precisely what I did. Including the collection of several religious symbols and statuary from people who offered to make donations—which I then arrayed on a stone table at the front of the chapel. The table eventually began to serve more or less as a multidenominational altar.

For light, we had to get creative. Without electricity we couldn't use or recharge our flashlights. One of the native plants had inedible roots that, when their pulp was crushed and pressed, yielded a thick sweet-smelling oil. All of us began using it in small clay lamps, so that the chapel remained open sometimes long after sundown.

For myself, I had just one small room in the rear with a clumsy door made of salvaged native wood. My cot was actually the same stretcher Chaplain Thomas had been carried on—now with clay blocks at the feet and the head to hold it knee high above the ground.

Life in the valley assumed a kind of surreal normalcy.

With the rigidity of military regimen practically dissolved down to a small core of stalwart officers and older NCOs, people formed their own small communities and townships. Roads sprang into being where feet crossed between the villages. A civilian constabulary of former MPs and several volunteers formed up to take care of the few actual crimes anyone might recognize as being worth policing—namely, theft and murder. Which was extremely rare. With so much room in the valley and only a few thousand of us to go around, anyone who didn't much like his neighbors could easily move away.

Farms sprang up wherever there was water to be had. People with green thumbs quickly began to figure out how to coax some of the native plants and even a few of the smallish animals into domestic capacity. There was talk of formalizing plans for an elaborate series of canals and ditches that would divert water from the streams and small ponds in the foothills, down to the thirsty valley floor.

It wasn't an easy existence, but it was an existence all the same.

And since the mantes had practically vanished—save for the occasional patrol that passed through now and again, just to remind us who was in charge—we could almost forget ourselves.

Almost.

Fulbright surprised me when she went into the preaching business. In addition to my chapel, there had been at least a dozen other structures built in the valley that were dedicated to some religious purpose. And people who'd never given religion much thought during their lives on Earth suddenly began picking and choosing which churches or religions suited them best.

While I went with a soft hand, some others were pounding the pulpit. Which was fine. Whatever people needed to hear to get them through the to the end of each day, and to the tail of every week.

And while I was still technically only the Chaplain's Assistant, people had begun to more or less treat me as if I was Chaplain Thomas's surrogate: rendering me the same deference and respect that they might have rendered him. I'd have objected to such treatment if I'd not realized that the behavior had nothing to do with me, and everything to do with the fact that many people simply needed to revere someone or something other than themselves. Who I was was not as important as what I represented—as the personification of the chapel itself.

I never got the big crowds that Fulbright—Deacon Fulbright—sometimes got. But the regulars were friendly, and of all manner of belief. From the hesitant agnostics to the devoutly theistic. Mine was the building that became known as the quietest space in the valley.

To come and hear with your heart, not with your ears.

Until that morning almost five years after the invasion, when my chapel door yielded a surprising and unlikely inquirer...

CHAPTER 51

"I WAS TOLD WHAT HAPPENED," SAID THE QUEEN MOTHER.

It was the next day, following my near-miss with death at the hands of the mantes onboard the Queen Mother's flagship.

She was in my quarters, alone. Though I could tell by looking at it that she'd already begun the process of dismantling her disc. Several compartments appeared to have been evacuated, leaving nothing but gaping holes. Though this hadn't affected the disc's impellers, which allowed it to float and travel freely.

"I was stupid," I said, "And it almost cost me. If I'd been thinking more clearly I'd have stayed put until you or someone I knew came back for me. I should not having been wandering through the ship alone."

"And my people should not have been seeking to harm you in direct violation of my orders," she said. Her speaker grill mechanism was still working too—I thought I detected anger in the mechanical tone.

"They will be dealt with," she said.

"Not too harshly, I hope," I said.

"They would have killed you," she said.

"Perhaps," I said. "It definitely seemed like it in the moment. But that lead trooper—the one around whom the others seemed to have rallied—he hesitated in the end. I got the sense from him that even though he didn't like me, he wasn't quite prepared to do cold-blooded murder. Had I been an armed human on the field of battle, I have little doubt he'd have tried to cut me down.

He wasn't prepared for me to offer no defense, save a challenge to his conviction."

"Boldly played," she said.

"Or stupidly," I said. "Sometimes the dumbest move is the move that gets the best results."

"Just so," she said. "I am currently engaged in some dumb moves of my own. As you can see, I have begun the process of deconstructing my carriage. It is an uncomfortable and not altogether orthodox process. I have had to reassure my flag officers several times that I am not ill—either in body, or in mind. I tell them it is an experiment, nothing more."

"And if they decide you are compromised to the point they can't trust your authority?"

"No mantis has ever usurped the Queen Mother," she said. "We have had quarrels. Even on very rare occasions, violent ones. But nobody has ever removed a Queen Mother without her consent. As long as I live, my word is law on this vessel, and throughout mantis space. Rest assured. And any who transgress my word... as I said, they will be dealt with."

I cringed, imagining what that could possibly mean for the dozen or so aggressive and aggravated mantes who'd molested me in the corridor the day before.

"But aren't we basically usurping the *new* Queen Mother's authority?" I asked. "So far as we know, this is the only ship on which you have any actual control. What if when we get to this staging area you've spoken of before, the new Queen Mother orders you stripped of your power? Or even killed?"

"As I said," she said, "there have been quarrels. I am hopeful that because of my successor's relative youth in her new role, and because of the unexpectedness of my return, that both she and the Quorum will acquiesce."

"But will they let you actually halt the war, when you were the one who was pushing for it in the first place?"

"My newfound position on the matter of the war will take some explaining. Of that there can be no question. I have been trying to formulate my plan. For when I must ultimately stand before the Quorum of the Select itself, and make my argument. Where once the mantis you call the Professor came to me, and persuaded me to halt the Fourth Expansion, now I must do the same. But not for the sake of mere research or curiosity. I must convince the Quorum that a permanent peace with humans is not only the most pragmatic course of action, but also the most moral course."

"Moral," I said, testing the word on my tongue. "I've never heard either you or the Professor use it like that before. Do mantes even have morals?"

"We have what you humans understand to be ethics, and we pride ourselves on our logic. But yes, underneath it all, there are rules by which our society operates. We need them to function, much as you do. We believe in . . . I think you humans call it, right and wrong? Though there is no spiritual component to these decisions. We do not fear for the future of our souls should we make wrong choices. Or . . . we didn't used to."

I looked at her, and saw the flush returning to the soft places on her body. Her shame was welling up again, just like it had before.

"I'd like to be able to lock my door," I said, trying to distract her.

"I . . . Yes. Yes, your technical assistants have already been told, and I have authorized it. It will be done."

"Thank you," I said.

"No need to thank me. It was my fault I exposed you to potential harm in the first place. Here again I have caused hurt. In fact, everywhere I look lately—my choices, my own actions—I cause *hurt.* This hurt does not seem to be connected to any physiological problem of any sort. I have researched this phrase you used—*absolution*—according to the Professor's own notes. I am afraid I do not see much use in any of the Earthly rituals he was aware of, as a result of his lengthy study on Purgatory. Save one. Confession—talking about my wrongdoings with someone else. That does seem to make a difference."

"Really?" I said.

"Yes. After we had our conversation in the observation bubble yesterday, I felt reenergized. Not relieved, per se, but I felt as if I had discovered a possible direction. There was *work* to be done. And I was determined to do it. So much so that I am afraid I took leave of my senses and left you to fend for yourself."

"It's okay," I said. "My technical helpers came to the rescue. And it's not like turnabout isn't fair play. When we were onboard the *Calysta* it was you who became surrounded by hostile enemies. So let us consider the debt evened, and the fault resolved. Done?"

"Yes, I think so."

I got up out of my chair and began to walk around the room.

"If you're feeling claustrophobic," she said, "I could arrange for an escorted tour."

"It's not the ship that interests me. It's the goings-on *outside* the ship. The battles still being fought while we race to begin the recall process. I fear a great deal, and hope against the odds."

"Myself as well," she said. "The vessel is moving at maximum possible velocity now. We will arrive at the first staging base very soon. Then it can be seen whether or not my words can pull us back from the heart of the storm I've created."

The door opened and my technician friends arrived. They almost bowed in the Queen Mother's direction—not speaking a word, but seemingly transmitting their greetings and deference carriage-to-carriage.

"We would like to know more about children," they said.

The Queen Mother looked at me. "Do you mind if I stay for this?"

"No," I said. "Though I can't say I'll be able to give good answers. I am not a parent."

"When human children are hatched," said one of the three, "are they afforded no assistance at all?"

"What do you mean by 'assistance'?" I asked.

"Technological," said another. "For the mantis, his or her first thoughts are in conjunction with the carriage-joining process."

"You mean," I said, "the newborn's first thoughts are as a result of the carriage-mantis mental interface?"

"Yes," they said. "The newborn begins learning almost immediately. It is a process that takes many of your weeks—as the fundamental skills and knowledge are slowly integrated into the young adult's mind."

"Almost like loading an operating system onto a blank computer," I theorized.

"Very much like that, yes," said the one who'd not spoken up yet.

"For humans it's not that easy," I said. "We have no machine-mind interface. Nothing to download or upload. The baby—what we call our version of a pupa—is totally helpless and dependent on its mother and father for food, protection, cleaning, you name it. The mother and father do it all."

"When does learning begin?"

"Immediately," I said. "But for us it's purely experiential. And it takes a long time. Most of us don't even know how to walk until we're many Earth months old. Talking takes longer still. In fact, language skills are a primary emphasis right up until true adulthood, and even then it's never a totally complete process. So you might say, our journey from infancy to adulthood never really finishes. At least not for most of us."

The three technicians drifted away to converse amongst themselves while I sat at my desk and sipped at a cup of cool water. I'd have loved a soft drink or something with a little zing to it. But at least my water didn't have dirt in it.

"You receive no template?" the Queen Mother asked me.

"What do you mean by that?"

"Our young adults are given a basic set of what you might call 'operating instructions,' which prepare them properly to interact with adults and the mantis way of life. This happens through the carriage interface, and the template is the same for *all* of us. Regardless of our station. It's part of what allows us to begin individuated training so early, and also what keeps our society cohesive and rooted in mantis laws and traditions. It is what makes us who we are."

"For us, all of that comes in time," I said. "But everything depends on the parents."

"No two parents give the same template?"

"Hardly. Though many try. A great deal hinges on traditions and communities, national original, ethnic identity, among many other things."

"Then the templates of one parent or group of parents could be totally different from the templates of another," she said.

"Yes."

"No wonder humans are divided against humans," she said.

I could hardly disagree with her.

"But it's not all bad," I said. "For most of us, childhood is a wonderful time of discovery and exploration. Barring a few bumps and bruises."

"You liked your childhood?"

"Yes," I said.

"Mantis young adults are raised in collective training," said the Queen Mother. "Depending on who mates with whom—the female, and the male—their eggs will be destined to form new generations of farmers, factory workers, warriors, technicians, computer experts, and also researchers like the Professor."

"Can mantes ever change jobs?" I asked.

"What does that mean?" asked one of the technicians; they'd jointly floated back over to listen to the conversation.

"Can a mantis decide for him- or herself that, say, he or she no longer wants to be a farmer and instead wants to be an architect?"

"Why would we do that?" asked one of the technicians.

I looked at the Queen Mother. This was a bit unsettling.

"Secondary templates," she said. "Once the basics have been disseminated into the young adult consciousness, then comes the preparation for productive application in mantis industrial society."

"So what was your secondary template?" I asked her.

She thought about it for a moment.

"I was female, so this of course put me on track for the Quorum of the Select at an early age. We have far more males than females among us. I suppose my template was decided accordingly."

"And these technicians," I said, tipping he head in their direction, "they must have been secondarily templated for starship maintenance."

"Yes," she said.

"Does that bother you?" I asked the technicians.

"Does what bother us?" they said in unison.

"Does it bother you that before you were even hatched—or pupated—that all three of you had your roles in mantis culture selected for you without your knowledge or consent? That you were in fact *programmed* for this specific work?"

They stared at me.

"We are what we are," they said. "How could it be otherwise? Each mantis does his part for the whole. We do not worry about how each of the different pieces of the machine feels about its function, simply that our specific piece works as well as it can, so that the machine as a whole works as well as it can. If we started doubting ourselves... it would lead to chaos."

"It *was* chaos," the Queen Mother said. "The Professor may or may not have shared this, but long ago, during the time of the First Expansion, the mantes were not nearly as cohesive as we are now. There was great discord and division, although I do not think it approaches what you have described as being common on Earth. When the earliest carriages were developed—it is believed—the Quorum of the Select mandated that all pupating mantes be given as much advanced preparation for their healthy participation in society as possible. It has greatly helped us to maintain peace and harmony ever since. Every mantis has his or her place, and every mantis is happy in his or her place."

I said nothing. Such language—spoken on Earth—had been used by rulers throughout history to justify castes and permanent stratification of society. Or worse. It was fairly grotesque to hear such language coming out of the Queen Mother's mouth. It was even more grotesque to see my three tech helpers happily agreeing with the Queen Mother. Yet another reminder that while mantis minds and human minds worked equally well, our thoughts could often be very far apart.

"So the Professor did not decide on his own to become a Professor," I said.

"He could have resisted this," she said. "But why would he?"

"Why would any of us?" said one of the technicians.

"When we are doing our work, we are happiest," said another.

I resisted the urge to shudder.

"It is not so for humans?"

I shook my head vigorously.

"Humans seldom have just one occupation in their lives. And while we spend a lot of time schooling, and parents especially can sometimes try to direct their children into a specific path or vocation, whether or not that child actually chooses to remain on that path or in that vocation for the long-term is a matter for the individual to decide."

Now it was the mantes' turn to give me the funny looks. All four of them backed away ever so slightly. The Queen Mother seemed especially uncomfortable, based on the agitation in her movements.

"You will leave now," she said.

The technicians exited without a word of protest.

"Clearly," I said, "there are great differences between our people, in addition to great similarities."

"Clearly," she said.

"This templating process you describe," I said, "if it were applied on Earth it would be considered grossly immoral."

"Why?"

"Because in the past when it has been applied—albeit externally, through a combination of indoctrination, force of law, and violence—it's been condemned. Either in the moment, or by history. As a rule, we humans prize our independence and our right to choose."

"Mantes are also independent," she said.

"Yes, but apparently only to a point. You're the Queen Mother because from birth you were *slotted* to be among the people who might be chosen for that role. The Professor was a researcher because he was preselected for the job. In most human societies we resist that kind of thing. Though, as I said, there have been governments, societies, and even religions which have tried."

"And what has your independence gotten you?" she said. "You said it, Padre: humanity squandered its resources and its potential by fighting with itself, instead of uniting and pooling all talent, energy, and material towards a common goal—or set of common goals."

I was really getting uncomfortable now. She must have smelled it in the air.

"I will now return to the delicate process of adjusting and removing components of my carriage," she said.

"Of course," I said.

She hovered towards the open door. Halfway out she turned back to me and said, "Just because we mantes have a certain way of doing things, and of being, and of thinking, I am not sure that means we're wrong."

"Just because *we humans* have a certain way of doing, and being, and thinking, that doesn't mean we're wrong either."

She looked at me.

I looked right back.

She left, and the door closed without another word.

CHAPTER 52

LATER THAT DAY, THE QUEEN MOTHER REAPPEARED IN MY doorway.

"We are near to arrival," she said.

"Good," I said. "The sooner we can get started, the sooner we can save lives."

"I want to apologize if I offended," she said.

"Me too," I admitted. "I feel like our last conversation didn't necessarily end on the friendliest note."

"I detected no music," she said

"It's a human turn of phrase," I said. "It means we didn't leave with the best feeling or understanding of each other."

"I see. Well, come with me, Padre," she said. "I would like to take you to our ship's command nexus."

I walked out into the corridor. Not only were the three technicians present, but a squad of armed soldier mantes as well.

"Royal guard?" I asked her, pointing to the troops.

"You could say that," she said.

We proceeded slowly, with all the other mantes on the ship giving us a wide berth as we passed.

Again I noted how wrong human assumptions had been regarding mantis ship design and architecture. No slime, no stench, no bizarrely nestlike or hivelike honeycombing. The bulkheads and the decks and the superstructure were as ordinary and, indeed, comfortingly plain as that which could be found aboard a Fleet vessel. I let myself peek through hatches that opened and closed along our route, which revealed other technicians and soldiers and mantes whose roles I couldn't guess at, moving to and fro in quiet harmony.

Though I suspected if I could "hear" the communication between their carriages, I'd be bombarded with a cacophony of conversation.

A tiny audible warble came from the ceiling.

"We have returned to conventional propulsion," the Queen Mother said. "It will only be a little while longer before we dock."

"Space station?" I asked.

"One of many," she replied. "This system is one of our most developed forward systems, near to what you would call the border between our peoples. A great deal of military and civilian traffic passes through this place. From here I can dispatch couriers to the other deploying bases, and attempt to begin the recall. I will also be able to assess how effective our offensive has been to date—how much damage has been done to human colonies."

"Or mantis colonies," I said.

The Queen Mother looked at me—her antennae curled with mild irony.

I figured she didn't need to be reminded of the fact that our most recent planet of residence had still been in play at the time of our departure. For all we knew, the Fleet had prevailed and the Queen Mother's flagship was the only mantis survivor to have departed. Or perhaps Fleet had been utterly smashed, and the world—indeed, the whole system—was in mantis possession.

We should know soon.

Suddenly, there was a rumble through the deck. Then another, louder rumble. A differently-pitched warble sounded in the air, and the soldiers around us quickly formed a defensive ring around the Queen Mother.

Her antennae were quivering.

"What's happening?" I asked.

"We are . . . we are being attacked."

"Attacked?" I said, startled. "By whom?"

A third, louder rumble. I stumbled and caught myself on the edge of one of the technician's discs.

There was a pause.

"Your Fleet," said the Queen Mother. "Human warships. Many

of them. The entire staging base is under attack. There are . . . we have come out of jumpspace into the middle of a battle!"

I blinked.

Of all the things I'd expected when we reached our destination, this hadn't been on the list. How Fleet had managed to locate the base was a mystery, to say nothing of how Fleet had found a way to spare the ships for a deep-penetration attack. Sakumora and his people had apparently been more clever than I'd given them credit for.

I remembered that Adanaho had mentioned stealth missions. Perhaps one of them had chanced across this place? That it was under siege either boded very well for the human side of the equation, or it was a desperate maneuver designed to distract the Fourth Expansion. Put them on a defensive footing. Buying time for Earth?

I suddenly had so many questions. But as had happened on the *Calysta,* there was no time. Like *déjà vu*, we were being plunged into a cataclysm entirely beyond our control.

The artificial gravity wavered. I felt my stomach waver.

A third, louder, bass-heavy warble began to sound continuously.

The armed contingent around us began to move. The Queen Mother seemed as confused as I was, what with herself, me, and the technicians all being swept down a side corridor—away from our original path through the bowels of the mantis ship.

"What's happening?" I yelled over the noise.

"Hull breaches," the Queen Mother said, her speaker grille belying the fear that she felt. "We are being boarded."

Boarded?

"Human marines," I guessed.

"Yes! My guards are tasked with defending me with their lives. We are being taken to a safe place within the ship where it will be difficult for intruders to reach. Padre, do not let yourself be separated from me. I cannot guarantee your safety otherwise."

I momentarily considered breaking for it and trying to find my way to an exterior passage—somewhere I might run into humans. The Queen Mother didn't really need me anymore. She'd be able to recall her people perfectly fine without me. And I certainly couldn't offer her any more protection than the guards who had been posted to her. With their armored carriages, replete with lethal weapons.

But then . . . no.

Any mantis happening across me during a hostile boarding action was liable to mistake me for one of the marines, and shoot me on sight.

I kept up with the Queen Mother as best I was able, jogging while the rest of them cruised on their carriage impellers.

We halted at the hatch for what appeared to be a lift tube.

The only thing distinctly different about the mantis ship was that there were no obvious buttons or switches. Everything seemed to operate by proximity sensor, or according to the silent broadcasts of the carriages themselves. When we waited at the lift tube door for too long—additional concussive blasts sounding through the ship, letting us know that there was precious little time to waste—the Queen Mother engaged in a quick exchange with her guards. The lot of them huddled: conversing carriage-to-carriage.

"This way," she said.

And suddenly we were moving rapidly away from the lift tube complex, back the way we'd come.

"Malfunction?" I asked.

"Emergency override," the Queen Mother answered. "Because we have hostile forces inside the vessel, all means of mechanized travel are suspended until further notice. Per ship's protocol. We must hurry. If we don't get to one of the—"

The Queen Mother was cut off as we rounded a corner and came face to face with a squad of humans. The marines were clad in space armor not too different from the sort I'd trained in, back in the day. Only this model appeared even more flexible and robust than what I'd been wearing when I landed on Purgatory. The face plates were silvered against blast flashes, and each marine had his or her rifle up—the descendent model of the R77A5, no doubt.

There was an instant of hostile recognition between the Queen Mother's guards and the marines. Then the shooting started.

I flattened to the deck as weaponry belched instant death over my head.

Mantis warriors died. Human warriors died.

When it was over, the marine squad had been obliterated. But only two of the Queen Mother's guards remained, the others having been perforated by the automatic moose-caliber antipersonnel fire from the marines' rifles. Mantis gore and human gore was spread sickly on the bulkheads and across the deck. So much so that I wrinkled my nose and averted my eyes.

"Come," said the Queen Mother, and we were off again.

I lost complete track of which way we twisted or turned, as the imagery of the dead marines and mantes replayed over and over across my imagination. I'd seen it all before, of course. But somehow I never quite got used to it—the instant and graphic taking of life. Those marines had had families. The mantes? Probably young. And while obviously slotted for their roles, at least entitled to *some* kind of future. I permitted myself to feel a moment of pity for them, before we were again confronted by a squad of marines.

Just how many men and women had been tasked with taking our ship? Surely, this was not an accident. There had to be many ships at the staging base. Not all of them could be enduring simultaneous boarding actions. Could they?

I hit the deck again. Only, this time I wasn't so lucky. One of the rounds from one of the marines grazed a rib. I screamed and rolled onto my side, clutching at the sudden wound. The blood felt hot and slick on my fingers, and for an instant I panicked, imagining a quick bleed-out.

But when both the marines and our royal guard had mutually annihilated each other, I slowly sat up and realized that nothing vital had been hit. Just the rib had been cracked, and I'd need a hell of a lot of stitches to sew the skin back together.

The Queen Mother had been hurt too. One of her forelimbs had three bleeding bullet holes in it. It dangled uselessly across the top of her disc, which appeared to have taken a couple of rounds itself, though it still functioned.

One of the technicians had also been killed.

The marines were a smashed mess of bodies.

Looking around dumbly, I vaguely heard the echoes of other rifle reports much further down the corridor from us. The marines were attacking in force. Which way was safe? Could I protect the Queen Mother long enough for her to complete her task, or would the marines put a magazine of bullets through her, thinking she was nothing more than a common mantis shock troop?

I pushed myself into a standing position—ignoring the severe pain in my side—and went to pick up one of the human rifles that lay on the deck. A quick visual inspection confirmed for me that there were still rounds available, and also that the rifle's function wasn't too different from what I'd trained on many years before.

"What's the plan now?" I asked, gingerly stepping back to the Queen Mother. Our two remaining technicians fretted over her wounded forelimb.

"I do not know," she admitted—if the pain was as bad for her as it was for me, her speaker wasn't making it apparent. "It would seem your human troops have been far more efficient at penetrating the interior of this ship than I would have thought possible. The ship's crew will be sealing off every sector now, trying to bottle the humans up, at which point tactical counterstrikes will begin—in an effort to drive the marines off our vessel, or exterminate them where they stand."

"If my people find us before that, you're all dead," I said to the Queen Mother and the technicians. "I suggest you let me stay out in front. They might be hesitant to fire if they see me coming first."

"Your injury—" one of the technicians said, pointing with a forelimb at my bleeding side and ripped uniform.

"I'd do something about it if I had access to a med pack," I said. "But that's back in my room, and we're obviously not going to make it there any time soon. I'll just have to hope the bleeding doesn't get any worse. Sure hurts like a sunuvabitch, though."

If the technician wondered what I meant by that, he didn't ask.

"There is a maintenance passageway near here," the other technician said. "If we can reach it, I suspect we may be able to find a way to hide. Until either one side or the other is successful."

"Let's do it," I said.

The technician guided me with words as I walked, my eyes scanning ahead of me and the rifle in my hands at the low ready.

We occasionally passed dead marines and dead mantes.

The battle for the flagship quickly took on a surreal quality.

Assuming the marines weren't going to take my word for an answer, was I *really* prepared to fire on another human being? I'd come close to trying to hurt someone badly once. Maybe even kill him. I'd been talked out of it at the last second. For which I was quite thankful. Now, things were coming to a head. I really couldn't see any way around it: if the Queen Mother died, any hope for peace would die with her. Would it be wrong of me to fire on my own kind? Cause casualties? Even if it meant saving lives in the end? Long after the fact?

I wasn't sure I had the nerve. I hoped to hell I wouldn't have to find out.

Of course, any armed mantis that discovered us would just blow me to pieces. The rifle in my hands would guarantee it, whether I fired first or not.

Just short of a closed pressure door, the technician indicated a circular panel in the deck. He seemed to signal to the panel's motors with his disc, then the panel slid downwards and slipped away to the side, revealing a somewhat tall shaft that dropped for several decks.

It was mercifully empty.

I peered down.

"No good," I said.

"Why?" the Queen Mother asked.

"No ladder," I said. "I'll fall."

The mantes looked at each other, then at me.

"You must ride," the Queen Mother said.

I cursed, then walked to the rear of her disc and tried to climb up, growling at the pain it caused me. One of the technicians helped me up, while the other floated over and vanished down into the hole. Followed by the Queen Mother herself—with me riding shotgun—and then the second technician behind us. The deck hatch slid out and sealed shut over our heads.

And we were left with only the mechanical hiss and hum of the ship.

We weren't alone for long.

After maybe five minutes, a new threat presented itself. This time, from below. A trio of armed mantes floated into view, and challenged our presence in the shaft. I could hear none of it, of course, but I could see them peering up at us—up at me—and arming the weapons that projected out of slots on the front of their discs.

Neither the Queen Mother nor the technicians were so armed.

"Will they fire?" I asked.

"They would be insane to do it!" the Queen Mother replied.

"What do they want?"

"They say that as long as you are present with a weapon, they cannot trust that I am not under your control."

"They think you're my hostage?"

"Something like that," she said.

"Tell them I am just trying to keep you safe."

"I did. They refuse to believe me."

Just then the technician below us made a fatal decision—he rushed the soldiers.

To this day, I am not sure why. Maybe he thought it was the only way to distract the troops before they went after me—and the Queen Mother became a collateral casualty?

When the shooting started, I shouted a choice profanity, then leaned over the edge of the Queen Mother's disc—my wounded rib hurting me terribly—and began to empty the contents of my rifle's magazine. It was the first time in all my many years I'd been at war that I actually fired a weapon at the enemy.

While their rounds ripped into the technician, mine went into the soldiers. Sparks flew, and the shaft became a deafening funnel of sound. Within seconds, the three mantis soldiers were lying at the tunnel's bottom, their destroyed carriages and mangled bodies slowly smoldering. A familiar, acrid, gag-inducing aroma rushed up at us. The dead technician lay on top of the soldiers, his upper thorax blasted open and his fluids spilling out across the lot, making a hideous pattern.

"I'm sorry," I said to the Queen Mother, barely able to hear myself over the ringing in my ears.

"No," she said. "It was necessary. I am now afraid that we face enemies on every side. With my official guards gone, and the ship's watch suspecting that you are compelling me through force, the ship's command may have concluded that it's better to ignore or kill me."

"I promise I won't let anyone hurt you," I said.

"I believe that, Padre. But unless you can summon an army in our defense, you may not be able to keep your promise."

"Is there any way for us to get off this ship?" I asked.

"Yes," said the technician above us. "If we pass down two more decks, we can re-enter a secondary corridor that will lead us to one of the hangar decks. We could take an ancillary craft from there."

"It might be worth the risk," I said. "Anything is better than waiting here. If the marines find us, we're dead. If the mantis soldiers find us—especially with the bodies of their comrades heaped at the bottom of this tunnel—we're also dead."

"Right," the Queen Mother said.

We dropped silently to the deck indicated by the technician, reentered the ship proper through a side hatch, and began flying down the corridor outside. With the technician in the lead, we took two right turns, then a left turn—zooming past hurried crews of other technicians—and found our way out into a mammoth hangar even bigger than the one I'd seen when I first came aboard. For an instant I allowed myself to gawk, then I noticed the platoon of armed mantes bursting out of one of the far hatches—followed by what seemed to be a steady flow of humans in armor. All of them shooting at will. Rounds flying every which way.

"Go!" our technician said.

There was a small, slim craft perched on tripod legs. Perhaps big enough for half a dozen mantes. We cruised up and into the open hatch in the craft's belly.

"I sure hope to hell you're a pilot," I said to the technician.

"No," he said, "but the computer can fly for us."

"Make it happen," I said, hearing a little bit better each second as the ringing in my ears diminished. Which just meant that the violence outside in the hangar was all too conspicuous.

The Queen Mother settled to the deck, and I climbed off.

My side still hurt like shit, but there didn't seem to be much additional bleeding. I permitted myself to place my rifle on the deck, and sat down against one of the bulkheads—a hand clamped over my wound.

"Your face is wet," the Queen Mother said.

"I'm sweating," I said.

"Why?"

"Exertion, shock, adrenaline, whatever," I said, breathing deeply.

"Will you survive?"

"Probably," I said. "Had the bullet hit any closer to my center of mass, it would have punctured a lung. As things are, I will just need some superficial sewing up. Presuming any of us make it out of this."

"By leaving, we are abandoning the body of your captain, of course."

Damn. I hadn't thought of that. But what else could we do?

"There is a problem," the technician said as he floated back out of the cockpit.

"What?" I asked.

"All automated functions have been locked down. We cannot order this vessel to depart, nor can we signal the hangar airlock to give us passage."

"Let me try," the Queen Mother said.

I stared at the technician while we waited for the Queen Mother, who went into the cockpit to work her royal magic.

"I'm sorry about the two others," I said to the technician.

"They gave their lives in the Queen Mother's service. There is perhaps no more noble way for a mantis to die."

"Would your people *really* kill the Queen Mother? Rather than let her be taken by humans?"

"Quite possibly," the technician said. "It would be assumed that she was compromised—such that she could no longer function in her official capacity as the nominal leader of the Quorum of the Select. Even if she were captured alive, her authority would most likely be nullified."

"Meaning she could give no orders to any other mantes while she was in human custody?"

"That is correct."

I considered.

"Then I'm a liability," I said.

"Yes, and also no. You are an insurance token—that armed humans will be less likely to kill the Queen Mother while you remain alive to stand in their way. Yet my own people will consider you a threat. Someone not to be trusted. You saw manifestations of this when you were foolishly left alone to wander the ship unguarded."

I remembered the look of the soldier who'd had his serrated forelimb to my throat. How much he'd wanted to take my life—yet he'd not be able to do it.

"So it's a Catch-22," I said.

"I do not know what that means," the technician said.

"Old human phrase. It means we're damned if we do and we're damned if we don't. There is no correct option. We just have to pick a path and hope for the best."

The Queen Mother floated back to us.

"All of my command codes have been locked out," she said. "Nothing like this has ever happened to me before. I should have full mastery of every system on this vessel. Yet I am denied!"

If she'd been a human woman, she'd have been shouting in apoplexy.

Several extremely loud blasts shook the little craft on its landing legs—grenades.

How long before the fighting ruptured the outer hull? I suddenly longed for a combat suit—with a helmet. Vacuum would kill me as surely as bullets.

Another grenade exploded, this one so close it shook the craft and caused its emergency alarms to begin chirping.

"Well, we're not safe here," I said, looking from the Queen Mother to the technician, and back again. "Where else can we go?"

"I do not know," the technician said.

I remembered our exit from the *Calysta.*

"Don't mantis vessels have lifeboats?"

"What is a lifeboat?" the technician asked me.

"Small emergency vehicles. They're placed throughout the vessel. Spaceworthy. Can stand up to reentry if necessary."

"No," the technician said.

"*No?*" I said incredulously.

"They would be considered superfluous."

"What happens if one of your ships is disabled?"

"Our large vessels are constructed such that they always carry sufficient ancillary craft to effect an escape."

"But not in our case," I said, exasperated.

The technician simply looked at me.

The sound of human boots slamming across the deck began to echo up through the open belly hatch of our ship.

"Looks like we're in for it now," I said. "You two get back into the cockpit. I'll try to talk to these marines."

The technician and the Queen Mother did as they were told.

I kept my rifle at the low ready as a trio of space-armored figures pulled themselves up through the hatch.

We all stared at each other for a second.

"I'm Chief Warrant Officer Barlow," I said. "Fleet Chaplains Corps."

They continued to stare at me, their face plates still silvered against blast flashes.

"Who's your NCOIC?" I asked. "I'm here on a vital mission that can potentially end the war. I need to talk to whoever is in charge."

The three armed and armored marines looked back and forth between them, no doubt communicating via wireless. Then one of them dropped back down out of the hatch. When he returned, there were three other marines with him. They scrambled up into the ship and formed a horseshoe around me, weapons also at the low ready.

One of them had the chevrons and rockers of a platoon sergeant stamped onto his chest.

He walked up to me—confident in his strides.

When we were almost face-to-face, he carefully reached up to his collar and hit the release for his helmet. There was a small hiss, then he one-handed the helmet off his head.

"Oh my God," I said.

CHAPTER 53

"LONG TIME NO SEE," THUKHAN SAID.

"Batbayar?" I said, not quite believing my eyes. Like a ghost, someone I'd not seen since the end of IST was suddenly standing before me. I forgot all about the sounds of fighting and weapons fire outside the ship. For that instant, there was only me—and him. How long had it been? The better part of two Earth decades?

His face was sweaty, and there was an old, ugly scar that ran from his left ear, across his forehead, and up into his much-receded hairline.

"So they made you a chief," he said, looking me up and down. "I guess life in exile wasn't *all* bad for you."

"Nor you," I said, pointing to his rank emblem on his chest.

"I earned everything I got," he said defensively, face stern.

Shit, I thought. *Really? Were we going to go right back at it again? Like teenagers?*

"No doubt," I said. "Look, I meant what I told your squad. I'm on a mission that can end the war. I don't know how Fleet's managed to spare the manpower for this assault, much less boarding and seizing ships, but we can—"

"We know about the Queen Mother," he said flatly.

I stopped short.

"How?"

"That escape pod you came down in? From the *Calysta?* Captain Adanaho left an encrypted text message inside. We spent days combing the planet for you as a result. You'd have been in safe custody except for the fact that a mantis counter-patrol found you in that canyon shortly after Fleet marines found you first. Our response force didn't get there in time to do much more than pick up the pieces, but when we didn't find either you or Captain Adanaho, we knew you'd been taken offworld. Based on Adanaho's information, we used our stealth intel to figure out the closest mantis staging system."

I wondered how Fleet had managed to make the jumpspace crossing in less time than the mantes themselves—maybe the Queen Mother's flagship had loitered too long in real space, during one of its periodic stops? I remembered that there had been several. If human ships had rushed headlong, with no interruption . . .

"It's vital that the Queen Mother be allowed to initiate the recall," I said. "That was our whole reason for coming here."

"Where is Captain Adanaho?"

"Dead," I said.

"Killed in action?"

"Fratricide, if you must know. The marines who found us in the canyon were shooting indiscriminately, once the mantis counter-patrol dropped down on top of us. Her body's in stasis on this ship."

"We don't have much time," Thukhan said.

"Tell me about it. Is your objective to claim the Queen Mother as a prisoner—for use as a bargaining chip?"

"Essentially," he said. "That was Captain Adanaho's stated desire, and Fleet Command agreed with her assessment. We need the Queen Mother alive."

"It's no good," I replied. "Her own people already consider her to be under my control, and they've cut her out of the loop. Unless she's perceived to be operating according to her own will, they won't listen to her. Not even their automated systems are responding to her codes."

"It's true," said a vocoded voice.

The Queen Mother floated out of the cockpit.

The marines brought their weapons up, but Platoon Sergeant Thukhan waved them down with a knife-hand sweeping to the deck.

"Queen Mother," Thukhan said officiously, "I've got specific orders from Fleet Command to take you into custody. Please come with me, and you will not be harmed."

"It's a dead end!" I shouted. "Didn't you just hear what I said? She's no good to us as a prisoner. Her own people won't *care* if we have her. Our only hope is to let her go. Let her do what she has intended to do ever since Captain Adanaho died. In fact, I am *ordering* you to let her go."

"I don't have to recognize your authority on this," Thukhan said.

"Bullshit, *Sergeant.* Protocol is that you're obliged to followed the lawful orders of a superior officer, and that's me. You're certainly free to file a protest through your company commander, but at this moment I've got rank, and I'm using it."

Thukhan got nose-to-nose with me.

"I could kill you right now and nobody would say a word," he breathed.

The hostility in his eyes was oh-so-familiar.

"Yeah, you could," I said. "But I have to think if you've survived this long—reached your current rank—that you've learned a thing or two since we were knocking heads back in IST. You don't respect me and I don't respect you. But this isn't about us. This is about the future of Earth. Our survival, as the human race. I don't know what kind of strategy Fleet thinks will turn the tide against the mantes, but the numbers don't lie. We've caught up to them in terms of some of their technology, but not in terms of population. Way more of them. Less of us. They have more planets, and have had more time to populate them. They also work far better as a society than we do, if what I've learned in the last few days is accurate. So I don't care what kind of tricks intel has cooked up—stealth ships, or whatever—the mantes are the ones who are going to eventually win. Battle by battle. Planet by planet. They will drive us back to the brink, and then push us over it. *Unless* we help the Queen Mother complete her recall."

Thukhan glared into my eyes, his jaw flexing.

"Think about it," I said. "How many battles have you fought on the ground? In space? When could we actually claim to have had an upper hand? Never, that's when."

"So we just let her go?" he said indignantly. "A lot of people died for this mission. You always were a pussy, Barlow."

"And you were always determined to fight the world at every step," I said, staring him right back in the eyes. "Even fighting people who never had anything against you in the first place."

"Please," said the Queen Mother to Thukhan. "I am defenseless. I have no weapons. Your superior officer is correct. In your custody, I can do nothing. I must be allowed to reach the staging base. I can attempt to effect a cease-fire. Without such a cease-fire, I firmly believe that the human species will die. We have thousands of ships and potentially billions of soldiers at our disposal. How many humans are there in the entire galaxy? How large is your Fleet? Not large enough, I suspect."

"It's just a matter of time," I said, my expression pleading.

Thukhan's eyes went from me, to the Queen Mother, then back to me.

"No," he said. "My orders were quite clear. Now if you'll kindly get out of the way, *sir*, I'm going to carry out those orders."

"Eff that," I said, refusing to move.

"Out of the way, cunt—"

"No way," I said, standing fast. "I'm giving you a direct order to back off and—"

The little craft was rocked by another blast, this time directly against the ship. Everyone inside was thrown to the deck. I fell on my wounded side, and screamed because of the pain.

"My people now respond to yours," said the Queen Mother.

I pawed my way over to the open belly hatch and peered out. If the marines had achieved a period of shock and surprise, the mantis backlash was that of a relentless wave. Hundreds and hundreds of mantis troops were belching out into the hangar from numerous hatches along the internal bulkheads. Marines were getting mowed down right and left, unable to hold position as the mantes swept across them.

Thukhan came up beside me and looked out as well. He spat curses, and then ordered his squad into motion. They formed up around the Queen Mother, weapons aimed at the open hatch while Thukhan put his helmet back on and resealed the collar.

"You better get ready," Thukhan said over the external speaker in the side of his helmet. "Something tells me they're not going to care if you're a marine or not when they hit us."

"No!" I yelled.

I sat up painfully and looked at the Queen Mother.

"Can't you order them to stop?" I said.

"I've been completely cut off from the command nexus," she said. "Short of trying to face them in person, there doesn't seem to be much I can do."

"No way," Thukhan said. "I'm not letting her go."

I stared hard at her, then at Thukhan—who had his rifle up,

and was clearly prepared to start shooting at whatever came up through the hatch at us. Or the Queen Mother, if she tried to make a break for it.

Outside the hatch, all human resistance was being put down—in merciless fashion. The weaponry of the mantes didn't sound precisely the same as human guns, but it was obvious that Thukhan, his squad, and I, were shortly going to be the only humans left alive in the whole hangar.

Then...

I couldn't wrap my brain around it.

The end. Death. And not even a hero's demise. We'd die stupidly, for stupid reasons.

I couldn't accept it. I *refused* to accept it. To go through so much and come all this way...

I suddenly remembered what Adanaho had whispered to me moments before she had died. And I thought again of the hateful mantis soldier who'd been unable to kill me, despite his desire. Simply because I refused to offer any resistance. I watched the moving wall of mantis troops close around our little ship. At best, Thukhan and I had seconds to live.

I closed my eyes, and the world got strangely quiet. All I could hear was the rhythm of my own blood hammering in my ears.

I knew I had no right to plead. But—

Alright, I thought quickly, *if ever there was a time in this whole lousy life when I needed help the most, God, this would be it. Please. If you are there—if the spirits of people like the Professor and Captain Adanaho matter at all—let me make a difference just one last time!*

I dropped out of the hatch and rolled, the pain in my side almost too much to bear. When I stood up, I threw my hands into the air—no rifle.

I held them high.

"*We surrender!*"

My eyes were closed, of course. I couldn't bring myself to watch. When the rounds hit, I just hoped they'd hit in such number that I'd never know it.

Only... they didn't.

"*We surrender!*" I yelled a second time.

I could hear the humming of their discs so close, I could almost touch the metal.

I dared to open my eyes.

A small sea of mantis warriors had surrounded the craft, all of them aimed in towards me with their weapons trained and their postures as aggressive and menacing as could be. Yet, not a one of them attacked. They simply looked at me, their individual antennae vibrating and shivering with mixed expressions of surprise and confusion.

My rifle sat useless on the deck at my feet. I kept my hands in the air, despite the immense pain in my side, and the additional flow of blood that I felt running down into my waistband.

One of the mantis soldiers hovered forward until the edge of his disc touched my sternum.

"I have seen images of you. You are the human called *Padre.*"

"Yes," I said.

"The Queen Mother had respect for you. Does she live?"

"Here," the Queen Mother's voice said as she hovered down out of the ship. "This human—indeed all of these humans—are under my authority. They are not to be harmed."

I turned my head back to see Thukhan and the others standing at the hatch's edge, their rifles nowhere to be found and their arms raised high; just like mine. I wrinkled my brow at Thukhan, who was looking down at me with an almost astonished expression.

The Queen Mother hovered up to the mantis warrior in front of me, and they appeared to communicate silently between them—carriages networked.

She turned to Thukhan and the other marines.

"Climb down," she commanded. "And come with me."

The marines did as they were told, and the mantis troops made a corridor through which she rapidly passed.

I struggled to keep up with Thukhan as he and the others marched quickly. Hands still over their heads.

"I thought for sure you'd go down fighting," I said to him.

"I couldn't pull the trigger," he said. "When she saw you jump out the hatch, she moved right past me, and I *couldn't shoot her.* Something inside just sort of said it wasn't worth it. Especially when the troops on the deck didn't open fire on you. I know you think I'm a complete asshole. But I *do* value the lives of my marines. You'd just better be right, about this working out in the end."

I watched the side of his head as we walked quickly. He deliberately didn't look back, though I am sure he could see me out of the corner of his eye.

"Where are we going?" I shouted to the Queen Mother up ahead. Our lone technician had fallen in behind me, with the heads and eyes of the mass of mantis soldiers in the hangar swiveling to watch us as we went.

"The command nexus," she said. "We must communicate with my fleet, and yours!"

CHAPTER 54

THE TRIP TO THE FLAGSHIP'S EQUIVALENT OF A BRIDGE WAS resumed.

"If you're still locked out," I yelled ahead, "how in the hell are we supposed to get there?"

"I will make us a way," The Queen Mother said.

I didn't have the breath to argue. The pain in my side had become almost too much to bear standing up. I began to fall behind. Thukhan—of all people—slowed, then put a shoulder under the arm on my good side, and helped me forward.

"You'd better be effing right about this," he said to me.

"Yes," I wheezed. "I certainly hope I am."

We pushed through scene after scene of human and mantis carnage. Fleet had committed at least several companies of marines to taking the ship, and so far as I could tell—as we wound our way down several corridors—Thukhan and his squad might be the only ones left alive.

When we were confronted with shut bulkheads or stalled lift tubes, we took still other turns through other corridors, passageways, and even a short trip down another maintenance shaft—albeit a shallow, single-story affair. All the while, rumblings through the structure told us that the war outside the flagship was ongoing, even if the fight within had come down decisively in the mantes' favor.

Finally, we arrived at a very large set of sealed pressure doors.

The Queen Mother hovered defiantly before them, trying her

codes. When they did not work, she floated up to them and banged her functional forelimb on the metal several times.

Two small hatches to either side of the doors popped open and armed mantis warriors came out, their weapons trained on us all. The Queen Mother glared at them, her antennae erect and dignified.

"What are they doing?" Thukhan asked.

"She's demanding entry," I guessed. "The guards have orders from inside to not permit her—"

The Queen Mother faced back towards us, and pointed with a forelimb.

"—and she's indicating we're unarmed," I said.

Several moments passed.

Finally, the large doors unsealed and hummed open on their motors. Inside, a contingent of harried mantes were clustered around several oval tables that projected out of the deck. Holographic displays were suspended in the air over each table, and though the scene was mostly silent, it had the look of tremendous agitation.

When the Queen Mother floated into their midst, every mantis in the command nexus stopped to watch her. She looked around at them, antennae still erect—challenging any of them to deny her right to rule.

I stared at the holographic imagery over one of the tables. Differently colored symbols were spread across the air: some of them blinking, others swirling, and still others gradually disintegrating until they were but wispy motes of nothingness.

"How many Fleet ships?" I asked Thukhan quietly.

"Classified," he said.

"Oh, come on," I said. "The only one who doesn't know at this point is me," I said.

"Twenty," he said. "The mission briefing told us ten would go in hot against the staging base, while the rest would hang back near the system's most likely exit points—for mantis ships coming out of jumpspace. We hit everything that came through, hoping that one of them would be yours. And that the Queen Mother would be alive and aboard."

"What about the rest of the war?" I asked. "How bad has it been?"

"Fleet won't say," Thukhan said, keeping a straight face. "But we're here, right? You said it yourself. How *could* Fleet Command commit so many marines and ships? Draw your own conclusions, Chief."

So. I'd been right. Seizing the Queen Mother was a desperate gambit. I wished to hell I could hear what she was saying to her subordinates.

"Do they accept your authority?" I asked.

"On this ship, for the moment, yes," she said. "But until the battle with your Fleet attack armada is concluded, the staging base is refusing my requests."

"Do we have any officers aboard who can talk to Fleet?" I asked Thukhan.

"Marine captains arguing with Fleet generals? Good luck. Besides, did you see anyone left alive to ask?"

"No," I said. "But what was the plan, assuming your boarding parties were actually able to take the Queen Mother into custody? Surely you have a signal."

"We do," he said.

"Well," I said, "what are you waiting for?"

"If I use it, Fleet will be expecting immediate liftoff from one of the assault carriers that's resting on the hull of this ship, and I don't even know if any of those assault carriers are still intact."

I looked to the Queen Mother.

"Well?"

She quickly discussed it carriage-to-carriage with her officers.

"No," she said. "All of the human ships which had attached to our hull have been destroyed. As was the main vessel from which they were launched."

Thukhan sighed, then pulled his helmet off. The rest of his squad did the same.

"Then we're screwed," he said.

I watched the holographic display. It wasn't hard to guess which color was assigned to Fleet, based on the dwindling numbers.

"Won't we retreat?" I asked him.

"No," he said. "The orders were to bring the Queen Mother back alive."

"Or?" I pressed.

"Or... the briefing didn't give us instructions beyond that point. Bring the Queen Mother back alive. That was all."

I suddenly felt faint. Whether because of shock from my injury, or the realization that nothing could be done to stop the battle.

"Please put me down," I said to Thukhan.

He walked me over to one of the bulkheads—mantis eyes staring at us as we walked into the command nexus—and helped me take a seat on the deck. I hugged my hurt side under one arm and kept the opposite hand clamped over the wound as I slowly put my knees up and leaned my forehead onto them.

Sick. I felt sick at the fact that nothing could be done.

"Talk to the Fleet," I muttered.

"I told you—" Thukhan said, but I cut him off.

"No, not you. Queen Mother, talk to my people. They obviously know who you are and they know your value. Send out a blanket broadcast. Platoon Sergeant Thukhan will know the encryption key for our combat network. If you broadcast to our ships using that key, it should tell them something about your intentions. Maybe they'll have the good sense to listen, and back off, before your ships finish tearing our ships to pieces. Once the remainder of our ships clear out of the system, your staging base should allow us to make contact and issue new instructions on your side. Right?"

"That is probable," she said.

I looked up at Thukhan. "Give her the key."

A few moments later, the Queen Mother was floating in front of a second oval table with a camera and an audio pickup projected from the surface.

"Human vessels," she said, "I speak to you now as the Queen Mother: ruler of all mantes throughout all the galaxy. Your continued attack on this mantis star system is futile. Your ships will be destroyed unless you cease and desist. Now. I will command my own forces to allow you to jump to safety, but you must cease fire and withdraw all combat troops from all mantis vessels. Signal me that you will comply."

Moments stretched on in silence.

One of the holographic images over one of the tables changed from tactical display to real-time external image. I got a look at a very-bright sun far in the distance, followed by a large gas giant world. The mantes' space stations appeared to be in orbit of the gas giant—probably manufactured on-site from the ores present in the loose ring of tiny asteroids. It was impossible to see distinct ships, but occasionally a sudden flash would indicate the detonation of a warhead, or the going-up of a reactor. Tiny colorful halos surrounded small dots that were moving visibly.

Again, color coded for either human or mantis forces. It was pretty obvious that the Fleet force was outnumbered five to one.

The Queen Mother repeated her imperative.

Still, there was nothing.

"It's no use," she said.

I growled and slammed my fist several times on the deck.

"Help me back up," I said to Thukhan.

"What for?"

"Just effing help me back up," I said.

He hesitated, then stooped down and put his arm back under my arm on my good side.

He helped me around to where I could stand next to the Queen Mother.

"Are we on?" I asked.

The Queen Mother looked to one of the bridge staff, who said nothing, but whose antennae flexed slightly.

"You are now," she said.

The pain was excruciating. I hoped I could enunciate well enough to be intelligible over the broadcast.

"This is Harrison Barlow of the planet Purgatory. You all know me, and I'm told you know of Captain Adanaho by now. Who is dead. By our own hands. People of the Fleet, we're slitting our own throats. You have to trust the Queen Mother, she's good as her word. Withdraw! Withdraw and save yourselves. This war only ends if we take the first step. The Queen Mother is going to recall her armadas. But it can't happen until you all disengage first. I helped stop the war once—saved us all, or so Adanaho thought. Well, now it's time for me to stop the war again. Withdraw! Before it's too late."

I'd almost shouted the last part, and clasped my wounded side while gasping for breath.

"Is there nothing you can do for him?" The Queen Mother asked Thukhan.

"You killed all of our medics," Thukhan said.

"Wait," one of the marines said. "If we could put the chief into one of our armor suits—"

"One that's not full of holes." Thukhan said gruffly.

"What would that accomplish?" The Queen Mother asked.

"The suits have automatic medical response systems design to staunch the flow of blood and prevent infection, if ever the suit is compromised and the wearer wounded."

"Forget about me, what about the Fleet?" I said through clenched teeth.

Silence, for almost a full minute.

Suddenly the few remaining human ships in the real-time display began to break off and regroup, headed away from the gas giant.

"That's it," I said. "They're breaking and running."

"But we've received no signal—"

"Do what you have to do," I said, "but keep your end of the bargain. Keep your people from annihilating my people."

The Queen Mother's antennae wove a quick, thoughtful pattern in the air, then she spun to her officers and they had a silent conversation for about ten seconds.

The sound of the ship changed, and the real-time hologram began to shift.

"What's happening now?" Thukhan asked.

"Since I cannot give direct orders to the staging base as a whole, yet, I have ordered this vessel be put in the path of any mantis vessels which fire their engines in pursuit of your Fleet ships."

"Will that work?" I asked.

"We shall find out," she said. "Meanwhile, I have ordered that an armor suit be stripped from one of your dead, and brought here. So that whatever aid can be rendered for you, will be done."

"Thank you," was all I could manage.

The pain in my side had turned wicked, to the point I wondered if I'd pass out.

"Back down," I wheezed.

Thukhan—my oldest enemy—complied without a word.

Sitting and leaning against a bulkhead definitely felt better than standing. I allowed myself to close my eyes and breathe shallow breaths as the minutes ticked by: our flagship maneuvering to intercede on behalf of the Fleet's leftovers. Would our ships interpret this as a hostile act, and fire? Would the mantes themselves interpret this as a hostile act, and fire?

"Hang tough," Thukhan said, sitting down beside me. I opened my eyes to see him with the other marines arrayed in a circle around us.

"You know, there was a time when I wanted to break your head open," I said, a small smile creeping onto my lips.

"I know," Thukhan said.

"How?" I asked.

"I've got ears, stupid. I remember that night when I was in the head. I could hear you and Capacha talking. It's good you didn't try anything, because I'd have almost certainly killed you."

"You could have killed me today," I said, putting my head back and reclosing my eyes. My mouth was getting dry and a mild lightheaded feeling had begun to grip me.

"Yeah, I could have," he said.

"You were going to kill the Queen Mother," I said.

"Yeah."

"So why didn't you? What happened?"

There was palpable silence, then I heard him swallow and lick his lips.

"I'm tired of the wars, Barlow. New, and old. Do you know how long it's been since I set foot on Earth? How many engagements I saw, up close and personal?"

"That scar on your head says too many," I said.

"Effing right, too many. But what else was there? For you, the war took a long holiday. But for the rest of humanity? Every single day of the armistice was spent building up for the resumption of combat. Every piece of industry on every planet was put to work manufacturing armor, weapons, ships, you name it. We didn't know how long the ceasefire would last, and we didn't trust the mantes to let us have any kind of edge, so we worked like bastards. Trained, and trained, and trained. For the moment when the shooting would start again."

More silence.

"Got anyone in particular you're anxious to get back to?" I asked.

"No," he said.

Silence.

"But I'd like to," he said, this time almost so quietly I wasn't sure anyone else could have heard him.

And suddenly the picture of the man—a picture I'd had in my head for years—gradually began to dissolve away. I'd thought him a menace once. A spiteful, cruel menace. And maybe he was, at a certain time. But the war had changed all of us. Far more than any of us could have imagined at the beginning. In my heart, the little nugget of acidic resentment which had borne Thukhan's name melted away, to be replaced by a tiny warm spot of pity, mixed with understanding. I too had not seen Earth in a very long time. I decided then and there that if the Queen Mother was actually successful, and we were able to pull things back from the brink, that I was going to go home. And see if I couldn't rediscover what I, Thukhan, and probably a lot of other people had lost along the way.

CHAPTER 55

I PASSED OUT. NOT SURE WHEN. MAYBE BECAUSE OF THE PAIN, maybe because of the blood loss. When I came to I was back in my quarters. My upper torso encased in the top half of one of the armor suits I'd seen Thukhan wearing. There was also a human female sitting on my chair at the side of the bed, her chin on her chest while she quietly dozed. She didn't have any armor on, though she wore the undersuit of someone who'd come aboard wearing armor. I didn't recognize her as one of the squad that had been with Thukhan in the flagship's command nexus.

My side was mercifully pain-free.

"Hello," I croaked, suddenly realizing I was parched.

She stirred and looked over at me.

"Hey, Chief," she said.

"How long was I out?"

"A few hours. Long enough for me to sew you up a bit and get the bleeding stopped."

"Medic?" I asked.

"Surgeon, actually," she said. "This ship picked me up in a lifeboat. When they demanded to know my occupation, and I told them, they brought me directly here and ordered me to fix you up."

"Seems like you did a good job, ma'am," I said. "I can't feel a thing."

"That's the local anesthetic," she said. "I had some in my kit I took onboard the lifeboat. And a good thing, too. Ideally we'd have you in a sterile wrap, but the armor will have to do. You won't be able to take it off for a few days. Not until the wound has mended enough to peel the self-sealing foam away from your skin without causing more bleeding. Your rib cage . . . well, if you've ever cracked a rib before, you know it's just something that takes time."

"Thanks," I said. "How many other survivors have we picked up?"

"Many," she said. "Now we're waiting to see if the Queen Mother can negotiate her way back into her own fleet's good graces."

"It's the only chance we have," I said.

I closed my eyes and let myself enjoy the comfort of my pillow.

"Can I ask a question?" the surgeon said.

"Of course, ma'am," I said.

"The Queen Mother's not like I expected her to be."

"You should have seen her back when I first met her onboard the *Calysta.* No doubt you're aware of how that all transpired?"

"I got a briefing," she said. "We all did. General Sakumora's plan—Fleet Command's overall strategy—hasn't been working as anticipated."

"Can you tell me," I said, "how bad it's gotten? How badly are we losing?"

"It's difficult to say," she said. "I came directly from Earth onboard the *Penultimate.* Supposedly she was the toughest, most deadly ship in the inventory. We got assigned to a special deep-strike mission which was, I later learned, hot on your tail. We wanted the Queen Mother. Enough to devote ships like the *Penultimate* to the job. I think she lasted longer than some of her sisters, but since I'm sitting here now I think you can figure out that even our best ships aren't cutting it against the mantes' combined firepower."

"More of them, less of us," I said quietly.

"That's about right."

"Which is why the Queen Mother must succeed," I said.

"Do you really think she can get them to pull back?"

"Either she can do it, or we're finished," I said. "All depends on the mantes recognizing her authority as their supreme leader in this situation. It's why I knew the second we landed—I don't even know what that stupid planet is called, if it's called anything—that she would be the key to stopping the fighting."

"She's certainly not like the warriors," the surgeon said.

"She was more like them at first," I said, "because she wanted the war as much as we—the Fleet—did. She came prepared to die so that her side would be fully committed."

"What changed?"

I opened my eyes and stared up at the ceiling. Took an experimental deep breath, felt my side twinge just slightly, and settled for a medium breath or two. Then licked my lips.

"Water, please," I said. "Before I become a shriveled apple."

A plastic straw was put to my lips and a hand lifted the back of my head up off the pillow.

I swallowed greedily.

Then my head was let back down, and the cool bottle of water was pressed into my left hand.

"May I ask your name, ma'am?"

"Shelby," she said. "Major Shelby."

"Thanks for patching me up," I said.

"It's my job. I'm just glad I didn't get blown to smithereens. When the *Penultimate* was breaking apart, I figured the mantes would begin picking off the survivors. I floated through space for hours before the Queen Mother's flagship snagged me. And a whole bunch of others. They're keeping us all down in one of their big hangars, as a group."

"Prisoners?" I asked.

"Not precisely. The Queen Mother addressed us all as *guests*, which is probably better than any of us could have hoped for. We destroyed a number of their ships before the *Penultimate* went up. I'd have expected them to be raging for blood at this point. So far... I can't even tell if they're annoyed. How do you read these aliens?"

"It's a learned skill," I said. "Spend enough time around them, and you figure it out."

She laughed a bitter laugh.

"I'd rather go back home, and not see another one of these scary mothers ever again."

I grunted my understanding.

A day later, the Queen Mother appeared in my doorway.

"I have good news," she said.

I was propped up in my bed, nibbling on a ration bar Doctor Shelby had given me. The doctor watched the Queen Mother—and the technician who'd survived with her, from the trio originally assigned to my service—with a mixture of revulsion and nervousness.

I immediately noticed that the Queen Mother's wounded arm was missing.

"They amputated?" I said, startled.

"The damage was too severe," she said. "So the decision was made to remove the damaged limb."

There was not even a stump where the shoulder had been. The chitin appeared to have been patched and fused.

"Did it hurt?"

"Yes," she said. "But it's a small thing. A replacement will grow back, in time."

"You can do that?"

"We've always been able to do it. Our biology is very resilient. A lost limb is only a temporary inconvenience."

"Wow," I said, thinking about what it would be like if humans possessed the same innate ability.

"Anyway, what's the news?" I asked.

"After a good deal of discussion, I have convinced the officers in charge of this staging base to accept my directives."

"Will the other staging bases do the same?" I asked.

"We shall see. I will shortly be transferring my flag to a fast courier, which will depart—under escort—for the next larger staging base, deeper into our space."

"You have to go around convincing your base commanders one at a time?" I said. "That will take . . . too long! Lives will be lost."

"I know," she said. "Those mantis ships under direct supervision of this specific staging base will withdraw—once couriers have reached them. But there are protocols which even I must follow, and there will be a great many of my officers who will not want to trust my motives. At first. It certainly took all my persuasive effort to achieve the results I wanted here."

"Why can't you just *order* them to stand down?" Shelby asked.

"I tried that at first," the Queen Mother said. "And when I was rebuffed, it made me extremely angry. Enough so that I wanted to order this ship to attack the staging base's own command nexus. But I knew that would be a pointless and suicidal gesture, so I opted for a prolonged dialogue. They didn't want to trust me at first, but I am still the Queen Mother whether they like it or not. So they listened. And I argued. And argued. And argued. Until they finally accepted what I had to say."

"Can you trust that their allegiance will stick?" I asked.

"What does that mean, in this context? Stick?"

"Will they follow your commands without question from this point forward?"

"These particular officers? Yes. I believe I have convinced them of the moral necessity for cessation of hostilities."

I raised an eyebrow.

"That must have taken a lot of fancy talk," I said.

"Talk, yes. A significant amount. But I am encouraged. That these mantes can be swayed, tells me that others will be as well. My successor chief among them. Because it's vital that she have the same conviction I now do—that the eradication of the human species is not essential to the progress and health of our dominion in the galaxy. Otherwise, the possibility of war will always exist between our species. I do not think there will be a third opportunity to avoid the genocide of the human people. Already, I am told, much damage has been inflicted on your space—your colonies. This grieves me deeply. I would not have given it a second thought before. But now? Now . . . I do not want to be known as the Queen Mother who eradicated humanity. Not after Captain Adanaho gave herself up for my sake. Not after everything I've learned. I could not live with myself if I did not try to undo what I had done. I must make sure that no others in my wake make the same mistakes that I have."

I nodded my understanding. The manifestation of the Queen Mother's conscience was complete.

"What happens to the humans on this ship?" Shelby asked.

"Once the remainder of your survivors have been picked up—we are still finding more lifeboats, even at this moment—we will aim to negotiate for your exchange."

"We've taken *mantis* prisoners?" I said, surprised.

"My officers and I assume so, until proven otherwise. Regardless, all of the humans on this ship will be returned to a human colony world as quickly as we're able to effect negotiations for their safe release."

"Good," I said. It would be nice to be back with humans again.

The Queen Mother hovered over the deck, expectantly.

"There is something else," she said to me.

"Yes?"

The Queen Mother faced Shelby.

"How long before Padre is healthy enough to function without your supervision?"

Shelby pursed her lips.

"Assuming he doesn't bang that broken rib around, a couple more days. But the real question now is infection. I've dosed him heavily with a spectrum antibiotic, but without knowing what kind of microbes and bacteria he's been exposed to on this ship, or on that planet you were both stranded on, it's impossible to say whether or not he's out of danger."

"When will we know for sure?"

"I'd say, give it a week. If he's not running a fever and the wound itself appears to be mending without gangrene or other complications, then he'll be okay."

"Will you consent to travel with him until that time?"

"Wait, what?" I said.

"Padre," the Queen Mother said, "I would like you to stay on with me. Be my companion as I visit the other staging bases. To plead my case."

"I'm no good to you," I said. "Nobody on your side cares what a lone man would say."

"It's not for their benefit that I want you to remain," she said.

"It's not?"

"No. Padre—Harrison—it may sound odd, but I have come to consider you . . . I think of you as my friend."

I stared at her. The only mantis who'd ever said that to me had been the Professor.

Shelby's eyes were wide, and she looked from the Queen Mother, to me, and back again.

I swallowed hard, then said, "I'm honored."

"Will you consent?" the Queen Mother asked my doctor.

"Sure," Shelby said.

"Thank you," The Queen Mother said. "The sooner he can be made ready to travel, the better."

"Are you in too much pain to walk?" Shelby asked me.

"I made it to the toilet and back. Hurts like hell now that the meds have worn off, but not so bad I can't manage. It would be better if I could get the top half of this suit off."

"Forty-eight hours," Shelby said.

"Okay," I said.

Then I looked back at the Queen Mother.

"It's an agreement."

CHAPTER 56

THIRTEEN WEEKS LATER, I WAS IN ORBIT AROUND EARTH.

It took a long time for the Queen Mother to convince her forces, and longer than that to convince Fleet that the Queen Mother's overtures of peace were sincere. Several human planets had been destroyed, along with several mantis worlds. And hundreds of ships. For the first time, the fight had not been one-way.

Millions were dead. Mantis and human. Past a certain point, body count ceased to matter. What mattered now was that the Queen Mother and her top officers were getting ready to meet with Fleet Command and its top officers—with the intention of signing not just a cease-fire but a permanent treaty of nonaggression.

My uniform had been stitched, cleaned, and prepared for the occasion by my mantis aides. They'd managed to get almost all of the blood out of the fabric—both mine and Adanaho's. There remained just a vague discoloring of some of the lighter piping.

Adanaho herself rested in a stasis casket. The mantes had spared no effort preparing the body. The transparent lid of the casket showed Adanaho in a flowing one-piece gown woven from traditional mantis silks. I'd told them how to go about it. They'd wanted her presented to Fleet Command with as much dignity as could be mustered—a token of their good will, and also in honor of Adanaho's act of sacrifice in defense of the Queen Mother.

I stood staring at Adanaho's face while our mantis shuttle maneuvered through Earth orbit in order to dock with the Fleet space station on the far side of the world. Thankfully there was gravity. Something I hoped human engineers would replicate soon. We'd done so well with other aspects of mantis tech.

The Queen Mother stood next to me. No disc. A small package of electronics had instead been attached to her thorax, with flexible straps: a translator box and speaker grill for communications.

The mantis guards at the hatches did have discs, polished and bright. The guards themselves were rigid with respect.

"She was too young," I said sadly, not daring to touch the captain's casket. Adanaho looked pristine now. Immaculate. I didn't want to disrespect what she'd accomplished, by treating the casket like mere furniture. I had decided it was a kind of monument, both to the horrible bloodshed which had taken place, and to the new shoots of fresh possibility which had sprouted amidst the ashes.

"And I am too old," said the Queen Mother. "Age has made me cynical. I once thought the one you called Professor to be an eccentric. And now it is I who find myself transformed beyond reckoning."

"Do you miss your carriage?" I asked.

"Oh yes, all the time," she said. "But after our recovery from the planet's surface, you were right. It became apparent to me that there could be no going back. Not for me. Your captain was also correct. Our carriages have come to define us in ways we neither understand nor suspect. It took having mine ripped away from me to make me see what we mantes have lost in the long time since we first achieved sapience."

"And what is it you think you're regaining?"

The Queen Mother considered my question for a moment, then she said, "Illumination."

I raised my eyebrows. "Oh?"

"If I understand the human use of the term, it means an emergence into a state of deeper understanding—of the universe, of the self, of the meaning of both."

"That's one way to look at it," I said. "What will you do now?"

"Once the treaty is signed and reparations meted out, I will call the Quorum of the Select together and the new Queen Mother will be permanently installed. She helped me when I needed her help to effect the new peace. She's earned her seat."

"So, you're just... *quitting?*" I said, surprised.

"I must. Already I am an oddity among my people. They need someone who can lead them during this transition, and it cannot be me."

"But the treaty is *your* idea," I said. "You said it yourself once. What if the new Queen Mother decides to throw it away and restart the war?"

"We do not behave so rashly, despite what you may think, Padre. It took us a long time to reach the conclusion that war must be renewed. It would take an even longer time for us to reach the conclusion that the new peace must be destroyed. There is an additional human name circulating in the Quorum now. The heroism of Captain Adanaho—for my sake, and for the reclamation of the cease-fire—will live eternally in the memories of the mantes."

I bowed my head, eyes closed, remembering the captain's last words to me. They'd hit me in a place so deep I'd not even known it existed. And whether she knew it or not, the captain had bound me to this alien who now stood at my side—the matriarch of all I'd once feared.

I also remembered the Professor. The one who'd originally sought me out of curiosity, and upon whom so much had depended in the long run. That he'd died trying to protect the three of us—Adanaho, the Queen Mother, and myself—only seemed to cement the unspoken pact. Blood for blood. The life of a mantis hero for the life of a human heroine, each given freely so that there might be a future for both races.

If I had anything to say about it, the Professor's prominence in human lore would be every bit as great as Adanaho's was becoming among the aliens.

Aliens. I smiled slightly and shook my head. Time to get that word out of my system. The mantes had proven to be every bit as *human* as any woman or man I'd ever known. To include their capacity for regret, and a longing for redemption.

"And once you're free of responsibility," I said to the Queen Mother, "where will you go? Home?"

"No," she said. "I will need time to properly dwell upon what has happened; what *is* happening. I do not yet fully comprehend what it is I am becoming without the carriage. I cannot say I am regressing, nor am I standing still. I feel as if I am pupating all over again. Only this time it's happening inside of me. In my mind. In my . . . soul?"

I arched an eyebrow at her use of the word. But said nothing.

"I will need," she continued, "a place of quiet refuge. Somewhere I can meditate. I think that's the right human word? I feel as if I am seeing the world and everything in it for the first time, all over again. I must be free of distractions. And I will need to be in contact with someone of whom I can ask questions. Many questions."

"There must be many planets in mantis territory suitable for this," I said.

"No," she replied. "Only one."

"One?"

"Yes. It's a sparse world. Not much to look at, really. Upon which there is a single, modest chapel."

A tiny thrill went up my spine.

"And I expect you'll be wanting me to go with you," I said.

"Only if you wish it. I cannot compel you to do this thing. You have come far enough, out of necessity. This thing I now ask . . . humbly out of desire for your continued companionship."

I thought about it for a long moment.

"It's okay. I'd have gone back to Purgatory even if you didn't ask. But not before I've had a chance to visit Earth again, and make proper goodbyes to the many people I left behind during the first war."

"Of course."

"Thank you."

"No, Padre, thank you."

"It's going to be difficult," I said. "This journey you're proposing to take. In all the thousands of years of human history, countless men and women have walked the same path. The results have not always been good ones. There can be no guarantees. You might get frustrated. Or worse."

"That is why I will need you, to be my guide."

"But I'm just—"

"Padre, what did Captain Adanaho tell you? What would her *spirit* say if it could speak to you now?"

I looked through the lid of the casket.

"That I can't put off the inevitable," I said.

"Then we shall walk the path together?" the Queen Mother asked.

"Yes, I think we'll have to."

"Good."

A small chime in the compartment alerted us to the fact that the mantis shuttle was on final approach for dock. I took another long look through the top of the casket, then straightened my uniform and followed the Queen Mother out into the corridor that led to the gangway hatch.

CHAPTER 57

EARTH.

It had been a long time since I'd stood on my home planet's surface. Things were just as crowded as I remembered them being. The Fleet put me down in Los Angeles, and from Los Angeles I caught a train to the Bay Area. There were several old friends in San Francisco with whom I wanted to catch up. But even more importantly, there was a person specifically from my POW days I needed to see. She'd been one of the first ones to go home when the Fleet returned to Purgatory in the wake of the original armistice. And she was the closest thing to a friend I'd had during our time behind The Wall.

I found her in Oakland. Living in a small apartment listed in the Fleet registry.

Not the best high rise I'd ever seen, but not the worst. The elevator took me up to the eighty-seventh floor. I pushed the buzzer button next to the front door's key card slot.

I heard someone approach the door on the other side. For a moment the light coming through the peephole was occluded, then the door's locks snapped open and the door swung inward.

"Harry," she said, her eyes wide. "What the hell are you doing back on Earth?"

"Good to see you too, Diane," I said. "A lot's happened since I saw you last. May I please come in?"

"Sure," she said, and moved out the way while beckoning me in with her free arm. I noticed immediately that she'd dedicated the entryway wall space to a giant floor-to-ceiling tile mural. The scene depicted was of a beach at sunset: white sand, dark blue waves, and an orange-to-yellow sun half-submerged behind a glistening horizon.

"Nice," I said. "Who did it?"

"Me," she said.

"I didn't know you had the skill."

"There wasn't much of a chance for me to show it off when we were on Purgatory. Harry, it's been *years.* What's going on with you that you needed to sleuth me out?"

"You know about the new treaty with the mantes?"

"I'm not part of active-duty Fleet anymore, but I've still got my hand in via Fleet Reserve. I know Fleet ceased offensive ops after the mantes' leadership called a truce. Your name kept coming up in the nonclassified reports. When the reports said the treaty signing would be held in Earth orbit I wondered if you'd finally decided to come back. Got a place to stay yet? If you want I can talk to this building's manager. There's some lovely balcony units available on some of the other floors."

"I won't be staying," I said. "There's other business that's come up. I wanted to talk to you about it before I do anything else."

"Take a seat," she said, gesturing to one of the two small sofas that made an L-shape in the apartment's small living room.

"Do you want anything to drink?" she asked.

"No thanks," I said.

She sat down across from me, her hands straightening and smoothing the lower half of her plaid day robe. Her ordinarily wavy hair was pulled up in a tight bun, out of which the occasional unruly lock projected. There were extra lines on her face which hadn't been there before, and she seemed less effervescent than I remembered. Had times been hard? A quick eyeball scan of the apartment told me she was doing as well as could be expected, financially. Fleet made sure all of us former POWs got back pay for time served. Not a massive amount of money. But enough to get a fresh start. Was Diane Fulbright doing anything else with herself now that she'd officially transitioned to civilian life on a full-time basis? Or was she staying on with the Reserve just long enough to earn a pension?

I decided these questions could wait until later.

"The Professor is dead," I said.

"I'm sorry to hear that," she said. "When war broke out again I figured anyone and everyone involved in crosscultural contact was at risk. Until news of the treaty arrived, I feared you and the Professor both might be in a lot of trouble, if not dead already. When the news said that a human identified as 'Padre' had been instrumental in getting the top mantis in the Quorum of the Select to agree to talks, it was impossible to not think of you first. Heck of a way to get into the history books, Harry."

"Yeah, about that. History's not quite done with me yet. The Professor gave his life to protect me and the top mantis, someone the Professor called the Queen Mother. She's passing her mantle to a new Queen Mother, and also decided to pick up where he left off. She wants me to go back to Purgatory with her."

Diane stared at me, one eyebrow raised.

"Are you?" she asked.

"I think I have to," I said.

"Why?"

"It's a long story."

"Okay then, let's have a drink—whether you feel like it or not."

Moments later I had a wide-rimmed glass in my hand, with a pungent bit of amber liquor flowing around in the glass's bottom. I took a quick swig—fire to the throat!—and set the glass on Diane's little wooden coffee table.

Then I told her everything that had happened. About how the Fleet had commissioned me as a Warrant Officer. About how the Professor's inquiries into human religion had hit dead ends. About how Captain Adanaho had sought me out at the request of Fleet Command, and the subsequent and dramatic events which had followed on.

Diane listened carefully, occasionally taking the barest of sips from her own glass. When I was done with my story she shook her head and smiled ruefully at me.

"You're damned lucky to be alive," she said.

"Yes," I admitted. "That thought has crossed my mind many times."

"Did you pay your respects to Adanaho's family yet?"

"No," I said, squirming on the sofa cushions. "I honestly don't know how to go about it. Her aunt is the only one she was close to, or so it sounded like to me. I don't have a name nor an address, though I am sure I could find it through the Fleet registry; just like I found you. More than that, though, I wouldn't know what to say. Adanaho's aunt doesn't know me from Adam. Fleet's having the body interred during a very highbrow ceremony to mark the official transition from wartime to peacetime. That's in a few days. Should I wait until then? Maybe her aunt will show up for the event?"

"You sound like you're afraid," Diane observed.

"Yeah, I am, actually," I said.

"Of what?"

"Captain Adanaho died believing in me. Told me I'd been chosen, whatever that's supposed to mean."

"Seems pretty obvious to me," Diane said with a small smile.

"Oh?"

"You're the olive branch, man. The peace-bringer. Some people think that can't have been by accident."

I made a sour face.

"Like I told the captain before she died, nobody has any idea how much pressure's been put on me over the years. The man who pulled the rabbit out of his hat. Now, twice."

"That's true. When I got back to Earth you'd already become something of a low-level historical celebrity. When people found out I knew you from our years together on Purgatory they always asked me about you. I tried to tell them you were just a regular guy who did what he thought was right in the moment. Most people accepted this at face value. But not all."

"Well, Adanaho was in the latter category," I said. "She seemed to think there was a higher power at work, through me."

"Is that so bad?"

"Yeah, it's bad!" I said, standing up and pacing across Diane's living room to the galley kitchen. "Pilgrims used to come to the chapel and expect me to be some kind of guru. Always, they went away disappointed. You know me, and you know how I worked. I was never a preacher. I only kept the chapel open so that people could come in—"

"—and find their own answers," Diane finished for me. "Yeah, yeah, Harry, you've laid that line on me a hundred times before. It's a good line. Really, it is. Because I know you believe it."

"A line?" I said, feeling the heat rise under my collar.

She grimaced, realizing she'd upset me.

"Bad word choice. Look, I agree, you were never cut out to

be a traditional pulpit-thumper the way some people have always seemed to think you should be. But it cannot be denied that you just happened to be the right person in the right place at the right time, and who also had the right ideas. Once may be coincidence. Twice? Even I have to start wondering."

I walked back from the kitchen and plopped down onto the sofa again, frustrated.

"I can't do it alone," I said.

"You mean, go back to Purgatory with the Queen Mother?"

"She won't be the Queen Mother by then," I said. "She'll be just like the Professor: a mantis who's desperately seeking enlightenment at the hands of an inept human. What if I blow it this time, just like with the Professor?"

"Didn't you just tell me that the absence of the disc seems to have had a profound effect on her?"

"Yes."

"And isn't the Queen Mother—or whatever she's going to call herself later—essentially vowing to do without a disc from now on?"

"Yes."

"Well, there you go. Seems to me that's the missing ingredient. If what Captain Adanaho theorized is true, and the disc was somehow suppressing natural perceptions, then it stands to reason the Queen Mother's quest for spiritual awakening will garner significantly different results."

I wanted to believe my old friend. I really did. But...

"Come back with me," I said, finally putting the question on the table.

"What?" she said, startled.

"Like I said, I can't do this alone. I need help. I need... someone with *real* faith who can help me."

"You've always seemed to be a faithful soul to me," she said, "although you were always too wishy-washy about it for my tastes."

"Wishy-washy?"

"Again, sorry, bad choice of words. Harry, from what I could tell, you were always afraid to commit. To pick one of the *flavors,* as the Professor called them, and dive in headfirst. Make the effort. Do the work to deeply and truly understand one particular religion."

"My job was to serve everyone, and I—"

Diane ran a thumb across the air in front of her throat.

"Save it. That's been an excuse. Sounds to me like you know that if you go back to Purgatory with the Queen Mother, you won't have any excuses to hide behind."

"You're kind of pissing me off," I said to her, and meant it.

"You're the one asking *me* to come back with you," she said. "Sounds to me like all you really want me around for is as a crutch when the questions get too hard, or too uncomfortable."

I fumed quietly on the sofa. Had coming to Diane's place been a waste of time? A mistake? I wanted very badly to get up and go. But something held me in place. I slowly downed the rest of my drink and stared at my shoes. Civilian shoes. I'd picked up a set of cheap clothes in the spaceport after I'd landed. Was I angry simply because Diane was telling me what I'd suspected all along, yet had not had the courage to admit to myself?

"Crutch or no, I still want you to come," I said softly.

"I can't," she said.

"Can't, or won't?"

"Can't."

"Got a nice job? Something you can't walk away from?"

"You might put it that way," Diane said, though she wasn't smiling.

"Not that it would take much," I said. "You and I both know that Purgatory's a cozy little acre of hell."

"In a different time and place I might have said yes," she said. "But a lot has changed for me since I came back to Earth. I've got responsibilities here that I can't just walk away from."

I looked around the apartment—clearly a bachelorette pad.

"Not a husband?" I said.

"No."

"Are you a mom now?"

"No."

"Then what's the problem?"

She stared at me—eyeballs to eyeballs.

Then she dropped her gaze.

"I'll think about it," she said.

"Think quickly. Once the treaty is signed, the Queen Mother is headed back to her people—and I am going with her. Once she's handed over her responsibilities, we're going back to Purgatory."

Diane looked at the floor of her apartment, mouth turned down in a frown.

"There was a time when you could not have paid me enough money to go back to that damned planet," she said. "I hated it there."

"We all hated it there," I said.

"Not you. At least not enough to leave."

"I had a job to do."

"So do I."

"Is that your answer, then?"

"Like I said, I'll think about it."

"I won't blame you if you say no," I said. "But I'd be thrilled if you said yes. Thanks for having me in. It's really good to see you."

She looked up at me with a slight smile.

"It's good to see you too," she said.

We chattered a bit more. Small talk, mostly.

Then I let myself out the way I'd come in.

CHAPTER 58

THE TREATY SIGNING WAS A SPECTACULAR EVENT.

Hundreds of Fleet officers and thousands of civilian officials crowded the plaza at Fleet Headquarters, North America West. It had been built on the bones of the old United States Navy air base on Whidbey Island, off the coast of Washington State. Mobs of spit-and-polished men and women moved to and fro, their passes and ID tags hanging from lanyards on their necks, while the press—with their ID tags and their passes hanging from similar lanyards—interviewed anyone and everyone they could get their hands on.

Myself especially.

I'd not expected that.

But Diane had been right: my status as a celebrity had been cemented by the cease-fire. And now that we were officially closing out the war, my name was on everyone's lips: as the guy who pulled off a miracle.

I mumbled my way through question after question, trying not to sound too stupid, but feeling too much like I'd felt when people visited me in the chapel: expecting me to dispense insight, wisdom, or guidance. So I told them the truth. That I'd just done what I thought was the right thing, and we'd all been lucky that it was enough to make a difference when it counted.

If the reporters were disappointed, they didn't show it.

There were other men and women—other officers—plainly prepared to hold forth, both politically and philosophically, on what the treaty signified.

When I could, I stole away to one of the verandas that had a view of the ocean. The wind coming in off the water was tangy and brisk, but with the sun out and the sky clear, things weren't cold. I looked down over the historical airfield which had been preserved next to the much larger and more industrial-looking spaceport, with its gantries and towers and hangars filled with aerospacecraft. Not too different from Armstrong Field, where I'd first trained as a recruit.

One of those hangars held a mantis ship.

I could just barely make out the ceremonial mantis guards arrayed around the hangar, with an equal number of Fleet marines—in full dress uniforms—arrayed around the guards.

Unlike when I'd been aboard the *Calysta,* I knew now that the marines had no ulterior orders. Even Fleet Command had been convinced that peace was necessary, following the loss of over two-thirds of their capital ships. We'd been on the run when the Fourth Expansion was brought to an official halt: our offensive blunted, pulverized, and beaten back. It would have been a matter of months until Earth itself became the target.

Something I found surreal, as I watched gulls circling and drifting in the air over the beach at the far edge of the old airfield.

For a brief moment I imagined kinetic impact weaponry or hydrogen bombs coming down on the island. Or, if the mantes were smart, far out in the Pacific. Drop a big enough asteroid into the water and the tsunami would do most of the work. At least for the coastal areas where much of the civilian population was concentrated, as well as a good deal of Fleet equipment and manpower.

But now, all was quiet.

When it came time for the official signing to begin, I took my seat along with the rest of the Fleet personnel.

One after another, generals and several civilian statespeople took the podium to make their speeches. I sort of tuned out—old military habits dying hard—while I looked across the dais on which the podium sat, to where the Queen Mother and many of her officers were in formation. Their antennae waved lazily in the breeze, while their eyes were directly on the podium proper.

Occasionally I saw the Queen Mother move her head, looking in my direction. I smiled slightly, hoping she noticed that I noticed her.

Then I got a shocking surprise.

General Ustinov, overall commander of Fleet in its entirety, had one of his colonels approach the podium with a small box.

"And now if Chief Barlow would please present himself," Ustinov said, his Russian accent distinct.

I reflexively shot up out of my chair and muttered apologies as I made my way to the aisle and then up to the edge of the dais. I looked up at Ustinov—flanked by his other generals—and saluted.

"Warrant Officer Barlow, reporting as ordered," I said.

The general—and all around him—also saluted.

When they dropped their hands, I dropped mine.

"Come on up," Ustinov said, pointing to a spot in front of the podium.

I stepped onto the carpet and proceeded to where I'd been aimed, then stood at rigid attention. When one of the colonels whispered under her breath for me to do an about-face, I spun on a heel and faced the crowd, which was composed of Fleet, civilians, and mantis personnel alike.

The outdoor amphitheater was packed.

I swallowed hard.

"None of you need an introduction to this man," Ustinov said into the microphone on the podium. "But I wanted him to receive special recognition for his contribution to this moment. In war, generals have to plan for the worst-case scenario. Having discussed things with my counterparts in the mantis military, my understanding is that we were both convinced that the other side would strike. At any moment. So that when hostilities did renew, we threw ourselves into the melee with all our energy. Yet it was a chaplain's assistant who took the initiative to seek an alternative path. A path we're now walking, for the sake of mankind's future in this universe. Chief Barlow, please remain at attention while I and all the other people of Earth give you a well-earned round of applause."

The amphitheater came alive with clapping, as men and women rose to their feet. In addition to the clapping, there were cheers from the civilians, some of whom where pounding their hands together so hard—with tears in their eyes—that I blushed despite myself.

After thirty seconds, the applause died down, and the civilian people began to return to their seats. The military folks remained standing. Out of the corner of my eye I noticed the Queen Mother walking slowly up to the podium.

The colonel's voice hissed for me to do another about-face. I did as I was told. Ustinov stepped away from the podium and walked up to me. The colonel trailed, box in hand.

"Stay with it," Ustinov said quietly to me. "I know it's painful being the focus of attention like this, but we've only got two more small matters to attend to. Colonel?"

The box sprang open on hinges. Two small metallic items gleamed within. I didn't dare look down—just kept my eyes straight ahead.

A major walked to the podium and cleared her throat, using a small pad to read from while she spoke into the microphone.

"Attention to orders. In accordance with the wishes of the President-Secretary of the Alliance of Earth Nations, and per the directive of the Chair of the Colonial War Contingency Congress, Harrison Barlow's brevet rank of Warrant Officer is removed. Barlow is hereby promoted to the rank of Captain, Chaplains Corps, per special appointment by General Ustinov, Commanding General, Fleet Command."

Ustinov reached up and plucked the bars from my collar.

"You won't be needing those anymore," he said softly, still smiling.

Out of the box came captain's clusters identical to what Adanaho had worn. I swallowed thickly as the general pinned them in place.

"Furthermore," the major said into the mic, "Captain Barlow is awarded the Interstellar Medal of Valor, in recognition of his sacrifice and hardship in the service of the highest ideals of the Fleet, and the Colonial War Contingency Congress. Captain Barlow's actions, in the face of overwhelming odds and at the risk of his own life, were directly responsible for the successful cessation of combat."

The general gently and expertly applied the strip at the top of the ribbon—from which the solid metal disc of the medal hung—to my chest, where the strip sealed instantly against the artificial fabric of my dress uniform.

"Now give us one more about-face," Ustinov said.

I spun.

The Queen Mother walked to my side, her eyes looking out into the human crowd.

"There was a time," her vocoded voice said, now made large through the amphitheater's sound system, "when my people thought ourselves the sole, supreme intelligence in our universe. We travelled the stars and saw none to match us. When twice before we encountered sapience, we extinguished it, believing that the universe was ours alone to develop and rule. I was a product of that thinking. There was no room in my mind for humans. Two people changed my thinking. One of whom stands before you. The other does not. Like so many of your people, and mine, she was a victim of my limited thinking. And though I cannot bring her—nor any of the other dead—back, I can tell you now that we mantes *are* committed to peace. We will learn to make room in our minds, and also, in our *hearts,* for human beings. This I promise you with my own life."

Thunderous, titanic applause. Like a sound wave beating against me. When it finally died down, the major at the podium continued.

"The Colonial War Contingency Congress Star of Honor is posthumously awarded to Captain Ndiya Adanaho, Intelligence, in recognition of her supreme bravery and sacrifice in the service of all humanity. Captain Adanaho's clear thinking and ultimate sacrifice are in the highest tradition of her branch, and the Fleet as a whole. On behalf of Fleet Command, we ask that Captain Adanaho's next of kin approach the podium to receive the award."

A tiny old woman in a conservative shawl stood up from the front row of civilians and walked slowly up and onto the dais. Not a sound was heard as she came to stand beside me. A second box was brought forward and pressed into her hands, with Ustinov quietly speaking words of condolence and thanks.

Out of the corner of my eye I could see tears leaking down the woman's brown, wrinkled face. I suddenly felt the overwhelming urge to kneel at her feet and plead forgiveness—for not saving her niece.

But I kept my bearing.

There was no applause this time. As a whole, we bowed our heads for a respectful moment of silence.

The rest of the event was something of a blur for me. I went back to my seat as ordered, and observed the actual signing with a mixed mood of relief and exhaustion. I also kept an eye on Adanaho's aunt, who had returned to her seat, and who wasn't looking at anyone in particular while she continued to cry. She just rubbed the box in her thin-fingered little hands, clutching it occasionally to her face while those around her reached out their hands to pat her shoulders and express condolences.

When it was all over, the crowd surged down and onto the dais, bubbling with talk.

I remained seated, leaning this way and that to try to keep an eye on Adanaho's aunt, but was upset to discover that the old woman had disappeared.

I got up and began to gently pushed down through the mass of milling bodies—accepting thanks and handshakes and congratulations as I went—until suddenly I felt someone's hand grab my forearm and pull me aside.

It was Diane. In full dress uniform.

"Kudos, Harry," she said, smiling at me.

Her finger tapped my medal, then my collar.

I bowed my head and sighed.

"Adanaho was the real hero. She *earned* her rank. And her medal. I didn't do much. I couldn't even save Adanaho when it mattered."

Then I noticed Fulbright's uniform.

"*Captain* Fulbright?" I said, looking at her with eyes wide.

"You never asked me my rank when I told you I'd stayed on with Fleet Reserve. I didn't feel like going through the rest of my career as an enlisted woman. So I put in my packet for a direct commission two years before the fighting got started again. Looks like we're both going to be playing *ossifer* now, Harry. Same branch, too."

The Queen Mother approached, with General Ustinov in tow.

"The ripple effects of the treaty will take time to spread throughout mantis space—and the Quorum of the Select. We will have to detour to meet the Quorum on our way to Purgatory, so that my successor can officially take over again. Do you mind the extended space duty?"

"No," I said.

"Very good. We will depart your planet at the rising of tomorrow's sun. Until then, I have further officiousness and ceremony to attend to, at the behest of your civilian leadership. Will either of you be coming for that?"

"Not if I don't have to," I said, looking at the general.

"I think I'll allow for some personal time," he said. "Since you've got one last evening on Earth, it's up to you to decide how you want to spend it. Report to the flight line at ten-hundred tomorrow, ready to climb aboard the Queen Mother's ship."

I *yessirred*, saluted, he saluted back, then Diane and I bade farewell to the Queen Mother and looked for a quick exit.

CHAPTER 59

OAK HARBOR WAS LIT UP LIKE A CHRISTMAS TREE. FOR A HISTORICALLY military town, the mood was quite festive, with Fleet personnel and civilians alike mobbing the sidewalks and chattering happily amongst themselves. To look at the place you'd not have guessed that until very recently, humanity was at war.

Diane and I had agreed to dine at the Crestwood, a somewhat upscale establishment on the roof of one of the newer residential towers. Which was fine, as we'd stayed in our dress uniforms.

The *maître d'* showed us to our table. Much of the roof had been covered in hydroponics equipment so that trees and bushes grew at regular intervals. Artistically designed modern fountains were spaced among the trees, their gurgling making a gentle chorus while shimmering bouquets of multicolored light emanated from the fountain bottoms.

"Magical," Diane said as she looked this way and that.

"I asked around: where was the best place to take a lady to dinner?"

"Do you always try to impress a girl like this?"

"Actually, I've never tried to impress a girl, period."

I laughed at my own joke. Diane didn't.

"Sorry," I said. "My date humor's a little rusty."

"When's the last time you even went on a real date? Like, with a girl you'd like to take home with you when it's over?"

I blushed.

"A long time ago."

"You mean to tell me that all through the armistice, you never even—"

"No," I said. "And to be totally honest about it, I'm not sure I missed much. The bulk of the women went home once The Wall was gone and Fleet ships came back to Purgatory. Just like you, they couldn't wait to get back to civilization. The few that stayed, already had families."

"What about visitors?"

"What about them? I'm not exactly one-night-stand material."

She looked at me with her head cocked to the side.

"No," she said, appraisingly, "I guess you're not. You always were a nice guy. Earnest. You seemed more devoted to Chaplain Thomas's wish for the chapel than anything else. Some of us used to joke that you were like a monk or a nun in that way. Married to the church, so to speak. And yet, you're still unsure of your convictions. Even after all you've been through."

"Which is exactly why I wanted you to come with me," I said.

She looked away.

A table waiter arrived and we placed our orders: grilled chicken and vegetables for Diane, a small sirloin with baked potato for me. And a bucket of ice with a wine bottle in it. Not that either of us intended to get tipsy. It just seemed appropriate for the occasion.

When the waiter left I turned the tables.

"So why did you pick the Chaplains Corps?" I asked.

"Well," Diane said, swirling a bit of wine around in the bottom of a long-stemmed glass, "it seemed like a good way to put my money where my mouth is. I am the Deacon, after all."

I gazed at the other Crestwood clientele: men and women, well heeled, affluent, or at least not hurting for means. They laughed and talked and ate, and seemed to be carrying on without a care in the world. I immediately felt more like an outsider than I ever had among the many weeks I'd tarried on the Queen Mother's ship—bound for the treaty signing in Earth orbit. The mantes were elegantly simple in their own way. A logical and deliberate people. Not frivolous.

"What's wrong?" Diane asked, noticing my expression.

"Sorry, I was woolgathering."

"I could see that. But what about?"

"It's just . . . well . . ."

Our food arrived before I could complete my thought, and

soon we were bantering over mouthfuls: about the whereabouts of mutual military acquaintances, family members, old school buddies, and what was in store for us in the future. Diane had retrained through Fleet education assistance to do data analysis in hospital administration. Not the most glamorous profession in the world, but she had a knack for it—or so she said—and it paid the bills. When she wasn't drilling with Fleet Reserve in her other capacity.

I talked mostly about recent events. How close I'd come to dying several times onboard the Queen Mother's ship. Diane just nodded and listened, occasionally sipping at her glass.

Then the conversation sort of died out.

My half-finished thought hung uncomfortably in the air. Both of us knew it. I cleared my throat and tried to speak, but as if on cue, my phone buzzed in my uniform's jacket pocket.

"Hold on," I said.

I put the device to my cheek.

"This is Ch—I mean, Captain Barlow," I said.

"This is the Queen Mother," said a computer voice.

"Yes, ma'am, I was just talking about you."

"With the officer named Fulbright?"

"Yes."

"Good. Tell her I want to talk to her."

I raised my eyebrows.

"Oh really?"

"Please pass your device to her now."

I slowly handed the phone over to Diane. Her brow was knit and she looked at me with a questioning expression, I mouthed the words *Queen Mother* and shrugged.

Diane took the phone, "Yes, this is Captain Fulbright, how can I help you, Queen Mother?"

Diane listened for several moments, then pressed the HOLD button.

"What's up?" I asked.

"What did you *tell* her about me?"

"Nothing," I said. "All I told her was that maybe I might have an old friend coming back to Purgatory with me. It wasn't a sure thing. I just wanted to make sure the Queen Mother was cool with it."

Diane looked at me for a long moment.

"I think the Queen Mother expects an answer," I said.

Diane kept looking at me. I reached across the table and grabbed one of her hands in mine. I squeezed tightly.

"Only, when we go back together," I said, "let's do it *right.* Okay? The way you're supposed to. Diane... Diane, I want you to be my wife. I know it's crazy. We haven't seen each other in a long time. But being here, talking to you, I'm just thinking about how a man only gets to have so many second chances in this life. I should have proposed to you back on Purgatory, before the armistice. I told myself then it wouldn't be worth it. I thought you'd turn me down anyway. We were just friends. But this thing with the Queen Mother, and all that's happened to me... Diane, it's time I stopped hiding from what I know to be true in my heart."

If I'd shocked her, she didn't show it. Her expressive eyes—touched with just enough shadow and liner—examined me across the table. Evaluating carefully. Her lips barely moving while we stared at each other's faces.

From out of my cell phone's tiny speaker I heard the Queen Mother's voice ask, "Hello, Captain Fulbright, are you still there? What's your final answer?"

Diane looked silently at me for a second or two more, then she pressed the TALK button and put the phone back to her cheek.

"Yes," she said, smiling widely.

CHAPTER 60

FLEET PUT DIANE AND ME BOTH ON INDEFINITE ORDERS. AS official attachés for the duration of our trip to Purgatory. We were deemed *cultural* exchange officers. Many mantes had remained behind on Earth in a similar capacity. The Queen Mother and her official party had been the first mantes to ever see any portion of Earth society—in an informal setting—and a small group of them had been left behind, to form the first official mantis embassy to another sapient race, in the entire history of their species.

Meanwhile, on Purgatory, we were starting over from scratch. My chapel, and everything else in the mountain valley, had been razed to the ground when hostilities were renewed. There was nothing left. Not even bodies. The mantes had dropped a very small asteroid right down into the middle of the valley proper, and that was the end of that.

Now, two former human residents of Purgatory had returned. This time, to a different valley altogether.

Our new home was quite a bit different from our last on this world. A beautiful mountain lake spanned the bottom of the valley, with healthy meadows of Purgatory grass stretching into the foothills on all sides.

The drop pod from the drop pod carrier made a decent enough shelter, until Diane and I could get the new chapel built. And we had crates filled with Earth seed to begin growing crops. Plus some Earth livestock to boot. Tending them was certainly a learning process, as neither Diane nor I had ever been farm kids back home. But we managed.

With the Queen Mother's help, of course.

That wasn't her official capacity anymore. The exchange of power at the Quorum of the Select had been as similarly officious—in mantis terms—as the signing of the treaty had been in human terms. Much speaking and acting-out of formal ritual. Though Diane and I had been forced to use a translator to tell us what was going on, as everything had been done silently—mind to mind.

When I asked her what we should call her now, the former Queen Mother was at a loss for words. Even she had no idea.

"You'll need a name eventually," I said.

She thought about it.

"I should use the station in which I function," she said. "Much like you called the Professor by his function."

"So what's your function now?" Diane asked.

The former Queen Mother considered at length.

"I think we shall call me... Pilgrim."

Which was good enough for all three of us.

Pilgrim's new arm was growing back rather rapidly. She looked comical with this little pee-wee version of her big forelimb, waving about and gesticulating, its chitin looking fresh whereas all the rest of her was well-seasoned.

I took it as a good omen. But it wasn't the only one.

Diane and me, well... we were getting to know each other like never before. And for once in my life I didn't feel like I was the only one being expected to answer all the questions. Of which Pilgrim still had many.

For relaxation and exercise, we all spent about as much time as we could hiking around the valley. If the planet had a garden spot, this seemed to be it. And by day, work meant assembling the chapel proper, or tending the little farm that surrounded the growing chapel walls. If Pilgrim was annoyed at having to exert herself with so much physical labor, she didn't show it. In fact she appeared to rejoice in it every bit as much as Adanaho had rejoiced in the challenge of her own toil—liberated from VR.

Occasionally Pilgrim explored her flight envelope with her wings. We'd all climb up to the top of a bluff or other high point at the valley's edge, and she'd go running as fast as she could, shooting off into the air and spiraling elegantly around and around, back down into the valley floor, sometimes even getting as far as the shoreline of the lake before she'd put down.

It was a beautiful thing to see.

At night, Diane and I would go to our bed, and do some exploring of our own. Newlyweds that we were, it was clumsy stuff, at first. But there was time enough for learning. And when we were lying in the rumpled blankets, we'd look up through the drop pod's portholes at the stars in the sky above.

Bright, and pure, and promising as they'd never been before.

"So, Chaplain Barlow," Diane said to me as I felt myself sliding towards slumber.

"So . . . Missus Chaplain Barlow," I said in reply, smiling in the dark.

She giggled, and wrapped an arm around my shoulders while snuggling up to my ear.

"Back on Earth," she said, "you told me you were done hiding from truths you knew in your heart. I'm pretty sure at this point I know what that means."

"That I've always loved you?" I replied. "Yes."

"No, silly. That you've finally accepted God."

I lay there, feeling her warmth next to me, and thinking that it was pretty difficult to remember any time when I'd felt quite so content. An old and reflexive part of my brain wanted to reject her words. But that part had steadily grown more quiet over the days since we'd returned to Purgatory.

"Chaplain Thomas seemed to think there was a reason we got spared, back during the first war," I said. "He thought it was part of God's plan. I said he was talking nonsense at the time. But now . . . what else am I to think? Yes, I've accepted God. More than that, I've accepted the idea that forging peace with the mantes was only the first step. I've got to help Pilgrim find and accept God too. She's just the first. There will be others like her. Other mantes. I am sure of it."

"I am too," Diane whispered, kissing my ear. "You know, you were always in the back of my mind, Harry. The one guy I kept wondering about, when the nights got lonely. I thought I'd never see you again, especially when the war cranked up a second time. Watching you walk into my place that afternoon in San Francisco . . . I knew it wasn't an accident."

"No, I don't think it was either," I said.

We kissed deeply, then pulled the blankets over us—the distantly gentle lapping of the lakeshore serenading us to sleep.

— THE END —